NEVER AS IT SEEMS

ISBN 978-1-948613-06-4
Library of Congress Control Number: 2020908097

This book is a work of fiction. Any references
to historical events, people, or places are used
fictitiously. Names, characters, places, and
events are products of the author's imagination,
and any resemblances to actual events or places
or persons, living or dead, is entirely coincidental.

Edited by Ruth Beach
Front cover image ©2020 Stacie Gerrity
Book design by Stacie Gerrity

Printed in the United States of America

Sunny Day Publishing, LLC
Cuyahoga Falls, Ohio 44223

www.sunnydaypublishing.com

I stand amid the roar
Of a surf-tormented shore,
And I hold within my hand
Grains of golden sand—
How few! yet how they creep
Through my fingers to the deep,
While I weep—while I weep!
O God! can I not save
One from the pitiless wave?
Is *all* that we see or seem
But a dream within a dream?

—Edgar Allan Poe

Never As It Seems

J. Joseph Thomas

Prologue

Robert Balfour II desperately wanted to be a great author, a prolific novelist like his father and grandfather before him. Having the proper pedigree, and possessing a work ethic second to none, his lofty aspirations didn't seem all that unrealistic.

But the passing years proved him wrong. After writing dozens of failed manuscripts, his shortcomings became apparent to all, especially to himself. He'd all but given up on his dream until he met a Navajo shaman who led him down a different path, one that included a night of wild revelry and experimentation. By morning's light, Balfour had been unwittingly transformed. The hack novelist would soon become a highly acclaimed writer, one who would garner a Nobel Prize for a work entitled *The Unlikeliest of Heirs*. Literary critics called it "a book for the ages."

The fact that he couldn't duplicate his magnum opus wasn't all that surprising, considering the level of its brilliance. But what was puzzling was his inability to follow it up with anything even remotely printable. His rise to the top of the mountain had been meteoric, dizzyingly spectacular, shockingly brief, and very perplexing.

What had happened to the Nobelist who penned *The Unlikeliest of Heirs*? Why had his writing skills suddenly dried up?

Theories were offered of course. Plagiarism was hinted at, or perhaps a ghostwriter lurked somewhere off in the shadows. Some even suggested that his novel had been a gift from God, an answer to a prayer. Balfour had certainly prayed for help often enough. It stood to reason that if the Almighty could guide the Prophets out of the wilderness, then why not lead the inept Robert Balfour out of the darkness?

He, however, had his own theory about his lone burst of literary brilliance, and it had nothing to do with divine intervention. He suspected that his inspiration had come from a much darker place.

UNIVERSITY HOSPITAL, OCTOBER 13, 1985

Who was the patient in Room 502? No one working at University Hospital had a clue. It was quite clear, however, that this mystery man was suspended somewhere between this life and the next, that he was sleeping away his last days on earth, and that he'd been admitted to University Hospital with no driver's license, Social Security card, or wallet. So, needing to call him something, the unimaginative staffers on the fifth floor dubbed him "Patient X."

Making this situation even more intriguing was the fact that the doctors assigned to his case had no idea what was wrong with him.

So little information it seemed, despite the fact that his collapse and subsequent coma were well documented by dozens of bystanders who'd witnessed his blackout and tumble down the front steps of the hospital. Unfortunately, none of the eyewitnesses knew his name, and no one had come forward to identify or claim him, even after a week in ICU.

To those who stood by helplessly, the most vexing aspect of the Patient X case was that, though comatose, he appeared to be an otherwise healthy, middle-aged male who'd taken up hibernating.

Of course they'd run the tests, an exhaustive battery of tests. Blood panels, X-Rays, brain and body scans that all showed that X's deteriorating condition made little sense. No medical red flags had sprung up either. He looked to be a fit, fifty-something who'd collapsed while wearing an expensive jogging outfit, three-hundred-dollar running shoes, and teeth too straight, unmarred by fillings, and dazzlingly white to be anything but caps.

By any method of evaluation, the mystery man—in all likelihood a local—appeared to be someone meriting an All-Points-Bulletin, neighborhood search party, or at least a missing person's ad in the local newspaper.

Three specialists—Drs. Kern, Lamb, and Johnston—representing neurology, cardiology, and internal medicine were assigned to the case as four nurses rotated through varying shifts. Nurse Esther Bailey, being the one in charge, was the most visible.

On day eight of the Patient X vigil there was a new development, a new voice was heard in Room 502, one dripping with barbecue sauce and drawl. "It defies everythin' in medical science, but there's no doubt this man's slip-slidin' away from us for no apparent reason."

The staff watched as the visiting troubleshooter, a Dr. Myron Spenser, lifted one of the patient's eyelids, then the other. After clicking off his penlight, he turned to the half-dozen staffers who'd been patiently waiting for some kind of profound utterance. Instead they got an elongated *hmmmm*, and an absurdly axiomatic, "Certainly comatose, but not in the traditional sense."

Nurse Bailey, already tired of Dr. Spenser's histrionics and hubris, could barely contain herself. The nationally renowned diagnostician, who'd come to them from the prestigious Baylor University Hospital, had thus far proven to be a major disappointment.

Oblivious to the staff's mounting restlessness, he moved down to the patient's ankles as if chasing a phantom pulse. "We should also note that the response is stronger in the right ankle. Not all that unusual in cases involving total immobility."

After moving back up to X's flat abdomen, he poked, prodded, and observed a bit too cavalierly, "Kind of ironic, this one's quite the physical specimen. Obviously kept himself fit and trim. Hardly seems a likely candidate for all of this."

Nurse Bailey finally spoke up. "Dr. Spenser, have you ever seen a case like X's before? I mean he has no symptoms, and all his tests have come back negative."

"As a matter of fact I have," he answered. "Three times in as many decades." He stopped and checked X's pupils again. "The fact that the pupils aren't dilated is a little different, but this case is eerily similar to one I collaborated on a few years back at the Mayo Clinic."

After tapping both knees with a rubber mallet for reflexive responsiveness, he returned to his Mayo Clinic story. "The patient at Mayo, he too had no apparent pathology. No genetic markers. Nothing."

"Did he die?" one of the nurses asked brusquely.

"Yes, and it was the damnedest thing. He seemed to do it right on cue."

After Dr. Kern asked for clarification, Spenser explained, "Well, it was almost as if he waited for the entire first shift gang to arrive. Then he opened his eyes, mumbled something, and then just faded out."

"Faded out?" Nurse Bailey repeated skeptically.

He took pains to emphasize the *fading out* part of the story with a fluttering wave of his hand. "Yup, like I said, almost as if he'd willed himself to die."

"You think that's what X is doing," challenged Dr. Lamb, *"willing himself to die?"*

The resentment that hung in the air was palpable, but the wizened doctor seemed oblivious to it all. "I really don't know," Spenser answered while gently probing the patient's neck glands with gloved fingertips. "What I do know is that this kind of case, well, let's just say that the boys over at JAMA start toeing the mark, licking their chops. Believe me when I tell you, this man's condition is that rare."

"Boys over at JAMA," Bailey fumed internally. The man was a sexist in addition to specializing in buffoonery. Having said that, Spenser was an old friend of her boss, the man who signed her checks. So she bit her lip.

"Very frustrating no doubt," Spenser went on, apparently loving the sound of his own voice. "But you have to admit that this kind of case still titillates, does it not?"

His examination concluded with a perfunctory scoping of ears and nostrils before slowly peeling off his gloves and dropping them individually in the trash as he left the room. The gesture carried an unmistakable air of finality. The examination was officially over.

The others exchanged looks ranging from doubt, to disgust, to relief that Spenser appeared to be done with whatever the last hour was supposed to have been. Nonetheless, with little expectation, they dutifully followed him into the hall. Credentials, press clippings, and friendship with their boss aside, their assessment was unanimous— Dr. Myron Spenser appeared to be either an aging charlatan, or at the very least a pompous windbag.

"Look, I'm sorry," he apologized insincerely. "The prognosis for this man is as bleak as it is confounding, but in my humble opinion, there's nothing more you can do for him, except make him as comfortable as possible, and hope for the best."

Nurse Bailey, up to her neck with the arrogant Texan, emoted, "So let me get this straight Doctor Spenser, you came all the way from Baylor to tell us what? That our patient is dying! With all due respect sir, we already knew that."

The doctor tried to muster some empathy by awkwardly patting her arm. "I know this is all very disconcerting, and I wish I could offer some deeper insights. Nothing short of a miracle is going to save him now."

It seemed a strange moment for the clueless interloper to crack a smile, but that's what he did right before adding, "But on the brighter side, the trip wasn't a complete waste of time."

The group waited for the rest of it. Some inane, folksy punchline delivered by the ivory tower academician. Maybe something along the lines of *"It was a pleasure meeting y'all. Dr. Blanchard has put together a great bunch of docs here."*

Instead, what tumbled out of his goatee-fringed mouth next was a stunning announcement, a real game changer. The first major clue that might lead them to uncovering X's true identity.

"Now, I can't be absolutely positive, but I'm pretty sure I know who your Patient X is."

She'd heard he was back, living in the old neighborhood after a nineteen-year absence. She'd heard all the other stuff too, the really bad stuff. The stories about Jason Scarza's perjury conviction, his assaulting a fellow Navy SEAL, his two-year stint in the brig, and his dishonorable discharge from the US Navy. When Little Italy's rumor mill began spinning out of control, saints and heroes seemed to fall much farther and harder than mere mortals.

The final days of Scarza's military career got more scandalous with each re-telling.

Olivia Jardine, however, would believe none of it. The young man that she remembered from the old neighborhood was irreproachable, a knight in shining armor, a defender of the defenseless, and a poster boy for the entire Italian-American community. She couldn't imagine a man like that lying under oath or attacking someone without provocation.

....

The Scarza home sat at the end of 123rd Street. It was a carbon copy of the other houses in this blue-collar neighborhood that bordered Cleveland's most prestigious burial grounds, Lake View Cemetery. The surrounding homes, all modest multi-family frame dwellings, featured big front porches, postage stamp yards, and colorful histories filled with love, pride in their Italian ancestry, devotion to church, and a pervasive, dark connection to Mafia lore.

Since garages were little more than useless appendages when Little Italy suddenly sprang to life at the turn of the 20th Century, everyone in the neighborhood was forced to park their cars on the hilly, narrow streets, giving Little Italy a cramped feel, just like many of its dwellings that were bursting with three-generation-living arrangements.

This tiny hamlet, born out of necessity, was predominantly settled by Italian stone cutters and sculptors who were brought over to carve monuments and memorials for the rich and famous who'd chosen to have their bodies forever interred in Lake View. Great grandfather Scarza was one of those original stonecutters.

Passed on from generation to generation, it was Grandma Scarza who eventually inherited the family house. She lived on the first floor, and after he was court-martialed, her grandson Jason, still licking his wounds, took up residence on the second floor.

Jason Scarza had been back six weeks when Olivia learned of his return. And as far as she was concerned, the timing could not have been better. She had a nasty situation on her hands, one that even the police couldn't help her with. Someone who spewed out euphemistic jargon might have labeled it a "jurisdictional problem," one that only a native son could fully understand, and hopefully arbitrate.

Besides, she was dying to see Jason Scarza after all these years. Was he still as handsome as she'd remembered, a god walking among mere mortals? Or, was he broken as reported? She was about to find out for herself.

Olivia "Livy" Jardine, in all her twenty-nine years, had never lived anywhere but Little Italy. She was deeply rooted there, anchored by staggering commitment and comforting familiarity. She knew everyone in the tiny community, as they did her.

She was very pretty, a talented artist, personable, and fun to be around. She cared about people, especially the old, the infirm, and even those societal throwaways that people crossed the street to avoid.

Perhaps this affinity toward the eccentric and troubled had something to do with her mother's various afflictions that often manifested themselves as paralyzing neuroses. As a paranoid schizophrenic, hoarder, and agoraphobe, her mom required constant supervision. Warding off her mother's imaginary demons had become a full-time job for Livy.

So she held on for dear life, even during those last dark years of her mom's life. If anything, she drew closer as if holding tighter might ease her mother's pain. It didn't. Livy lived with her, shopped and cooked for her, took her to doctors' appointments, accompanied her to church, and read her stories until the tortured woman fell asleep.

Living on Mrs. Jardine's small disability check also proved problematic, especially at the end of the month when everything came due. Incredibly, Livy accomplished this monumental stewarding feat, sans a nine-to-five job, using a special skillset and loads of hutzpah. Baking pies from the Jardine kitchen and peddling them to the local bakery for instance. Selling her paintings at a local art gallery, using her interior decorating skills to help color-challenged neighbors, walking dogs, and occasionally playing canine psychologist. Her uncanny connection with dogs earned her the title of The Dog Whisperer of Murray Hill.

On the threshold of thirty, the possibility of ever marrying seemed the stuff of fairy tales. This pessimistic outlook about marriage seemed an odd turn since she'd grown up a stone's throw from Holy Rosary Church, the very citadel of holy matrimony. She'd witnessed first-hand some of the most lavish weddings one could ever imagine, and as a little girl peeking through the privet hedge that bordered the church grounds, each of these marital extravaganzas had a coronation-like feel—a sumptuous ball featuring gorgeous flower arrangements, black tuxedoes and flowing gowns.

It was all dizzying fun to little Olivia. Prince and princess, bride and groom, they were one and the same. The whirlwind trip through the adoring throng, the rice shower a baptism for young lovers, the limo pulling away with the *just married* sign and tin cans attached to the bumper—for the imaginative child, it was as if the happy couple was being whisked away in a horse drawn coach to Camelot.

As Livy grew older, however, fairy tale endings gave way to a gritty, more brutal reality. Her dad would never walk her down the aisle because he went A.W.O.L. when she was ten. Her mom, zonked out on prescription meds, wouldn't be adequately present to help her plan her own wedding, let alone help pay for it.

Since her mother's care was so all consuming, there'd be no prince knocking at her door either. Her few encounters with men were usually brief, meaningless tussles in the dark. Mere chemical experiments that proved both unfulfilling and emotionally draining.

And so Livy's nightmarish, merry-go-round existence whirled on hopelessly until one day it all came to a screeching halt. A blood vessel in her mother's head burst. The coroner's report called it a cerebral hemorrhage; Livy called it a merciful act from a merciful God.

In any case, what her mom left in her tumultuous wake was more of the same—chaos, heavy debt, a house filled with unwanted junk, an over-mortgaged home, and funeral arrangements to be made.

On the flip side, Livy's mom was finally at peace, as was she. Now free to crawl out from underneath the wreckage that had been her mother's chaotic life, things were about to get very interesting.

Philomena Aveni was passionate about old books, art, and maintaining Little Italy's Italian-American culture. Unfortunately, teaching Algebra to snooty suburban kids excluded all three. So buoyed by a meager inheritance that included her deceased aunt's flower shop in Little Italy, she quit her job and moved into the tiny apartment above the shop. The rest was easy as cleaning house, changing inventory, and renaming the place Philomena's Art Gallery and Bookstore.

Robert Balfour strolled into the bookstore wearing a jacket, a tie, penny loafers, and a mustache so thin it looked like it had been penciled in. After a quick, disdainful look around, he asked, "Miss, would you happen to have a copy of *Romola?*"

Philomena gave him a quizzical look prompting Balfour to add, "George Eliot… Her greatest work…The gem that nobody ever reads."

"Including me, I guess," she said self-deprecatingly.

Her comment prompted him to take a closer look at the woman standing before him. The Ohio State sweatshirt, tattered blue jeans, high-top tennis shoes, unfashionably large pink eyeglasses, and silly bun pinned to the top of her head offended his sensibilities more than he'd cared to admit. *Why would Philomena hire someone who looked so unprofessional?*

Then she surprised him by offering her hand. "Hello Mr. Balfour. I can't tell you how happy I am to finally meet you. Oh, and I'm Philomena Aveni by the way."

He shook her hand reluctantly.

"I've read *The Unlikeliest of Heirs* three times," she gushed. "It's like nothing else I've ever read!"

"Three times?" He whistled softly. "A card-carrying masochist, eh."

Philomena's giggle brought a smile to his face. No one ever thought he was funny. But within seconds, he was back in character. "Your shop? This haphazard arrangement…Is it functional?"

She'd heard all the stories about the eccentric writer who lived on top of the hill. She'd also heard that he was totally unfiltered. Taking no offense, she responded, "It may not look like it, but there's a method to my madness, one that can best be explained via a grand tour." She stopped and smiled. "And lucky for you, that can be accomplished without moving an inch."

He turned and followed her pointing finger. "That section, it's obviously the bookstore. It may look a bit puny and disorganized, but it's mighty. Romance, murder-mystery, horror, gothic classics. Every bin and shelf clearly marked. Unfortunately, the aforementioned *Romola* is nowhere to be found."

He was a man who rarely connected to other human beings. But Philomena seemed different. Warm, intelligent, and fun, he instinctively liked her.

"And this part of the shop?" he asked as he turned toward the opposite side of the room.

"That's my meal ticket. Though books are my passion, I sell art for a living. That's why every nook and cranny is filled with paintings, mostly from local artists I might add."

Balfour, with Philomena on his heels, moved closer to several of the pieces. Finally, he settled in front of street scene. Vivid and garish, the textured piece was eye catching.

"You like that one?" Philomena asked.

"Wow, this is really good. The artist has really captured our little corner of the world. I especially like the men playing *Morra* on the sidewalk."

He took a closer look at the signature on the bottom and asked, "Does this Livy have a last name?

"Jardine. I have several more of her pieces. Her portraits are especially good."

"Hmm, very talented indeed."

"All pricing is negotiable," she added with a smile, sounding like a salesperson for the first time.

"Good to know." With that he turned toward her and extended his hand. "It's been a pleasure. I like your little establishment very much."

"It's been my pleasure. Please stop in again. I'll see if I can get my hands on a copy of *Romola* for you. Might read it myself."

He was halfway out the door when he noticed a cork bulletin board covered with index cards. Handymen, babysitters, apartment hunters, and dog sitters, all trying to make connections, but it was one card that caught his attention:

Need a dog walker, or dog whisperer who actually loves dogs? Call Livy at K91-WOOF!

He looked back at Philomena, and asked, "Not the same Livy, is it?"

Philomena nodded.

He looked at the card again before asking, "Is she any good?"

"Well, I don't have a dog, but from what I hear, she can straighten out even the most twisted, tormented little mutt."

"Wow, this is my lucky day. I just happen to have one of those."

MR. CHEEVES

Philomena called Livy to give her a heads up. Robert Balfour had taken her card. Expect a phone call.

The very next day Livy was standing at the Balfour gate, and as gates went, it was a massive, spiked deterrent to anyone who dared approach the sprawling estate that sat atop Mayfield Road. Two signs were posted on each side of the gate. NO TRESPASSING—VIOLATORS WILL BE PROSECUTED TO THE FULLEST EXTENT OF THE LAW! and GUARD DOG ON PREMISES!

Leather heels clicking on cobblestone pulled her attention from the warning signs to the driveway. A man, she guessed to be Balfour, was being dragged along by a small, barking dog. *Guard dog* indeed! By the time he'd reached the gates, the miniature Jack Russell had nearly barked itself hoarse. Perspiring and slightly winded, Balfour managed an introduction of sorts. "You must be Livy!"

She nodded and smiled. Philomena's description of the man had been spot on: "Tie, jacket, penny loafers, and a skinny, pencil-augmented mustache. And he has this slight British accent that's phonier than a three-dollar bill. He looks and sounds like an actor straight out of a Forties movie."

"Nice to finally meet you, Mr. Balfour."

He motioned her forward before pressing a remote-control button. The formidable gate creaked and moaned its way shut. A loud, latching clunk signified there was no turning back.

He gave her a quick once-over before they started the trek back up to the house. Without looking in her direction he candidly observed, "To be honest Miss Jardine, I was expecting someone a bit younger. Perhaps one of the university girls trying to earn some tuition money."

She'd heard that he was very eccentric, brutally frank, and occasionally unaware, but she was still taken aback enough to sputter and stutter a weak response. Trying to salve the sting of his words, he said, "I'm sorry. That came out all wrong. You're anything but old. And quite lovely too."

She smiled politely, but the truth was she preferred insulting and insensitive to creepy and lecherous. This wasn't how she expected the job interview to begin. With nowhere else to go, she got back to safer ground.

"I take it this little guy is the infamous Mr. Cheeves?"

Before Balfour could respond, the dog answered the question with three resounding barks that reverberated throughout the neighborhood before resuming his impression of an Iditarod contestant.

He nodded toward the animal. "As you can see Miss Jardine, you've got your work cut out for you."

She forced a smile. "That's why I'm here, right."

"So I see you found the place," he said awkwardly trying to fill the silence as they approached the front door. Evidently, small talk was not his forte.

She was now picking up on the British accent that Philomena had also observed, something she'd normally would've asked about, but thought better. As far as she knew the man was born and raised just up the road and that left only one explanation—the accent was fake, an artifice intended to impress. So she simply followed his lead. "Oh it wasn't hard. I grew up just down the hill. FYI, in the neighborhood, your house is referred to as the Taj Mahal."

He smiled, apparently pleased by the comparison. While holding the front door open, he motioned for her to enter. "Won't you come in Miss Jardine."

"Please call me Livy. Everyone else does."

"And Livy is short for what?"

She barely heard his question. The foray was that stunning. The double stairway, solid cherry from step to balustrade, rose up from both sides of the marble entrance to meet an upper walkway that led to sleeping quarters and god-only-knew what else. The ornate, crystal chandelier probably cost more than a luxury car. Livy felt like she'd just been transported back in time. The Tara Plantation came to mind.

"It's short for Olivia."

"Olivia," he repeated with the last syllable ascending a half-note. "Such a beautiful named to be chopped into little pieces. May I call you Olivia?" He didn't wait for a response or her permission. So from that moment on Olivia it was.

"We can talk in here, Olivia," he said, pointing to a den just off the foray.

Books and paintings everywhere, all screaming *anglophile on the premises. Fox hunts, English cottages, Windsor Castle, the Balfour coat of arms. It was Merry old England perched atop Mayfield Hill.*

He pointed her to a well-worn, cranberry-colored leather chair, while he sat a safe distance away on a love seat. Mr. Cheeves was off his lap and sniffing Livy's shoes and ankles liked she'd bathed in gravy. A few well-directed strokes encouraged him to leap onto her lap.

"Ah good, he seems to like you," he said. "Not true with most people." Balfour laughed. "Like master, like dog I guess."

Livy was beginning to relax, as was Mr. Cheeves, who flipped over on his back exposing his pink belly and other unmentionables. A belly rub was apparently on his mind.

Balfour couldn't conceal his joy at the scene before him. Mr. Cheeves was the only family he had left, and lately his behavior was zanier than usual. His vet could offer no solutions, thus Livy Jardine, the dog whisperer.

"So he's a puller," she began while still petting the dog. "Not so unusual for Jack Russells. They're a handful."

"I'm aware, but there are other things. Worrisome things."

She looked up when she heard him strike the match against the sole of his shoe. The smell of sulfur wafted across the room, as he continued to puff orange life into the pipe bowl. Satisfied that it was a fiery-go, he continued, "He hasn't been himself lately. He's had accidents in the house, not many, mind you, but he hasn't done that since he was a puppy."

"There could be a lot of reasons for that. Has he seen a vet recently?"

"Yes of course. The man was of no help. He offered some nonsense about Cheeves acting out because I leave him alone too much."

"Do you?"

"Do I what?"

"Leave him alone too much?"

"If locking myself in my study to write counts."

Pouting child came to mind as she pressed him for more. "How old is he?"

His tone lifted. "Eight. He'll be nine in September."

She smiled, he sounded more like a proud parent than a dog owner. "So is there anything else? Is Mr. Cheeves eating okay?"

"Yes."

The dog chose that moment to rejoin his master on the love seat. Livy was observing the man as well as the dog. Robert, while appearing to have it all, evidently had very little. Mr. Cheeves appeared to be it.

After he took a deep draw on his pipe, he said, "As you've probably noticed Olivia, I am honest to a fault. I just can't help myself."

He stopped and pointed to his temple. "I have a thought up here, next thing you know, I spill it. Put a nickel in, and the gum ball just comes tumbling out."

Not certain where all of this was going, she simply nodded and waited for some kind of punch line.

"Total candor can be a good thing, or it can be bad." Another puff on his pipe seemed to get him back on track. "I'm rambling, sorry." He stopped. "Ya know, I can't remember the last time I had someone visit my home."

"What a shame. It's such a lovely home."

He forced a smile. "Look Olivia, let me get to the point. I believe in first impressions." He paused a long moment before finishing. "Truth is, I like you, and more importantly Cheeves likes you."

Livy was relieved, the smile on her face said as much.

"And though I've done no background checks, you're hired, if you want the job."

She was stunned. "But we haven't discussed terms, fees."

He raised his hand to stop her. "If you fix my boy here, I will be very *appreciative*."

"I can't believe he invited me," Philomena effused. "An afternoon tea at the Taj Mahal. Who woulda believed it."

"He really likes you," Livy said. "And he especially loved your shop."

"He said that?" Philomena giggled like a schoolgirl. "Well, I was floored when you called me. I've passed this place hundreds of times always wondering what the insides looked like. And now," she stopped to fling her arms out, "here I am."

"Well, you can thank Mr. Cheeves. Best student I've ever had."

"I know this is gonna silly, but, my first thought was, what does one wear to an afternoon tea at the Taj Mahal?"

Livy looked her over. "Well, I certainly approve of your choice. I didn't think you owned a dress."

"Actually, I own two…You think the pearls are too much?"

"No, they're a nice touch. But the purple eyeglasses?"

"They match the dress," Philomena rationalized as she looked around the room admiringly. "Wow, this place is really spectacular. It's a lot bigger than I imagined."

"The man does have impeccable taste."

"Yes he does." After a quick spin around the room Philomena asked, "So what's he like?…I mean you have spent hours with him."

Livy thought for a moment before answering, "Smart, quirky, kind, and there's a sadness about him."

"He's sad, about what? He's got all this."

"Maybe melancholy is a better choice of words. I think he's lonely."

"But now he has you."

"Me? No, no. My job's done here. Cheeves is a new man."

"This arrangement doesn't have to end." She grabbed Livy by both arms. "Have you told him about your situation? Ya know, your mom's debts, and how bad things are?"

"No, I can't do that."

"Livy, Cassandra's throwing you out at the end of the month. If I wasn't already sleeping on the couch, you could stay with me."

"I'll think of something."

Balfour bounced into the room making a beeline to Philomena. After kissing her on the cheek, he said, "Welcome to my home! You look lovely, Philomena."

All aflutter she responded, "As do you Mr. Balfour."

He then pointed in Livy's direction and said, "And this woman, is she a miracle worker or what? In just one week, she's turned Mr. Cheeves completely around."

Philomena was beaming. "I told you she was good,"

Livy scratched Cheeves behind his ear. "If only my other clients were as smart as this little guy."

As Balfour was setting the tea tray and cookies on the coffee table, Philomena glanced out the window and spotted two thugs in leather jackets cleaning the garage gutters. They looked like two large dandelions popping out of the 18th green at Augusta, unsightly and completely out of place.

"According to the vet, his doggie IQ is off the charts," Balfour boasted, "and he's such a character. Totally irreplaceable. When he's gone, I'm done. No more dogs for me."

"He's one of a kind, that's for sure," Philomena agreed purposefully. Without knowing it, Balfour had just cued her next line. "Hey, I've got an idea. Maybe Livy could paint Cheeves' portrait? You know, maybe a way to immortalize him."

Balfour lit up. "What do you think, Livy? Ever paint a dog before?"

"No," she said as she looked over at Philomena, whose eyes were blinking dollar signs, "but there's a first time for everything."

He put his cup down. "So, how much would you charge?"

Philomena cleared her throat, a signal for Livy to take no prisoners. "I don't know, I'd have to think about it."

"You do that. And while you do, I'll pour us more tea?"

"Okay, but first I've gotta visit the little girls' room." Livy said as she jumped up.

Philomena immediately moved next to Balfour on the couch. After clearing her throat, she began haltingly. "Mr. Balfour, may I share something with you?" Now barely above a whisper, she added, "Something of a very personal nature?... It involves Livy."

With wrinkled forehead, he offered his ear. "Of course."

Though already knowing the answer, she asked, "Has Livy told you anything about her mother?"

"Not really. Only that she was a schizophrenic, and that she died several months ago."

"Well, there's a lot more. And believe me, none of it's good."

He looked around anxiously. "Maybe we should wait for her to return before we say anything more. Livy is a very private person."

Philomena chuckled. "Oh no, it's nothing top secret. She and I have talked about all of this a bunch of times."

"Okay, if you say so."

"You see, her mother left a mountain of bills that Livy feels obligated to pay back. Making matters worse, the bank also took the family home."

"Their home? God, that's dreadful."

"Yeah, that's why she does all these odd jobs."

"My goodness, and here I am, trying to negotiate with her like she's a common street vendor. I feel like a real heel."

"And ever since she lost her house, she's been living with a girlfriend. The rent's really low. The problem is that Cassandra is allowing her boyfriend to move in. So, Livy's out. I'd have her come live with me, but the area above the gallery is little more than a glorified phone booth. I sleep on a pull-out couch."

"So, what are you suggesting?"

"You have an in-law suite out back, right?"

"I do, but…"

"Look, Livy's skill set is nothing short of astonishing. I was thinking, maybe after she paints Cheeves, assuming she does, she could do your portrait as well?"

When he didn't respond immediately, she added, "Or, and please don't take offense Mr. Balfour, this place could use a freshening up. Some redecorating maybe."

He smiled. "And let me guess. Livy's an interior decorator too."

"That's right. Believe me, there's nothing our gal can't do."

He smiled. "She doesn't know anything about this, this little chat. Does she?"

"No, she'd be mortified if she did."

Just then Livy returned all smiles. "So, what did I miss? Mr. Cheeves balk at the idea of sitting for a portrait?"

Balfour looked over at Philomena and then back at Livy. "You know, I've been waiting for just the right moment to spring something on you. It's a little crazy."

Livy recoiled a bit. "That sounds kind of ominous."

Robert laughed. "Ominous no, vain yes... I've been toying with the idea of having my portrait done as well."

Livy joked, "Well maybe I can give you the family discount rate."

Balfour got up and repositioned next to Livy. "Listen, I've got something in mind, something you can nix it if it sounds too creepy."

"Whatever it is, it can't be any creepier than catching your gutter guy peeking in the window while I was sitting on the toilet."

"He did what?" Balfour ranted. "He'll be dealt with later!"

Philomena tried getting back to the matter at hand. "So Mr. Balfour, what were you saying before the peeping Tom interrupted?"

"Look Livy, I've got an in-law suite out back, some expensive projects in the works, including some possible interior decorating, and I was hoping that you and I could come to some kind of mutually beneficial arrangement."

Livy immediately looked at Philomena who was suddenly fascinated by the roses in the Persian rug. "So let me get this straight, are you suggesting one of those quid pro quo deals. A place to stay in exchange for what 'Judas' over there sometimes likes to call my 'special skill set?'"

"Yes. That's exactly what I'm suggesting."

She shook her head. "I don't know. You barely know me."

He nodded. "That's very true, but you'd have your own entrance, key, kitchen... And I'm declawed."

Philomena laughed a little too hard, fearing that Livy was about to blow a very generous offer.

"Okay, but once all the work is done, I insist that we rewrite the contract."

The live-in arrangement worked beautifully for several weeks. Livy, who painted both portraits before tackling the refurbishment project, felt good about her stay at the mansion. Robert was pleased with her work, and Mr. Cheeves loved the additional company.

Then the unexpected happened. Somewhere between the paint strokes and fabric swatches they became friends, unlikely friends who shared dreams, disappointments, and even some dark secrets. Not quite the grist priests and shrinks dissect, but it was close enough.

Then Robert got sick. A flu bug he called it. Whatever the mystery illness was, it left him weak and listless. Even Mr. Cheeve's antics and affection didn't rouse him from his lethargy. Livy, who'd just received news from Buffalo that her Uncle George had passed, was torn. Her favorite relative would soon be laid to rest, but leaving a sick man to attend a funeral seemed an irresponsible thing to do. And no one could ever accuse her of being irresponsible.

Of course Balfour would have none of it. She needed to be with family at a time like this. He convinced her that he was feeling better, so much so that he was thinking about accepting a long standing invitation from a friend who lived in Washington D.C. He'd tour the Smithsonian, visit the White House, maybe even go to a Washington Redskins game.

"I might still be gone when you get back from Buffalo," he said as he gave her a final hug. "Be safe and have a good trip," were his last words to Livy.

Returning to an empty house wasn't particularly worrisome, but when days passed without a post card or phone call, Livy became alarmed enough to alert the police, who in turn directed her to a UH nurse named Esther Bailey. "Robert Balfour," the nurse informed her, "is here at the hospital. He's comatose but stable." The fact that they had no idea what had caused the coma was the proverbial straw.

So with no idea what was wrong with him or how long he might remain non-communicative, Livy was committed to spending her days at his bedside, and her nights living in a mansion that wasn't hers, in spite of the fact that they'd only met weeks earlier.

Complicating her plans to hold down the fort, at least until Balfour's status changed, were a series of threats made by a pair of gang members—AKA, Balfour's voyeuristic gutter guys—who'd suddenly taken umbrage with her staying at the mansion. A dead cat in the mailbox, a slashed tire, and a number of breathless phone calls all intended to drive 'the poacher' out.

To her great consternation the cops at the Third District CPD didn't seem all that concerned about these threats. After all, she was a Jardine. Crazy mother, therefore crazy daughter. As syllogisms went, it was flawed, but the message was clear—the police were done chasing down Jardine boogie men. Livy was clearly on her own.

Although her head was on a swivel looking for bad guys in hiding, she hated guns and violence, which meant that the can of mace in her purse was her last line of defense, unless Jason Scarza could be recruited for bodyguard duty.

....

A recent downpour had come and gone, but the unpleasant mugginess remained. Another thunderstorm appeared imminent, bad news for a low maintenance, two-feet-on-the-ground-kind-of-gal who'd uncharacteristically tortured her curly hair into submission with a hot flat iron to impress a man she hadn't seen since she was ten. She didn't need a mirror to know that all the primping had failed, miserably. With her auburn curls now in full rebellion, the little-orphan-Annie-look prevailed.

Livy Jardine, with expectations bordering on the fantastical, had dressed that morning to accentuate the positive. Her bright colored sundress was cut short enough to show off her shapely legs and open-toed heels flattered her well-sculpted feet. Unfortunately, the uneven sidewalk and deep puddles made her choice of footwear problematic.

When the Scarza home came into view, she could almost feel Jason's presence and the possibility quickened her pulse, a response that surprised her. Toughened by years of crushing family responsibilities and an endless string of romantic disappointments, giddiness was no longer in her emotional repertoire. An ingenue she was not.

The stomach flip-flops, welcomed or not, caused her to revisit her expectations. Why was making a favorable impression on this guy so important to her? Certainly the threats made by neighborhood thugs were scary enough, and no doubt she could use the services of a bodyguard, but something else was at play. Perhaps her motives were better suited to a Harlequin plot.

The fact that she hadn't called ahead to announce that she was coming only added to her anxiety. What if Jason Scarza didn't remember her? Or he slammed the door in her face? Struggling with self-doubt, she started to turn around when she heard the sound of a whirring saw coming from the direction of the Scarza house, a homing signal of sorts that beckoned her onward.

She quickened her pace, and within moments she'd spotted him working on his grandmother's porch. Shirtless and on his knees, he appeared to be sanding a piece of wood.

From the sidewalk in front of the house, he came into clearer focus, especially his brawny back. It was a mural of colorful tattoos and scars that ran together like a seamless, sensual piece of art. And his face, appearing etched and gaunt, reflected a tough life lived. His dark brown hair was liberally streaked with gray. Boyishly handsome had morphed into middle age, albeit a ruggedly handsome middle age.

Why she was surprised by his seasoned look, she didn't know. After all, he was nearly twenty years older than the last time she'd seen him. Perhaps the obscenities of war had taken their toll, or maybe it was the cruel way his services were terminated by the country he loved. Whatever the reason, he looked different.

She stopped short of the porch with hands on hips waiting for him to look up, hoping he'd recognize her. She'd harbored a crush on that face since a long ago July 4th weekend, a fact that she wasn't ashamed to admit.

Everything about that day was burned into her brain. The parade, the fireworks, her Aunt's Jocelyn's new baby, and crossing paths with Jason Scarza for the first time.

And what a first impression it was! Though only a grade-schooler when she saw him in action that first time, the word "hero" suddenly had a face. From that day forward Livy cut out newspaper clippings about the high school phenom, and the Naval Academy All-American quarterback.

The fact that he'd become a highly decorated Navy SEAL was pretty much kept under wraps until he did something so heroic that he was invited to the White House to be feted. That story made the local newspapers, and her scrapbook.

And now, after so many years he was back on her radar screen.

Just a few feet away, he appeared to larger than she remembered. Broader, more muscular, definitely better suited to body guarding.

Not wanting to startle him she cleared her throat. Still nothing. Maybe he'd lost some hearing in battle, she reasoned. It seemed cruel that he'd travelled back to her from a lifetime ago, and yet now seemed out of reach.

Enough was enough, she wasn't a silly schoolgirl. The hello was on her lips when a dog lurking from behind the screen door struck preemptively. His loud barking froze her in her tracks and snapped Scarza's head in her direction. Quick to his feet, he grabbed for a tee shirt that was draped over the porch rail. "Hush Milo," he commanded. "You're scaring the young lady."

She wanted to say, *please leave the shirt off,* but offered an apologetic smile instead. *Young lady* had a nice ring to it, and his dog was a black Lab, named Milo. *How perfect is that,* she thought. Talk about completing life's circles.

It wasn't much of a journey back to the day when Scarza stopped by little Livy's house to give her a rescue dog named Milo, also a black Lab. *That can't be just a coincidence,* she reasoned hopefully.

"Can I help you, Miss?" Jason asked while slipping on his shirt.

His voice hadn't changed after all those years of crawling through jungles and killing fields across the globe. Masculine and warm, it still resonated with kindness. She remembered that voice as if that very special holiday weekend was yesterday. That's when she'd heard him for the first time from her aunt's bedroom window. A ten-year-old house guest with big eyes and curious ears drawn to an open window by a howling dog and an unforgettable showdown.

The scene was still vivid in her mind. Below her, in the neighbor's yard, a tense confrontation between Scarza, then a high school kid, and her aunt's neighbor Bruno Lentoni. She also remembered trembling because Bruno was so menacing.

A notorious Mafia foot soldier, Lentoni was in a foul mood that morning. He'd just flown in on a red-eye from St. Louis, and it was the one-year anniversary of his wife's death. The last thing he needed was to come home to find dog shit all over the house, and a police citation about his animal disturbing the peace tacked to his front door.

Truth was, the dog missed Donna Lentoni almost as much as Bruno did, but that didn't change the fact that he was in for a beating. And it didn't matter that the punishment was inflicted using a rolled-up *Life* magazine. Bruno held nothing back. The dog howled piteously with each blow causing Jason Scarza to halt his morning run, hopefully to stop what appeared to be blatant animal abuse. The fact that the abuser was the *most* notorious, dangerous man living in Little Italy made the situation dicey.

The folks living in the neighborhood knew better than to challenge anyone connected to the Dante crime family. It was tantamount to suicide. Of course this rule wasn't written anywhere, it was understood, an immutable law. You place your hand over an open fire, you're going to get burned. You go against the mob, you take a long ride to a New Jersey swamp. Why that scary truth didn't deter young Jason, even he didn't know.

"Whoa Bruno, that's no way to treat Jupiter. He's a good boy."

Bruno wheeled around, exposing bared teeth and a holstered gun.

"Just move on kid. This don't concern you."

"Of course it concerns me. No animal should be mistreated like that."

"Look Kid, if you're smart, you'll back off. Go home, get some milk and cookies. Go iron your letter sweater 'cause high school football heroes don't mean shit to me."

Unfazed, the young man stepped across the sidewalk and onto Lentoni's lawn. "Whatever you say, just give the dog a break, okay. He's had enough."

Bruno tried to rein himself in. This ballsy kid wasn't just any pain-in-the-ass, he was the neighborhood hero. "How can I put this so you'll understand? The dog doesn't concern you. He belongs to me. So, do me a favor. Go screw yourself. Or better yet, go screw your girlfriend."

Young Scarza smiled, but found none of it amusing. "Ya know Bruno, it's not just me who cares about dogs." The kid paused before throwing caution to the wind. "Enzo Dante, he owns dogs. You knew that, right? I don't think he'd be happy about Jupiter getting smacked around like this."

Even the little eavesdropper watching from the window above winced at that one. Everyone in Little Italy, including Livy, knew Enzo Dante's reputation, knew that he was "The Don" of the Cleveland crime family.

Bruno, a large man with a wolfish face turned scarlet as he stepped ever closer to Scarza. Bringing Enzo into the conversation had just escalated the crisis. "Why you little punk, are you threatening me?"

The young man never flinched, retreated, or raised his voice. He maintained eye contact throughout as he continued advocating for Jupiter. "No, of course not. Just trying to keep our little guy over there alive."

"Kid, kid, kid," the gangster hissed menacingly as he rested his hand on his holstered pistol, "maybe you should be more worried about keeping yourself alive. Capish?"

Livy buried her face deeper into the lace curtain. Everything had just gotten much uglier.

"I get it Bruno. Believe me, the last thing I wanna do is disrespect you."

Bruno had a reputation for being both volatile and violent, which made the steely stare-down that followed seem to last an eternity. But the gods were evidently smiling on Jason that day, for when that forever moment had passed, the mobster's gun remained holstered.

No gun play, that was a good thing. Taking that as sign for him to tiptoe forward, the boy continued, "So how 'bout this Bruno. What if we can make everybody happy here? I think I may have a solution for you, for Jupiter too."

Bruno held his hand up. "My god kid, you don't quit. Those are some big balls on you, coming into my yard," he was huffing and puffing as he ranted on, "giving me orders. You gotta a frickin' death wish or something?"

"No, but I do have a plan. What's the harm in listening?"

"Christ kid, maybe I'm the one who should be calling the cops."

Jason laughed, *that one was funny*. Dropping his voice didn't prevent little Livy from hearing what Jason said next. "Look I run by here all the time. I see what's going on. The dog's always tied up. He gets no exercise. He craps all over the place. He barks a lot."

"So call the animal protective league. FYI, good luck with that, my nephew works down there."

"We both know that'll never happen." Jason paused a moment to make sure his next words came out just right. "Look, I know Jupiter was your wife's dog, before she died. She wouldn't want any of this either. Let me have him. I'll find him a good home."

Bruno stopped, took his hand off his gun as he turned back to face the cowering Lab. Truth was, he hated the mutt because he reminded him of his wife's last days and her losing battle with pancreatic cancer. "You'd do that?" he asked softly. "You know someone who wants him?"

"I'm pretty sure. Yeah."

"Someone who'll give him a good home?"

An odd question for a man who only moments earlier had been

mistreating the animal.

"A very good home."

Jason couldn't be sure, but he thought he saw a lone tear appear on the gangster's pock-marred cheek before he quickly turned away to ostensibly give Jupiter one last head pat. As he handed the leash to Scarza he cautioned, "No one, and I mean no one needs to know about all this. Understand kid? 'Cause if anyone finds out about all of this, our conversation out here, our little deal…"

He stopped short of saying it. The mobster's stock-in-trade was his stone-killer reputation. He was one of the most ruthless, and feared men in the America's underworld. Backing down to a kid who was barely shaving would not only cost him "contract work," but in all likelihood, his life.

Jason Scarza, wise beyond his years, knew all of that when he called out to Lentoni, "Hey Bruno, you did a good thing here this morning. Your wife would be proud of you."

"Yeah, yeah kid. Just remember what I said about our little talk. No one hears nothin."

Livy Jardine snapped back from that unforgettable moment, from Bruno Lentoni's yard, just like someone had clicked fingers and magically transported her from her aunt's house back to Scarza's front porch, a breathtaking ride that had whisked her across two decades.

Now here she was, all grown up and staring into the Caribbean blue eyes of one of her childhood idols. Brawny, graying, and marred by a nasty scar on his cheek and a Roman nose that veered left, he looked nothing like that baby-faced man-child who'd gone toe-to-toe with Bruno Lentoni.

She began haltingly, "Hi Jason. I don't know if you remember me. My name's Olivia Jardine. My friends call me Livy."

No reaction from Scarza forced her to prattle on. "My family lived next door to the Longos, ya know just around the corner."

"The Longos, over on Wayside Road?" he asked.

"No, that's the wrong Longo family." She stopped and tried a different approach. "Maybe you remember Milo. His real name was Jupiter."

YOUNG ROBERT BALFOUR

Anton Chekhov, O. Henry, and Elijah Balfour were the three names that most often topped the list of the 10 Greatest Short Story Writers of All Time. Dominating the era between the World Wars, Balfour, a Shaker Heights native, won every award relevant to his genre.

His son, Robert Balfour I, chose a different path. He wrote novels, and lots of them—fifty, give or take. Many of those books topped the *New York Times* Best Seller list, some for years at a time. And twelve of his stories were made into blockbuster movies.

Because of his staggeringly successful lineage it was only natural for young Robert II to presume that he too would grow up to be a great writer. All he had to do was buy an old Underwood, amass stacks of the finest stationery, settle into a comfortable chair behind a sturdy oak desk, one that overlooked an inspiring vista, perhaps even take up pipe smoking like the Balfours before him, and begin madly typing away. Crisp strokes, keys biting into the white linen paper creating characters that would stand the test of time. Of course New York's publishing moguls would ring his phone off the hook, after all he was a Balfour. The debates about who was the greater writer, father or son, would inevitably follow.

It was a surprise to no one who knew him that young Robert penned three manuscripts before graduating from high school. Unfortunately, none of them could be mistaken for literature. So his father convinced him that a degree in journalism might be a good back-up plan.

Attending journalism classes at Ohio State, however, didn't dull his zeal for yarn spinning. His 4.0 GPA was even more impressive considering that he'd written four more novels while earning his undergraduate degree. Again, all of these stories were subsequently panned by his father's publisher, and anyone else with even an ounce of literary acumen.

Seven stories, seven flops. Flawless syntax and a vast arsenal of adjectives couldn't save his muddled story lines, and vapid, cliched characters. He could wax poetic with the most grandiloquent writers, but in the final analysis, young Mr. Balfour lacked the one gift that all great authors possess—the ability to tell a story.

So by his mid-twenties young Balfour Junior had lost confidence completely. He'd failed miserably at the only thing that really mattered to him. A deep depression followed. Once emotionally stalled, he began drinking in earnest.

Now very concerned about his son's declining condition, Balfour Sr. got his son a job as a sports reporter for the Cleveland *Plain Dealer*. He also suggested that being out on his own might help him grow as a person.

"Travel more, try new things, and experience life," advised his father. "Once you've done that, who knows, maybe something will click for you."

So he moved out of his father's house in Shaker Heights into a gated mansion on top of a hill that abutted a cemetery, the same cemetery that had given birth to a tiny hamlet called Little Italy. He wasn't certain about the logic of it all, but desperate times called for desperate measures.

Something had to change. He needed to think differently. Fresh scenery might give him fresh perspective, and fresh perspective might be the catalyst needed to stimulate an imagination that had been scarred over by numerous failures. Who knew, if interesting locales in Western Europe could spark Ernest Hemingway's creativity, perhaps Little Italy, acting as his muse, could do the same. The writer that was trapped inside him could only hope.

9

JOHNNY EAGLE | MARCH, 1961

Balfour's first job as a writer for the *Plain Dealer* sent him to Tucson to cover the Cleveland Indians' spring training camp. He had mixed feelings about the assignment. Though he liked baseball, it wasn't one of his passions. Politics seemed a better fit, but he couldn't deny the fact that he needed the job. So to get his father off his back, he hopped on the first plane to Arizona making sure that he'd packed his PRESS CORPS badge.

The Cleveland Indians' pre-season camp was filled with talented players, many with interesting backstories, but it was a batting practice pitcher, Johnny Eagle, who caught Balfour's journalistic eye. Considering the fact that the only person on the baseball food chain lower than the batting practice pitcher was the batboy, Johnny Eagle was an interesting choice of subject matter.

What made the Native American's story so compelling was how quickly greatness had been snatched from him. At the start of the 1941 season the young Navajo was the best pitching prospect in all of baseball, by seasons end, he was little more than broken equipment tossed onto the scrap heap. His pitching days were over before he reached voting age.

Motivated by pity, the Indians' brass offered Eagle a job as a batting practice pitcher. Twenty-three years later, he was still tossing batting practice on the Cactus League circuit.

Balfour, using the Native American angle as a hook, decided Eagle's story was much larger than grown men playing America's favorite past time. Hopefully, by using the Navajo Reservation as his backdrop, his readers would become more aware of the dire plight of the reservation Indian.

The Johnny Eagle interview began in earnest on day two of training camp. More accurately, the evening of day two. At Balfour's insistence it took place in a one room house that Eagle had grown up in, one that he still called home. Situated on the outskirts of the reservation, some might've described it as a modest dwelling, others a shack. The living area featured four chairs, a table, one lamp, a pull-out couch, a stove, refrigerator, and a toilet and shower barely concealed by a beaded curtain.

Balfour found the Navajo interesting to talk to, innately intelligent, and extremely worldly for someone with such humble roots.

Considering the fact that Eagle's tribe had long ago been relegated, in a most inhospitable way, to alien status in a land that was theirs to begin with, he still managed to carry himself with a kind of regal dignity.

The rookie reporter found Johnny to be an interesting interview. The subjects they discussed were far ranging and sometimes bordered on the profound. The writer was most curious about life on the reservation. Surprisingly, baseball was barely mentioned.

"So your teachers, the ones on the reservation, they were Catholic missionaries?"

"Not all of them," Eagle answered. "But it was a priest, Father McAdams, who influenced me the most."

"So you're a Roman Catholic?" Balfour pressed.

The Navajo smiled broadly, evidently finding considerable humor in the question. The toothy grin revealed missing molars on both sides of his mouth. Evidently, dental care benefits didn't come with pitching batting practice. "Not really. The God of the Catholics sits on a throne in heaven, mine is everywhere. In all things."

"So you're an animist?"

"Why put a label on everything?" the Navajo asked, as a sage might. "We walk this earth for a very short time, and then we die. We can take nothing with us on our next journey because we own nothing. We're merely tenants living on someone else's land."

Balfour squirmed a bit in his chair. The mansion that he'd just purchased, the one perched high above Little Italy, was blatant materialism run amok. High gates, private property signs, and a host of security cameras screamed—**this is mine, get your own!**

"Eventually," Eagle went on, "we close our eyes for that very last time and become one with our ancestors. One with the cosmos. It's all one big circle my friend."

"So you're definitely not a Catholic," Balfour observed wryly, "and yet, you wear a crucifix around your neck."

"A gift from Father McAdams." Johnny got up and walked to the stove and brought the coffeepot back with him. After refilling both cups he set the pot down on the scarred table and continued, "Truth is, I'm who I am today because of that priest. He was tough, but he taught me how to read, how to think critically." He took hold of the crucifix and held it out for closer inspection. "I wear this cross to honor him."

Balfour, though a nominal Catholic, found Eagle's reason for wearing the crucifix somewhat blasphemous, but decided not to go there. Instead he kept it light. "Did he teach you how to throw a baseball too?"

"As a matter of fact, he did." The Navajo paused to chuckle. "The man built a baseball diamond smack dab in the middle of the reservation. And he caught hell for that."

"Why?"

"Dunno exactly. Probably had something to do with graft and corruption. Indian agents are some of the most corrupt bastards on the planet."

He looked around the shack. *Desert land nobody wanted, drafty shacks with few amenities. All gifts of the white man, and pretty shabby ones at that.*

"Father McAdams was something alright. He loved baseball, the Brooklyn Dodgers in particular." Johnny smiled as he recalled all the hot-stove debates they'd had, and the pointless passion of it all. "Duke Snider was his guy. Said he was better than Willie Mays."

Balfour sat back, slurped his coffee while studying the Navajo's etched face. He looked every inch the Native American with his long black hair pulled back into a ponytail. Though his large hooked nose dominated his face, it was his piercing black eyes that were his most salient feature.

The Navajo stopped talking about baseball as he grew more pensive.

Balfour was not about to interrupt the nothingness of the moment. Sometimes, good things come from moments of nothingness. He'd let Eagle decide the drift of the conversation.

The silence was finally broken with a chuckle, then came the really good stuff, the weighty stuff. "This really is something, ya know, you and me meeting like this."

Balfour nodded, but said nothing.

"The irony of it all." He paused. "It's funny, the silly game of baseball of all things, brought us together. We were two strangers on a very big planet with absolutely no chance of ever meeting. And yet here we are, a pretty unlikely match if you ask me."

Balfour couldn't agree more, but he didn't see the irony in their newly forged relationship. His narrowed, searching eyes said as much.

"You don't see it? It's almost comical. You flew all the way out here to write stories about professional baseball players. Instead, you wind up here, miles from the team's camp, on an Indian reservation interviewing me, a batting practice pitcher. And to make it even more laughable, down deep, you'd rather talk about anything but baseball."

Balfour shook his head and laughed. "You picked up on that huh?"

"It was hard to miss, especially knowing your background."

Surprised by the reference to his background, Balfour blinked twice before asking, "My background? You know about my family?"

"A little. I know you come from a family of great writers."

"Yeah, my grandfather wrote short stories, my dad novels." Robert sighed, his ambivalence quite evident. "Very successful, the both of them."

"I know, Father McAdams was a big fan, of your dad especially. The man can really spin a tale."

Robert grew pensive. He'd moved out of his father's house, travelled across a continent to get himself out of his father's long shadow, and now here he was, once again the underachieving offspring of one of the world's greatest writers.

Balfour nodded, and then for no apparent reason added, "Ya know, he got me the job at the *Plain Dealer*...No doubt had to call in lots of favors."

Eagle gave him a long look. "You say that like it's a bad thing."

Robert rolled his shoulders and contorted his face.

"You can't condemn him for that Robert. He was just doing what fathers do."

"Maybe so, but it still hurt."

"How so?"

"The way he went about it. Pretty much said that I lacked talent. That I'd never be a novelist. He basically told me to pack it in."

"I hope not his exact words," Eagle said softly.

"Not quite verbatim, but close."

Eagle grimaced, "Ouch! That's pretty rough stuff."

"No doubt. But to be fair, he wasn't wrong about any of it. I've got a big stack of dusty manuscripts in my den that prove he's right."

Eagle waited for the rest of the postmortem, and when it didn't come he observed, "Kinda sounds like you've given up on yourself too?"

Robert shrugged his shoulders. "Thought I should concentrate on this gig, ya know. I owe the old man that much."

Eagle hesitated a long moment. "So if you don't mind me asking, how many manuscripts have you written?"

Robert shrank back, almost embarrassed to say the number out loud.

"In all, sixteen novels and five short stories." He shook his head. "Even sadder, I'm a Balfour for chrissakes. Publishers would've sacrificed their firstborn to run my father's next book. And yet, not a single one of them showed a lick of interest in my stuff. It was devastating. It almost destroyed me."

Eagle rocked back in his chair and opened his mouth as though he was about to speak, but stopped himself, prompting Robert to ask, "What?... Just say it."

"Well, I think this might be a good time to tell you something. Something about me."

Robert sat up straighter anticipating a possible confession, the outing of some dark secret.

"In my tribe, amongst my people... I'm considered a Shaman."

Robert bit his lip to keep from smiling. "You mean like a holy man?"

"Well, I prefer to think of myself as a healer... An herbalist who also dabbles in the metaphysical."

The Navajo studied Balfour's reaction closely. It was obvious that the job title had amused his guest. "FYI, after my pitching shoulder shredded, I took some classes at Tempe. Psychology, Philosophy, Religions of the World."

"That doesn't surprise me at all. You're smart, and obviously introspective."

"I realize that twelve semester hours is only a drop in the bucket, but if you factor in Father McAdams' wisdom and tutelage, all the research I've done on my own, and my exposure to tribal medications..."

"Tribal medicines?" Robert scoffed, "You mean hallucinogens."

Eagle nodded, then reached into the pocket of his flannel shirt and pulled out a small plastic bag that contained a brown powder. After placing the bag on the table he asked, "This assignment of yours... profiling a bunch of dumb jocks...do you honestly think that's gonna change anything in your life?"

Balfour, not sure what Eagle wanted him to say, merely shrugged his shoulders.

"That's what I thought." Eagle said forcefully. His mood and tone had changed. He was now in *closer* mode. "So, your failure to emulate your father's greatness almost destroyed you? You did say that, right?"

Robert nodded.

"Look, I wasn't kidding before when I said I'm a Shaman. I have powers. I've helped people before."

Robert was having a hard time taking Eagle seriously. "Helped them how? Get 'em high?"

"I helped them open up their minds. Broadened their horizons."

"Were any of these people as pathetic as I am?" he asked skeptically.

The Navajo moved his finger back-and-forth in pendulum fashion. "Do not mock what you don't understand my friend."

"I'm not mocking you Johnny. It's just that I'm way beyond…"

"Beyond what?"

"Believe me, it's too late for me. I'm a lost cause."

"There's no such thing," Eagle countered as he nudged the baggie across the table until it was within Robert's reach. "Believe me, I can help you. You came here looking for my story. Maybe I can help you rewrite yours. Help you realize your full potential."

Robert frowned. Suddenly things had gotten a bit too intense for his liking. Angrily he asked, "My potential to do what? Be a better sportswriter?"

Eagle got up and purred, "You can be anything you want my friend. The sky's the limit." Balfour watched as he dragged his chair closer. The next thing he knew the Indian was practically whispering in his ear. "I know we just met, Robert, but I like you. My gut tells me you're a good man. My gut also tells me that you've got one great novel in you."

"And you think that little bag will do the trick?" Robert smiled warily. "You do know that I'm a recovering alcoholic?"

"Completely irrelevant," Eagle declared confidently. "It's mostly peyote…Not addictive…LSD has twice the kick."

Balfour arched his eyebrow. "*Mostly* peyote?"

"Look, I'm an herbalist. And a very creative one at that." He pushed the bag a little closer. "Take it. Spread your wings, soar like an eagle."

THE ARTIST

"Little Livy? You're Milo's little Livy?" Scarza wore dumfounded well, a Martian sighting would've stunned him less. "Why the last time I saw you, you were this tall," he gushed while lining up hand to hip.

Livy was pleased by his reaction, that he remembered her at all was remarkable. And unless she was mistaken, he seemed genuinely glad to see her. "Well, I *was* only a fifth grader at the time. So..."

"Yes you were, and mature beyond your years."

Surprise furrowed her brow. "And how would you have known that?"

"Because I canvassed the neighborhood. Asked a lot of questions. I needed to find a suitable home for Milo."

"You did?"

"Yup, everyone I talked to gave me your name, and after I heard that you'd just lost your own dog, so I thought, the perfect match."

"Wow, you actually canvassed the neighborhood," Livy gushed.

"Yup, Milo deserved the best."

Livy looked over at the dog as he panted and slobbered all over the front screen. "And you named your own dog Milo. I think that's so sweet."

He chuckled. "No, that mutt doesn't belong to me. I'm just dog sitting for the people across the street. They're in Vegas, getting married."

"But the name?"

"His real name is Howard. I like Milo better. I think he does too."

She laughed, shuffled her feet while scrambling for the next topic to keep the conversational fires burning. The saw and birdhouse that cluttered the porch floor looked like possible icebreakers. "You make birdhouses?"

"Yeah, amongst other things. As it turns out, I like working with wood. Who knew? Coffee tables and rocking chairs might be more profitable."

"I can relate. I paint whatever sells best."

He smiled and nodded, all the while wondering why she was standing on his front porch, why she'd just dropped by after nearly two decades. Thinking it impolite to ask, he pursued the inane instead. "Ya know, given a little more time, I would've recognized you, even minus the pigtails."

Livy, who wasn't above using self-deprecation to lighten the mood or escape uncomfortable situations, joked, "Yeah well, a little humidity and a few drops of rain and this is what you get, all wild and woolly. More kinks than a cheap garden hose."

Feeling like a stand-up comedian who'd just bombed on stage, she regretted the garden hose analogy the instant the words left her mouth. *What could she possibly have been thinking?*

Jason chuckled, but he was smart enough to say nothing about her wayward hair. A veteran of guerrilla warfare, he knew booby traps, and this definitely was one.

Unnerved by his steady gaze and broad smile, nonsensical verbiage just continued to roll off her tongue, most of it having to do with the curse of having red hair. Mercifully, Livy was rescued from herself by someone standing behind the screen door who suddenly called out, "Jason, who's the pretty girl?"

Before he could answer, his grandmother was standing next to him wearing a white apron over a floral cotton housedress. The red stains on her apron matched the tomato sauce that coated her wooden spoon, the one she was waving about as though it was a maestro's baton. Her black geriatric shoes were all laced up, and her nylons were rolled down to mid-calf. A gold crucifix adorned her large pendulous breasts. Her thinning white hair was pulled straight back into a bun.

"Gramma, this is Livy," Jason answered. "Livy Jardine."

"I know who she is," the old lady teased as she playfully jabbed his arm. "She's a neighborhood girl. I recognized her right away. She's the artist."

Livy was flattered. Being called "the artist" was a new experience for her. She reasoned that being called "the" anything was a separator of sorts, and she considered that to be a good thing. "It's very nice to meet you Mrs. Scarza."

The old lady threw a beefy arm around the young woman and pulled her closer. "It's Gramma Scarza honey. Better yet, just call me Gramma."

They just stood there gawking at her like she'd stopped by to sing a telegram, but when that didn't happen, Gramma took Livy's hand and pulled her toward the door. "My grandson's got no manners. Come into the house. I just baked some bread."

Livy looked to Jason who sanctioned the invitation with a shrug and a smile. "Okay, but just for a few minutes. I've gotta be somewhere this afternoon."

The home, like its owner, had seen better days, but that didn't lessen its value. To Gramma Scarza, it was a precious heirloom, a museum of family history. Her grandfather and father were born in an upstairs bedroom, as was she. They also died in the same room. It was all so cyclical, all the births and deaths strung together like pearls on a string. Was there a better way to define history?

"This here is the kitchen," she announced with a sweep of the hand.

Everything about the room was oversized, including the stove, double-doored refrigerator, elongated cabinets, and a huge kitchen table that seated eight. A yellow oil cloth that featured an array of fruits and vegetables, covered the table. The double hung window placed above the sink offered little sunlight and a big chunk of the neighbors' gray clapboard siding. Unlike Gramma's kitchen, housing was tight in Little Italy.

The smell of garlic filled the air, as did the sweet smell of freshly baked bread. Culinarily challenged for much of her life, Livy found the aromas intoxicating, mouth-watering even. Gramma, a reader of minds, purred, "I don't mean to brag, but everybody in the neighborhood says my homemade bread is the best on the Hill. Even better than DiCorpo's Bakery."

"The best on the Hill," Jason seconded, while patting a gut that was washboard flat.

"And you came just in time," Gramma added exuberantly, "I just fried some peppers and sausage. We'll eat, but first I wanna show you the rest of the house."

It was dinner time somewhere, thought Livy as she followed Gramma into the living room, and hungry or not, they were going to feast. Gramma Scarza had spoken.

The living room featured sepia-toned photos of men wearing three-piece suits, ties, fedoras, and their women were all gussied up in long dresses, white gloves, and towering pompadours. It was Ellis Island meets *GQ.* Every shelf, table, nook-and-cranny either featured someone who'd impacted the house, or Gramma Scarza. Religious statues and crucifixes were scattered here, there, and everywhere.

On a more amusing note, most of the living room furniture was covered with clear plastic. With Gramma Scarza up in years, it wasn't silly or cruel to ask, why?

Standing in the middle of the room, Gramma suddenly looked even smaller than her five-foot-stature. Her voice seemed to get smaller too. "When I was a little girl my father would sit right over there, listening to the radio. He loved opera. My mother would be next to him, sewing." Her eyes misted up. "And my brother and I would play Jacks on the floor, right there by the coffee table. They're all gone now...It all seems like just yesterday."

Jason swept in to protect his grandmother from her own memories. He felt that her heart had been tugged on enough. "C'mon Gramma, Livy's hungry. Let's have some of that bread while it's still hot."

The old lady, not quite done yet, pulled Livy along. "Hang on, I wanna show Livy the den. And while you're at it, put Howard in the back room. He's slobbering all over the furniture."

"But Gramma, the den's a mess," he protested.

She ignored him and trudged on. "Right this way honey. Wait 'til you see this!

The room was cluttered and dusty, and filled with every award that Jason had ever garnered. Dozens of trophies of every size and description, medals for bravery, scrap books filled with achievements, photographs of athletic glories and barrack buddies.

Embarrassed, he grabbed Livy's arm and began to kid. "Okay folks, the shows over. Let's move it along." But before he could get her to exit the room, Livy spotted something in the corner, a large mystery item that was blanketed by a white sheet.

"It's a piano," Gramma volunteered. "Jason's piano."

"You play?" Livy asked, more than a little surprised.

"I used to."

"He sings too. Like an angel. He still gets calls from agents."

"All ancient history…Believe me, no agents are calling."

"He played in a band in high school," Gramma added. "He and Calvin Short. They were on TV…Jason was even offered a music scholarship to Julliard."

"Julliard?" she asked, obviously impressed.

"It sounds more impressive than it really was. Believe me, it was all kid stuff."

Livy sensed his reluctance, but asked anyway, "Would you play something for me? Even a few arpeggios will do… Please."

He shook his head. "Maybe some other time. Let's eat."

Fried peppers and sausage on homemade bread—talk about your lip-smacking-wipe-the-olive-oil-from-your-chin-kind-of-hedonistic pleasure. Gramma glowed. Nothing made her happier than feeding people. Coffee and her homemade anise flavored biscuits brought brunch to a tasty close.

For Livy Jardine, the visit had been wonderful, yet somehow felt weird. Virtual strangers had invited her into their home, fed her, treated her like family, and yet, just a few hours earlier, they might have passed her on the street without a single word being exchanged.

Weirdness aside, Gramma Scarza had proven to be an unexpected ally, albeit a very transparent one. To her way of thinking, her grandson, struggling with some weighty issues, needed a special someone to get him through these very dark days. And then Livy showed up, apparently an angel sent from heaven. There was little doubt that her round-the-clock Novenas had finally paid off. Now, they just needed a push, a little jumpstart—this one coming from a lovable cupid armed with wooden spoon instead of a bow-and-arrow.

With little time to lose, her matchmaking attempts bordered on clumsy and comically direct. They started with, "Just like two movie stars, you two make a such a handsome couple." And ended with, "I pray to God every single night," she stopped to cast her eyes ceilingward and cross herself before finishing with a dramatic flair, "that Jason gives me some grandkids before I die."

Of course they talked about other things too. Jason's upstart furniture business and Livy's budding art career dominated most of the lunch conversation, but as they were clearing the table, Gramma Scarza, out of the blue, asked Livy, "The name Jardine, is that Italian?"

Livy, having grown up in Little Italy, recognized the question to be a loaded one. The standard joke on the Hill was, *everyone was either Italian or wanted to be Italian.* If one's name didn't end in a vowel, he or she was ostracized. The bias was especially applicable when looking for a mate.

"It's French Gramma," Livy answered honestly. But after seeing the old lady wince, she quickly added, "but my mother was 100% Italian."

Obviously relieved, Gramma said, "Probably Siciliano. A lot of redheads live in Sicily. Teresa Trivisonno, for instance, she came straight over from Messina. Talk about a carrot top."

And so, they pretty much discussed everything from recipes to canines, everything but the reason Livy had shown up on their doorstep.

So with no conversational openings presenting themselves, she found herself on the porch in Gramma Scarza's crushing embrace.

"Now don't over-do it with the sugar," the old lady cautioned her, "biscottis aren't supposed to be sweet. Remember, let the anise do the talking."

Livy took the recipe from her hand and gave Gramma one last hug. "Thanks for everything. I really enjoyed myself."

The old woman was safely in the house when Jason said, "It was great seeing you again Livy," while extending his hand. "You'll have to come back real soon."

Emboldened by Gramma's warm acceptance, she went for the hug instead of the handshake. It was a good, long hug. More importantly, Jason hugged her back. His hard body felt good up against hers.

She started down the porch steps before wheeling around. "I've gotta ask, aren't you even a little curious? Ya know, about why I stopped by today?"

He laughed. "Of course I am. I just didn't want to be impolite."

"So, you woulda let me just walk away without knowing."

"Okay, okay. I'm asking now. Why'd you stop?"

She climbed back up onto the porch. "It's kinda complicated. A bit awkward actually." She pointed to the glider at the end of the porch. "Can we sit for a second?"

The prolonged hug and move to the glider greatly pleased Grandma Scarza who furtively watched their every move from behind a living room curtain. God's plan, her plan, they were one in the same. More importantly, all her machinations seemed to be working.

"Do you remember my mother?" seemed a strange place for Livy to start her narrative, but Scarza ran with it.

"I remember that she was tall. And that she seemed... a little reserved."

"That's because she'd actually taken her meds that day."

"Whatever. I was just so happy that she agreed to take Milo in. The rest of the visit was just one big blur."

"Well, one visit doesn't reveal much." Livy glanced up at the neighbor's giant maple tree. Its fall foliage was a spectacular blend of reds and golds. *If only she had her paint supplies.* "My mom," Livy began again with a heavy sigh, "she was a very off-beat character." She paused to reconsider her choice of words. "Well, I'm being generous when I say off-beat."

She shifted, he shifted, their knees brushed, electricity arced between them. They both tried to ignore the spark as Livy forged on, "When I was little, her antics were kinda fun. She did off-the-wall stuff, like this one time when she put three cigarettes in her mouth and lit them all at once."

Jason smiled, "That's really not so crazy. I saw Red Skelton do it on TV once. The audience thought it was hilarious."

"Oh it gets worse. Another time my mother and I were shopping downtown when she decided that we should jump into the Public Square fountain. She almost got us arrested for that one."

He stopped smiling. He sensed that things were about to get much darker.

"Her stunts, they really started getting out of hand. Dangerous even. As a kid, I realized that something was seriously wrong with her."

"What about your father? How did he handle all of this?"

"How did he handle it?" She stopped to take a deep breath. "Well, one morning he says that he's going out to get a newspaper, and he never comes back. Not a word since. Never showed at my mom's funeral... He could be dead for all I know."

Jason had also lost parents, but he'd never been abandoned. Gramma had seen to that.

"So, it was just she and I. I couldn't leave her, so I passed on the idea of going to college and stayed home. For the next nine years, I watched her get sicker and sicker. She died last year."

"Oh, I'm so sorry."

She stopped him with an upheld hand. "Believe me, it was blessing."

Howard, AKA Milo, chose that moment to bark at the postman who was walking on the other side of the street. Grandma's hand suddenly appeared from nowhere to grab the dog's collar. The dog disappeared as a prop might in a magic act.

The interruption gave her pause to reflect on her mission. Talking about her mom was never a good idea, and an even worse idea would've been asking Jason to get involved in her mess. It was way too much, way too soon. The last thing she wanted to do was drive this great guy away.

It was at that moment of clarity that she decided to abort the mission, and her trumped up afternoon appointment was the perfect ploy. A quick glance at her watch prompted, "My God, I've lost track of time. It's almost one... I've gotta run."

He stood up with her as she continued, "I've been rambling on like a babbling idiot. I'm so sorry."

"Don't be." He smiled, took her hand and gently pulled her back down onto the glider. "What's the matter? Don't you think I can handle it?" He then brushed an unruly curl away from her eye. His fingertips were in no hurry to leave her face. "How bad can it be?"

Her heart fluttered. "Look, I can't even handle it, whatever *it* is.

I'm trying to spare you, that's all." She removed his hand from her face but continued to hold on to it. He made no attempt to disconnect. Gramma saw it. They were holding hands. Oh my God, a kiss seemed imminent.

"My mom, she had no idea about money. She lost our house, maxed out credit cards, blew her disability checks on bingo and lotto cards." Livy stopped herself to take a deep breath. "And then what did I do after she passed? I decided to clear the family's good name. Square up all my mother's debts."

She chuckled at the irony of it all. "To clear the family's *good name*. What a joke. A mentally unstable mother and a deadbeat father… The Jardine legacy."

"We control what we can control," he offered gently. "What matters most, you were there for her until the end. You were a good daughter."

"Thanks. I'll tell you one thing, my mom's madness kept me on my toes. Made me really resourceful. To survive, I've had to wear many hats. Which brings me around to the very sticky situation that I now find myself in."

"Ah, a sticky situation. My bailiwick… I just happen to specialize in sticky situations."

"Well, kinda think really, really sticky, like… quicksand."

"Quicksand…Funny you should mention quicksand. I've been neck deep in the stuff, and yet, here I am."

She took a moment to study his face before plowing straight ahead. "Okay, you asked for it. Here goes…Ya know the big house on top of the Hill?"

"The Balfour mansion?"

"That's the one. Well, the guy who lives there, none other than Robert Balfour himself, calls me about a month ago and asks me to straighten out Mr. Cheeves."

"Whoa, back up. Who's Mr. Cheeves?"

"Balfour's dog. One very mischievous Jack Russell I might add."

"Mr. Cheeves is a dog?"

"Yup. Ya see on my business card, I call myself a dog whisperer. You wanna hear my phone number?... K91-WOOF."

"Very clever."

"That's me, clever to a fault."

Jason, more than a little amused, asked with a straight face, "So did you straighten out Mr. Cheeves?"

"Yes, and while I was busy doing that, Balfour asked me to paint his portrait and the dog's as well."

"You painted a portrait of Mr. Cheeves?"

"Yup, and the little guy actually smiled for me…I'm not kidding." She grew more serious as she added, "Balfour was really appreciative, and really nice."

"I thought he was supposed to be a curmudgeon. A recluse."

"Well, he kinda is, but strangely we hit it off. So much so that he asked me to move in. Ya see, he has this in-law suite in the rear of the house. It's completely off by itself with a separate entrance and all."

Because she felt Jason recoil a bit, she quickly added, "Believe me, the offer was on the up and up. No funny business either."

With Jason still not convinced, she explained further, "I know the whole thing smacks of lechery, but I was homeless at the time. My roommate found love and I found the pavement."

"And Balfour knew all of this?"

"Yes, Philomena cued him in. In fact, the whole thing was actually her idea."

"Who's Philomena?"

"My best friend…My business partner."

Jason, becoming more smitten by the moment, smiled. "You actually have a business partner?"

"Yeah, she owns an art gallery next to DiCorpos. She sells my pieces."

Jason mulled it all over before segueing back to Balfour's mansion. "The fact that you were even inside the mansion is remarkable. To my knowledge, the closest anybody has ever gotten to that place is a quick peek over the cemetery wall."

"Well, that's not exactly true. But I'll get to that part in a minute."

"Good, another sidebar. I can hardly wait."

She shook her head. "I'm boring you, aren't I? I tried to warn you that this whole thing was complicated and messy. And now you're bored."

He squeezed her hand and moved closer, almost as if he was about to kiss her. "The one thing you aren't is boring."

With her heart racing, she gave a passing thought to initiating a kiss, but thought better of it. "Look, truth is, I'm beginning to bore myself, so I'm going to stop now. The rest of this sad tale can be saved for another day."

"You'll do no such thing. Tell me, what happened at the castle? And why you really come knocking on my door?"

"The long and short of it? Robert Balfour stroked. No, no, check that. I really don't know if he stroked, but he did wind up in a coma."

"Coma? What happened?"

"From what I've heard, he was out jogging when he went down. Conveniently, he collapsed right in front UH. He's been a patient there ever since. Strangest part, no one seems to know what's really wrong with him."

"So, your benefactor's in a coma laying in a hospital bed, and you're living in his house." He hesitated. "I don't see the problem, I mean, he gave you a key to the place. You're not trespassing or anything."

"I'm not finished. It gets even more bizarre. It seems he left a will."

Jason smiled. "Most people do."

"Yeah but do most people leave everything to someone they've only known for a few weeks? If he dies, I get everything. The house, bank accounts, investments, everything."

Jason decided the moment was right for some levity. "What, no provisions for Mr. Cheeves?"

"Not funny. Cheeves died last week. Broken heart I'm guessing."

Scarza shrugged his shoulders. "I have to admit it's hard to figure, but there's really nothing to fret about, other than Balfour's illness. There are worse things in this world than being the only heir to a large fortune."

"Worse things? Ya mean like receiving menacing threats."

"What?

"Yeah, at first it was a slashed tire on my friend's car. Next, I found a dead rat in my mailbox. Then a few days ago a man wearing a ski mask approached me on the driveway. Told me to pack up and leave the Balfour house, or else."

"Did you go to the police?"

"Yes, they pretty much blew me off after they heard that my name's Jardine. Lumped me with all my mother's bevy of paranoid-driven 9-1-1 calls."

A vein in Jason's temple had emerged, and his cheeks had reddened. "Do you have any idea who this guy is?"

"I can't prove it, but I think it's the gutter guy. Kyle Mangini."

Jason's eyes widened. "Mangini! I went to school with that low life. His brother Leo too."

"I know. I asked around. Thus this visit, and this very convoluted, crazy conversation."

He chewed on her story for a few moments before responding, "So what's Mangini's connection to Balfour, and you?"

"I guess for the past couple of years the Mangini brothers have been trying to ingratiate themselves to Balfour, pretty much volunteering for any odd job that he wanted done."

"Odd jobs? Like…"

"Cleaning the gutters, cutting the grass, re-roofing the carriage house, tuning his car, shoveling his drive. Anything and everything."

"That doesn't sound like the Kyle I knew. He was lazier than sin, and his brother Leo was even worse." He paused. "Do you think they knew that Balfour was ill?"

"I don't know. But they worked really cheap. Even gratis sometimes."

"Gratis?"

"Actually," Livy explained, "that part's not so surprising. I mean as generous as Robert was with me, he was incredibly stingy when it came to his other dealings. He said he couldn't help it. It was the Scotch in him."

"But Balfour had to suspect that something was up. Strangers don't do favors without expecting something in return."

"That was Kyle's point. He said that he and Balfour had an understanding. That he had a will to prove it, and that I was squatting. He wanted me out of the house, ASAP."

"A will huh. I can only imagine what that document looks like. These guys aren't too swift." Jason clicked his fingers. "Hey, what about security cameras. Maybe they were caught slashing that tire."

"Every camera has been mysteriously disabled. Maybe they're not as dumb as you think."

"No, they're pretty dumb. Amoral and stupid can sometimes be a very lethal combination."

"So what should I do? Maybe I should pack up and leave?"

"No, that's exactly what they want."

Grandma Scarza had heard enough. Through the front door she bolted moving faster than any octogenarian had a right to. While waving her wooden spoon wildly, she erupted, "Those Mangini boys have always been bad boys! Livy, you come stay with us."

A group hug ensued, and while still in the grasp of his distraught grandmother, Jason got Livy's attention with a roll of the eyes. He knew that Grandma Scarza wanted no more trouble for her boy, and the old lady was savvy enough to know how a confrontation with the Manginis might end. Her grandson needed no more brawls, legal hassles or jail time.

Livy watched as he moved his lips without uttering a sound. "I'll take care of it."

Though his words were reassuring, there was something in his eyes that frightened Livy.

12

CHAMPION

He couldn't stop thinking about Livy. Certainly she was pretty, but her appeal went much deeper. She was intelligent, easy to talk to, extremely candid, funny, and managed to pass the most stringent of all tests—winning over his grandmother. He felt like he'd known her for a lifetime, and in a way, he had. The fact that she was being harassed by vermin like the Manginis kicked him into protector mode.

Even before Livy had exited his grandmother's yard, Scarza had formulated a plan to free her of any further Mangini thuggery. It was a simple plan really—fight intimidation with intimidation. To do that, he needed to meet with Kyle Mangini face-to-face.

He'd known Kyle since they were first graders at Holy Rosary School. Even as a child, Mangini wanted to be a gangster, a notorious hoodlum like Al Capone. No big surprise there, for decades Little Italy had been a haven for mobsters who lived large, bought expensive cars, and dated beautiful women. The fact that they carried guns and never punched a time clock made their lifestyle even more alluring. To Kyle Mangini, mobsters were rock stars.

Kyle, with an IQ south of ninety, quickly found his ceiling in the mob hierarchy. Never someone the capos could trust with tough decisions, he became a grunt for the real gangsters, little more than a gangland wannabe.

So rather than being a minnow in a very large mob lake, Mangini struck out on his own by forming a gang called the Sons of Sicily Social Club. Petty thieves and drug dealers mostly, they attempted to ramp up their bad boy image by wearing leather jackets and riding motorcycles.

Everyone in Little Italy knew about Mangini's upstart gang making it quite easy for Jason to locate them. Every Saturday afternoon the Sons of Sicily met in the back room of the Mayfield Rd. Billiard Hall to play Poker. The stakes were high, the beer plentiful, and the conversation was typically vulgar and profane because that's the way bad guys were supposed to talk.

Though advertised to be a motorcycle club that espoused the Sicilian culture, the Sons of Sicily, never ones to shy away from the grandiose, stated their purpose for being in bold letters above their clubhouse entrance. It read, **"SONS OF SICILY—N***eighborhood watchdogs, head busters, vigilantes***! Outsiders BEWARE!**

So, even though they may not have been Hell's Angels, walking into the Sons of Sicily clubhouse uninvited was ill-advised. Since most of the members bordered on the psychotic and carried guns, Jason knew the risks when he walked in, unannounced. Curiously, Mangini's gang didn't seem all that surprised by the drop-in.

"As I live and breathe," Kyle shouted enthusiastically as Scarza walked through the door. "Jason Scarza. Here in the flesh. Honoring the Sons of Sicily with his presence."

Scarza replied with a nod before positioning himself directly across from Kyle. The dingy room, a converted storage area, featured warped paneling, a dozen cases of Budweiser stacked in a corner, a large flag of Italy draped across an entire wall, a couple of dusty bowling trophies sitting on a knick-knack shelf, two bar stools positioned outside the inner circle, and a round poker table surrounded by six folding chairs. One long bank of fluorescent lights bisected the water-stained acoustic tile ceiling. Since there was no window, the smell of beer, heavy smoke, and mildew collided in a most unpleasant way.

"Goddam paisan, you got bigger! What's up with that? Roids man?"

The members around the table, thinking their leader was amusing tee-heed a bit, then quickly put their menacing-face back on. Bottom feeders the lot of them, their common sartorial thread was a black leather jacket with a skull-and-crossbones on the front, and *Sons of Sicily* written on the back.

The inner circle included two skinheads, a guy sporting a mohawk and lightning bolt tattooed on his cheek, and a stout young woman with cropped blonde hair, nose, lip and eyebrow piercings. The name

Walter was tattooed on the side of her pale neck.

That left the Mangini brothers doing their best John Travolta impersonation—slicked back black hair and a cigarette dangling from the lip. They could have passed for twins except Kyle was much bigger than his younger brother. Two nondescript freaks, who were slouched on the stools in the shadows, completed the grouping of usual suspects.

"It's been a long time, Kyle," Scarza managed, the weak stab at civility being the best he could muster under the circumstance. They were, after all, the same men who'd been psychologically torturing Livy.

"Come to play some cards?" Leo asked while wearing a cat-who-ate-the-canary grin. "It's a twenty dollar buy-in."

Scarza quickly sized up the situation, and didn't like what he saw.

His surprise appearance didn't feel much like a surprise. Evidently, the gang knew he was coming. "No thanks Leo, I didn't come here to play cards."

"That don't matter," Kyle said. "It's just good to see ya Bro, especially after what you've been through."

Scarza, who'd anticipated the rest of the taunt, girded himself for the onslaught. He made such a great target these days. His sudden fall from grace had been more like a death spiral. For lifetime losers like Kyle Mangini, it was a rare opportunity to gloat, to go on the attack like hyenas watching and waiting for that moment when the fallen can't rise up to defend themselves.

"Man, when I heard what happened, I was shocked. I still can't wrap my brain around it. Just can't imagine you, you of all people, spending time in the brig." His smile was pure evil as he tacked on one final barb, "Is it true what they say about prison life. You know, how everyone becomes someone's bitch?"

Before Jason could respond, another man quietly entered the room and took his place behind Kyle. This guy, though quietly unassuming, demanded closer inspection. He looked like a comic book caricature of the missing link—squat, powerfully built, flat faced and grotesquely ugly. His eyebrows were scarred over, and his nose was pancake flat.

There was little doubt this gorilla knew his way around a boxing ring or a back alley.

The appearance of the newcomer set Leo off. Barely able to contain his exuberance, he clapped his hands while shouting, "Walter, you finally made it. And just in the nick of time."

Scarza, expecting a grunt-like response from the ape, got instead, "Heidi's directions left a lot to be desired. Sorry I'm late."

Kyle read Scarza's questioning look. Pointing to the only woman at the table, he began, "I'd like to formally introduce you to Heidi, Walter's kid sister."

Heidi looked at Jason as though he was raw meat and she was a starving lioness. "I heard you was Special Forces," she hissed, "but you don't look so special to me."

Jason had to smile. What a menagerie, and Mangini was the perfect ringleader. "So now that the gangs all here, what's next Kyle. Bear wrestling, cock fights, what?"

Kyle smiled. It was six to one, and that didn't even count his secret weapon, Walter. "You're right Scarza, I think the time's come to cut all the bullshit. Let's just get it out into the open. We know you talked to the Jardine woman."

Before Scarza could ask the obvious, Kyle quickly explained, "That's right we know. A little birdie told us."

"So I talked to her," Jason admitted, "and now I'm talking to you. Maybe we can come to some kind of an understanding."

"Understanding? Fuck that! The bitch is squatting on our property. We want her out of there, or there could be dire consequences."

Dire consequences? Jason smiled. Either Kyle had bought himself a dictionary or Walter had classed up the gang. "You know what they say about honey and vinegar."

Leo, champing at the bit for the main event to start, shouted out, "Honey, vinegar! Nobody gives a fuck about cooking. Are we gonna do this thing or not?"

"Whoa, let's slow down here," Jason cautioned, "if Balfour actually willed his house to you, I say. God bless and good for you. You two finally caught a break."

Not knowing how to respond to that, Kyle, wearing a confused smile, kept nodding his head vigorously. It sounded as though Scarza was siding with him.

"Can I see the will?" Jason asked as he watched Walter shift a bit closer. "You have got a will, right?"

Fury replaced confusion as Mangini shouted, "No, you can't see the fucking will. As a matter of fact, you have no say in this matter, that matter, or any other fuckin' matter."

Jason, with both eyes on Walter, let Kyle rant on. "Just because you and that woman are shacking up, that don't give you the right to come strollin' in here playing big Navy SEAL savior."

Jason smiled. "You think that's what I'm doing, playing?"

Kyle was so livid that he pulled a gun out of his belt and pointed it at Jason. With his handing shaking, he screamed, "Now what do you have to say? I could end this right now. Just give me a reason motherfucker."

"Cool it Kyle," he ordered evenly, "you don't want to make a mistake here."

"Mistake! Did you hear that boys?" After a grunt or two from the Sicilian Club misfits, he tacked on, "You still don't get it. I'm in charge, not you."

Scarza sighed, "Maybe it's time we change the rhetoric."

Disgust registered on Mangini's flushed face as he threw his hands into the air. "Rhetoric. Listen to this fuckin' guy. His back's against the wall, his life's flashin' before his eyes, and he's still tryin' to lord it over us."

Leo jumped in, "Put a hole in him Kyle. Drill the motherfucker!"

Kyle motioned for his brother to sit back down. Then he collected himself enough to continue, "Listen to me and listen good. We're getting nowhere fast. So, I'm gonna make you an offer. Take it, don't take it. I don't give a fuck 'cause truth is, I don't like you, and I never did."

At that most critical moment, Scarza knew the dispute wasn't going to end peaceably.

"See this card table," Mangini began deliberately, "it's round. Kinda like King Arthur's table."

Jason was surprised by the historical reference, obviously comic-book-inspired.

"The way I see it," Kyle continued as though he was holding court, "we're like two powerful lords fighting over the same castle."

Walter's face was partly obscured by a shadow, but Jason thought he saw the man beginning to salivate.

"Some lords like me, well we don't bloody our hands over trivial matters. We're above it. So, we have seconds. I believe the medieval term for them is champions."

Jason shook his head. It was like Rocky Balboa trying to play Hamlet.

"So, let me guess," Jason broke in. "Walter's your champion?"

"He's my champion. Indeed he is!"

"And?"

"And after the battle's fought, the winner takes all, in this case, the Balfour estate."

"Aren't you getting a little ahead of yourself. Balfour's still alive."

"Barely. It's just a formality, like you're gonna be after Walter pummels you to within an inch of your life."

While chuckling, Leo demonstrated what an inch looked like by holding up his thumb and index finger. "Within an inch, baby boy."

Like chimps at the zoo, Leo's antics seemed to incite the rest of the gang members who started pounding fists into palms while pointing at Jason. The only person who abstained from the histrionics and chest pounding was Walter, who watched with cold detachment and dead eyes.

Now it was Scarza's turn to be impatient. "So is that it, or are there more bullshit rules of combat?"

"No more rules, but maybe something you should hear." Mangini paused. "Walter's what some in the business might call a ringer. Twenty-one pro fights, he won 'em all. They were grooming him to become the next light-heavyweight champ until he got in trouble with the law. Unfortunately, they suspended his boxing license."

"Twenty-one fights, twenty-one knockouts mother fucker," shouted Heidi. "He even killed a man in the ring, beat him to death."

"His ring name," chimed in Leo with his spittle flying across the table, "was *Kid Impervo.* You wanna know why?"

Jason eyes turned to Walter. His mood seemed to change when Leo mentioned his moniker. Suddenly animated, he began shuffling his feet like a prize fighter waiting for the bell to ring.

Kyle, who wanted to deliver the juiciest part himself, waved his brother off. "He's called Kid Impervo because he's impervious to pain."

Kyle expected more of a reaction from Jason. When he didn't get one he continued, "Ya see, he's got this medical condition. A very rare one. It's called congenital anala...anala something or other."

"Analgesia," Walter announced. "Congenital Analgesia."

"Point is, my brother can't feel pain," Heidi interrupted as she rose to her feet. To her perverted way of thinking the situation seemed to call for some kind of show-and-tell exercise.

Jason watched as she raised a beer bottle menacingly over her brother's head. The thought that she might be bluffing was quickly quashed when she delivered a blow that could only be described as pure savagery. How that bottle stayed intact was anybody's guess. The loud thunk made Jason grimace. She smiled and then hit him again with the same result. Lumps formed instantly on the man's shaved head with nary a flinch or whimper. Diagnosis confirmed—Walter had congenital analgesia all right, complicated by having a moronic, sadistic sister.

"So there you have it," Kyle said proudly. "my man's a walking, talking, feel-nothin' wrecking ball motherfucker. Full disclosure complete."

"Seems pretty formidable," Jason said with little emotion.

"Fuckin' A," Leo erupted, "Walter's a fucking Sherman tank."

"Now you know the truth," Kyle began calmly. "Nobody in their right man would want any part of Walter." He paused. "But I also know how badly you wanna please your lady. So, if you like, I'll try to even the playing field a little."

Surprisingly, Scarza found himself becoming more intrigued.

"Should I go on, or has the sight of my champion made you shit your skivvies? Maybe, you can even wave 'em around like a white flag of surrender, if they're not too stained."

Jason smiled. He knew exactly how he was going to attack Walter, if it came to that. The fight would last less than thirty seconds, he guesstimated.

"I'll take that as a yes. Since Walter is so special, I'll relax the rules, ya know, so you'll have a fighting chance. So, how about this. Boxing, kick boxing, even that Karate bullshit, it's all good."

"Knowing about my training," Jason said, "that's pretty generous."

"And, because we grew up together, I promise I'll call him off before he kills you. I'll even drive you to the ER after he does what he does."

Kyle smiled. He was enjoying what he perceived to be the ultimate humiliation of Little Italy's native son, the college hotshot, the Navy hero. "And believe me, you're gonna need some serious medical attention."

"So, let's say I do this," Jason said, "and by some miracle I win, what guarantee do I have that..."

Kyle raised his hand in the air. "If you beat Walter," he began with a sincerity that felt genuine, "I'll back off your girlfriend, I swear it on my mother's grave."

Jason looked him in the eye. Somehow he believed him. "Okay."

Leo was on his feet ranting obscenities while smashing his fist into the wall. "Right now! It's happening right now!"

Within minutes both men were bare-chested and poised for battle. Now snorting like a wounded bull, Walter raised his fists in front of his face and marched straight into battle. He expected to fight a boxer but got a ninja warrior instead.

It was all so quick. Jason going airborne, and suspending his body in midair for what seemed an eternity. Then came the kick to Walter's solar plexus. Like a cobra's strike, it was swift, and deadly accurate. Though the Club of Sicily's champion may not have felt the blow, it registered in his brain nonetheless. He was down, out, and completely immobilized inside of fifteen seconds. The battle for the castle was over, or was it?

Heidi, leaving nothing to chance, had stashed a Louisville Slugger behind the beer cases. Her brother hadn't even hit the floor before she had the baseball bat in her hands. The violent blow to the back of Scarza's skull produced a loud thud, and the crunch of flesh and bone giving way to wood. The blood splatter from the wound found Heidi's neck and white t-shirt, and the feel of his warm blood on her skin stirred something primal in her. Her war whoop was a signal for the others to join in.

13

NAVAJO RESERVATION | SPRING OF 1961

"Look, I've taken this stuff myself. It has no side effects."

Balfour could feel Eagle's breath on his neck. The Navajo was that close. "Just tell me what's in the baggie Johnny, besides the peyote."

"Mushrooms, miscellaneous herbs. A touch of this and that. All nature's bounty man."

"I don't know about any of this. I can't afford to get wasted tonight. My editor's expecting my first installment tomorrow."

"Relax kid, you'll make your deadline. In fact, the peyote might expedite things," Eagle winked, "if you catch my drift."

"You should be more excited," Balfour gently scolded, "the folks back in Cleveland are about to find out who Johnny Eagle really is."

Eagle didn't respond. Instead, he let his eyes do a dance of seduction as they darted back-and-forth between the plastic baggie and the reporter.

Robert retreated and sighed, "Why are you pushing so hard? Why is it so important that I do this?"

"Because I like you. You're good people. You actually care about us. You see this reservation for what it really is, a concentration camp. A zombie factory!"

Robert stared at the peyote, and shook his head.

Disappointed, the Indian backed off, picked up the baggie, and moved back across the table. "I'm sorry man, I just wanted what was best for you." He paused. "But, it's obvious that you're not ready."

"Ready for what? Tell me again. I take this drug and then what? God talks to me? I get smarter? What?"

The Navajo frowned. "You're very negative my friend, and that's a big part of your problem."

Balfour's smile was one of resignation. "You're not the first person who's told me that."

"Look at it this way, what I'm offering is a kind of awakening.

Maybe even a rebirth."

"Awakening?"

"I know you're skeptical. And that's understandable. But, if I'm exaggerating, even a little bit about how wondrous this stuff is, I'll gladly forfeit my shaman license."

"You don't have a shaman's license."

They both laughed. "Okay, how 'bout this. You try my little bag of magic, and I'll give you some dirt on a couple of the players, star players at that. Booze, drugs, women. Believe me, some super scandalous shit. The people back in Cleveland will eat it up. You might even get a big raise."

"I don't want gossip, I want a guarantee that I'm gonna come out on the other side of this so-called *awakening* with my brain still intact."

"For the tenth time man, it's safe. Just fasten your seatbelt. You're in for the ride of a lifetime."

"And that's what scares me."

Eagle threw his hands up. "I don't get it. In one breath you tell me you're unhappy with your lot in life, and in the next, you refuse to try something new, something that might change everything for you."

"You're right. Maybe if the deadline wasn't tomorrow."

"Deadline," he scoffed, "who wants to read about a washed up Indian who tore up his shoulder a hundred years ago."

Eagle's young protege was showing signs of waffling, so he kept pounding away. "The time is now my friend. It's time to soar, to touch the sky. Get you a little taste of the ambrosia."

Balfour shrugged. Maybe it wasn't so crazy after all. What did he really have to lose? The dead-end job that his dad had gift wrapped for him? He'd listened to that timid, ever-cautioning voice in his head for twenty-five years and what had it gotten him? He was stuck in neutral, paralyzed by a fear of the unknown. Afraid to die, afraid to live, but mostly he was afraid that the mounting pile of dusty manuscripts stored in the bottom of his closet would be his only legacy.

Johnny Eagle, now sensing submission, eagerly looked on as

Balfour picked up the baggie. He appeared ready. The confidant, the guru suddenly became the seducer. The moment the baggie's contents were ingested, Eagle maneuvered Robert back toward the pull-out-bed. It was a mere five step journey. Being supine was the best way to enjoy the trip.

"Just lay back man, close your eyes, don't fight it Robert."

It didn't take long for the drug to kick in. Preconceived notions about exploding skyrockets and armies of white-robed seraphim serenading him with a chorus of "hallelujah" never materialized. He did experience a warm glow, an accompanying serenity, and the fragrant smell of hyacinths and lilacs. He was free-floating, adrift in a place where, off in the distance, a woman was calling his name. Then a soft hand touched his cheek.

Was he dreaming, or did he really have company? Or the more likely scenario, he was experiencing a drug-induced hallucination. When he tried to open his eyes to find out which, his eyelids felt heavy, his limbs were rubbery. Fearing the possibility of an overdose, panic began sweeping over him until he saw the blurry outline of a woman who was bent over him. She smelled good, like lilacs and hyacinths.

He wanted to reach up and touch her face to make sure that she wasn't just a figment of his imagination. It was then that the woman whispered something that he couldn't make out, but before he could utter a sound or protest, she kissed his mouth. The sensuality of the kiss quelled all his fears. Whatever parallel universe this was, the mystery woman had him completely under her spell. Her touch, her deep kisses aroused him like he'd never been aroused before.

Her mouth melted into his as she lightly stroked his full-blown erection through his jeans. On the brink of ejaculation, she undid his pants and climbed on top of him. And that quickly, he was inside her. This kind of passion, this stallion-like vigor was new to him. Now was the time for exploding skyrockets, and an army of seraphim belting out the lyrics of "Hallelujah."

She was an incredible lover. She'd taken him places where mere mortals seldom go. And all the while she rhythmically moved up and down on him, she kept whispering. "Emanuelle. Emanuelle. Emanuelle."

What happened after they'd finished making love, he wasn't completely certain. He did remember they'd talked for a long while. Her voice, like her touch, was soft, mesmerizing, hypnotic even, causing him to drift in and out, his eyes too heavy to open.

The next thing he knew a rooster was crowing. Intrusive and annoying like the buzzing of an alarm clock, this was not the sound one might expect to hear in Avalon.

Dawn had broken, and when he awoke Emanuelle was gone. Determined to find her, he rushed to get dressed, all the while thinking she couldn't have gotten far. She was definitely of Native American descent, and probably lived somewhere on the Navajo Reservation. How hard could it be to find her?

So door-to-door he went describing a statuesque woman in buckskin, a woman named Emanuelle. He canvassed the Indian lands for most of the morning, but no one knew her, or of her. It was like she was a phantom, a woman that Eagle had materialized for his pleasure only. Or maybe it was just the peyote at work?

For days he tried to piece together the details of that amazing night, but all he could remember were the kisses, the magical fusing of their bodies, her deep honey-coated voice, and the name—Emanuelle.

It seemed odd that they'd talked, for what seemed like hours, yet the specifics of the conversation had escaped him. Blanks, that's all he was drawing. What had they talked about? Were promises made? Deals struck? What secrets were shared? Perhaps Emanuelle was the enlightenment, the inspiration that Johnny Eagle had promised him?

Tormented by so many unanswered questions, Robert Balfour II had only one place to turn for answers—Johnny Eagle.

14

A DEBT REPAID

A concussion, two cracked ribs, assorted facial lacerations, and a bruised kidney put Jason Scarza in a hospital bed down the hall from Robert Balfour. Two Cleveland Police detectives came calling soon after.

"My name's Detective Ambrose. This is my partner Ed Lange."

Jason tried to sit up straighter but his injured ribs objected.

Still navigating through a concussion haze, he tried to anticipate why two cops were paying him a visit. He hadn't phoned them or pressed charges, and the Manginis certainly wouldn't want the police nosing around in their clubhouse shenanigans.

The next words out of Ambrose's mouth sent off alarm bells in Jason's already throbbing head. "We're from homicide."

He racked his brain trying to make sense of it. *Homicide!* Who got killed? Not a single murder scenario presented itself, not really all that surprising since Heidi had bashed his skull in with a Louisville slugger.

"I hope you don't mind us asking you a few questions," Ambrose began apologetically. "You look pretty uncomfortable, so we'll be brief."

Jason heard the detective's words, but nothing was registering. He was too preoccupied with trying to piece together the fuzzy details of the billiard hall debacle to produce any kind of scenario where a corpse might be involved. As far as he knew, he was the closest thing to a homicide victim carried out of the Sons of Sicily Clubhouse that fateful Saturday.

Detective Lange, seeing the searching look in Jason's eyes, asked, "Are you okay? Did you hear what my partner just said?"

"Yeah, yeah. I heard him. You have questions that need answering, may I ask about what?"

"Let's start with your relationship to Kyle Mangini," Ambrose said, without really addressing Jason's inquiry. "It's our understanding that you two go back a long way."

Kyle Mangini, Jason agonized. *If he'd initiated this visit from the cops, it spelled trouble, especially since control of the Balfour estate was still up in the air. Framing Jason for some unsolved murder would take him out of play, leaving Livy to soldier on alone.*

Remembering nothing after he'd kicked Kid Impervo in the chest was definitely complicating things. Maybe the Manginis hadn't needed to frame him at all. Was it possible that the one, well directed blow to Walter's solar plexus had caused a mortal injury?

"Yes," Jason answered, "we've known each other since grade school."

"So, you'd characterize your relationship as close?" Lange deduced.

With each question asked, Scarza became more wary. The sobering truth, his court martial was still an open wound, and his history of violence was well documented. Any association with the unsavory Mangini boys and their shady dealings could put him back in jail.

"We knew each other. I never said we were close."

While Detective Lange played secretary, Ambrose probed deeper, "You went over to the Sons of Sicily clubhouse last Saturday afternoon, is that right?"

"Yes it is."

"Were the Mangini brothers responsible for all of this?" Ambrose asked while pointing to Jason's assorted bandages.

Though uneasy about incriminating himself for whatever vagary the cops were driving at, he chose to answer honestly, "I'm guessing so, since they were the last faces I saw before the lights went out."

Detective Lange stopped writing long enough to add, "Thirty-two stitches to close that head wound. They worked you over pretty good. Lucky for you that guy from the pool hall walked in when he did."

"Who walked in?" he asked thinking it would be nice to add a missing piece to a story that had more holes in it than a gopher field.

Lange answered, "His name's Tommy Lorek. He mistook the

Clubhouse for a bathroom, or you'd be in the morgue instead of in here. You might wannna thank him when you get outta here."

"So what happened exactly," Ambrose jumped back in, "how did the ruckus start?"

Still in the dark about their purpose or their line of questioning, Jason kept it brief and sketchy. "Well, we got into an argument. Next thing I know, someone blindsided me."

Seeing the cops exchange knowing looks was enough to prompt him to ask, "Detectives, what's this all about? Why all the questions? Did the Manginis contact you? Have they accused me of something?"

Ambrose, obviously surprised by Jason's inquiries, returned question for question. "You haven't heard?"

"Heard what?"

"The Mangini brothers, they were found last night, in a dumpster down at Edgewater Park."

Lange added, "Both shot in the eyes."

The news stunned Scarza. Only yesterday they were alive, and obnoxious as any two humans could possibly be. Today their bodies are in the morgue. "You say that someone shot them in the eyes? Did I hear that right?"

"Yup," Ambrose answered, "with a 9mm Glock."

What had all the earmarks of an execution, seemed unwarranted for lightweights like the Manginis. Contract killers usually had worthier targets than these two wannabe losers. Still, Jason would've been lying if he said he wasn't relieved that they were dead.

"We also found the body of a young woman in the same dumpster," Lange added rather casually. "Shot in the back of the head…9mm Glock. The same weapon."

"She was a Pittsburgh girl named Heidi Gadsky," Ambrose added. "Her brother Walter identified her body this morning."

Lange smiled and shook his head admiringly, "Gadsky was one scary-looking dude. Kinda reminded me of a pitbull." He paused, "By any chance, do you know this Gadsky guy?"

"Yeah, we met at the Clubhouse."

The two detectives suddenly stopped talking, hoping the prolonged silence would give Jason a chance to process the murders, and do a little embellishing. Maybe volunteer a plausible explanation for all the mayhem.

Jason didn't bite, but that wasn't to say he didn't have theories about the murders. *There was little doubt that someone was cleaning house, or clubhouses.*

"Mr. Scarza, these killings, they have mob hit written all over them. We don't know much about the girl, but the Manginis had a long list of enemies. Having said that, it still seems pretty unlikely that your assault and their murders weren't somehow connected."

Though he was not about to verbalize it, Scarza was in full agreement.

"Now we know, with your injuries and all, you couldn't have been involved directly, but maybe you know someone. Someone who might've wanted revenge, ya know, for what these guys did to you?"

Lange quickly clarified, "We're thinking old guard here. You know, someone who's still around. Maybe still somehow connected."

Jason pondered that one for a long moment. No one came to mind.

It was his understanding that most of Little Italy's mobsters had recently been jailed by the Feds.

"Mr. Scarza, can you give us any names. Or, at least a clue where we might begin our investigation?"

Jason gave it a few seconds, and for whatever reason, Bruno Lentoni suddenly popped into his mind. The old timer still lived in the neighborhood. As a matter of fact, just down the street from his grandmother's house. Could he be Jason's avenger?

"Sorry officers. I can't think of anyone," he lied. "You've gotta remember, I've been away for a long time. Only been back in the neighborhood for a coupla months."

After the cops left, Scarza's mind raced back some twenty years, to Lentoni's yard, to that poignant moment when big Bruno, feared mob enforcer, gratefully handed over his dog's leash. He remembered the stone killer's eyes getting weepy, his tone humble and childlike when he asked, "You'd do that for me kid? You'd find Jupiter a good home?"

Scarza also recalled a conversation that he had with one of Livy Jardine's neighbors a few weeks after he'd given Jupiter to Livy. That same neighbor told him, that on several occasions, he'd seen Bruno walking by the Jardine house, apparently checking on his wife's dog and the suitability of his new owner.

If Jason was right, Bruno Lentoni finally had a chance to show his gratitude, and maybe his wife's too. Executing the Mangini brothers very well could've been a debt repaid in full.

15

A SURPRISING DEVELOPMENT

The Robert Balfour watch had stretched into a third, agonizing week. The handful of caregivers and staffers who stayed the course were losing hope as their vigil had become a test of endurance, a siege really.

Without Balfour's wealth, he probably would've been shipped to a nursing home that specialized in end-of-life care. Instead he got round the clock care in one of America's best hospitals.

Livy and Jason tried to see him daily, but after spending hours at Balfour's bedside, they were beginning to question the merit of such visits. Balfour was non-communicative. His eyes may have fluttered open occasionally, and he'd moaned a few times, but the man was, for all intents and purposes he was little more than a zombie. They had no way of knowing if he even knew they were there.

The one day that Livy hadn't gone to the hospital, she got a phone call from Nurse Esther Bailey. "You should get down here. Mr. Balfour surprised us a bit this morning."

Right back to where she didn't want to be, Livy found herself in Balfour's room waiting on Esther Bailey's arrival. She'd stayed away this day because she was frustrated, the hopelessness of Robert's situation had finally worn her resolve to a frayed nub.

Even his room, sterile and drab, was starting to close in on her. No pictures, no drapes, a mounted TV that no one watched—welcome to room 502, AKA, the dead zone.

Livy found the clash of disinfectant and bedpan especially unpleasant this day. Of course, Robert wasn't complaining. He'd slept through all the hospital routines. The switching of IV bags, the hourly check of vitals, the occasional scan, and the flirtatious exchanges between a nubile LPN and the married resident on call. Whether it was the beeping of dispassionate monitors or the squeaking gurney wheels, Robert remained oblivious to it all.

Winded and apologetic, Nurse Bailey rushed into 502 waving a fistful of papers. "Sorry I'm late. I wanted to get my hands on the latest print-outs before we talked."

Obviously disappointed, Livy pointed to Balfour and groused, "The way you talked on the phone, I half-expected him to be sitting up, or at least sucking jello through a straw."

Still smiling, Esther put her arm around Livy. "My dear, my exact words were, *he surprised us a little.* I never said that Jesus Christ had raised him from the dead."

Livy's tone softened, "I'm sorry, it's just so sad. Hour after hour, day after day, he just lays there, and no one ever comes to visit him."

"I know, I know, but let me show you something." The nurse opened the folded print out. "Look right here, see this line. See that spike."

Livy nodded, but the EEG readings looked like the work of a preschooler handed his first pen, or a seismograph that had run amok.

"We monitor his brain activity once a day using a print-out like this one. It's called an electroencephalogram. One of the things it measures is Hertz or frequency levels... In layman's terms, brain wave activity."

Livy gave the print-out a perfunctory look, then nodded. Thus far she was more confused than impressed.

"A normal reading is 8.0. Since the day he arrived, Robert's has fluctuated between a five and six, until this morning."

"So what's his level now?" Livy asked hopefully.

"A 6.3."

Livy sat down heavily. "That's doesn't seem like much improvement."

"Maybe not, but it's a step in the right direction."

"I don't know," Livy said. "I see his eyelids twitch. Occasionally he even groans. All of it makes me wonder, what's actually going on in that brain of his?"

Bailey sat on the arm of Livy's chair. "We're confident that he hears sounds. Decoding those sounds is where it gets kinda dicey."

"Does he dream?" Livy asked.

"Well, he's not brain dead. So, I'm guessing, yes."

Livy shook her head. She made no attempt to conceal her frustration. "So, what you're saying is, he's in a kind of purgatory, suspended halfway between this life and whatever awaits him on the other side?"

"Yeah, something like that." She patted Livy's shoulder. "I know it's not easy seeing him like this, but it's important to remember that your visits are making a difference."

Livy dropped her voice as she glanced in Robert's direction. "So, is he hearing us right now?"

"Probably."

"God, that makes me feel even sadder."

The nurse hooked Livy's arm and led her into the corridor. "Look, I won't kid you, he's still in alotta trouble. To turn this thing around, we're gonna need to get really lucky. A minor miracle would be nice."

"Ya think," Livy said with all the sarcasm she could muster. "Your team still doesn't know what caused all of this. How do you find a cure if you don't even know the cause?"

Esther had no response for that one, so Livy ranted on, "Even that big shot doctor you brought in from Texas, what'd he do? Identified Robert from some book signing tour in Houston. Big whoopie."

"Granted, Dr. Spenser was less than advertised, but he did bring *you* to us. That's huge!"

Livy was hesitant, but she had to ask, "Look, my knowledge of medicine could fit into a thimble, but what's happening to Balfour, it seems way beyond weird. Am I wrong about that?"

"No, it's one of the strangest cases I've ever been a part of."

"I mean, nothing makes sense," Livy kept on. "I know this is going to sound insane, but is it possible," she hesitated again, "that Robert's condition might somehow be self-induced?"

"Self-induced? You mean like psychosomatic?"

Livy nodded. "Look, Robert's a sweet guy, but he's also a very odd duck. He doesn't, or didn't, see the world as most people see it."

"I'll have to take your word for that. I've never even heard his voice."

Livy's eyes welled up. "When I was painting his portrait, we had some really interesting conversations. Actually, his story was quite sad."

"Many people live sad lives, and they don't end up like this. Now, why would you think that his medical condition might have been self-induced?"

"For starters, I found a notebook in his desk last night. A spiral notebook."

"Okay, you found a notebook. And..."

"Well, at first glance I thought it was some kind of diary, but I was wrong. It was too disjointed. Nothing made sense. He did mention a woman named Emanuelle a bunch of times. Her name was practically on every page."

"Emanuelle? The same woman that Robert never located?"

"Yup, the one who broke his heart."

"Okay, so our guy was shot down like a million other guys, who, by the way, aren't in comas."

Livy shook her head. "Ya know, I should've brought the damn notebook down here. Then maybe you wouldn't be so negative."

"Sorry, keep going. You think his coma may be self-induced because..."

"Well, Balfour claims that he'd had some great epiphany. His exact words were *The scales have fallen from my eyes.*"

"Poetic yes, mad no.

"Okay, how about this," Livy pressed as she opened her purse and took out a piece of paper. "There was a long list of strange names. I wrote a few of them down, especially the juicy ones. Take a look at this."

Esther grabbed the paper and began reading aloud. "Cornelius, Mephistopheles, Valdes, Faustus..." She suddenly stopped and looked at Livy. "These names, they're all out of the same book... *Dr. Faustus.*"

"And how do you know that?"

"Miss Cameron, 12th grade English Lit... You've never heard of

Dr. Faustus?"

"Sounds vaguely familiar," Livy said unconvincingly.

"The book was about this guy, Faustus, who sold his soul to the Devil. Actually the whole deal was negotiated by the Devil's agent, Mephistopheles."

"A deal with the Devil!" Livy raised her hands above her head triumphantly. "And there you have it. The great mystery's been solved."

Esther smiled while shaking her head. "Don't tell me, you think Robert Balfour struck some sorta deal with Satan? Is that what you're proposing?"

"I didn't say that."

"What did you say?"

"That Robert was screwed up enough to believe that he'd sold his soul to the Devil."

"Or, maybe he just liked the book," Esther offered lightly. "Christopher Marlowe is considered a great writer, *the book*'s a classic."

Livy shook her head. "Look, you had to see the notebook. Robert's gibberish bordered on the deranged. He seemed especially enamored with the words *homo fuge.*"

"Homo fuge," Esther repeated. "Definitely Latin,"

"I looked it up," Livy said. "It's Latin alright. Something about man taking flight."

Esther shook her head. "Man, this guy was all over the place." She reflected a bit before adding, "Maybe we're looking at this thing all wrong."

"Whaddya mean?"

"Maybe this isn't as much about him inducing his own illness as it is him inducing his own madness. Total obsession can be a very dangerous thing."

"You may be right, but what makes me think that it was the other way around are the dates."

"What dates?"

"The first entry in the notebook was dated 10/31/61."

"Okay," Esther responded, still sounding unconvinced.

"That was the date his novel was published."

Still not all that impressed, the nurse managed another questioning "okay?"

Livy quickly added, "And the last entry in the notebook was dated 10/31/85."

"10/31/85?" Esther's eyebrow shot up. Things had just gotten a bit more interesting. "That's two weeks from today. Did he post an entry?"

"Get ready for this one... Lake View Cemetery...Section 48, plot 12."

"Whoa!" Esther exclaimed. "Tell me the plot belongs to Robert?"

"I checked it out this morning...Yes it does. So we're talking book-end dates. A beginning and an ending."

"A beginning and an ending? You're not suggesting that..."

"Is it all that crazy? For years the man, by his own admission, couldn't write a lick. And then, in a drug-induced state, he meets a mystery woman who both mesmerizes and inspires him to write one of the greatest novels ever written. This same woman then vanishes into thin air..."

"I know. You've already told me about Emanuelle, the Indian enchantress. Who, lest I remind you, may or may not be a real person."

Livy dug her heels in. "Robert thought she was real, and that's all that matters."

"I admit it sounds like a great story line, but two facts are indisputable. One, the woman has never been found. And two, we can't ignore the fact that Robert was stoned out of his mind when she supposedly appeared to him..."

"True, but she was the catalyst, the muse, the inspiration for the book."

"Maybe."

"One great book, and no more," Livy continued on. "Robert never got another piece of literature published after his masterpiece. Doesn't that strike you as odd?"

Esther shrugged. "Perhaps he had just one great novel in him. It's possible."

"Yeah right, like a comic strip cartoonist painting *Night Watch* or *The Mona Lisa*."

"Well, when you put it that way."

"I know Robert wondered about it himself."

"He told you that?"

"Yes. Even his own father was skeptical. Asked him about a ghost writer."

"So where does that leave us. And please don't tell again me that he struck a deal with the Devil."

"No, of course not." Livy answered. "But all that matters is, Balfour thought it might have been possible. In his tortured mind, Emanuelle may have been his Mephistopheles."

"That's insane. How would he not know if he did or didn't strike a deal?"

"Who knows. I think he had a drinking problem once. He dabbled in drugs too. God only knows what else he ingested on that reservation."

Esther chuckled. "Still, it's quite a stretch if you ask me."

"And yet, nothing about any of this makes sense. I mean we've got a seemingly healthy man wasting away in a coma. And quite possibly, the coma may have been self-induced."

"So now what?" Nurse Esther asked rhetorically. "We circle Halloween as his day of reckoning and wait to see if he dies on cue?"

Livy answered, "Do we have any other choice?"

"Okay," Esther said, "let's assume for a second that your theory is correct, how did Balfour determine that this particular Halloween was his day to die?"

Livy shrugged her shoulders. "You're the expert on *Dr. Faustus*. I was hoping you could tell me."

"Okay, let's try this again. Faustus wanted knowledge and power. So as the story goes, he asked the Devil to make him really smart. In return, he traded his soul. The Devil, after granting him his wish, gave him twenty-four years to enjoy this gift before he came to claim his soul. You can guess the rest."

Livy smiled knowingly. "Do the math. 10/31/61 begins the timeline. 10/31/85 ends it...Twenty-four years to the day!"

Esther was beginning to believe. "Wow, this is freaky."

"Yes it is."

"Well, if all of this is true," Nurse Bailey added, "then Robert Balfour is about to do what no man has ever done before...prophecy the day of his own death."

16

A COMPLICATED MAN

The news of the methodical execution of the Mangini brothers spread across Little Italy like a prairie fire. The town bullies' violent end was mourned by no one except their grieving mother.

Lisa Mangini had tried to raise her boys to be god-fearing, hard working, and honest, the antithesis of their absentee father who was serving a twenty-five-year stretch at Leavenworth for drug trafficking and armed robbery. Unfortunately, she failed.

With her husband away she tried to steer her sons away from the Mafia culture that permeated Little Italy in the Sixties, but it was a battle that was unwinnable. She knew that long before she was called to the morgue to identify her sons, both shot through the eyes.

Of course, she understood the significance of their fatal wounds. The message was clear enough. They'd messed with the wrong people, mob people, and they'd paid the ultimate price.

Alone after her husband was imprisoned, the young mother of two, void of family and wary of judgmental neighbors, had no one turn to until she met Donna Lentoni. They met at University Hospital while Mrs. Lentoni was convalescing from Whipple surgery—a procedure that removed parts of the pancreas, duodenum, and gall bladder in hopes of curing her pancreatic cancer.

The wee hours of the morning were especially difficult for Mrs. Lentoni. Not only did her pain level seem to intensify after midnight, but coping with her bleak prognosis—two, maybe three years to live—proved very difficult. So, she prayed incessantly while waiting for daybreak, and Bruno's next visit.

Mrs. Mangini, who worked third shift at the hospital as a cleaning matron, watched Donna's struggles from behind a cleaning cart in the hall outside her room. Finally, she got the nerve to approach the patient hoping to pick up her spirits.

"Excuse me Mrs. Lentoni," she approached timidly, "my name is

Lisa Mangini. I work here. I'm part of the cleaning crew."

As Donna struggled to turn on her side to face her visitor, her eyes appeared red and puffy. Her prayer book, floppy and worn from hours of reading and supplication, fell from her bosom to the edge of the mattress. Though profoundly tired, she responded politely, "It's nice to meet you Lisa."

Lisa asked softly. "How are you feeling tonight?"

"A little better. Trying to get some strength back in my legs. I'm supposed to go home Friday."

"Friday. That soon huh?"

"I know, I feel the same way, but the doctors insist I'll be ready." She paused, and misted up before lamenting, "I feel sorry for my poor husband. I can't do much for myself, and he's got his own health issues."

"Oh I'm sure he'll be delighted to have you home."

Donna shrugged. Her eyes welled up again. "He's a good man, but my illness, well it's almost more than he can handle."

Lisa nodded. "Can I get you a glass of water, maybe some ice chips?"

"Thank you no. You're very sweet."

Lisa, not certain if Donna wanted to talk about her cancer or her surgery, treaded lightly, "I hope you don't mind, but I overheard the nurses talking about your surgery."

Donna forced a weary smile. "Well, it's not exactly classified information."

"Some kind of Whipple procedure I heard? Seven hours of surgery?"

"Procedure my ass," she joked. "They practically gutted me. If I didn't need my heart, they would've plucked that out too."

Both women laughed. "I'd show you my incisions, but no one sees me naked except Bruno, and half the damn hospital. I swear one of 'em was the guy who cuts the grass."

At least she'd kept her sense of humor, thought Lisa. Or more likely, she was whistling in the dark.

"Well, I probably should get back to work. My boss makes his rounds about now. Don't wannna get fired." Lisa patted Donna's hand. "Try to get some rest."

Mrs. Lentoni watched her walk away, only to see her wheel around. "Oh, I almost forgot, I brought you a little something." She fished around in a deep pocket of her uniform and pulled out a small cardboard box. "This is for you. It's not much."

Donna turned the box this way and that as though the box itself was the gift. And then the tears came. Happy tears, sad tears, a tidal wave born of the realization that for the first time in her life, death had a face. *Ask not for whom the bell tolls, it tolls for thee* was now more than a line in a poem meant for someone else's ears. The grim reality of her situation slapped her across the face with a kind of impunity that only death can deliver.

Mrs. Lentoni took a deep breath and collected herself. *What was she getting so melodramatic about? It was a little gift for crying out loud, from a woman she'd just met.*

"You really shouldn't have," Donna managed in a quaking voice.

"It belonged to my mother. Helped her through some really tough times."

Donna opened the box carefully sifting through the excess cotton padding. "Rosary beads. They're beautiful. The color's so unusual. A mauve maybe."

"They came all the way from Naples. They're over two hundred years old."

She shook her head. "I can't accept this Lisa."

"Of course you can. When you get better, you can return them." Lisa made sure that Donna had fresh flowers for the rest of her stay at UH, and during Lisa's dinner breaks she'd share whatever she'd packed for herself, especially the homemade desserts.

Their friendship continued outside the hospital setting. Whenever Mrs. Lentoni's health would allow, she'd have her new friend over for tea. They talked for hours, mostly about family and faith. Jupiter, her black Lab, never left her side.

The one subject they never discussed was Bruno's occupation.

Donna died one day shy of the three years promised her with Bruno, Lisa, and Jupiter at her bedside.

....

The Mangini brothers' funeral was staged like a cut-rate, off Broadway play. Bruno Lentoni, the impresario, was also the writer and director of the Holy Rosary production of *Even Vermin Get a Final Send-off.*

Most of the characters in this farce, with the exception of Lisa Mangini, were masquerading as someone else, or those pretending to care about the deceased. Father O'Hare, the venal parish priest, was at the top of both lists.

The supposed protector of virtue and the defender of truth at Holy Rosary Church was actually neither. Frequenting strip clubs, drinking excessively, and abandoning his vow of celibacy with great frequency—his life was one big lie.

The fact that Father O'Hare was both greedy and corruptible, however, helped expedite Bruno's elaborate plan for a funeral that no one seemed to want, except for the mother of the dead men. This priest, like Judas, could be bought. How else could two evil men, who'd been excommunicated years earlier, be entitled to a proper Christian burial? The answer was simple. The cleric's itchy palm had been greased with a tidy stack of C-notes all taken from Bruno's rainy-day fund.

The setting was perfect. Holy Rosary Church, though not quite the Cathedral of Notre Dame, was still beautiful. Soaring ceilings that featured murals of angels-on-high holding pious poses, impressive stained-glass windows adorned with a pantheon of saints, and wood-working second to none. A huge organ loomed from its overhead perch. Baskets of beautiful, fragrant flowers filled the altar area. The *impresario* had spared no expense.

The officiating priest, who didn't disappoint sartorially, took his place behind the pulpit wearing a flowing kelly green satin robe with a large white cross prominently displayed on his chest. His matching green mitre, standing tall on his head, looked almost Vaticanesque.

The two rosy cheeked altar boys, wearing white robes, had positioned themselves well behind the Priest.

The rest of the sparse gathering was scattered around the cavernous church waiting for the mass to begin. Mrs. Mangini, wearing a black dress, sat in the first row next to Bruno, who was also cloaked in black—suit, shoes, tie and tinted eyeglasses to ostensibly conceal *his sadness*, not the hypocrisy that soured his belly. Behind them sat three women who worked with Lisa Mangini at UH.

In the back of the church the hearse driver was chatting with a maintenance man like they were at a ballgame. Two girls that no one seemed to know, huddled together off to the side. Their ratted hairstyle, excessive make-up, and black leather jackets indicated they might be Sons of Sicily groupies.

That left only Walter Gadsky, a last-minute arrival who made a bee-line to the front pew. "Mrs. Mangini," he began earnestly with his hand extended, "I'm Walter Gadsky. I'm really sorry for your loss."

She struggled to place him as she shook his hand, "Thank you for coming Walter. Were you a friend of my sons?"

Bruno couldn't take his eyes off Gadsky. He was pure Neanderthal. His broad chest and huge biceps taxed the fabric of his cheap shiny blue suit. His tight collar practically garroted his size 22 neck.

"Not exactly. I just met the boys recently, but my sister dated Leo for awhile."

"Your sister?"

"Her name was Heidi. She was also murdered last week."

Murdered! It was a blunt assault on the senses. Bruno wasn't certain if Walter was just incredibly insensitive, or looking at his flattened nose and scarred face, punch-drunk-challenged.

In either case, Lisa jumped to her feet and embraced him. While they hugged Gadsky's eyes turned slowly to Bruno. The look was long and penetrating. It was then that Bruno realized that Walter hadn't come to pay his respects, but he'd come searching for answers. He'd apparently dropped his sister's name to stir the pot, to get a reaction from Bruno.

Bruno gave Walter a nod as the young man backed away from Lisa. It was a subtle gesture, a brief dip of the chin, but one that left Walter guessing. Now more intrigued than ever, Gadsky positioned himself so that he could better study the old man who oozed clout from every pore of his body.

The young man could attempt to analyze the man in black to his heart's content, but there was no way for him to fully understand the meaning of the nod, nor the fact he'd been spared the fate of his sister because of some twisted moral code that governed an amoral man.

The reports that had gotten back to Bruno about Walter were conflicting. Yes he battled Jason, but after regaining consciousness, he tried to pull the other gangbangers off of Scarza. Because of this good deed, Walter Gadsky had been spared. The subtle exchange was a reprieve of sorts. The nod was intended to be a tacit message—*by the grace of God kid, by the grace of God!*

Bruno was after all a unique breed, an enigma, a righteous stone-killer. The oxymoron seemed the perfect description for a man who killed over seemingly trivial things, like favors owed from long ago.

Remembering the good Samaritan, for instance, who found a home for his wife's dog. Or perhaps repaying the woman who'd given mauve rosary beads to a dying woman. Little things never to be forgotten, debts worthy of repayment

No doubt Bruno was a paradox. Understanding how the same man who executed two men in cold blood could turn around and pay thousands of dollars for a sham funeral just to bring peace and closure to their grieving mother was next to impossible? Somehow violence and tenderness managed to co-exist inside Bruno Lentoni.

"Thank you, Bruno," Lisa said tearfully, "for everything. My sons would've been buried in a potters' field if it wasn't for you."

He squeezed her hand. "It was the least I could do."

She cried even harder, her shoulders heaved uncontrollably causing her friends behind her to pat her back and whisper comforting words.

"Don't cry, Lisa," Bruno said helplessly. "They're in God's hands now."

It wasn't a total lie. He didn't say anything about them being in heaven.

One mass for two brothers was unorthodox perhaps, but certainly an exigent way to bring closure to an ugly end to lives lived so despicably. The sparsely attended service said as much.

Walter stared at the two urns that sat beneath the altar. He was having a difficult time imagining that two strapping bodies could be reduced to a small pile of ash, cinder, and indestructible orthodontia that could fit into container no bigger than a jewelry box. To Walter, incinerating someone's flesh and bones was tantamount to destroying their souls. At least he'd secured his sister's soul by giving her a proper burial.

"I don't know how you got Father O'Hare to agree to a mass for my boys," Lisa whispered into Bruno's ear, "but thank you. Thank you so much."

Bruno just squeezed her hand harder. He'd run out of balm, he'd run out of lies. He wished his wife was had been there. She would've known a better way to comfort Mrs. Mangini.

With the mass coming to a close, it finally struck Walter that all the significant players in the Jason Scarza beating had either fled for their lives or we're dead, except him of course. Raising the question—why had he been spared? And that was just one of many questions that had tormented him since his sister's death, questions that had brought him to Holy Rosary Church that morning. Perhaps the old guy in black had some answers for him.

The funeral mass moved along at a mercifully accelerated pace. The final blessing and the application of holy water were the final touches.

A final look in Bruno's direction gave Father O'Hare the nod of approval he was seeking. The last thing the priest wanted was a dissatisfied gangster who hadn't gotten his money's worth.

"Eternal rest grant unto thee," the Priest said as he sprinkled more holy water, "and may perpetual light shine upon Kyle and Leo Mangini. Amen!"

Lisa, relatively composed until that moment, buckled, but didn't go to the floor. Once the priest saw that she was securely in Bruno's grasp, he ended the proceedings in business-like fashion. "The ashes will summarily be taken to Lake View where they will be interred. The Mangini family thanks everyone for coming."

In the final analysis, Bruno Lentoni's lethal response to the assault on Scarza was unprecedented in gangland's lurid lore. The hit on the Mangini Brothers had nothing to do with mob business, profits, or an ambition to move up the organizational ranks. It was, however, reciprocation at its highest, most personal level. Good deed for good deed, an eye for an eye, you hurt mine and I'll hurt yours.

Somehow Bruno Lentoni had managed to juggle mayhem and mercy, law and anarchy without a pang of remorse. Unquestionably, he was a complicated man.

17

A DREAM WITHIN A DREAM...ARIZONA, 1961

The potent desert sun hadn't yet flexed its muscles, it was too early in the day for that. Peeking over the eastern horizon, the hazy orb appeared to be checking out the comings-and-goings on the Navajo reservation, this particular morning more interesting than most. A beautiful woman in flight was indeed a rare sight in this wasteland.

The Spring of 1961 had been unseasonably cool and rainy, bad news for a Major League team who headquartered in Arizona for one reason—the warm, dry weather.

Robert Balfour, feeling the chill through his lightweight windbreaker, zipped up and took a quick survey of the eastern tract of the Navajo reservation. What he saw was far from picturesque.

A handful of shacks dotted a two-lane gravel road that eventually tapered off into nothing. A dusty truck or car parked here or there, some actually in running condition, added to the feelings of utter desolation. There was no greenery to speak of, only an unending arid landscape adorned by a handful of stunted cacti. Underfoot, several emaciated, squawking chickens busily pecked at pebbles.

Balfour, shielding his eyes with his cupped hands, scanned the entire horizon until he was back to where he'd started from. *So this was Johnny Eagle's neighborhood in the light of day. Some might've called it hell, and not been wrong.*

Surprisingly, Eagle's dilapidated Ford pick-up truck was right where they'd left it the night before, and the keys were still in the ignition. All of which raised the question— where was he?

Perhaps the dozen oil spots that polka-dotted the dirt around the truck were reason enough to abandon the vehicle. *Probably used more oil than gas*, Balfour surmised. Still, the rusty old junker was better than nothing at all, especially since he had a search to conduct, a mysterious woman to find.

So he climbed in, turned the key, and held his breath. The fuel gauge read less than a quarter tank. Gas stations on a reservation or unicorns grazing in Central Park, choose the more likely. In any case, he needed to get lucky. Finding Emanuelle quickly was imperative.

Of the several dozen houses that Balfour had checked out, half were vacant, the others responded to his inquiries as though he was an alien searching for the mother ship. It was on this journey that he stumbled upon a store, a kind of weathered oasis sitting in the middle of an inhospitable land. Two men were sitting on the porch, the front door was flung open, and the sign mounted on the corrugated steel roof read, "Big Earl's General Store."

By casual glance, the two Navajos looked to be twins. Sporting ten-gallon hats and spurred boots, they looked more cowboy than Indian. The cigar stubs wedged in the corner of their mouths were unlit. Their hands were busily whittling something out of nothing, or after a closer look, maybe nothing out of something. They did stop long enough to give Balfour the once-over before getting back to their wooden thingamajigs.

The place smelled like a melding of spicy stew and foul-smelling cigar, not quite nauseating, but offensive nonetheless. He followed the "Sundries Sold Here!" sign to a crudely constructed counter that featured a planked top that was marred by assorted nicks, gouges, cigarette burns, and an oversized jar filled with beef jerky. Hunting knives, rifles, ammo, chewing tobacco, hats, canned goods, and animal traps were on display in helter-skelter fashion throughout the store. It was all there somewhere, the trick was finding it.

The place appeared to be unmanned until the owner emerged through a beaded curtain. Expecting a mountain man named Big Earl, Robert saw a little person instead. Broad faced, dark skinned, hawkish nose—he was definitely Navajo. A miniature version of Johnny Eagle, so compacted that he needed a stool to stand on to work the counter.

His tone was big, baritone rich, and accusatory. "Is that Johnny Eagle's truck I see out there?"

"Yes, it is. My name's Robert Balfour. I'm a friend of Johnny's. I'm here covering the Cleveland Indians for the Cleveland *Plain Dealer*."

The little man lit up, reached under the counter and grabbed a Cleveland ball cap. After yanking it down over his ears, he proudly proclaimed, "It's nice to meet ya. My name's Earl, and I own this establishment."

Balfour did his best to look impressed, but Earl knew better. "It's not Sears Roebuck mind you, but this reservation ain't no friggin' suburbia neither."

"You could've fooled me," Robert replied with a smile.

Earl gave him a quick once over, then effused. "I love the Tribe. They're my favorite team."

Robert smiled. If Earl only knew that he was an impostor playing sportswriter, the Navajo could've saved his breath. "Yeah, I think they have a chance this year," Balfour lied while thinking that two could play this game, "with the Yankees being in a rebuilding year and all."

"I agree. If only the Indians hadn't traded away Rocky Colavito."

"Worst trade ever made." Robert moaned. "Frank Lane's got shit for brains."

Earl nodded. "Worst General Manager in baseball. The man doesn't know his ass from a hole in the ground, that's for sure."

Balfour smiled. He was convinced that a quick look behind the counter would've produced baseball caps for a dozen other teams that also trained in the Arizona desert. And if Balfour would've introduced himself as a writer covering the New York Yankees, the little man would've donned a Yankee cap and complained that Roger Maris was stealing Mickey Mantle's thunder.

Entrepreneurial success, especially in the middle of a wasteland, demanded a Bedouin aptitude for doing whatever it took to sell product and eke out a living. Listening to Earl tickle the ears, Robert guessed that he was more Bedouin than Navajo.

When Earl removed his hat, the small talk ended. "So Mr. Balfour, *what can I do you for?* I know you ain't interested in no gopher traps."

Balfour checked his watch. His article was due in six hours. "Well Earl, the long and short of it is, I'm trying to find someone... A woman."

Earl broke into a wide smile. "Ain't we all."

Balfour smiled. Evidently doing a little corny schtick wasn't beneath Big Earl. He half expected a rim shot from the boys sitting on the porch.

"Her name is Emanuelle."

Balfour hoped for instant recognition, but got a shrug and a blank stare instead. *How many women on this damned reservation could be named Emanuelle?*

"She's slender, tall, has long black hair. She's very pretty."

"Sorry man, that description rings no bells. Maybe Charlie and Lefty might know her."

Earl hopped off the stool and scurried outside. "Either of you two know a woman named Emanuelle?"

The twins shook their heads in unison without bothering to look up, evidently whittling wood was that captivating.

"Sorry Mr. Balfour. I've lived on the reservation for thirteen years. Lefty and Charlie a lot longer than me. My guess? Emanuelle ain't of these parts."

"Okay, thanks." Robert paused looking for a new angle to pursue before exiting the store. "Johnny left his truck this morning. Any idea what that might mean?"

"Probably means he hitched a ride with George into Tucson. George is my second cousin. He's a used car salesman. That pile of crap out there, it was George who sold it to Johnny."

Way too much information. It wasn't long after the "scintillating" used car salesman was introduced into the narrative that Balfour said goodbye to Big Earl, Lefty, and Charlie. Finishing his article before attempting to hook up with Johnny Eagle made the most sense. Surely, the man who'd inserted Emanuelle into his life would know her whereabouts. But first things first, his editor needed a story.

………

Later that afternoon he tracked Eagle to a bar near the Indians' practice facility. Johnny had already knocked down a couple of beers while waiting for cousin George to pick him up.

Balfour walked straight to Johnny's barstool, tapped him on the shoulder, and dangled the truck keys in his face. "Forget something, Johnny?"

Eagle jumped off the stool, threw his arms around Balfour, and vigorously pounded his back. It was like they hadn't seen each other in years. "Dude, you're glowing. Got some bounce in your step too." Eagle winked, "Didn't I tell ya! Soar like an eagle Baby!"

Robert pulled up a stool. Several veteran players eyed them from a nearby table causing Balfour to drop his voice, "So where'd you run off to last night?"

"I stayed with a friend. Two grown men sleeping in a single bed?... People will start to talk."

"You're a riot," Robert said as he yelled out to the bar tender. "Can I have a Pepsi please."

"How'd you find me?" Eagle asked.

"Big Earl."

"So, you met Earl. Man makes the best rabbit stew in these parts."

"And Charlie and Lefty too. A barrel of laughs, those two."

Eagle chuckled before edging closer to Robert. In a voice barely above a whisper he asked, "So tell me, how was it?"

Balfour took a deep breath, smiled and just let it all out. "Just like you said it would be... Incredible."

"I told you."

"Yes you did."

"I gotta tell ya, I was a little worried. Never seen anyone conk out that fast. Lights out Baby!"

Robert took a swig of his soda. "Ya know, there for awhile, I could barely open my eyes. And my body, well, it felt like everything was moving in slow motion. Almost like I was underwater or something."

"Goes with the territory," Eagle responded dismissively, "but I will tell ya that you had this shit-eating grin on your face when I left."

Robert playfully poked the Navajo in the ribs. "We can probably blame Emanuelle for that."

Eagle's smile suddenly disappeared. "Emanuelle?"

"You know, I guess we could call her my *dream girl*."

Eagle still looked confused. "You're dream girl? Someone back in Cleveland, or maybe a Tucson girl?"

Robert gave him a quizzical look. "You're busting me, right?"

"About what?"

"Emanuelle. Ya know, the woman you set me up with."

Johnny studied his face to gauge his sincerity. Balfour wasn't kidding.

"Look man, I didn't send Emanuelle, or any other woman to your bed last night. I got you high, and that was it. The rest was up to you."

Balfour was beginning to panic, to doubt himself, maybe even question his own sanity. His mind, now racing in reverse, was attempting to piece together the events of the previous night. "But, I was sure that this woman…this Emanuelle…that she was real. I swear to God she was there, in your house. She smelled like lilacs."

Eagle chuckled. "If you say so."

Grasping at straws, Robert pressed, "Well then, could someone else have made *the arrangements*?"

Trying to keep it light, Eagle answered playfully, "Are you crazy? It was just you, me, and the peyote. The masked man and Tonto don't need no third wheelers."

Reeling from the cognitive dissonance, Balfour turned sullen.

"Okay, now you're starting to worry me," Eagle said. "Maybe you're still hung over."

"No, I'm clear as a bell," Robert snapped.

The Navajo shook his head. "Okay, let's go back to square one. A woman named Emanuelle, she showed up at my house, after I left? That's what you're telling me?"

Robert nodded.

"So, what actually happened between you and this Emanuelle?"

"You know damn well what happened. We had sex. Mind blowing sex."

"Wow, so the peyote took you in that direction." Johnny observed. "I guess that can happen."

"C'mon Johnny cut the crap. I'm not angry. In fact, just the opposite. I just wanna find her. She left in a big rush like she was leaving the scene of a crime. I didn't even get her number."

Eagle, trying to be more supportive, asked, "Okay, how 'bout a last name?"

Balfour shook his head.

"This is weird," Eagle agreed, "unfortunately I can't help you."

Visibly upset, Robert ranted, "I even canvassed the reservation. Nothing. Not a trace of her."

"I don't know what to tell you man. Unrequited love's a bitch."

"This has nothing to do with unrequited love," Balfour snapped. "She took off for some other reason." Balfour looked miserable as he continued, "Earl was no help. Neither was Lefty or Charlie. They'd never heard of any Emanuelles living in these parts."

Johnny hesitated to say the painful obvious. "Maybe that should tell ya something."

"She's not a figment of my imagination, if that's what you're trying to say." He paused. With jaw locked and eyes narrowed, he vowed, "One way or another, I'm gonna find her, no matter how long it takes."

The Navajo shook his head. "That kind of thinking can fuck you up Bro. Maybe it's time to flip on the reality switch."

Unhappy about Eagle's indifference, Robert looked away.

"You gotta shake this. You didn't miss your deadline, did you?"

"No I didn't, by tomorrow you're gonna be famous, at least in Cleveland Ohio."

"Cleveland, eh. Did you at least make me look good?" he joked.

"Yup, not quite a superstar, but close."

Johnny laughed. "Did you mention my special powers? I could use more clients."

"Ya mean more victims like me?"

The Navajo suddenly looked contrite. "Hey, I'm sorry man. I thought the peyote might give you a new perspective on things. Get you off the snide."

Balfour shrugged. "In a way it did. My editor loved the article."

"Great! It's official then, you're unblocked. You're well on your way. Who knows, maybe you'll even write that great novel now."

"I'd settle on finding Emanuelle?"

"Emanuelle again." Eagle sighed deeply as he squared up to him. Now face-to-face he began slowly, "Listen to me Robert, when you told me that you'd taken hallucinogens before, you were being straight with me?"

"Yes. I've experimented with LSD... Twice."

"So, you've not a virgin. You've tripped out before, right?"

Robert nodded.

"Then I don't get it. None of this should be all that surprising. When one experiments with hallucinogens, one usually hallucinates."

"Okay, enough with the condescension. It's almost like I'm back in my father's house playing his whipping boy again."

"Sorry, but I don't seem to be getting through to you. This girl. Emanuelle. She's an illusion man. An hallucination."

"But I saw her, touched her, made love to her."

Eagle just shook his head. He was done talking.

"Look Johnny, I know you don't believe she's real, but I need your help. Even though you think I'm crazy, I want you to ask around the reservation. Around greater Tucson even. You know a lot of people."

"You want me to ask about this girl?"

"Yes. Find out who she is, where she lives, anything."

"And if I can't find her?"

"Then maybe you're right. I made her up. She never existed."

Eagle shook his head. "None of this is healthy man. If you're not careful Robert, you're gonna lose your job."

"Not to worry. I resigned an hour ago."

....

Weeks of scouring the reservation and the greater Tucson area had turned up nothing. Emanuelle had either vanished, or maybe Johnny Eagle was right, she was merely an illusion, a dream within a dream.

18

THE INDIAN AND THE PRINCESS

Emanuelle, real or imagined, proved to be an inspiration for Balfour II, a muse most certainly. Johnny Eagle had, after all, made promises to the dysfunctional writer. "Sample the peyote and the scales will fall from your eyes," the Navajo guaranteed it. "There might even be a great novel in your future," he teased. And as it turned out, he wasn't wrong about either.

A mere six months had passed since Robert left Arizona, yet it felt like eons ago. Now back in his father's house, he was the prodigal son returning home. It took but a few minutes for him to realize that everything was different, everything but his father's rigorous daily routine. It was etched in stone.

Rise early, complete a strenuous physical workout, wolf down a light meal, and then write until eyes and imagination grew weary. After a quick power nap, the prolific author would rise and repeat the entire regimen. He was a Spartan armed with pen, not sword.

Balfour Jr. entered the house just as his father was completing the workout phase of his morning, and whether he did it for his son, or for the benefit of the master designer who'd installed obsolescence into man's DNA, he finished by slamming down the barbell, and shouting defiantly, "Two hundred pounds, twenty reps! Fuck you old age!"

Robert's father was a driven man to be sure. He had to be the best at what he did, which was writing novels. His measuring stick was the *New York Times* Best Seller list, more specifically, repeatedly topping that list, and in the process, ultimately besting the man who'd sired him.

He made no attempt to soften his approach or apologize for his blinding ambition. When he appeared on Jack Paar's *Tonight* show an arrogant Balfour Sr. did nothing to endear himself to the host of the show when the first words out of his mouth were, "Actually I'm not a big fan of the *Guinness Book of Records.*" After staring down the TV monitor, he took a shot at his host, "But I guess I should thank them for finally getting me on your show."

Paar, who made a living sparring with testy guests, smiled and continued unfazed. "Fifty-one novels. Your books have topped the *Times* Best Sellers list fifty-one times—a new Guinness Record, congratulations."

"Yeah, but fifty two sounds a lot better."

"So," Paar began again, "how does one man write so many best sellers? What's your secret?"

It was apparent that Balfour had been asked the question many times before. His robotic response was, "A voracious curiosity about all things, a love of language, and most importantly, an aversion to sleep."

"So no leisurely strolls through Central Park then?" asked Paar facetiously.

Balfour smiled. "When they start equipping the park benches with typewriters, I may take up walking. Until then, number fifty-two beckons."

It was obvious to anyone paying attention that Jack Paar wasn't fond of men whose talents and egos were greater than his own. So he took another pot shot at his guest, this one far more personal in nature. "The volume of your work truly staggers the imagination, and yet not a single Pulitzer," Parr jabbed. "I believe your old man garnered five of those, didn't he?"

The author sat stunned for a moment, rose to his feet, made an obscene gesture, and stormed off the NBC set. The interview was over.

This was the man who raised Robert, the man who expected perfection from his only son, but got painfully flawed instead. Ordinary was not something Balfour Sr. accepted or tolerated. So young Robert was set up to fail, and he didn't disappoint, until this day.

This visit would indeed be different. Everything had changed. The fact that he'd abruptly resigned from his job with the Cleveland *Plain Dealer* was all but forgotten as he sat across from his father, who was eying him while sipping his coffee.

"So, am I still disowned?" Robert asked his dad playfully.

"Hey, joke all you want. I had to call in a lot of favors to get you that job, and you didn't even make it a week. It was embarrassing."

"Sorry, but I launched myself into this," he said while pointing to a hefty manuscript that was located on the coffee table in front of them.

Senior stared down it. "Seven hundred pages, quite ambitious to say the least. I'm more than a little surprised that you brought it to me first."

"Well, I needed an honest opinion, and maybe some help fine tuning it, you know before I submit it. You were the first person I thought of."

"Fine tuning? That might prove challenging. It's nearly perfect." Senior placed his hand on the manuscript as though it was a Bible used in a swearing-in ceremony. He patted it affectionately before shifting questioning eyes in his son's direction. "And you wrote this."

Statement or question, Junior wasn't sure. However intended, his father's last words sounded more accusatory than laudatory.

"That *is* my name on the title page," he answered assertively.

Senior shrugged, then offering a weak apology. "I'm old, I'm jaded, what can I say."

"It's just that I've never been accused of plagiarism before. Probably because I've never written anything worthy of the accusation."

"I only ask because of the huge disparity. Please excuse the feeble metaphor, but *swill to caviar* with a click of the fingers. Well, some book critics might think that transformation rather *perplexing.*"

Junior chose to ignore the "swill" and focus on the "caviar" part of the analogy. "So you liked it?"

"What's not to like. The writing's brilliant, the language is elegant, the imagery powerful." He stopped and cleared his throat. "I do however have a few questions."

"Okay," Junior responded warily, "shoot."

"So, let's start with your mythical King Kordon. I want to make sure I understand him. He's a conqueror, a powerful ruler of a great empire."

Robert interrupted, "Think Charlemagne."

"Okay, so we're talking about a ruthless ruler who's crushed foes and executed thousands on a whim? Death is no stranger to him. And yet, when faced with the prospect of his own death, he unravels? Starts questioning everything?"

Junior responded. "Up until that point he thought he was invincible, an immortal demi-god. When he found out that he was truly dying, he began to search for existential answers. Was there a God? What does it all mean? Why do men die? Is there an afterlife? The kind of questions that have confounded man since the beginning of time."

Senior nodded. "Okay, and since he's not a religious man he turns to the wisest men in his kingdom. Invites them to his castle for a great debate. Kinda like a jousting tournament using brain not lance."

Junior smiled. "Exactly, and because he has no heirs, the wisest contestant takes all. Kordon's crown, his kingdom, his wives… Everything."

"You did a brilliant job with your Five Sages by the way. Their arguments, the philosophical models they espoused, all so creditable, one brilliant stroke after another. Socrates, Descartes, Kant, they were all so cleverly disguised."

"Thank you. That was the most challenging part of this project."

"Which brings me to Malik," Senior said, "Kordon's bastard son."

"You didn't like his character?"

"On the contrary. I loved the character."

"But…"

Senior hesitated. "I don't know, maybe I missed something, but the way Malik sneaked into the competition as a last-minute replacement for Sage Number Five, it left me needing more. It didn't ring true."

"Okay, any suggestions would be appreciated."

"You might want to beef up the relationship between Malik and Sage Five. A far-flung empire was up for grabs, and the Sage simply handed his lottery ticket to the boy? The why is important, their relationship even more so "

Junior waited for more criticism that never came. "Other than that, it's perfect, especially the relationship between father and son, especially poignant was the scene where Kordon crowned Malik. I was actually moved to tears…A monumental feat these days."

Junior thought he detected a cracking in his dad's voice almost as if he was still emotionally invested. "And when he told the King that he was his son, wow! Talk about a moment. It touched me right here," he said pointing to his heart.

It was Junior's turn to be moved. "It means so much to me that you like it. Do you have any other suggestions?"

"None. The rest is perfection. I especially loved the fact that these so-called men of wisdom were humbled by a young, unlettered blacksmith who saw life for what it really was. I'm stealing a line from your book now—*We're born to procreate, keep the line moving, and then we die. It doesn't get any simpler than that.*"

"Multiply and fill the earth," Junior paraphrased. "It's straight out of the Scriptures." Junior smiled. "That part I plagiarized."

"So, when did my atheist son become a proponent of creationism?"

"When a Navajo shaman, who was educated by Jesuits, popped into my life."

Senior shook his head admiringly. "Using Malik as your storyteller was also a brilliant stroke. Using first person narration can sometimes be a slippery slope, and you handled it deftly."

Robert was speechless. His father's effusive praise was completely unexpected.

Senior waited a long moment before dropping a bombshell, "So, how did you find out that I was dying?"

"What?" Junior asked taken aback by the question.

"Well, I'm guessing that your King Kordon character is loosely based on me. Am I wrong?"

"Um, maybe bits and pieces."

"And I certainly recognize Malik," he said with a wink, "son." When Robert didn't respond, Senior added, "Which makes me terribly sad by the way." He fought back the tears and asked again, "So, how did you find out?"

Robert hesitated. "Charles called me."

"I'd fire that old man, except good cooks are hard to find these days."

Robert moved to the couch, next to his father. "So, what's the prognosis?"

"Maybe a year. The oncologist suggested a chemo regimen, but chemo brain would make writing impossible, and I plan to continue writing right up to the bitter end."

"Dad, if you want, I'll move back in."

"No, I appreciate the offer, but we'll keep things as they are."

"It's your call, but maybe you should rethink the chemo thing."

"Nah, that's not gonna happen." He sat back and stared at his son. "Ya know, your story is better than anything I've ever written, and that goes for your grandfather too."

Robert beamed. "What a tremendous compliment. Thank you."

"After you tighten things down a bit, I'll take it over to my publisher in person, but I should warn you, expect a little flak."

"What kind of flak?"

"Like I said before, *swill to caviar.* Critics are going to be curious how this great metamorphosis took place."

Junior shrugged. "Actually, I'm not sure myself."

Senior smiled. "So, what happened out there in the desert? What, or who inspired this beautiful story?"

He smiled. For the first time in his life he felt like he was on equal footing with the great Robert Balfour I. "You didn't see the dedication page?"

"I saw it. I thought maybe you were just…"

He could've finished his father's thought. Probably something disparaging like, *just trying to impress the publisher, or maybe even remind anyone assigned to reading the manuscript that the man who wrote this novel was the son of the most prolific writer of all times.*

"Dad, my tribute to you, I meant every word of it. I know we've had a rocky relationship, but you're my greatest inspiration. I've patterned my whole life after you. You're a brilliant writer."

Senior smiled. "So you're not going to tell me what happened in Arizona?"

Junior shrugged. "In a nutshell, I met an Indian, and a Princess."

Balfour Sr., remaining stoic to the end, rose to his feet and gave his son a truncated hug. It was a signal that they were done with all the father and son stuff. His praise was as hard to hang onto as the last tick of the clock.

As they neared the front door, Junior pulled up. He was not about to leave without addressing another issue, one almost as important as the novel itself. "Dad, I have one more favor to ask. It's kind of important."

The dad checked his watch. He should've been banging away at his typewriter hours ago. "Okay, you've caught me in a very charitable mood. So, make it quick. What's the favor?"

"Well, there's this woman I met in Arizona."

"Hah!" His dad threw his head back and laughed. He'd always feared that his son might've had latent homosexual tendencies. Good news all around. First the brilliant manuscript, and now his son was searching for what he presumed to be a lost love. "So was she the Indian, or the Princess?"

"The Princess."

"And does this Princess have a name?"

"Emanuelle."

"Lovely name. Exotic beauty I'm guessing."

He wasn't about to share any of the particulars of the one glorious night that he and Emanuelle had shared, he couldn't. An X-rated rendezvous wasn't grist for family discussion. They'd never even had the birds-and-bees discussion. "She was unbelievable, that's all I'll say."

"Was?"

"Oh no, she's still alive."

"Well that's good. So what's the problem then?"

"I can't find her. She's disappeared."

He could tell his father's penchant for creating murder/mystery scenarios had just kicked into gear. "When you say she disappeared…"

"No, there was no foul play or anything like…" He stopped himself short. He really didn't know that for certain.

"Okay, somehow you've managed to lose an intriguing, amazing woman. Sounds like the basis for another great novel."

"Dad, this is serious. I need to find this woman."

"Okay, so how can I help?"

"Well, I've tried for months to find her without any success. Even hired a private investigator."

Without a millisecond of hesitation the father asked, "You want my team on this?"

Robert immediately felt better. He could share delicate information with a PI that he couldn't tell his father, information that they'd need to locate Emanuelle. Besides, his father's investigators were the best this side of Scotland Yard.

"I'd really appreciate your help Dad."

And that quickly, Bryson & Sons, Private Investigators extraordinaire, were on the job.

19

ROCK AND ROLL IS HERE TO STAY

So much had happened since Livy dropped in on the Scarzas on that rainy October morning, not so with Robert Balfour's mysterious medical condition. Forget all the medical jargon. Three weeks and holding steady, the man was still in a deep sleep.

Livy, taking Grandma's advice, had moved into the Scarza home. Their cozy third floor suite had a new tenant.

Hearing the raindrops pelt the roof above was comforting, but knowing that her champion slept directly below made her feel safer than she'd ever felt before. Their close proximity also stoked her imagination. It wouldn't be the worst thing, she fantasized, if in the middle of the night he somehow got disoriented and crawled into her bed by mistake, or simply knocked at her door.

Livy's presence had the neighbors abuzz, especially with the Mangini threat forever vanquished. Why not live in the comforts of the Balfour mansion? Certainly Robert Balfour wasn't going to object.

If pressed, she would've had difficulty giving reasons for her choice of humble abode over opulent living. Gramma's loving, nurturing presence aside, living in the Balfour mansion seemed an odd fit for her. Perhaps the Mangini brothers weren't that far afield when they once called her a squatter.

Even with Balfour's eleventh-hour will now in play, she couldn't dispute the fact that her claim to the mansion seemed sketchy at best, especially after factoring in her latest theory about Balfour thinking that he'd somehow struck a deal with the Devil. Questions about his state of mind at the time his will was amended certainly would arise. Further clarification and resolution could only come if Balfour suddenly woke from his slumber.

Jason was at the breakfast table drinking coffee and reading the morning paper when Livy came down for breakfast. Gramma was where she always was, at the stove. Bacon, scrambled eggs, thick slices of homemade bread slathered liberally with butter, and a huge bowl of blueberries made for a tasty start to the day. My god could this woman cook, Livy lamented. Gaining three pounds in a week was all the damning testimony needed.

"Morning everyone," Livy said cheerfully. "Smells wonderful Gramma."

The old lady motioned her over. "Help me out honey, the toast's almost ready. Did you sleep good?"

"Like a baby."

Jason smiled at her as she returned to the table with a stack of toast. She was sporting a new look—baggy running shorts, sweatshirt, ball cap, not a stitch of make-up, and high top Keds sans socks.

His smile remained in place for a bit too long prompting her to demand an explanation. "What?"

"Nothing," he answered while diving back into the newspaper.

"There's no *nothing* here," she sparred, "come on, out with it."

"It's just that, well, you kinda look like a jock." Her raised eyebrow caused him to quickly retreat, "Don't get me wrong, I like the look, especially the ponytail, the way it sticks out of the back of the hat and all."

"So, you think I look like a tomboy?"

"No, no. Sassy, saucy, athletic. I'd call it the Evonne Goolagong look."

"Who?"

"Great Australian tennis player...A really cute tennis player."

Gramma looked relieved as she joined them at the table with the eggs and bacon. Her grandson had just extricated himself from a self-inflicted jam, but she tacked on another compliment for good measure. "Never saw you wear a ponytail before Livy. It's really cute."

"Thanks, it's not much of a ponytail. My hair doesn't grow very fast. It took months to grow this nub."

They all dug in, which pleased Gramma. She was feeding people, and her grandson looked happier than she'd seen him look in years. "Oh, I almost forgot, Livy," Gramma said as she sipped her coffee,

"Some lady called all upset. Said her dog growled at her."

"Did she leave a name and number?"

"Yes, it's on the coffee table." She paused, "You should charge more dealing with potzos like her."

"You're probably right. With business picking up, I should be more selective."

Jason got up to refill their cups. While standing over Livy he asked, "So, I take it that you're not going to the hospital this morning?"

After dunking toast into her coffee she responded, "I already talked to Esther this morning…. Big surprise, no change."

"Well, he survived another night," Jason commented, "at least that's something."

Gramma winked at Jason then mouthed the words, "Did you see? Livy *fooned* her toast."

Livy could read lips, even when Italian slang was the language of choice. Demanding to be let in on the inside joke, she repeated "Fooned?"

"It just means that you *dunked* your toast," Jason volunteered. "Now you're one of us. Not exactly an exclusive club, I might add."

Livy gave Gramma a smile and thumbs up before getting on to more pressing matters. "I thought I might go up to the house this morning. You know, to check on things."

"Balfour's house?" he asked barely able to conceal his annoyance. She nodded.

"To check on things. You mean more snooping around."

She grabbed Jason's arm and pleaded, "Come with me, puleeze. Lately, that place creeps me out."

"I don't know. Last time we were there, I felt like a grave robber."

Gramma got up and left the room without saying a word. It was 8:30 sharp, time for her morning constitutional. Four prunes a day was the secret to her success.

"That's ridiculous. I just need a little more time in the library."

Jason shook his head. "You're still looking for that damn book?"

"Yes, I think that *Dr. Faustus* is the missing piece to the puzzle."

Jason put the sports section aside and addressed her fully. "All of this searching because of that bizarre notebook. Livy, it's pure gibberish."

"You may think it's gibberish," she said angrily, "but Esther agrees with me. The notebook helps give us the *why*."

"The man's totally delusional. Deals with the Devil? C'mon."

Her face flushed as she pulled back from the table. "For the hundredth time, I'm not disputing that he's delusional. I'm just trying to better understand what happened to him. How did he get to where he is now? And I think the book may shed light on all of this, this madness."

He knew he'd stepped in it. Alienating Livy was the last thing he wanted to do. "Look, I'm sorry. I know you're just trying to help this poor guy out. I should be more supportive."

"Do you mean that? 'Cause I feel like I'm alone on an island with all of this. Who knows what the hell's wrong with him, and worse, nobody seems to care, except for Esther and me."

"Believe me, you're not alone. Look, how about this, I've got an appointment downtown this morning, but after that, I'm free. We'll head up to Balfour's house about four. How does that sound?"

"Okay, that sounds good." Though appreciative, she was also feeling left out of the loop. This was third time, since she'd moved in, that Jason had unspecified *business downtown,* which both spiked her curiosity and aroused her suspicions. Who was he meeting? And what was the big secret?

Gramma re-entered the room with a renewed bounce to her step. Re-adjusting the belt on her dress confirmed it. *Operation Prune* had been a total success. "This time don't forget Jason," Gramma said, "invite Calvin over for dinner. That boy's a beanpole."

"I will. Listen, with rush hour traffic and all, I should get dressed."

Livy waited for him to leave the room before she approached the weakest link in the chain. "Gramma, who's Calvin?"

Gramma looked toward the doorway and then back. "I told you about him, remember? He and Jason had a band in high school. They even made a record together."

"Of course you did. So, what's the big secret?"

"Whaddya mean honey?"

"Two old friends having a beer together, just reminiscing about high school. So, why wouldn't he tell me about meeting with Calvin?"

Gramma hesitated. "Because I think it's more than that."

Livy squirmed a bit. "That sounds kind of ominous."

Gramma shrugged. "All I know for sure is Calvin's back from Vegas, and from what I understand, he's got some kind of gig down in the Flats. Jason's not saying for sure, but I think he wants Jason to join his act."

Livy laughed. "Listen to you. He's got a *gig*. You sound like one those...those cool hepcat musicians."

"Me a hepcat, that's funny."

"So," Livy began again, "I still don't see what the big secret is."

"Actually, I'm praying they do get back together," Gramma said, obviously off on her own tangent. "It would be good for both of them. Calvin's had problems with booze, and Jason..." She stopped herself. The old woman's eyes suddenly filled with tears as she unloaded, "All of that bad stuff the Navy said about him, they were all lies. I've been so worried about him. He needs his music. Of course he needs you too, even more than the music."

"So you think there's a chance he'll do it?" Livy asked excitedly.

"This is the third time they're meeting. Between me and you, I think they've been rehearsing secretly."

"This is big," Livy effused. "I only wish he would've shared some of this with me."

"It's because he wasn't sure." Gramma hesitated while checking the doorway again. "You didn't hear this from me, but I think Jason wanted to make certain that Calvin was off the wagon."

Livy chuckled. "You mean on the wagon."

"Don't get smart," the old woman said playfully, "ya know what I meant."

"Wow, this is exciting. I'd love to hear them perform."

"Oh you will. And believe me, you've never heard music like this in your whole life. Jazz, boogie-woogie, rock-and-roll."

"I can hardly wait."

Gramma nudged her with an elbow. "So why wait?"

"What?"

"But you can't go downtown in sweat clothes."

"But I wasn't invited."

"So what? Who says you need an invitation?"

"I don't know, I respect Jason too much to just elbow my way into his plans. He'll think I'm pushy."

"Listen to me, sweetheart. Men don't know what they want. The sooner you realize that, the better off you're gonna be. It took my husband three years to propose to me. I got him though. Tricked him into marrying me because I knew it was for his own good."

Livy chuckled. She adored the old lady. Her special kind of wisdom didn't come wrapped in sheepskin.

"Listen to me honey, I know my grandson. I see the way he looks at you. Believe me, he wants you at his side. Now, go get dressed, I'll handle my grandson."

20

Gramma spoke, and Jason listened. Livy would tag along as they met Calvin Short at the Blue Note Club, a hip, new musical venue located on the east bank of the Cuyahoga River.

"I would've asked you to come along," he explained, "but I thought you might be going to the art gallery. You said something earlier about a buyer for one of your pieces."

"I called Philomena earlier. The man backed out. Besides, I'm dying to meet Calvin."

"Well, I'm thrilled for the company. I hope you won't be bored."

"Is this outfit okay?" she asked, sounding completely out of character. "I'm not overdressed am I?"

Jason noted that it was the same outfit that she'd worn the first time they'd met. Bordering on sexy, the dress exposed enough leg to turn heads. "You look amazing, but we do have a bit of a trek ahead of us, so you might wanna rethink the heels."

"A trek? How long a trek? she asked as she changed shoes.

"You'll see," he said back over his shoulder as he headed down the front porch steps.

It was a gorgeous day for late October, a perfect day for a walk and more queries from Livy. "We hoofing it down to the Rapid Station?"

"No."

"Cabbing it then?"

Jason took her hand as they walked on. "I can't tell you. It's kind of a surprise."

"Ah, so we're talking some kind of a romantic gesture then," she said playfully. "Maybe a hansom cab ride?"

He chuckled. "Ya know, you ask an awful lot of questions. Has anybody ever told you that?"

"Only you. C'mon, fess up. I know we can't walk all the way down to the River."

"Be patient, we're almost there."

"Almost there," Livy exclaimed as she stopped to look around. "But we haven't even left the neighborhood."

They walked on until Jason pulled up abruptly. Vic's Butcher Shop, a very unlikely stop along the way, loomed in the foreground. Her quizzical look demanded a response. "No, we're not here for sirloin." He then pointed to a narrow brick driveway that ran alongside the building. "Follow me, it's back here."

Up the drive they walked until they saw it. The small building, though crudely built, did have an overhead door. Livy quickly realized that they had stumbled across one of the rarest commodities in all of Little Italy—a garage.

While Jason searched for the right key, Livy teased, "Is this yet another part of the sprawling Scarza empire?"

"No Miss Smart Ass, Victorio Trammel owns it," Jason shot back over his shoulder as he hoisted the overhead door open. After ducking out of the way of an exiting sparrow, he added, "Don't let appearances fool you. Forty a month is a real bargain."

By all appearances, single car garage was a generous description. The meager illumination provided by a single bulb couldn't conceal the shoddy masonry work. The courses of brick strayed from the parallel as mortar haphazardly oozed from between the joints. The slanting ceiling line and gravel floor made Vic's rental fee appear to be 'grand-theft-garage.' But at least the roof didn't leak.

Dominating the small area was a tarp draped over what could only be a car. Jason yanked the cover off like he was doing a magic trick while shouting "Voila!"

Livy whistled admiringly. The vintage, chartreuse green automobile looked to be in mint condition, and yet here it was, hidden away and gathering dust like it was some dark family secret. Wrong place, wrong time, wrong everything! This beautiful anachronism, the one that smacked of a bygone era when Americans worshipped their cars, Henry Ford, and mega horsepower, belonged in a showroom, not a crypt.

Jason patted the hood of the car as if it was a family pet. "It's a 1950, V-8 Ford Sedan. It's got 300 horses under the hood."

"Three hundred horsepower!" Livy exclaimed. " Beautiful, and a gas guzzler."

"Yeah but when this car rolled off the Detroit assembly line, gasoline was 29 cents a gallon," Jason explained. "Do you believe that?"

"How do you know that?" she asked as she peeked inside the car.

"Because I was there. I lived the Fifties. Things were good back then."

She eyed his powerful, fit torso and teased, "You've held up remarkably well for an old guy."

He ran his hand over the hood and boasted, "Back in the day my sassy friend, hot-rodders would've drooled over this little baby."

Livy still not certain why Jason wanted her to see the car, asked, "Who does it belong to?

"Me. This was my dad's car."

"Really. And you keep it in here?"

"Yup, Victor's more than my butcher. He's also a good friend and my mechanic."

Livy whistled. "Just look at that black leather interior," Livy said. "Everything's in pristine condition."

"My father was a fanatic when it came to this car. Get in."

"What? We're not taking *this* downtown are we?"

"Yup, get ready to be stared at. This car is almost as extinct as the T-Rex."

Barely out of the garage Livy observed, "It started right up."

Jason smiled. "Like I said, Vic's my mechanic."

She got quiet for a moment then had to ask, "So this arrangement with Vic, how long has it been going on?"

"Since my parents were killed. Even when I was in the Navy, Gramma's paid Vic to take care of it. He loves this car. Has offered to buy it a hundred times."

"Rent, maintenance, and TLC for $40. That's quite a bargain."

Jason smiled. "Yeah, and he's had a thing for Gramma for forty years. She's led him on shamelessly."

"So green beauty is no ordinary car," Livy summarized.

"No, this car is all that was left of my father."

"Besides you, right?" she was quick to correct.

Wistfully, he began filling in the blanks for her. "You know the last time I saw my parents alive, they were in this car, waving goodbye to me and Gramma."

Livy clammed up. The floor was all his. This was inner sanctum stuff. Perhaps he'd share things with her that he'd never told another living soul, besides Gramma of course.

"My father worked for General Motors in Cleveland," seemed as good a starting point as any. "He had a very good job. Upper management, actually." He stopped to chuckle. "Upper management at G.M., and the man never went to college. Can you imagine that happening today? He was really smart."

The acorn didn't fall too far from the tree, she thought. A 4.0 GPA at the Naval Academy wasn't too shabby.

"And he was a great athlete. He played for the Cleveland Rams back in the early Forties, before he blew out his knee." He chuckled again. "My father used to joke that the only two things he ever got from playing professional football was a bad knee and a great wife."

With that amusing nugget out there, Livy didn't know which line of questioning to pursue—*Had Jason meant the Cleveland Browns when he said the Rams? Or, how did playing football land his father a wife? She chose the latter.*

Scarza's answer was short and to the point. "The Rams quarterback had a younger sister named Alice. She liked my dad, so he set 'em up. And that was that."

For Jason, being in that old Ford was better than leafing through any family photo album. The memories, some of them olfactorily inspired, were still powerful and vivid. Smells came with accompanying images. The faint scent of his mom's White Shoulders perfume, for instance, triggered visions of her sitting at her dressing table dabbing perfume behind her ears.

The stale smell of Lucky Strike cigarettes had permanently fused with the car's interior. Though a disgusting reminder of a disgusting habit, it was his parents' disgusting habit.

As a little boy watching from the backseat, he recalled being fascinated when his dad pushed in the cigarette lighter that was located on the dashboard waiting for it to pop out. While holding the red hot lighter to his cigarette tip, he would caution his son to never play with the lighter, or smoke for that matter.

Jason pushed the lighter in and said, "My parents both smoked. Back then everyone did. No Surgeon General warnings to alarm anyone."

"My mother smoked too," Livy joined in. "Just one more tranquilizer I guess."

He pointed to the radio with pride. "And this was way ahead of its time. Stereophonic, state-of the-art speakers in front and back."

To Livy, it just looked like another car radio.

"My father loved music. He played the guitar and the piano, and could he sing. He was a baritone. Sounded like Sinatra, at least he thought so."

Livy chuckled. "I heard Gramma singing the other day. Believe me, your dad didn't get his voice from her."

"Tin ear. Didn't stop her though. Family sing-alongs were big in our house and she wasn't going to be left out."

Livy silently lamented. Jason, even if it had only been for a fleeting moment, had experienced an Ozzie and Harriet childhood. In her house, there was no laughter or music. Instead, there was a blighted outlook, and frequent police visits.

"Sometimes my parents would pick up the rug, crank up the music, and dance. My mother loved to jitterbug."

Jason slammed on the brakes to avoid a dog that had crossed the road.

"Look at that poor thing," Livy said, "he's lost. Maybe we should stop."

"He's not lost. He lives in the firehouse up the block." He looked over at Livy who looked skeptical. "You remind me of my mother. She would've stopped for the dog too. She took in strays of every description."

"I've always thought," Livy said, "that God should have a special place in heaven for animal lovers."

"That's weird. My mother used to say that too."

They drove past the firehouse just as the dog walked in. Jason turned to Livy and smiled. "Told ya."

"That makes me feel better." Livy took a moment to take in his ruggedly handsome profile, one that featured a square jaw, aquiline nose, and full lips. "Your mom sounds like a fascinating woman. Tell me more about her."

"Well, everybody loved her," he stopped to reconsider, "well, with one exception. I heard it took quite awhile before she won Gramma over."

"Really. How could that be?"

"It's simple. My mother wasn't Italian. German, English, Hungarian, but not a drop of Italian blood. To Gramma she was the *American* girl."

"And that was it? Whew, off with her head! Thank god I'm half Italian."

"And she was taller than my dad. If memory serves, a couple of inches. And when she wore heels, she absolutely towered over him."

"And that bothered Gramma?"

"Yup. *Husbands should be taller than their wives, children should be seen and not heard, and women who frequent bars are floozies.*"

Livy laughed. "I can picture her pacing back and forth in the kitchen waving her spoon pontificating to anyone who'd listen. *Husbands should be taller than their wives!* ...The woman's hysterical."

"Yup, my Gramma's a trip. But I can't imagine the world without her in it."

Livy chimed in, "Amen to that."

"When I was real little, she spent so much time at our house, I actually thought she lived with us. You know, she taught my mother how to make her own tomato sauce, homemade pasta, biscottis. Well, you've seen for yourself what a great cook she is."

Livy hesitated. Jason had left a major part of the story lagging behind the rest, the part about his parents sitting in that Ford saying their final goodbyes. The car seemed the key to the telling of the tale.

She watched as he put on the left turn signal before exiting the main road. The long winding road that led down to the Cuyahoga River was marred by potholes and mud puddles. It proved to be a bumpy ride down to the riverbank and the Blue Note Club.

Up until that moment Livy hadn't paid much attention to roads, construction cones, or speed traps. Jason Scarza was her foreground. She loved spending time with him, perhaps that was just another way of saying that she was falling hard.

"We're getting close," Jason offered with his eyes glued to the rutty road. "It's dead ahead on the left."

Livy could see the river much clearer now. It was muddy, swift, and wide. A barge carrying iron ore was wending its way up the river. They were nearing several buildings that backed up to the water. She guessed that one of those had to be their final destination.

"So we're almost there and I still haven't heard what actually happened to your parents. Gramma already told me they died in a plane crash, but little else. Maybe if I know everything, I can better understand."

"Better understand what?"

His tone wasn't defensive or snarky, neither was her reply. "What you're feeling."

"It's all ancient history now. So why rehash it?"

"Because I wanna know everything about you and your family."

He sighed heavily. It was a story he rarely verbalized, but he'd do it for her. "Well, it all seems like yesterday. Gramma and I were standing on her porch, waving to my parents. Every little detail burned into my brain, in technicolor no less. My dad was wearing a blue suit and red tie, my mother was wearing a green dress, with this silly white hat that sat on top of head, the kind that Jackie Onassis used to wear."

"A pillbox hat?"

"Yeah, she was wearing a pillbox hat, and these long white gloves."

Livy gave him a playful jab in the arm. "Not bad for a jock."

"What I remember most was how happy they seemed," a fact that, in the retelling, ironically seemed to evoke great sadness in Jason.

He stopped talking long enough to focus on a tugboat that was tooting for attention. He appeared to be stuck, so he pretty much repeated what he'd said moments earlier. "Yup, they were all dressed up, happy, and waving. That's how I remember them. Then they just pulled away in the car, and that was it."

Livy, powerless to comfort him, merely played his sounding board.

"Of course Gramma was my rock. She was worried that I couldn't handle my parents leaving me for a few nights. She kept telling me that they'd be back on Sunday. That the flight to Michigan was short, and how important the trip was for my father's job."

When one rogue tear trickled down his cheek he made no attempt to wipe it away. "It was freaky the way the whole thing played out. A kinda perfect storm scenario. They should never have been on that plane."

He stopped when Livy handed him a tissue. "Gramma told me that the president of General Motors had thrown this big week-end bash at some resort on Mackinac Island. My father's boss, over a martini or two, apparently had sung my dad's praises to the head honcho. Normally that's a good thing, right?"

Livy stopped herself. The question was rhetorical.

"Wrong! The boss, who always got what he wanted when he wanted it, said he needed to meet my father in person, ASAP, and bring the wife along he insisted. Tickets for the flight would be left at Burke Lakefront Airport that same afternoon."

The story telling came to an abrupt halt when they pulled up in front of The Blue Note. Only one other car was in the parking lot, a candy apple red Cadillac El Dorado with a vanity plate that read *Elvis Who?*

Jason pulled up next to the Caddy, and turned off the key. He then turned lo Livy and announced, "We're running late, and Calvin's a little intense these days. How 'bout I finish this tale of woe later."

"Whoa, whoa, hold on a sec. Don't leave me hanging? Tickets for the flight would be left at the airport, and then what?"

"Believe me, Calvin's in there right now, having a fit?"

"Then give me the condensed version."

He hesitated. "It's kind of a bummer."

"My middle name's *Bummer*...Livy Bummer Jardine."

He took a deep sigh. "Well, the rest of it reads like some cautionary tale. One that warns happy people that life can chew you up and spit you out at a moment's notice. That bad things can happen to good people."

Livy saw it for the first time in his eyes, unadulterated anger, and not just about his parents' fatal plane crash, but also about what happened to him in the Navy. Framed, prosecuted, and disgraced, the bad guys wound up on the winning side of the ledger, he wound up in the brig.

"Well maybe you're right Jason, bad things can happen to good people, but wallowing is counterproductive. I should know. I've wallowed plenty."

"You, wallow?" he asked incredulously. "You're one of the chirpiest, most resilient people I've ever met. Talk about having the ability to make lemonade out of lemons."

"Thanks, and you're one of the nicest, kindest, bravest people I've ever known. And as crazy as this sounds...I think I'm falling in love with you."

Stunned, she wrung her hands and looked away. The words had just tumbled out of her mouth—"I think I'm falling in love you."

She was mortified. Their relationship, barely a week old, had progressed from incessant flirting to messing around on the couch after Gramma had gone to bed. And suddenly all that was changed with the utterance of seven little words, words that one could never take back. Brave, powerful words that hung in the air like his mother's White Shoulders perfume.

Jason was smiling as he took her face in his large hands and searched her eyes to verify that her soul and the words were in sync.

It was at that moment that he knew. He'd found his soul mate in the oddest of places—a neon green time machine filled with cherished memories of loved ones he'd lost.

The kiss that followed took her breath away, the ensuing hug even more meaningful. They held on for what seemed like forever, as their hearts pounded as one, and their minds disengaged from both the tragic past and the uncertain future. For that one moment, they were alone in the universe.

Livy didn't need to hear the horrific details of the ill-fated flight that took his parents' lives. The small prop plane, the one that went down in the middle of Lake Erie, left nothing behind. No recovered wreckage, no bodies, no little black box. Lake Erie had swallowed them up and would remain forever mum.

21

A BLAST FROM THE PAST

Calvin Short and Willie Dunham, AKA the *Dueling Pianos,* had been a Las Vegas Strip favorite for many years. Doing eight, high-energy shows a week, however, eventually took its toll, as did the excessive drinking and partying. The act was dying of natural causes when Dunham decided to go home to Phoenix and his father's construction business.

Short, who'd lost a significant amount of vocal range, struggled to make it as a solo act, eventually losing his job at the Flamingo Hotel and Casino to a magician. He was finished on the Strip, and pretty much everywhere else.

Washed up at forty-nine, he returned to Cleveland to lick his wounds. It was there he caught a huge break when the headliner at the Blue Note Club was badly injured in a car crash. The club owner sorely needed a replacement act and Calvin was agreeable, especially after he'd heard that his high school band mate was out there, scrambling to put his life back together.

Livy and Jason walked into The Blue Note hand-in-hand. First impression, the place was cozy and inviting. Brick walls, low ceilings, Tiffany lamps, a bar straight out of the Roaring Twenties, and cafe tables positioned close enough to the stage to see the performers' facial pores made the venue even more intimate. Two grand pianos practically kissed on a slightly elevated stage, and a small, scuffed up dance floor sat adjacent to the stage. Everything was where it should have been, except for Calvin Short.

"Are we late?" Livy asked while doing a slow three-sixty.

"No, we're right on time. He's gotta be here somewhere. That's his Caddy parked right outside."

"I noticed the vanity plate," Livy said, "does he have some kind of beef with Elvis Presley?"

"*Elvis Who*," Jason explained, "was the first song that Calvin ever wrote."

A raspy voice coming from the shadows added, "And the first demo we ever cut."

They turned to face the voice. The man who stood before them appeared to be a cheesy composite of several rock and roll headliners. In his gold lame jacket, he was gaudily accessorized with bling of every description, and his horsey-tooth smile was so broad it almost unhinged his jaw. Skinny to the point of vanishing, he spread his arms as if to embrace the whole world as he shouted, "So, you must be Livy. Come here, and give me a big hug."

Enveloped in his wingspan, she managed a "Nice to meet you."

Calvin stepped away to get a better look. "Well darlin,' our boy said you were pretty, but he definitely didn't do you justice."

Short threw his arms over their shoulders and steered them in the direction of the pianos. "Livy, my gut tells me that I owe you big time for getting Jace to agree to doing this gig. Is my gut right?"

Livy shook her head. "I don't think so. Maybe Gramma Scarza is the one you should be thanking."

"*Gramma* Scarza is it," he purred as if a light bulb had just been switched on. "Sounds real cozy and family like. Kudos Jace."

"Behave yourself, Calvin," Jason cautioned benignly

He then reached for Livy's hand. After kissing it, he said, "No Darlin, I think I thanked the right person the first time."

With the introductions out of the way, the two men went straight to their respective pianos while Livy took a seat in the front row. While finger rolling his way through several arpeggios, he asked, "Did Jason tell you anything about our last practice session?"

"No, I wasn't aware there was one."

Calvin laughed producing a phlegm-rattling hack. "Not surprising. He was probably reconnoitering the state-of-me before committing," he coughed again then resumed, "ya know, with my decadent lifestyle and all."

"That's ridiculous," Jason responded unconvincingly.

Calvin chuckled. "The man's like a mother hen."

"Can we please get to it," Jason said impatiently, "this ship sails in a week, and we still haven't nailed anything down yet."

Calvin looked out at Livy. "This is gonna take a while. You want some coffee, or maybe something a little stronger?"

The three beer bottles that sat on top of Calvin's piano were hard to miss. Evidently Calvin Short hadn't escaped the Las Vegas firestorm without some baggage and plenty of scars.

Livy shook her head, crossed her legs, folded her arms across her chest and waited for the show to begin. She'd accompanied Jason to the Blue Note with no expectations. How good could Jason be? He played in a high school band like thousands of other delusional kids who'd bought a guitar and taken a few lessons.

"I gave it a lot of thought last night," Calvin began. "How about we kick the show off with *Crocodile Rock*?"

Jason shrugged. "It's your call Calvin."

"I mean, it's up tempo, it'll get the crowd going." He looked across at Jason who looked unconvinced. "It'll be the perfect ice breaker for you."

"The song's good, but you should open," Scarza insisted. "You're the headliner. People will be expecting you to open."

"C'mon Mate, you absolutely killed it Tuesday. You did the Rocket Man proud."

"Yeah but it's your name's on the marquee, not mine."

"Okay, how about this. We both sing it."

Short initiated the song with a one-and-a-two-and-a three. Both men, in perfect sync, started pounding out chords. The energy was incredible. Jason's voice was rich and smoky, Calvin's raspy and raucous as they belted out,

I remember when rock was young,
Me and Suzie had so much fun.
Holding hands and skimming stones,
Had a gold Chevy and a place of my own.
But the biggest kick I ever got,

Was doing a thing called the Crocodile Rock.

Livy was floored. They were really, really good.

"So, it's decided. We open up with *Crocodile Rock*," Short said as he leafed through a song book. "I think for the first few weeks we divvy things up to showcase your strengths. You do the oldies-but-goodies, and I do the more current stuff. How does that grab ya?"

Jason nodded. "Good. Sounds like a plan."

The next two hours featured a process of sifting, trial-and-error really. From Sinatra to Springsteen, the Stones to Louie Prima. Broadway show tunes to heavy metal, all without a score or any sheet music. Goose bumps ran up and down Livy's spine. She'd reach deep down into her purse to see them perform.

By noon, the Dueling Pianos went silent. "It's all good Jace," Calvin said after gulping down what was left of his last beer. "I think we got ourselves a foundation. Crowd requests will take care of the rest of it."

"Are we too top heavy with the up tempo stuff?" Scarza asked. "Don't we need to change pace a little. Maybe throw in a ballad or two?"

"Ballads are like Sominex, Jace. They put people to sleep."

"Even if they're requested?"

Calvin answered, "Well, if a ballad is requested, you're singing it."

Jason understood Calvin's anti-ballad stance. He'd clearly lost some range. "Okay, are we done for today?"

Calvin motioned him over to his piano. In a near-whisper he said, "I gotta tell ya man, you and Livy, you look right together. Right as rain!"

Jason smiled then joined Calvin on the bench. He eyed the empty beer bottles. "Are you okay Cal?"

"Yeah, why?"

"It's a little early in the day, don't you think?"

"I know, I know. It won't affect me on stage. It's just that I'm going through a rough patch right now. A minor transition of sorts."

He forced a phlegmy laugh before adding, "Just in case you haven't noticed, Cleveland ain't Vegas."

The refrain was familiar, one sung by many military lifers. After recognizing the *twelve-pack-lie*, Jason chose to ignore it. "Okay then, same time tomorrow?"

They shook hands. "Same time tomorrow. And Jason, thank you for saving my ass."

Calvin, looking more vulnerable than he'd ever seen him, moved Jason. Keeping it light seemed the way to go. "Yeah well, seven hundred a night and tips. That ain't bad for a navy jailbird."

Livy had questions, lots of questions on their ride back to Little Italy. A sampling—*Why hadn't he told her that he was such a talented musician? How did he play without sheet music? And what was the real reason that he'd changed his mind about performing with Calvin Short?*

"If I know the key of a song," he explained, "I don't need any music. Then it's just a matter of playing the cords in that particular key. The rest is all in my ear."

She looked confused.

"I studied music theory, took composition courses, and my father taught me the rest. Without sounding boastful, I was kind of a child prodigy. Thus the music scholarship to Julliard."

"But I thought football was your great passion."

"I liked football, but I loved music."

"So why didn't you go to Julliard. Why did you choose the Naval Academy?"

"It's a long story."

She smiled and interlocked her arm in his. "Are we in a hurry?"

"Okay, you want the truncated version? I met John Glenn."

"The Senator?"

"He wasn't a Senator when I met him. He was still an astronaut. He came to our high school to give a motivational speech. He was amazing."

"Okay."

"Even though I was just a kid, I was majorly impressed. The way he talked, the way he carried himself. Not to mention the fact that he was the first American to orbit the earth. I mean, c'mon. Who wouldn't be impressed?"

"So, Beethoven was out, and rockets were in."

"Well, it was a little more complicated than that. Glenn told our class how important it was to pursue one's dreams. Then he shared his dream with us."

She teased, "Let me guess, first man to Mars?"

Jason smiled. "You wouldn't be so glib if you would've met the man."

"Look, I'm locking my lip, and throwing away the key," she said trying to be serious. "You see that? There goes the key right out the window."

"Ya know, if you're not careful, you might not get an invitation to the premier."

"Really?" She said as she jabbed his ribs playfully. "Ya know, if you didn't invite me, I think Calvin would."

Jason smiled. "Wow, that was cold."

"Don't worry, Calvin's not my type. You in bling and gold lame? I don't think so. No, I prefer men who wanna grow up to be an astronaut."

"There you go again, busting my chops."

"Oh c'mon, I may not be a huge John Glenn fan, but Jason Scarza, now he's a different story." She paused before asking, "So don't leave me hanging. What was John Glenn's dream?"

"Simply put, he wanted to help people. That was it. Helping people. And he felt the best way to do that was to go into politics."

"So you reset your sights to a career in politics?"

"Well, not exactly. Let's just say that he caused me to alter my course. A scholarship to Julliard was exchanged for four years at the Naval Academy. I figured a stint in the Navy, early retirement, and then maybe run for national office."

"So what happened?"

"I stayed a year too long. The rest reads like your worst nightmare."

Moments later they arrived back at Victor's garage. The walk back to Gramma's house, unlike the rest of that frenetic morning, was one without chatter, clever repartee, or declarations of love. Instead, they walked in silence processing the morning's happenings to the accompaniment of a few boisterous birds, rustling leaves dancing to the rhythm of the west wind, and the snap of twigs underfoot.

Livy found it hard to believe that in one morning, she'd pried open the chest of secrets that was Jason Scarza's life. Love, hate, great fortune, incredible misfortune, dreams made, dreams crushed—he'd revealed it all to her, a fact that made her feel good about their future together. She just had one more question for him. "So Jason, what really made you change your mind about Calvin Short's offer?"

They stood on the porch as he mulled the question over. "On a more sophomoric level, perhaps I just wanted to impress you."

"Well, you certainly did that."

"And then there was the debt I owed Calvin, the one that I can never repay."

Livy drew closer as he explained. "When I was in the brig, Cal phoned Gramma to check on her. When he found out that she wasn't doing so well, he flew in from Vegas to visit her."

"Wow, what a sweet and thoughtful thing to do."

"It gets better, Over the course of my two year sentence, he flew in three times. Even gave Gramma money." He paused. "Cal never told me about the visits or the money, but Gramma did."

After hearing about Calvin's good deeds, Livy did some soul searching. Re-thinking her feelings about the smarmy Mick Jagger clone required her to take a closer look at herself. She'd prejudged him based on his gaudy outfits and tasteless jewelry, when she should've been focusing on his heart and good deeds. Book covers, gift wrappings, and candy red El Dorados—none should be used to examine the soul of a man.

Robert Balfour spent a fortune on books, some of which he'd never even read. His collection of first editions, one that included the complete works of Dickens, Melville, and Poe, was very impressive.

Jason Scarza was awestruck as he strolled the perimeter of a room that had a feel of aristocratic exclusivity. A hint of Balfour's cherry pipe tobacco could still be detected in the library. Combined with lemon scented furniture polish and a vanilla- candle, it produced an oddly pleasing scent. If old money and a Mayflower lineage could have been bottled as cologne, the place would've reeked of both.

While strumming his fingers across the leather bindings he was fully aware that some of the greatest wordsmiths to have ever walked the earth, all neatly arranged from A to Z, were at his beck and call. "I wonder what all this is worth?" he asked Livy as she walked into the room.

Livy, who'd already spent countless hours in the Balfour library, was amused by Jason's slack-jawed wonderment. She'd reacted the same way the first time Balfour had given her the grand tour. "Robert once told me that the contents of this room could buy him a villa in Monte Carlo."

"I don't doubt that. Here's a first edition *Jane Eyre*," he said while thumbing through the book, "I'm guessing six figures, at least."

"Amazing isn't it?"

"Yes it is," he agreed, "but then again, so is the Leaning Tower of Pisa, and we can't fix that either."

Livy stopped dead in her tracks. "And what's that supposed to mean?"

Jason started to answer but thought better. "Nothing. Forget it. We've got a book to find, clues to hunt down."

"No, no. What did you mean about *fixing* the Tower of Pisa?"

"Look, I know you want to find a cure for Robert, but the man's broken. He's Humpty-Dumpty and Rip Van Winkle combined, and nothing we find in this room, or any other room, is going to put him back together again…not even *Dr. Faustus.* Who by the way, is not where he's supposed to be, alphabetically speaking."

The edge to his voice was barely discernible, but it was there nonetheless. Livy had forced him to accompany her to the Balfour home just days earlier, and here they were again, performing act two of the same play.

He backed up into the middle room and threw his hands up. "Yup, we got books, and lots of 'em," he said with a theatrical flair, "unfortunately, none of them are titled *A Cure for Mysterious Comas.*"

"We don't need to find a cure for his coma," she responded wearily, "we just need to understand what was going on with Robert right before he lapsed into the coma. *Faust* seems our best bet to shed some light on what actually happened."

"Livy, your perseverance is admirable, but it's pretty obvious that we're spinning our wheels here."

She looked hurt as she reminded him, "You said that you wanted to support me. This doesn't feel like support."

"You know how Einstein defined insanity?" he asked while forcing a smile. "It's a person doing the same thing over and over again, while expecting different results. Sound familiar?"

She ignored him as she made her way over to Robert's desk. Things were just as she'd left them on her last visit. There was a photo of Mr. Cheeves, a bowl of miscellaneous office supplies, an ashtray, and a large calendar. What was new, however, was a yellow post-it stuck on the calendar.

She grabbed the note and began reading silently, prompting Jason to ask, "Who's the note from?"

"Philomena," Livy answered. "She was here earlier to pick up one of the pieces that I'd left here. We may have a buyer for it." Livy turned her attention back to the note and beginning reading aloud. *"I reduced the price of the lighthouse piece to $695. If that's not okay, give me a call later. And you might want to check the refuse can in the greenhouse. I'd* *suggest wearing gloves...And please be careful of the vase shards. "*

"The woman's a complete germophobe," Livy chuckled while scanning the room for missing vases.

"The greenhouse?" Jason repeated, obviously less than thrilled about the prospect of another wild goose chase.

Livy was already up and moving. "Off to the greenhouse we go."

As they opened the trash can lid the fetid odor rocked them back on their heels. Undeterred, Livy took a second look. This time she spotted what appeared to be a book, a badly burned one. Without a second's hesitation, she reached into the compost and pulled it out.

"Is that what I think it is?" Jason asked as he stepped closer.

After brushing off plant clippings, a withered bouquet, and a slimy substance of questionable origin, she examined the remains of the book more carefully. The leather cover was badly damaged but still intact, as were sections of a number of blackened pages. Moisture from the decaying compost had left stains that made the deciphering process almost impossible.

"Yup, it's our missing friend," She responded. *"Dr. Faustus.* And what a mess you are."

"Maybe if we dry it out," Jason offered with little conviction, "some of it might still be salvageable."

"That won't be necessary," she said. "The book's of little use to us now. The bigger question is, why would Robert set fire to it. It was his favorite novel."

"Certainly very pricey kindling," he added.

"So, why did he set fire to it?"

"Maybe he didn't," Jason offered. "This could've been the work of the Mangini brothers."

"Not likely. If the Manginis had broken in, cash and jewelry would've been their primary targets...Besides, those Neanderthals wouldn't have known Dr. Faustus from Dr. Ruth."

"Well, this development makes things much more interesting," Jason said as he looked over Livy's shoulder. "Robert destroying something this valuable adds credence to your theory."

"Ya think?"

"Absolutely," Jason answered. "Self-doubt haunted the man for decades. Did he write the damn book on his own, or did he get some kind of supernatural help? Even he didn't know for sure."

Livy nodded. "That's why he needed to find Emanuelle. It wasn't just about finding a lost love. For his own sanity he desperately wanted her to be a flesh-and- blood human being. Someone who wasn't a deal brokering demon masquerading around in a buckskin dress all doused in lilac scented perfume."

"Help me write a great book, and I'll give you my damaged soul," Jason summarized while shaking his head. "When you say it out loud, it sounds absolutely ridiculous."

Livy nodded. "It's a storyline straight off of these charred pages. Pages that Robert had memorized. For him, fiction had morphed into reality."

Jason was starting to believe. "Imagine the countless hours Robert spent replaying that one night in the desert. It would warp anyone's sense of reality."

"For twenty-four years this thing has haunted him," Livy tacked on.

"That's a lot of suffering," Jason agreed.

"The good thing is, it's almost over. If I've interpreted the dates correctly, D-Day's this Halloween. We've got a week left."

"But setting fire to the book," Jason retreated, "how did that help Balfour's situation? That part makes no sense.""

"Maybe not, but it's kinda like a leper who keeps looking at himself in a mirror," Livy added. "As the disease progresses, the leper hates the sight of himself, and the mirror too. So, he smashes it."

Good analogy. "The book was the mirror."

She held up the book again, this time more triumphantly. "And so I present Exhibit A, *Dr. Faustus*, our Rosetta Stone. The key to understanding Balfour's bizarre fate is little more than a bundle of smelly, charred paper. "

Jason shrugged. "I just have one more question. I know that the human mind is capable of believing just about anything, but, one would think that Robert would've remembered something of that night with Emanuelle, besides the obvious. How often does one strike a deal with the Devil?"

"It was all one big blur, that's the way he described it to me. A series of hallucinations, and lots of blanks. The man was sky high."

"A Shaman's magic potion and great sex," Jason summarized.

They both grew pensive before he added, "So, I guess I should apologize. I think you may have been right all along. Robert's coma could well be the culmination of some kind of self-fulfilling prophecy."

"Unfortunately my being right hasn't helped Robert. He's still laying in that hospital bed waiting for Mephistopheles to show up…to come snatch his soul."

"And we can't do a damn thing about it."

"Not necessarily true. I've given a lot of thought to this." Livy cleared her throat. "We've got one week to Halloween. A week is a long time."

"Okay, so what do you propose we do with this week?"

"Well. Nurse Bailey tells me that Robert can hear. So I was thinking, what if I made some audio tapes, tapes that can be used to plant a different message in Robert's brain."

"Subliminal messages," Jason interrupted.

"Kind of. You know, tell him that he's not sick, that all his tests results are normal, that he's not dying…Maybe even lie to him. Tell him that we've found Emanuelle, and she wants to visit him."

"You're talking about de-programming him."

"Exactly. Let the tapes run all day and night. Osmosis can be a very effective tool."

Jason nodded. "It sounds like a plan, assuming that we're right about this whole Faust thing."

"I know it's a big stretch, but no one over at UH has come up with another plausible explanation, or course of action. So, why not."

"So, we're down to last resorts."

"It's either this," Livy said, "or we wait for Halloween to come and go."

23

LAST MAN STANDING

People, like machines, wear out. Old age aside, often times it has more to do with the rocky shore giving way to the crashing wave. In Bruno Lentoni's case, the wave was a combination of conditions that included Type 2 diabetes, hypertension, and obesity; all contributors, no doubt, to his deteriorating condition, but it was his wife's grueling illness and subsequent death that took the heaviest toll.

With depression sapping his energy, he napped more frequently, sometimes falling asleep sitting up in his recliner while watching the six o'clock news. This was one of those times.

He was also dreaming more these days about his deceased wife, Donna. It was almost as if she was paving the way for their imminent reunion, calling him home. Oh, he was so ready for that.

These days, the dream was always the same. His wife was wearing a dress that he'd bought her for her birthday, the one covered in blue polka dots. He noticed that her hands were tan from working in the garden as she gave him a haircut. They were laughing as she teased him about his wild eyebrows and unruly nose hairs. "Your hair's growing everywhere, except on top of your head."

Warm and inviting like a summer rain, he loved her laugh. When she announced that she was going to can more tomatoes for her pasta sauce, or plant a fig tree like her father had done in the old country, he felt her strength once again. The dream was always so real, but when he went to kiss her, she wasn't there.

The disappointment was always crushing, suffocating even. His beautiful Donna was just an apparition, again.

But it wasn't the disappointment that jarred him back to reality on this occasion. Something or someone was in his den. His eyelids snapped open involuntary. He smelled the Old Spice cologne before his eyes could adjust to the shadowy figure sitting in the chair across from him. In spite of the sunglasses and ball cap, he recognized this man from the Mangini funeral. It was Heidi's brother Walter Gadsky. The gun in his hand, enhanced by a silencer, was pointed directly at Bruno. This was no social visit.

Bruno, a man with so little to lose, appeared surprisingly unruffled. Calm even. With suicide never an option for Lentoni, perhaps the kid would do him the favor. His voice was fuzzy and gruff from the long nap as he asked, "How'd you know it was me kid?"

Gadsky leaned forward, and removed his sunglasses. His voice was monotonic and lifeless like his eyes. "It was the way you looked at me at the funeral." He paused. "And, I checked you out."

Bruno shook his head, he'd been tracked down by a rank amateur.

Walter, for whatever reason, felt he owed his sister's killer more details about his methodology. "By the way, no one from the neighborhood ratted you out. In fact, everybody seemed too scared to say anything. They wouldn't even look me in the eye." He smiled, pointed to his temple, and gave himself one more pat on the back. "That made me even more suspicious...about you."

Bruno, always the old-time gangster smiled. One thing you could always count on, there were no rat-bastard stoolies living on the Hill.

"There was this one guy from Youngstown however," he continued on aimlessly, "now him, he sang like a canary, after I twisted his arm a little bit." The kid chuckled, evidently amused as he recalled those moments of violent coercion.

"Had to be Ray Scafotti," Bruno guessed.

"That's right. He called you one-bad-ass-mother-fucker. A pretty impressive endorsement from a guy whose stock-in-trade is knee-capping, don't you think?"

"Well, you can't believe everything you hear."

"Or believe what you see," Walter came back. "You're one tricky guy Bruno, what some might even call a paradox. Whack someone, then pay for their funeral. Good guy, bad guy, you wear both masks well. Truth is, I really wasn't sure you shot my sister until you just admitted it."

"C'mon Kid, that silencer tells me different. You came for me.

You're here to even things up. I'd do the same."

Walter studied the old man. What made him tick suddenly became important. "You believe in God, Bruno?"

"I used to." Not sure if this was the time or place to bring his wife into the discussion, he debated for a moment before opting against it. "I don't anymore."

"And yet, you don't appear to be afraid. Why's that?"

Bruno managed a weary smile. "I dunno. Maybe I'm too tired to care."

Satisfied with the response, he looked above Bruno's ridiculous comb-over hair-do to a shelf behind him. Nodding toward several photos he asked, "Is that your wife?"

"Was my wife."

"She's pretty. Got a kind face."

Though Walter sounded sincere, the inclusion of his wife into such ugly business set him off, "Kid, just get on with it. Do what you came to do."

Walter hesitated, the moment of truth had arrived and he was coming up short. Killing a man with a gun wasn't the same as beating him to a pulp in the ring.

"That's what I thought," Bruno taunted, "your sister had bigger balls than you do."

The pop was understated, the bright orange flash fleeting, and the pain excruciating as the bullet tore through Bruno's right slipper. "Son of a bitch!" erupted from his twisted mouth.

"Listen to me old man, you don't tell me when it's time. Got it."

Bruno already in shock, kicked off his slipper. There was a lot of blood, but it appeared that no arteries had been hit.

"So," Walter continued as though he'd just swatted a fly away from his picnic lunch, "I'm guessing that Jason Scarza was a close friend, or maybe somehow related to you?"

"Neither," Bruno answered through a grimace. The pain was intense. He was guessing that a bone had been shattered in his foot, "I was in his debt."

"What kind of debt?"

"Does it matter?"

"You gotta death wish you crazy old man? Just answer the frigging question."

Bruno, suddenly feeling like he was in the middle of an Elmore Leonard plot, answered apologetically, "Scarza rescued my wife's dog."

"Rescued your wife's dog," Walter scoffed. "You shot three people because of a mutt?"

Lentoni gave the kid a withering look. "Like I said, the dog belonged to my wife."

"I get it. You really loved your wife." Gadsky stopped, the revenge he'd plotted so carefully seemed to be taking a detour. He'd planned to sneak in unnoticed, pump a bullet into Bruno's skull, and get the hell out. But now, for whatever reason, he felt like talking.

"Now my parents, they hated each other. My father abused both me and my sister. I prayed every night that he'd die in his sleep."

The gangster was in too much pain to play family counselor. "Kid, I really don't give a fuck."

Walter ignored Bruno's hostility. "And Mrs. Mangini, what about her? You obviously cared about her too."

"What's your point Kid? You come here to shoot me or analyze me?"

"You're one strange hit man," he said, ignoring the question. "You kill the Manginis boys, then pay for their funeral. What's up with that?"

"It's complicated."

"You also bought and paid for that sorry-ass-excuse-for-a-priest, didn't you?"

Bruno just shook his head. *How did he know? Was it that obvious? Had Lisa Mangini figured it out too? He hoped not.*

"How much did that whole fiasco cost you?"

Bruno paused, then thought what he hell. "Ten grand?"

Walter whistled, "That's a lot of money for an old retired guy." The kid smiled. "You must be a good saver."

It was all so odd. Bruno, who'd never had the luxury of having a confidant, or priest that he could trust with his dark secrets, suddenly had one. Who better to confess your sins to than the last man you're ever going to see alive? Suddenly it felt right to share intimacies with his executioner. "I took out a mortgage on my house."

"Why in god's name would you do that?" Gadsky chortled. "Level with man, you and Lisa Mangini, you got something going."

"Watch your mouth," Bruno snapped, "show some respect."

"Then why the ten grand? You knock off her sons, then mortgage your house to pay for their funeral. That's insane."

Bruno took a deep breath. "Lisa Mangini's a saint. She was very kind to my wife when she was dying. They became good friends and I—"

"Ah," Walter broke in, "I get it. You were paying off another debt."

Bruno couldn't figure the kid out. Why all the questions, unless he was having second thoughts about killing him.

"Bruno my man, you're one noble bastard, aren't you."

Lentoni was beginning to squirm. His foot screamed for medical attention, and playing *64 questions* with Walter wasn't helping.

The kid let out a half-laugh. Something had apparently struck him funny. "It all seems right…fitting even…that you and me…both of us…we're in the same business. The business of repaying debts."

Walter stopped abruptly, and raised his gun. Bruno, anticipating the end, closed his eyes. But instead of a gunshot, he heard Gadsky's voice drone on. "The cops said that my sister probably never knew what hit her. Is that true?"

This was a first for Bruno, detailing the gruesome end of one of his victims. Walter's obvious pain prompted Bruno to answer honestly, "I know my business. It was quick. Real quick."

Tears streamed down Walter's face. "You know my sister wasn't all bad. She took good care of me after I had my brain surgery. I was partially paralyzed for six months."

He dropped his head to show a nasty scar behind his left ear. "The surgery didn't work. I still can't feel anything…I burn myself all the time."

"Well, she didn't do herself any favors hanging out with Leo Mangini," Bruno said, oddly trying to comfort the man who'd come to kill him. "That kid was rotten to the core."

Gadsky nodded, but now the only person he wanted to talk about was himself. "I'm a freak of nature you know. I black out all the time, and injure myself without knowing it. Christ, I'm impotent like a frigging eunuch. Worst of all, I'm tormented by this fucking, debilitating condition. I'm a freak of nature..."

Talk about irony. *A man who could literally feel nothing was in constant pain.*

Gadsky shook his head and sniffled back the tears. "And I'm a major fuck-up. Here I am, sitting face to face with my sister's murderer, having second thoughts. Heidi would be so pissed. Probably grab this gun from me and finish the job herself."

Lentoni looked down at his throbbing foot. *Because of his diabetes, it was likely that he was going to lose it. Strange thing to ponder, considering the fact that he was probably not going to survive the next few moments anyway.*

Walter seemed resigned to the weird situation he found himself in. A kind of finality had crept into his voice. "Ya know, you're nothing like I'd imagined you to be. But that shouldn't matter. You shot my sister. Put a big hole in the back of her head."

Something was happening, Bruno felt it. A roiling from within, a volcano was ready to erupt. An unlikelier pair of victims one could never find. They were two players in a Greek tragedy. Death seemed imminent, but for whom?

Walter, now completely broken, began to sob uncontrollably. "I'm sorry Heidi. I'm so sorry Sis."

Bruno watched him unscrew the silencer. That could be a good thing he reasoned. Maybe Walter had reconsidered. Perhaps he was going to abort the mission.

He got his answer shortly when the kid put the barrel of the gun into his mouth and splattered his brains all over the den's striped wallpaper.

Committing homicide is far more complicated than just pulling a trigger, as Gadsky found out the hard way. Suicide, on the other hand, can be a simple solution for those in pain, and evidently Walter wasn't just in pain, he was in agony.

Though Bruno had managed to escape another brush with death, the harrowing experience with young Walter Gadsky left him shaken. A good kid had died needlessly, and once again he was at the epicenter of the tragedy feeling more than a little responsible, a feeling he quickly squelched.

It was more about being pragmatic than being cold and heartless. Walter was dead. There was nothing left for Bruno to do except pay for another funeral, and soldier on like some wind-up toy. The rest he'd leave up to an estranged, ambivalent God, who for some unexplained reason, had chosen him to be the last man standing.

24

THE GET-WELL CARD

The cavatelli and meatballs dinner, a Gramma Scarza Sunday specialty, was delicious. The dinnertime conversation naturally drifted toward the previous day's mayhem at the Lentoni house. To spare his grandmother from all the gruesome particulars and unsettling implications, Jason omitted the fact that the young man who'd blown his brains out was one of the men involved in the Sons of Sicily clubhouse assault.

Gramma, never one to waste time or energy with fact checking, commiserated with Bruno. "This poor man can't seem to catch a break. First his wife gets sick, and then this happens, in his own home no less. That boy had to be potso in the head that's for sure."

Jason and Livy nodded. Shielding Gramma from Bruno's criminal activities seemed the least prickly path to traverse. So Livy stuck to wound assessment. "I heard Bruno could lose his foot."

"That's exactly what I'm talking about," Gramma bemoaned. "The man's cursed. Somebody's put the malocchio on him."

Many of the old-timers in the neighborhood believed so strongly in the evil-eye-curse that they wore the cornetto horn around their necks for protection. Gramma, relying on her many crucifixes and rosary beads, sought a different kind of insurance.

Jason, who hadn't shared his theory with anyone that it was Bruno who'd avenged his beating, avoided speculating about the reasons for Gadsky presence in the Lentoni home. No one, especially not Livy or Gramma, needed to connect those sinister dots.

With the dishes in the sink, and the coffee percolating, Gramma was on the move playing good Samaritan. "There's apple pie in the fridge. I've gotta run next door. Carmella sprained her ankle. I'm going to give her a hand with her laundry."

They held hands while they had coffee and pie. With Bruno Lentoni's misfortunes no longer a topic of conversation, things began to revert to the more mundane. "So how did your last rehearsal go?"

Suddenly Jason became more animated. "Quite well. I don't know how many people will show up Friday night, but I'm enjoying the whole process. I'd forgotten how much I loved the music."

"Good for you! And what about Calvin?"

It was a loaded question to be sure. Was she asking about his chronic hoarseness or his excessive drinking? He stayed clear of both. "Well, he's all fired up and raring to go. He can't wait for Friday either."

"Are you still opening with the Elton John song?"

"Yeah. We decided to go full bore from the get-go. *Great Balls of Fire* right on the heels of *Crocodile Rock.*"

She smiled and teased, "Sounds like a *gas* man."

He chuckled. "Smart ass. You are coming Friday, right?"

She leaned into him and kissed him. That was answer enough.

He sat back and sipped his coffee. "What about Balfour? Any changes since they started playing the audio tapes?"

"It's still early. But no, nothing." She wrung her hands together and sighed heavily. "I'm starting to have second thoughts. We're trying to de-program a man, who may or may not be hearing any of it, let alone processing it."

"What about the EEGs? Any change there?"

"No." Livy shrugged, shook her head before throwing her hands up. "But the docs have nothing else. So they figure, what the hell, let's keep the tapes rolling."

"The same tapes? I mean, have they added anything new? You know, change things up a bit. Maybe add some music."

"Jason," Livy scolded, "that's not funny."

"I wasn't trying to be funny. If music is therapeutic for the conscious, then why not the unconscious as well."

"Well, I guess I can talk to Dr. Kern about adding music, but I'm already on pretty thin ice at the hospital. Even Esther is starting to weaken."

"How so?"

"We're catching alotta flak from staff, and the doctors look at us like we're both crazy. They refuse to believe that Robert orchestrated his...what should I call it, his grand exit?"

"Well, you can kinda see their point. They're men of science, not science fiction."

"Maybe so. All I know is it's getting tougher and tougher to visit Robert. I've advanced from pest status to being the brunt of hospital jokes."

"Hospital jokes?"

"Yeah, I overheard two nurses doing me, mocking me. One of them was counting down to midnight as if it were New Year's Eve on Times Square, while the other one staggered around clutching her heart."

"Wow, that's really sick. How'd you react?"

"They never saw me, so I turned and walked the other way."

Jason put his arm around her and pulled her close. "I'm so sorry Livy, but this whole Balfour situation has become such an emotional black hole for you."

"Maybe, but it's never dull. Listen to this one. I walk into Robert's room and what do I find on his bed stand? A get-well card."

Jason pondered the possibilities before suggesting, "Another sick joke?"

"No, it didn't appear to be. It was from Johnny Eagle of all people. The return address was Mesa Arizona."

"You're kidding. The shaman sent Robert a get-well card? Is that even possible? I thought he was dead."

"Actually, he's not that old. If my math is correct, he's late fifties, early sixties."

"Was there a note?" Jason asked. "Did he say anything else? Ya know, like, have you *smoked any good dope lately?*"

She jabbed his arm. "I'm glad you're taking all this so seriously."

"Sorry, I couldn't help myself."

She reloaded and began again. "So the card got me thinking, how did Eagle find out about Balfour's illness?"

"Hmm, that's a very good question."

"According to Balfour, Eagle was the one who set this whole scenario in motion. So I figure, maybe Robert isn't the only one counting down the years. I'm sure that Eagle has a calendar too. Maybe he'd also circled this Halloween as the day of reckoning."

Jason smiled. "You got all that from a get-well card?"

"I don't think it's all that crazy. You don't see or hear from someone for decades, and then out of the blue, you get a card a few days before *doomsday.* That sounds like a lot more than just coincidence."

"I don't know Livy, adding a co-conspirator to an already unbelievable plot seems like muddying the waters even more than they already are."

She ignored him. "I'm telling you, Eagle was there at the beginning, whispering in Robert's ear. The peyote was his idea. And unless I miss my guess, he was involved with that mystery woman too."

"How can you be certain about any of this?"

"From conversations I had with Robert. He talked a lot about Johnny Eagle."

Jason shook his head. "Livy, maybe it's time to just back away from this thing. It's a dead end."

"Maybe it is, but I've gotta keep plugging away as long as Robert still has breath left in his body."

"I don't know. All of this upheaval because of one get-well card?"

"At the moment, it's all we have. I say we check out the card, and maybe flush out Eagle. I'm kind of curious what he's been up to all these years?"

"And how do you propose we do that?"

Livy smiled. "It just so happens that I know a guy."

"Well, Pinkerton's been dead for over a century, so I know it can't be him."

"Maybe someone even better than Pinkerton. How about Lawrence Bryson, private investigator extraordinaire."

"Who?"

"He worked for Robert's father, doing what, I haven't the foggiest."

"He sounds expensive," Jason guessed correctly.

"No doubt, but Robert once told me that, at his father's suggestion, he hired Bryson to help him find Emanuelle. Of course he never did, but he certainly knows things that no one else would. Maybe he even kept his old case notes."

"So, do you know how to reach this guy? Is he still alive, or even still in business?"

"Yes, yes, and yes. He lives in Las Vegas."

"Sounds like you've already contacted him."

"Yup, I called him and gave him Eagle's return address from the get-well card. He said he'd get right on it."

Jason shook his head. "Did you happen to discuss fees with him? PIs are like attorneys, the meter's always running."

"My love, that's what credit cards are for."

Livy picked up the phone. It was Gramma calling from University Hospital.

Livy panicked. "My God, what happened? Are you okay?"

"I'm fine. Carmella's ankle, it wasn't sprained, it's fractured. We're in the emergency room. Her son drove us. Don't wait up."

Jason didn't need the message relayed. He'd heard every word from across the room. Gramma's phone voice, affected by some hearing loss, made a megaphone unnecessary.

All that mattered at that moment was they were finally alone. The house was theirs for a few hours. They exchanged hungry looks as he swept in, picked her up in his arms, and carried her up the stairs. She threw her arms around his neck, girlishly kicked her feet while trying to play the role of the southern belle. Jason was suddenly her Rhett Butler.

Halfway up the stairs, she got giddy and wise cracked, "Ya know this is how men get hernias."

He shut her up with a kiss without ever breaking stride. She appeared light in his arms, but she was no wisp of a girl, Livy Jardine was a throwback to the Fifties and Sixties, an era when curvaceous women like Marilyn Monroe ruled the silver screen.

Once in her room, he laid her gently on the bed. It quickly became apparent that he was a very sensual, adept lover. He undressed her slowly, showing a kind of delicate curiosity, it was as if her body parts were unique to the species. When she was finally naked, he quickly stripped down to his boxers, but made no attempt to cover up his full state of arousal.

He spent an excruciatingly long amount of time lightly kissing areas that she'd never considered erogenous—toes, the back of her knees, the small of her back, her armpits, the nape of her neck. Like an overheated boiler, she was ready to explode when he finally placed his mouth on the wet nexus between her legs.

After several powerful orgasms, he finally mounted her. Half-crazed, he didn't bother to drop his shorts. He felt huge as she guided him in using both hands. They never stopped kissing as he continued to rhythmically pump her. She lost count of the orgasms.

He was totally selfless until he could contain himself no more. Several powerful shudders, and a shout-out to the heavens, and he was done. Gloriously spent, he fell to his side, lightly touched her face, her lips, her nose, and planted a dewdrop kiss on her mouth. His "I love you," was the perfect exclamation point for a love making session that had exceeded anything she'd ever read about or experienced before. Being both in love and in lust was a great place to be.

The persistent ringing of the telephone woke him. They'd slept for over an hour. Ten rings, eleven rings. Mumbling under his breath, Jason threw on his pants and hurried down the steps. Imagining the worst, he feared something had happened to Carmella, Gramma, or the most likely scenario—Calvin Short was calling from a bar, too drunk to drive home.

His "hello" was fraught with uncertainty.

There was a brief hesitation before a man asked, "Is this Jason Scarza?"

The caller's tone bothered Jason. The voice on the other end of the line sounded so official, impersonal, foreboding. "Yes I'm Jason Scarza. Who's calling?"

"My name's Kendrick. I'm a nurse. I called you earlier."

Jason blanked for a moment. No one had mentioned anything about a phone call, and certainly no messages left by a guy named Kendrick.

"I'm a caregiver for Rollie... Rollie Masters. He asked me to call you."

Scarza was too stunned to speak. Most of what he'd just heard was so incomprehensible that it didn't compute. Rollie Masters was trying to contact him? Why? Hadn't he inflicted enough damage already? Maybe he wanted to back the truck over Jason's fallen body one last time to really finish him off.

"Mr. Scarza, are you still there?"

"Yes I am. Listen Kendrick, I don't know if this call is legit, but…"

"Oh, it's legit. Rollie couldn't call you himself… It's kind of complicated. He wants to explain that part himself."

Scarza was part furious, part curious. Why was Rollie Masters trying to contact him? "Kendrick, I gotta tell you that I'm very close to hanging up."

"Please don't hang up Mr. Scarza, you really need to talk to Rollie. It's extremely important. Some might even call it a life and death situation."

"Life and death?" Jason repeated skeptically. "You're gonna have to give me a lot more than that."

"I can't. I've been instructed to invite you to Rollie's home in Germantown, and that's it."

Again Jason wanted to slam the phone down, but couldn't. The conversation had a cloak-and-dagger feel to it, one that left him more than a little intrigued. Something was going on, something way beyond strange.

"When?" just popped out of his mouth.

"As soon as you can get here. It's that urgent."

Jason took a deep breath. Never in this lifetime or the next did he expect or want to see Rollie Masters' face again, and here he was making arrangements to do just that. After a long hesitation he said, "I can be there tomorrow afternoon."

"Good, are you familiar with Germantown?"

"Somewhat?"

"Okay, Rollie lives on Riverside Drive, 7070. But there's more. You can't be seen entering the house. There's a park that backs up to his house. Come through the park. There's a walk-out basement entrance. I'll be there to let you in."

A basement door! Whoa, something major was afoot. The whole conversation had a gritty feel, like the good old days in the field.

"Mr. Kendrick, I have a question for you."

"Okay, shoot."

"You said earlier that you're Rollie's care-giver?"

"That's correct. Rollie has ALS."

"Lou Gehrig's disease?"

"Yes, he was diagnosed last year."

Jason was shocked into silence. Rollie Masters was a stud, every bit Jason's physical equal. It was hard to picture him slumped over in a wheelchair drooling from the corner of his mouth.

Jason was stunned speechless.

"See you tomorrow Mr. Scarza."

Gramma, hating Rollie Masters more than any man on earth, would never understand or support this clandestine meeting. After all, it was Rollie's lies, his crimes that had put her grandson behind bars, and gotten him booted from the Navy.

So Jason decided to shield her from the truth, invent some story about the Dueling Pianos needing more rehearsal time for the opening down at the Blue Note. As cover stories went, practicing well into the night didn't sound all that farfetched. And Livy could ad lib in case things went awry.

The Rollie Masters that Jason had known was a Marvel Comic Book character, a superhero with superpowers. He'd dodged bullets, leapt off cliffs, and walked through fire. He'd been an invincible warrior, a secret weapon of the United States Navy. But as his body began to fail him, questions arose about his future, his choices.

What does an invincible warrior do when a doctor utters the words that no one wants to hear—Sir, you've got amyotrophic lateral sclerosis?

One possibility was to throw oneself on one's sword, another was to invite an old friend/archenemy to one's lair. Rollie Masters had inexplicably chosen the latter.

26

Lawrence Bryson wasn't the stereotypical private detective. PIs are often former law enforcement types, anti-social misfits who don't play well with others, or people who grew up reading too many Mike Hammer novels. Bryson was none of the above.

The dapper, rail-thin detective graduated from UCLA, got his masters degree and doctorate from Stanford, and then went on to teach a World History class at USC. A few years later he was persuaded to join his uncle's private detective agency. Spying on cheating spouses of Hollywood celebrities proved to be far more lucrative than lecturing nineteen-year-olds who'd showed little interest in the Battle of Hastings changing the course of human history.

And all of this was before Robert Balfour Sr. entered his life. The famous author took a liking to young Bryson, even putting him on retainer as a researcher/private eye. Rumors began to circulate, whispers about their relationship being much more than that, at least according to the tabloids, but no could argue the fact that Lawrence Bryson's investigative work was exemplary.

Bryson's relationship with Senior's troubled son was a very different matter. In fact, they'd never even met. He was hired indirectly by Balfour II to find a mystery woman named Emanuelle, but every lead wound up a dead end. For the first and last time in a long career, Bryson had failed. He never did locate Emanuelle.

Then decades later, out of the blue, Livy Jardine phoned him to enlist his help locating Johnny Eagle. Of course she told him about the strange events that led up to Balfour's coma, and the perplexing get-well card. These eerie twists seemed to intrigue Lawrence Bryson.

"Perhaps in some crazy way," Livy explained to Bryson, "the get well card might be a key to Balfour's recovery."

Bryson thought her plan laughable, but his steep fees were anything but. So he reasoned, why not? Mesa Arizona was a lovely place to visit in the fall of the year.

Though Red Rock Manor was in the grim business of end-of-life care, primarily dementia cases, the facility looked more like a country club than a bleak final destination. The sprawling one-story structure, featuring cream-colored stucco walls, decorative shutters, red tile roof, and an abundance of windows, was surrounded by lush palm trees and vibrant yucca plants. The orange colored African Daisies, white Desert Lilies, and purple Sandbells pleased in a more ethereal way. *An upscale operation* was Bryson's initial impression.

Bryson had called ahead and talked to a nurse named Boris. Since he had no problem with Bryson's mission, Boris gave him the front door security code. "Four-three-two-one" seemed a breach of security in its own right, but there hadn't been any major breakouts since the facility opened its doors five years prior.

A frazzled old woman, wearing nothing but slippers and bathrobe, watched Bryson anxiously as he punched in the security code. No track shoes mind you, but she certainly looked ready to bolt. Seven grand a year to be imprisoned, it just didn't seem right. Of course, neither was having Alzheimer's eat into one's brain.

Warily keeping an eye on the robed woman, he waited for a staff member to intervene before he opened the door. The help came in the form of an obese LPN who stymied the woman's run to freedom with a gentle bear hug. The locked entry was as close as the desperate woman was ever going to get to the parking lot and the frightening world that lay beyond.

"Now Miss Elizabeth," cooed the LPN, "you know you have to get dressed up if you wanna go out." Infants were talked to with less condescension, Bryson observed. "So let's get you back to your room sweetie pie, and gussy you up a bit. Okay?"

Nurse Linda hooked Elizabeth's frail arm, winked at Bryson, and waved him on. No one else in the area seemed to have noticed the heart-wrenching scene that had just unfolded. Others, who were just a few paces away, totally ignored the quashed get-away attempt as though it was just another failed purse snatching on Times Square.

Bryson was soon to learn that what he'd just witnessed wasn't as much about callous indifference as it was the inability to process, or have the wherewithal to attend, even when desperate people were attempting desperate measures. Struggling to remember what you ate an hour ago, or the names of your children, had a way of negating just another foiled "jail break."

Once inside, Bryson took a cynical look around. It was all a slick attempt to sell a place of unspeakable degradation as a bright, airy social club for seniors who'd strayed a bit from the norm. The common areas were open and filled with faux activity, colorful artwork adorned the walls while Frank Sinatra's version of *High Hopes* was cheerily piped throughout. The only thing missing was party hats.

All of the staging was intended to impress guilt-ridden children or mates who were looking for a place to lock up that special someone who'd become too unpredictable and dangerous to keep at home. Miss Elizabeth, case in point, was somebody's wife, somebody's mother, just one lost soul among many lost souls.

Bryson approached the reception desk manned by a young woman chewing gum and reading a *Cosmopolitan* magazine. Her ID tag read Liza P. "I'm here to see Johnny Eagle, Liza."

Liza gave the PI a curious look. Eagle's typical visitor wore dungarees, flannel shirt, and a ten-gallon cowboy hat. Bryson's three-piece suit, bow tie, and fedora ensemble looked more GQ than Dodge City.

"Hmm, Johnny Eagle you say. I'm pretty sure that he'd still be at breakfast. Right this way please."

The dining room loomed ahead. Counting the tables and chairs, full capacity appeared to be thirty-six. The fancy tablecloths and chinaware, the affluent neighborhood, the lush manicured grounds, and the goodly number of attendants led the PI to one conclusion— Red Rock was an expensive place to while away your last muddled days. How Johnny Eagle could afford such digs was a question saved for another day.

"He's right over there," Lisa said while pointing to a man who was sitting alone at a table that was positioned near a window that overlooked a courtyard dominated by several mature palm trees.

"Johnny," she called out to him, "you've got a visitor."

Johnny blinked for a moment before jumping to his feet. He had a visitor, someone he thought he recognized from his days with the Cleveland Indians. The extended hand came first, then the coarse greeting. "Lefty you old son of a bitch, where'd you get the fancy duds?"

It was interesting to note that the energetic, lithe Navajo seemed misplaced in a sea of disheveled residents who were plagued by hunched torsos, fumbling fingers, vacant stares, and an obsession with lost objects from a previous life.

Eagle, the youngest resident in the facility, looked anything but feeble or compromised. Victimized by early onset Alzheimer's disease—one cruel fate heaped upon an even crueler fate—his mind was in rapid decline, but the rest of his body hadn't gotten the memo from his dysfunctional brain yet.

Bryson shook his hand while wondering what was the best way to handle the awkward situation. Should he correct Eagle or not? To successfully conduct the interview, the correction seemed a cruel necessity. "I'm sorry Mr. Eagle, my name's not Lefty, it's Lawrence Bryson. I'm a private detective."

His smile remained, the façade left intact. He'd grin and bear yet another indignity. Lately, nobody was who he thought they were. Names never matched faces, and faces never matched names. He covered up beautifully as he was wont to do these days. "Well I'll be damned. You look just like Lefty."

He slapped his thigh before veering even farther off course. "I shoulda known better. Once that old bastard retired to Laughlin, that was it. That shrewish wife of his won't let him leave the house."

Bryson, not certain if any of what he'd just heard was accurate or relevant, jotted it down anyway. *Lefty lives in Laughlin... With shrewish wife...Never leaves the house.*

"I tried to warn him," Johnny continued, "never marry a second cousin. They're too needy."

The PI momentarily debated asking Johnny if Lefty had a last name, but thought better. Eagle's glassy expression was answer enough.

"Johnny," the PI said in the least threatening way possible. "I've come to ask you a few questions about Robert Balfour."

"Robert Balfour," he shouted exuberantly. At last, someone worth remembering, a bridge to the past that hadn't yet been destroyed by a disease that was rapidly turning his brain into Swiss cheese. "How is Robert? Is he still writing books?"

Bryson, about to answer the question, was stopped in his tracks by a resident who wandered over, hovered over him for a moment before reluctantly taking the seat next to him. No introductions were made. The man just sat there eating his chocolate pudding while *openly eavesdropping*. An oxymoronic depiction of events no doubt, but there was no way for Bryson to know which bothered the confused man more, the fact that a stranger was occupying his chair, or that the cook had forgotten to put walnuts in his pudding.

Encouraged that the Navajo had successfully connected the right person and occupation, Bryson answered, "No, he's no longer writing. He's very sick. Actually, he's in a coma."

The man eating the pudding suddenly started to weep causing Johnny to pat his hand. "It's okay, Horace, it's no one you know."

Bryson watched as Horace perked up and got back to his pudding cup. With that disaster averted, the PI said, "Well, I'm guessing that you'd already heard about the coma. After all, you did send him a get-well card."

"I sent him a get-well card?" He thought things over for a long moment before responding. "Oh yeah, that's right. I did."

Bryson appeared pleased. *Things were looking up. Eagle remembered sending the card. Finally a breakthrough.*

"That foul ball nailed him good. Left an imprint on his forehead. You always gotta keep your eye on the baseball, even in the stands. "

Keeping Eagle on topic was exasperating, and that was before

Horace started crying again. Evidently comas and foul-balls greatly saddened him. But this time Johnny ignored the tears. "Ya know Lefty, back in the day, I was a great pitcher. Did I ever tell ya that I struck out sixteen batters in my first big league start?"

Eagle was meandering badly. Bryson had to get him back on track so that he could make a determination whether to continue the interview or scrap it.

"It's too bad about Robert Balfour," the PI started again, "he's really in a bad way."

Eagle shook his head. "Nah, he's okay now."

"He is? How did he get better?"

"I gave him a little something. Fixed him right up."

"Ya mean, like sending him a get-well card?"

"No, you gotta stay with me son! I gave him some peyote. Made him like new. I'm a shaman you know."

The interview had turned south, again. It was becoming more apparent that Eagle didn't have the wherewithal to send the card.

"So Lefty," Eagle asked, "is George still married to that white girl?"

Horace, apparently all cried out, decided to take his pudding and leave. Even the Jello guy saw the futility of the disjointed conversation.

Bryson, who decided that the peyote anecdote was the only spring board left available to him, asked, "So you gave Robert peyote? How did that go?"

The Navajo laughed out loud. "Poor bastard really tripped. But I'll tell you this Lefty. It was the craziest thing. Right after that, he wrote that book, the one that made him famous." He chuckled again. "I told him that he'd soar."

The guy was in and out, lucid, not lucid. He was on a time-warp machine that couldn't be turned off. Very little of the interview was proving helpful. Livy Jardine was going to be very disappointed.

"You know, I once struck out sixteen batters in my—" He stopped himself abruptly. Panic widened his eyes. He'd just caught himself repeating a story that he'd just related only moments earlier to someone that he no longer recognized. He had the same sinking feeling when he sometimes didn't recognize the face in the mirror.

He turned toward the window not wanting anyone to see the tears that were welling up in his eyes. Eagle had taken flight, and what was left behind was a mere formality, the long torturous wait for his brain to disengage, and shut down his ability to walk, swallow and breathe.

The PI walked away from the human wreckage that he'd left behind shaking his head. It had all been for naught. The Native American was too far gone to be helpful. But the question about the get-well card still remained—if Johnny Eagle hadn't sent the card, then who? Perhaps Nurse Boris would have some answers.

"You shouldn't feel bad," Boris began, "he's been all over the place lately. And getting more emotional by the day."

"I noticed." Not to appear insensitive, Bryson paused a long moment. "Boris, there's this guy back in Cleveland who's really sick. This man got a get-well card from someone in this facility."

Boris nodded enthusiastically. "Robert Balfour, right?"

"Yeah, that's right," Bryson responded more than a little surprised. "How'd you know?"

"I sent it. Well, actually Johnny asked me to send it. I wrote the note for Johnny. Believe me, it wasn't like a letter from home or nothing."

"Really, 'cause he didn't remember anything about the card."

"That's not surprising. Like I said, he's been way off his game."

"May I ask one more question Boris?"

"Shoot."

"How did you know. How did Johnny know about Robert Balfour's illness? Where to send the card? Any of it?"

"Oh that's easy. Freddy Graywolf stopped by."

Snow accumulation before Halloween was unusual for the Philadelphia area. So when Scarza trekked through Rollie Masters' backyard the icy slop was more a nuisance than a deterrent. Galoshes would've been helpful, however.

Rodney Kendrick looked through the peephole, unlatched several dead bolts before finally opening the door. He looked past Jason to the footprints in the snow. For whatever reason, Jason's tracks seemed to greatly vex him.

"Please come in Mr. Scarza. Rollie's waiting in the rec room."

Kendrick was powerfully built and moved with fluid grace. Former athlete, ex-military—either seemed a reasonable guess.

His gaze was penetrating. Brawn like his may have been a prerequisite for maneuvering invalids, but Mr. Kendrick looked to be more bodyguard than caregiver.

Scarza, less than thrilled by the prospect of seeing Masters again, tried not to scowl, but he couldn't help himself. It had been almost five years since they faced off in court, and his scarred knuckles were still a reminder of the fisticuffs that erupted outside the courtroom. The hatred he felt for Rollie Masters ran deep.

Making this situation even more mind boggling, they'd been best friends since boot camp, even visited each other's homes during holidays. Jason would've taken a bullet for Rollie, or given him a kidney. He expected reciprocation, but he'd gotten betrayal instead.

It all read like a B-movie plot. When a drug stash was found in Rollie Masters' locker, he blamed a comrade, a Lieutenant Jones, for planting the cocaine. His attorney claimed some petty argument over a woman had been Jones' motive for the "dastardly deed." So, it was Rollie's word against Jones.' Of course, being Admiral Masters' son, Rollie's word held sway.

But Jason knew the truth. Because his testimony refuted Rollie's account, Scarza found himself directly in the Admiral's crosshairs. A charge of perjury was leveled against Jason resulting in his court martial and two years in the brig. The ensuing fist fight, one that left Rollie's face unrecognizable, tacked on two more years for assaulting a fellow officer.

The entire nightmare flashed through Scarza's mind as he walked into the recreation room. And then suddenly Rollie was before him, sitting in a wheelchair listing to port like a sinking ship. Everything on his left side appeared to be compromised by his illness. The left hand was frozen into what looked like a claw, and the left side of his face was contorted. A blanket covered legs that had already begun to atrophy. The once-strapping warrior looked small as if someone had let all the air out of him. His eyes were pools of tears.

For Scarza, hate, fury, and revulsion were quickly replaced by pity.

Rollie saw the pity in Jason's eyes. He recognized the look, it was a look he was seeing more and more these days. After forcing a smile, he joked, "You should see the other guy."

Kendrick handed him a handkerchief so that he could mop up the tears. After collecting himself, he said, "I wasn't sure you'd come."

"Me either. Your guy here was very convincing."

"Kendrick's a good man. Special Forces himself, in another life."

Jason gave the place a quick perusal. What he saw was a buttoned up, secured area. The rear entry precautions came to mind, a nurse who looked anything but a nurse, and an underground room that felt more like a bug-proofed bunker than a billiard room.

"You gonna be okay," Kendrick asked his boss while keeping Scarza's in his sights. "I've got something that needs tending."

Jason waited for Kendrick to exit before commenting, "He's wiping out my tracks, right?"

He nodded. "How about something to eat? Kendrick's got quite a nice spread laid out on the bar."

"No thanks, I grabbed a sandwich when I stopped for gas."

Rollie studied him for a moment, then observed, "You look good man. Fit as ever."

"Well, you look like shit. When did all this happen?"

"Eighteen months, give or take," he began matter-of-factly. "It started with my left pinky, and got more ambitious as it went along. It's eating me up. Doctors say my case is one for the books. Very, very accelerated."

"I assume that you've gotten a second opinion?"

"Yeah, three of 'em, but all the Docs are singing the same tune. I probably won't be able to talk in a year or so. Swallowing will be the next function to go. Hopefully my heart will give out before I starve to death."

Jason started to speak, but stopped himself. There were no platitudes that could assuage a prognosis this grim.

"Bottom line? I'm fucked Jason, and that's all there's to it." He paused. "That leaves me with a very narrow window to try and make things right."

It took a moment for Scarza to put himself at the center of Rollie's redemption plan. "Make things right? Ya mean with me?"

Masters nodded.

Jason couldn't help himself. The laugh erupted from some bitter well deep inside him. "And just how are you planning to do that Rollie?"

"Listen to me Jason. It's not too late. I can make things right."

Even the broken, pathetic body and streaming tears couldn't stop Jason from venting what had been pent up inside him for so long. "Make things right? Which things? My fifteen-year-career up in smoke, my blackened reputation, the time I lost rotting away in the brig?...Good luck with any of that!"

"I'm so sorry man...So, so sorry!"

Jason shook his head, then ranted on. "I'm a registered felon. I can't even vote."

Masters pulled himself together and admitted, "Look, I was a coward, and the worst friend ever. I screwed you and Jones, and I'll rot in hell for it. But you've gotta believe me, I tried to make all this right even before the trial began, but my father blocked it."

Scarza had spent time at the Masters' home in Arlington.

Admiral Masters was a force of nature to be sure. The Quentin Masters' naval lineage could be traced all the way back to John Paul Jones. No one fucked with that kind of military pedigree.

"When I told him the truth and what actually happened in Honduras, he got this look in his eyes. He was absolutely scary. I had no doubt he would have killed me before he would've let me soil the Masters name."

Jason mentally replayed his visits to Rollie's home. His mom had always been gracious, his father, though a bit bombastic, had treated him like he was a second son. "So, you're saying that your father knew the truth all along?"

"Yes. He's dangerous Jason. That's why we're meeting like this. Believe me, he's capable of anything."

Kendrick returned. He blew on his hands to warm them. The look and nod he gave Rollie indicated that Jason's footprints were gone.

"Look Rollie, I appreciate what you're trying to do, but it's too little, too late." He paused. "Besides, if your father intervened last time, what makes you think this time will be any different?"

"Look, I contacted NCIS yesterday. The Agent who's handling the case is Lieutenant Commander Roger Coleman. He assured me that, if everything I've told him pans out, you might get a new trial in the next few months. With me deteriorating so fast, I really lit a fire under his ass."

Jason shook his head. This was the last news he'd expected.

"Think of it, a new trial. A chance to clear your name."

Jason took a deep breath. "Listen to yourself Rollie, do you know how naive you sound? This is never going to trial. Everything crosses your father's desk."

Rollie nodded. "That's why you're going to hang onto this."

From underneath his blanket he pulled out a videocassette. "It seems that my sanctimonious father has a penchant for rough sex, and apparently he likes to preserve the fun and games for posterity."

Scarza didn't bother to ask how he'd gotten the tape, but focused on how it was to be used. "And this helps me how?"

"Seriously Jason. What, no Machiavellian creativity skulking around in that Italian bloodline of yours?" He paused. "Think like a prick. It's you or him."

"You're talking about blackmailing a Four-Star Admiral in the US Navy?"

"Yes I am. Assaulting women is a court martial offense for admirals as well as ensigns." He held the cassette out in his good hand. "Here take it, but know that this is no ordinary smoking gun. My father goes down, the US military takes a hit that will rock the Pentagon to its very foundations."

Jason took the cassette reluctantly. "How long have you had this? More importantly, does your dad know that you have it?"

"Almost two years. Took it from his collection when I first started thinking about making amends. Just didn't have the balls to use it, until now."

"And he didn't miss it?"

"Not at first. He's got dozens of these things. One sicker than the next."

Scarza winced. "You said, not at first…"

Rollie had fire in his eye as he added, "Yes, he knows now. I told him right after I contacted NCIS."

For the first time Jason understood the secrecy of this meeting. Basement door entry, no tracks left in the snow. Knowing the power of the Admiral, they were all dead men walking.

"Actually, I threatened him. Told him if he interferes in any way, I go public with the tape."

Jason shook his head. "Rollie, what the hell were you thinking. Just because you're his son won't save either of us. You corner a grizzly, expect to get torn to pieces."

"No, that cassette is our insurance. He can't afford that going public."

"I see that as even more reason to worry. "

Rollie smiled. He seemed confident when he added, "I'm telling you we're okay. I've got a copy, and now you have a copy…just in case things do go sideways."

"Sideways?"

"Yeah, think of the tape as a kind of a failsafe, ya know if some accident should befall me, Kendrick, or Roger Coleman…"

Jason put his fingers to his temples. "You're talking crazy. Failsafe! What does that even mean?"

"Hey genius, you're supposed to be the smart one. Use your imagination."

They exchanged one last knowing look before Jason left the way he came in. The next time they'd see each other, their roles would hopefully be reversed. Rollie would don the mantle of shame that Scarza had shouldered for almost five years. A villain would be exonerated, and a hero would be vilified. Even scarier, all of these desperate turns and twists would be carried out under the nose of the evil puppet master, Admiral Quentin Masters. Hopefully, the switch would be accomplished without use of the failsafe, or body bags.

28

SLEEPING ACCOMMODATIONS

It was midnight, and Jason still hadn't returned from Germantown. For Livy, the slick road conditions were a concern, but Gramma was proving the bigger headache as she paced and fretted like a concerned parent on prom night.

"He's been gone all day," Gramma moaned while peeking out one of the front windows. "I ask you, what kind of rehearsal takes twelve hours?"

"It's a dress rehearsal Gramma," Livy lied, "and I think someone from the newspaper was going to interview Calvin and Jason afterward."

The old lady grunted her disapproval as she moved to the other window. "I'm telling you Livy, something's wrong. Jason's always been a thoughtful boy. He knows how I worry."

If she only knew the truth, Livy thought. On Gramma's social hierarchy, Rollie Masters was the lowest of the low, a pariah.

"Maybe we should call the police. Who knows, that motorcycle gang might be after him again."

Livy was running out of lies. The old woman's unrelenting pressure was starting to break down her resolve when the phone mercifully began ringing. Hopefully, it was Jason with some good news.

Gramma lunged for the phone, but Livy got there first. "Hello."

"Hello Livy, it's Lawrence Bryson."

Livy, always the quick thinker, knew Gramma wasn't going to bed until she'd heard from her grandson. So Bryson had unwittingly assumed the role of Jason Scarza. With Gramma sitting on Livy's every word, navigating through this conversation was going to be tricky.

"Hi," Livy said, while putting on her biggest smile, "I was beginning to worry."

Bryson hesitated, "It's a little early for that, don't you think?"

"I know. But everything is fine, isn't it."

Bryson, a tad confused by her odd responses, came back with, "Well, I wouldn't go that far."

With Jason still out there somewhere, Livy's entire focus had been on his trip to Pennsylvania. Now on the fly, she had to readjust her sights from Germantown to Mesa. "That sounds rather ominous."

Gramma, not one to stand on the sidelines very long, made her charge to grab the phone, but Livy nimbly sidestepped her. Most matadors would've been impressed.

"Yeah, I met with Johnny Eagle for maybe twenty minutes. It wasn't good. He's got advanced dementia."

"Well, that's a bad break."

"He did remember Robert though. Recalled giving him peyote." Bryson chuckled, "He also took some credit for inspiring his book."

"Did he mention Emanuelle?"

Gramma's face screwed up as she mouthed, "Who's Emanuelle?"

"No he didn't," Bryson answered.

"How about the card?"

Gramma threw up her hands in disgust. This time she vocalized her frustration. "What the hell are you two talking about? First it's this Emanuelle, and now somethin' about a card. Let me talk to my grandson."

"Who's that," asked Bryson warily.

"Who else? It's Gramma," she said as she warded the old woman off with one arm. "So what about the card?"

"He didn't remember sending it, but then again, he doesn't remember much."

"So, we're back to square one?"

"Not exactly. I got another name, a Freddy Graywolf. The nurse told me that this guy knew about Robert's condition, and which hospital he was in. In fact, the get-well card was actually Graywolf's idea."

"Really. That's very interesting."

Gramma, who'd had enough, marched to the kitchen to retrieve her wooden spoon. She began waving it in Livy's face. "Give me that damn phone Livy or so help me God I'm gonna give you a good wallop."

"Do you want me to follow up the Graywolf lead?" Bryson asked. "It means traveling to Phoenix."

Livy knew what that meant—Cha-ching! "Do it."

Though Bryson had already hung-up, Livy pretended that Jason was still on the line. "So, you'll be a little longer. And Calvin's still there? Good. Do you wanna talk to Gramma? Okay, I'll tell her. See ya later."

Looking both disappointed and relieved, Gramma threatened playfully, "And you, I should break this spoon over your head."

Livy laughed. "And I love you too."

Gramma sat heavily in a near by chair. "So, what did he say?"

"They're having drinks with the reporter. He said don't wait up."

Gramma sighed. "Thank God he's okay."

Livy threw her arm around her and kissed the top of her head. "I'll turn off the coffee pot and the lights. You go to bed. Jason said he was sorry he worried you."

Gramma gave Livy a big hug. "Goodnite, I love you honey."

"Me too."

Gramma stopped in the doorway. She looked exhausted but managed a wink. "Ya know Livy, there's no reason you have to sleep in the attic. It may have been a long time ago, but I was young once."

Scarza drove on through the night trying to get home before his grandmother awoke. Knowing how protective she was, he'd put Livy in the unenviable position of trying to hoodwink one of the most savvy old ladies in all of Little Italy. He expected a good dressing-down after he got back, from both women.

Once he reached Ohio, the roads cleared, unfortunately his mind had not. Having the Admiral's sex tape sitting on the passenger seat like a ticking time bomb was unsettling. What the hell was he supposed to do with it? How about, just for laughs, shake down one of the most powerful men in the entire US military. Yeah right! Maybe in another lifetime.

And then there was Rollie Masters, the man who'd initiated this whole mess and destroyed every fiber of Scarza's former life, quickly becoming a poster-patient for the Jerry Lewis Telethon. Hate turned to pity the moment Jason had laid eyes on him. Instead of cursing Rollie until the day he died, he now vowed to pray for him.

Learning that Rollie had contacted NCIS had taken him by surprise. With the possibilities being both exhilarating and worrisome, several questions arose. *Would the Navy Review Board want to open Pandora's box and begin proceedings to reverse his court martial conviction? That would set a dangerous precedent. More to the point, would Admiral Masters allow it?*

Jason gave the cassette another quick glance. An open crate of rattlesnakes would've been less lethal.

And there it was, the full gamut of emotions—a sniff of hope obliterated by a gale of uncertainty. Exoneration or extermination? Admiral Quentin Masters would probably make the final determination, and that was a frightening prospect, but being forced to use the sex tape as leverage was an even scarier one.

29

PENNIES, APPLES, AND CANDY CORN

Freddy Graywolf's trailer park was more prime rib than hamburger. The inside of his doublewide mobile home wasn't noticeably different than most suburban ranch homes across America. Surprisingly, Freddie looked every inch the quintessential yuppie in his khaki slacks, buttoned down shirt, and penny loafers. Lawrence Bryson had expected Sitting Bull, but got "Joe College" instead.

Freddy welcomed Bryson into his home as though he was an old friend dropping by to say hi. "Have you had breakfast yet Mr. Bryson?"

"Thanks for asking, but I'm not much of a breakfast eater. I grabbed a cup of coffee on the way over."

He fondled the business card that Bryson had given him. "Ya know, I've always wanted to be a private investigator, like Mannix or Magnum. Is it all that it's cracked up to be?"

Bryson smiled. "If you're referring to wild gun play and fighting off beautiful women, then no, it's not. All pretty dull stuff actually, but it does pay well."

Graywolf swaggered across the room and poured himself a cup of coffee. He was short, fit, and carried himself with a kind of confidence that bordered on cockiness. "So you said on the phone that you saw Johnny Eagle yesterday. How was he?"

Bryson's eyebrow shot up. "I would imagine about the same as when you saw him the day before."

Graywolf smiled sheepishly. "So not so good then."

"It was one of toughest interviews I've ever conducted," Bryson admitted, surprised by the depth of his own emotion. "The poor guy had a meltdown while I was there, and I think some of it may have been my fault."

"How so?"

"Oh, I don't know. One too many questions I guess."

"He's been on a steady decline," Freddie responded as though he was some kind of expert on dementia. "But lately, it's been especially tough to watch."

"Are you two close friends?"

Freddy answered, "Yeah, we go back a long ways."

"Can you be a little more specific?"

"Well, I first met Johnny in Vegas. I was a blackjack dealer at the Riviera, and he was this young, hot shot pitcher with the Cleveland Indians." Freddy stopped to shake his head. "A twenty-year-old Indian kid with money burning a hole in his pockets. Everybody wanted a piece of him."

"Including you?"

"We had a different kind of relationship...I sorta became his mentor."

The PI studied Graywolf. He was smarmy, but in an affable kind of way. Picturing him smokin' and jokin' with the hard-knocking casino crowd was one thing, imagining him as a mentor, well that was more of a stretch.

"But I won't lie to you. A lot of things changed after he hurt his arm."

"Like?"

"Well, he returned to his roots. Got more spiritual."

"Hurting his arm had to be devastating. Good thing you were there for him?"

"I'd like to think that, but truth is, he was there for me. Ya see, my pit boss fired me. He claimed that I had a scam going with this guy who was killing it at my table. He got me blackballed on the Strip, and everywhere else."

As Freddy droned on Bryson took note of a nearby photograph that included Freddy, an attractive brunette, and a young boy. It looked to be one of those over-staged family photos shot at a local department store.

"...And that wasn't the worst of it. I owed some really bad men," he stopped and touched the side of his nose with his finger, a gesture that Bryson recognized to indicate mob involvement, then finished with the obvious, "a lot of moolah."

A furtive glance around the room displayed several more photos of the woman, but none of the boy.

"Johnny bailed me out. Lent me…Well, gave me a big chunk of change. I think it was just about everything he'd saved from his baseball playing days."

"Sounds like he was more family than friend."

He nodded. The mist in his eyes appeared genuine this time around. "That's why this Alzheimer's thing's so tough."

It was time, Bryson thought, to come at Graywolf straight on. "Mr. Graywolf, do you know a man named Robert Balfour?"

"Not directly," Graywolf responded. "I know him through Johnny."

"Have you ever met him?"

"No."

The answer came without the slightest hesitation. The ring of truth was unmistakable. Bryson, more puzzled than ever, pushed a little harder. "But Nurse Boris over at Red Rock Manor told me that it was your idea to send a get-well-card to Mr. Balfour."

"Well, actually it was my wife's idea."

"Your wife?"

Graywolf pointed to the closest photo. "Yes, Emanuelle asked me to send the card, using Johnny's name."

The PI studied the photo. It had to be her. Balfour's mystery woman finally had a face, an identity. And evidently, she still remembered Robert. For the first time there was proof that Balfour's muse actually existed.

No pennies, apples, or candy corn for the endless stream of trick-or-treaters who knocked on the Scarza front door. Gramma Scarza was all in—full-sized-chocolate bars or be damned, no matter what the quality of costume or the size of the masquerader. Princess Leia and Rambo made appearances, as did Michael Jackson and Ronald

Reagan. All got rave reviews from the Scarza household.

Once the porch light was turned off, it was straight to the kitchen table for a freshly brewed pot of coffee and a rehash of Halloween, 1985. Gramma seized the opportunity to push her favorite, very transparent agenda. "Did you see the little Lemmo twins? They were so cute. They can't be more than four."

"Tweedle Dee and Tweedle Dum," Livy kicked in, "pretty clever costumes if you ask me."

"How about the Malone sweetie," Gramma purred, "cutest little Cinderella I've ever seen. She barely came up to her mother's knee."

Jason and Livy sipped their coffee and swapped knowing glances. Reverend Gramma was back behind the pulpit preaching a familiar sermon. "Mrs. Malone looks so happy. Ya know, she and her husband tried for years, then out of the blue, little Mia came along. Thank God for little treasures, huh."

Jason squirmed a bit. He hoped the maternity pep talk wasn't spooking Livy.

Gramma, afraid that her message was too subtle, asked, "So Livy, how many kids do you want?"

Livy looked at a squirming, red-faced Jason before volunteering, "Oh, I don't know. Maybe four. Two boys and two girls."

"Did you hear that Jason," Gramma erupted, while poking him in the ribs with her elbow. "Livy wants four children. Isn't that wonderful?"

"Yes it is, Gramma. Two boys, two girls. It all sounds so, so evenly distributed."

Gramma, who either missed his attempt at sarcasm or chose to ignore it, smiled triumphantly, slammed both palms onto the table, and stood up. She forced a yawn and announced, "It's been a long day, and I'm tired. Make sure everything's locked up kids. I'll see you in the morning."

With the stroke of midnight having come and gone without mishap, unless you counted the smashing of the pumpkin on the porch by some late-to-the-party-miscreant, October 31st had turned out to be just another day, and that was a very good thing.

Walking up the stairs hand in hand made it even better. The prospect of sleeping in the arms of the man she adored would never grow old. And for the first time, in a life that had been mangled by a mother's mental illness and a father's callous indifference, she thought seriously about having her own children. Jason Scarza had done that for her.

Everything was looking up. She could hardly wait for tomorrow evening, and Jason's well-anticipated debut at the Blue Note.

With so much to think about and look forward to, the Robert Balfour mystery had been moved to the back burner, or maybe completely off the stove. She barely noticed that doomsday had come and gone without the comatose author being claimed by the Devil. Happy people focus on happy thoughts, not wild, eerie tales of soul-snatching, and Faustian dealings.

The next morning at six-thirty sharp, Livy got a phone call from Nurse Bailey. Robert Balfour had passed away sometime around midnight.

30

SHIRLEY WATSON

By the time Livy got to the hospital Robert Balfour's body had already been transported to the county morgue. No doubt the case warranted an autopsy, one that would certainly pique the interest of the entire medical community.

Hopefully opening up Balfour's skull would shed some light on the great mystery, or reveal a brain ravaged by parasites, or blood vessels clogged by arteriosclerosis. Maybe there'd be a whole host of teenie-weenie green gremlins wreaking havoc in his cerebral cortex.

Jason, the most objective person in Balfour's inner circle, suspected the medical examiner would find nothing out of the ordinary. Sometimes crazy is nothing more than spending too much time alone with your own thoughts.

Nurse Bailey gave Livy and Jason big hugs. The first words out of her mouth were tinged with sadness. "He was alone at the end Livy. Alone."

Jason watched the sniffling women simultaneously reach for tissues. He was much more stoic about the situation. Like the poet, Scarza felt that any man's death diminished him, but aside from that, he barely knew the man. Livy, however, appeared to be devastated.

"So you said some time around midnight?" Livy asked through her tears. After Esther nodded, Livy pressed, "And why don't we have a more exact time?"

The nurse shrugged. "From what I understand there was a code blue on the floor. That might explain the confusion. And the monitors don't tell us much about the exact time of passing, nor the cause of death."

Jason left the pair out in the hall, and ventured into Room 502, Robert Balfour's home for almost a month. The windows were flung open, the bed was stripped, and the smell of bleach stung his nostrils. That quickly, all traces of the man had been wiped clean. It was as if he'd never been there.

Livy, who was still struggling with the idea that Balfour was alone when he passed, couldn't hide her irritation. "How is this even possible? There had to be somebody nearby. Floor nurse, orderlies, or maybe someone from the cleaning staff."

"Nope, no one. Like I said before, there was a code blue. I did talk to the cleaning supervisor this morning. I asked her who was scheduled for third shift in this wing. She gave me a name. I'm waiting for a call back."

The two women followed Scarza into 502, their thoughts much like his. The room was sterile, bare, and profoundly silent. The tormented writer was gone. Was it attrition that finally did him in, a self-fulfilling prophecy, or twenty-four years of constantly looking over his shoulder for the boogie man to come get him? Hopefully, the autopsy would give Livy some closure.

So there was little else to do except turn around and go home. Not once did it cross Livy's mind that she was the sole heir to a very large estate. She'd miss the quirky man who'd lived in the mansion on the top of the hill, the one she called her friend.

Just then, an aide called out from the nurse's station, "Nurse Bailey, someone named Shirley Watson is on line three."

Jason put his arms around Livy and gave her a big squeeze. She was trembling. He'd known all along that she worried a lot about Balfour, but he was surprised by the depth of her grief. Under the circumstance, getting her away from the hospital as quickly as possible seemed the most prudent course.

They were getting on the elevator when Esther ran after them. After grabbing Livy's arm she said breathlessly, "Let's go down to the lounge. I've got something crazy to tell you."

Bailey appeared much more animated as she ushered the pair into the lounge area. After closing the door behind them she erupted, "I just found out that Robert wasn't alone when he died. Shirley Watson was with him."

Stunned, Livy plopped down heavily in the nearest chair. "And who's Shirley Watson?"

"A woman on the cleaning crew, third shift."

"A cleaning woman was in the room with him when he died?" Livy asked, sounding more irritated than relieved.

"Actually, she was mopping the floors in the hall when it all started."

"Do you know this woman Esther?"

"No, she's a new employee. And, from what I've been told, she's been on the job less than a week."

"Less than a week?" Livy questioned, the edge in her voice was hard to miss. "And this is your source?"

Bailey grabbed for her hand. "Will you let me finish, please!"

"Sorry, but all this sounds kinda fishy to me."

"Oh, it gets better. Shirley told me that Robert died in her arms and…"

"In her arms? Now I know she's lying."

Jason placed a hand on Livy's shoulder, and gently advised, "Why don't you let Esther finish."

"I know her story sounds implausible," Esther said. "but it rings true, especially the part about thinking that she'd killed him."

"What?"

"Yeah, the poor woman thought she'd killed him because, when they clutched, his leads pulled loose. The next thing she knew, he'd expired."

"Then maybe she *was* responsible," Livy persisted.

"No, the leads had nothing to do with life support. They were merely monitoring his vitals."

Livy, still looking for a villain to blame, continued, "But she said that she was mopping the hallway. So what the hell was she doing in his room? Something doesn't add up. We need to do a background check on this woman."

"Stop! There's more. She said that Robert called her in."

"Is that even possible?" Jason stepped in. "The man hadn't spoken in almost a month."

Bailey shrugged. "I wouldn't have thought so, but when she said that he called her *Emanuelle*, I suddenly remembered the notebook, and how the name *Emanuelle* was plastered all over the place."

"*Emanuelle*," Livy whispered under her breath, as though the name was sacred. "He actually called her *Emanuelle*?"

"According to Shirley, she was frightened to go near him. His eyes were wild, his arms flailing. But he looked like he might fall out bed so she—"

"Why didn't she call for help?" Jason asked before Livy could.

"She did. No one came. No one was around."

"No one was around," Livy repeated. "Again, none of this adds up."

"Have you ever seen a code blue response? Makes a Chinese fire drill seem orderly. Anyway, she felt like she had little choice. So she ran to him, and he latched onto her and started weeping."

Livy was speechless. Perhaps it was true, and if it was, then at least Robert had found a modicum of comfort in his last moments on earth, deluded as they may have been. Perhaps he thought that he was finally back in the arms of his lost love, Emanuelle.

Jason, who was clearly caught up in Esther's account, asked, "So did this woman say anything else? Did he say anything, besides Robert calling out Emanuelle's name?"

"According to Shirley, his last words were, 'It's time. I'm ready.'"

31

PURE THEATER

Though Freddy Graywolf had been friendly and reasonably cooperative, there were obvious gaps in his story leaving PI Bryson with little choice. Emanuelle Graywolf would need to be interviewed, asked questions that her husband couldn't or wouldn't answer, no matter how embarrassing or compromising.

There was little doubt that Freddy Graywolf sent the get-well card to Balfour at his wife's behest, but the sleazy connection between Johnny Eagle, Emanuelle, her husband, and Balfour needed more bridging, something that Freddy had danced around very nimbly. So the PI decided to go directly to Emanuelle's place of employment, a bar in downtown Phoenix called Busters Drinking Hole.

He walked in from the bright sunlight into a smoky, dimly lit saloon. Even through the haze he spotted her chatting with a patron at the end of the bar. Striking and statuesque, she was hard to miss. Tall, slender, her hair was pulled back into a bun accentuating the kind of cheek bones that either God bestows on a chosen few, or is the deft work of a skilled plastic surgeon. Other than the faint crows' feet that bordered her eyes and a few flecks of gray in her hair, Emanuelle Graywolf did sixty proud.

She welcomed Bryson with a pleasant smile and a "what can I get you?"

"Do you have Dad's Root Beer?"

"We have Hires. Will that do?"

"Sure, with lots of ice, and a slice of lemon please."

"Interesting combination," she responded with a scrunchy, judgmental face.

He jumped up on a stool and placed his business card in front of him on the bar. When she returned with the drink she picked up the card, read it, and then eyeballed him. "I hope you don't take this the wrong way Mr. Bryson, but you don't look like a private investigator."

"No," he said while sipping his beverage. "What do I look like?"

"A CPA, or maybe a college professor."

Bryson chuckled. "Funny you should say that...I tried teaching for a bit, but it couldn't pay the bills."

"That is a problem," she said while wiping the bar with a towel. After giving him his card back, she came straight at him, "So how did it go with my husband? Was he helpful? Did he say nice things about me?"

Bryson's first reaction, this woman was difficult to read. Was she being open and friendly, or snide? He wasn't sure. "It went okay. He filled in a few blanks for me."

She nodded. "And you want me to fill in the rest, right?"

She had a pretty smile, and a relaxed way about her. She was welcoming without being blatantly flirtatious. "I did have a few more questions. Is this a good time?"

She threw her hands out. "As good as any. We've had only a handful of customers since we opened...Probably this damn heat wave."

"Okay then, why don't we start with your husband's version of the story. He said that it was you who suggested sending the get-well-card to Robert Balfour. Is that accurate?"

"Yup, it was all my idea."

He waited for more, but got a disarming smile instead. "Care to elaborate Mrs. Graywolf?"

"Elaborate huh." She took a deep breath. "Well, if it's ugly truths and sordid details you came to hear, you've come to the right place."

"Whatever you're comfortable sharing," the PI said as unobtrusively as possible. "Why don't we start with your relationship with Robert Balfour?"

She smiled. "So Freddy really didn't tell you any of it?"

"No. He said, on that particular subject, he was deferring to you."

She laughed. "So I gather he didn't tell you anything about my past either?'

Bryson shook his head.

"I should warn you Mr. Bryson, my life reads like a Charles Dickens' novel, if you throw in some war paint and eagle feathers. I'm afraid abject poverty and abused children weren't unique to Victorian England."

Bryson liked her mellifluous, honey-coated voice. For someone who'd been victimized by an abbreviated reservation education, she certainly articulated beautifully. "Okay, let it be noted, I've been warned."

"Well for starters, I'm proud to say that I am full-blooded Arapaho. I grew up fatherless on the Wind River Reservation in Wyoming. Cirrhosis of the liver made my mother a young widow."

"I'm sorry," Bryson responded lamely.

"Don't be. Alcohol is a recreational hazard for many reservation Indians." The lone patron in the place chose that moment to pound his empty beer glass on the bar. Taking no offense that the man was being boorishly impatient, she refilled his glass from the tap with a smile. Evidently, she was well trained in the art of placating ignorant, crass men.

She was back in a flash. "Now where was I?"

"Your father died young and—"

"Yes. To be fair, practically everyone's father died young on the reservation. Until the casino was built at Wind River, it was a horrible place to live."

She paused. "Then the gamblers started showing up, some from as far away as San Francisco. Apparently, one of these men spotted me on his way into Wind River. He must have liked what he saw because he approached my mother and offered to buy me…For five-thousand dollars! No deed, no title, just a straight cash transaction, like I was a used car, or stolen property to be fenced."

Bryson, half African-American, understood the concept of people being little more than chattel all too well. Nothing smacked of barbarism more.

It took her a moment to choke out the rest of it. "And unbelievably, my mother took the money." Emanuelle looked off to some distant corner of the bar. When her eyes returned to Bryson they were dewy. "I left that very day with a total stranger, crying my eyes out, just like I am now."

Her pain was palpable, and rightly so. When strangers sell young girls they're called human traffickers, but what does one call a mother who sells her own daughter? *An affront to all that's holy* sounded about right.

"I went voluntarily because my mother had four kids under eight. My stepfather, the biggest loser on the planet, took off with a Wild West show that was passing through."

Bryson sipped his soda and listened. She was on a roll.

"And what the government gave us to live on was a joke. We were all teeth and ribs. Hunger does strange things to people, even well intentioned mothers."

"How old were you?"

"Thirteen...A mature thirteen." She paused. "The man who bought me treated me badly. He had a mean streak a mile wide. We travelled from place to place looking for the next big card game."

She stopped, whatever she was about to divulge came out in pained spurts. "If he was on a losing streak, he pimped me out for stake money. It was awful. The utter shame of it." She stopped before admitting, "Once, I even tried to slit my wrists."

Freddy had neglected to tell him the part about the human trafficking. So Bryson's shocked countenance was genuine.

"And that's when Freddy came into my life. Unbelievably, my knight in shining armor won me in a poker game. Believe me, I was one hardened seventeen-year-old by then."

"Wow, I thought things like that only happened in old westerns."

"Well, it happened to me, and for the better. Freddy was sweet. He was crazy about me. He treated me like a queen, despite my past. I owed him everything. Eventually, we got married."

All very interesting stuff, thought Bryson, but no mention of Robert Balfour thus far.

"My husband told you about his debt to Johnny Eagle?"

Bryson nodded.

"Eighteen thousand dollars. Freddy owed a Las Vegas loan shark eighteen grand. There was no way he could pay it back, and this guy was no one to fool with. I'd heard that he'd maimed and killed people for a lot less."

"Freddy did tell me that Johnny Eagle once bailed him out of a big jam."

"Big jam!" She guffawed. "He saved my husband's ass!"

"Hey baby doll," the bar patron yelled out, "can you please change the channel. My show's about to start."

It took a few minutes for her to find the Wrestlemania channel. She returned wearing a grin. "Timmy's one of our regulars. Mensa's still mulling over his credentials."

Bryson chuckled. "How do you put up with guys like that?"

"Ah, he's harmless. It's the mashers and stalkers you've gotta watch." She took a moment, obviously trying to retrieve her last thought.

"So, I take it there were some strings attached to this *loan*?" Bryson re-directed gently.

She hesitated. "I know what this whole arrangement sounds like, but Johnny Eagle wasn't a pimp or extortionist." She stopped. "My husband has a lot of good qualities, but he's a gambling junkie. We've been forced to declare bankruptcy twice, because of his sickness. Johnny gave my husband every cent he had to keep him alive. To keep us alive."

Freddy's account had excluded any mention of his gambling addiction, a huge non-disclosure to the telling of this story.

"Let me reiterate, Johnny Eagle asked for nothing in return for his generosity. We had no way to repay him until I overheard him talking about some newspaper writer from Cleveland. He described him as a nice guy, a *hurtin' cowboy*. Very lonely and depressed. When he asked me if I'd cheer him up I agreed."

"By cheer him up…"

"No, he wasn't suggesting anything like that. What I did, I did on my own."

Bryson held up his hand. "Mrs. Graywolf, you're not obligated to tell me anything that is super personal, but frankly, I'm a bit confused."

"It's quite simple actually. Eagle told me he was going to give Robert some peyote, and I was supposed to appear to him like I was an apparition or something. Talk to him, be nice to him, be affectionate even. Nothing more."

"So what happened?"

"He was more attractive than I'd been told, and if I was being completely honest, my husband's impotent. Has been since he was forty. Prostate cancer...Implanted radiation seeds."

The PI wanted to spare her the telling of the rest of the tawdry tale, but he needed to hear all of it. So he continued sipping his soda while playing the good listener.

"So, one kiss led to another...Mr. Bryson, it had been a long time for me. I know that's no excuse for my behavior, but..."

"So you had sex with Robert Balfour that night?"

"Actually twice...I wish I could say I was ashamed about what happened in Eagle's home that night, but I wasn't."

She stopped to get Tim another beer, then returned. "It was the damnedest thing, though Balfour was spaced out on the peyote, he was very sweet, very romantic. We talked about everything, about nothing, and everything in between. He even quoted poetry to me. He was so smart."

Emanuelle leaned closer to Bryson and dropped her voice to a near whisper. "He even told me that he loved me...It was kind of nice to hear."

Bryson was impressed by her candor, her understated beauty, the way she turned a phrase. He now better understood Balfour's obsession with her.

"Don't get the wrong impression, Mr. Bryson, I still love my husband. He saved me from enslavement, and a really horrible man. The night with Robert Balfour was just that, one night."

"So, the whole mystical thing was pure theater?"

"Yes, I was supposed to be some kind of vision that would disappear with the morning mist, and that's exactly what I did."

"So Eagle directed this whole production to inspire Robert Balfour?"

"*Broaden his vistas* is how Johnny put it." She chuckled. "If I was being honest, I kinda liked playing Balfour's sexy, mysterious muse."

"Unfortunately, Balfour thought of you as something more. You know he searched for you. He even hired my company to find you… twice."

Obviously pained, she responded, "I had no idea."

"Yeah, after a while he just gave up. He eventually wrote you off as figment of his imagination. He would've loved the get-well card, if not for the coma."

"I feel really feel bad about that." She hesitated a long moment. "This may sound like a strange question, but would you call Robert Balfour a good man?"

Bryson thought that an odd question, but he answered it anyway. "I've known him since he was a child. He *was* a good, kind person who battled his share of demons."

"Was? You said was."

"He died last night. The cause has yet to be determined."

"My God, I knew he was sick, but I had no idea."

Bryson got to his feet. Emanuelle had filled in all the essential blanks.

"Well, Mrs. Graywolf, I thank you for your time and your candor. You've been very helpful."

"You're welcome, but before you go, may I ask you one last question?"

"Sure, go ahead."

"Did Robert ever get married, or have any children?"

"No, is that somehow relevant?"

"I think it might be, now that he's dead."

"How so?"

Emanuelle looked away, then back. "He has a son. Our son."

32

MAN IN THE CORNER

There were no flags flying at half-mast, no twenty-one-gun-salutes either, for Robert Balfour wasn't John Lennon or Elvis Presley. No one sitting in the Blue Note crowd that opening night gave a damn that a has-been writer, albeit a Nobel Prize winner, had just died. It was time to rock-and-roll baby, not to mourn.

The program began with three rock classics—*Crocodile Rock, Great Balls of Fire,* and *Johnny Be Good.* The crowd, clapping and singing along, went wild. Requests were plentiful, the tip jars overflowed with cash and lots of phone numbers.

Livy requested the Styx hit *Come Sail Away,* and Gramma giddily made her way to Jason's piano requesting *New York, New York.* She was almost as big a hit as the Sinatra tune as she pumped her fist in the air after returning to her seat.

Calvin Short, the gritty consummate pro, rose to the occasion. His tenuous voice was better than expected, but it was Jason who stole the show as he got more energized with every song. The women in the audience were drooling, a fact that hadn't escaped Livy or Gramma Scarza. The old woman patted Livy's arm and tried to comfort her. "Not to worry honey, it's only show biz."

Livy was surprised by Gramma's endurance. Three hours of grinding, pulsating, piano banging wasn't exactly her cup of tea, but none of that lessened her enthusiasm. "That's my grandson up there. That's my Jason!"

The animated crowd was up on their feet, dancing in the aisles, and completely immersed in the music, except for the powerfully built man sitting in the far corner nearest the exit. He was alone, wore all black, applauded politely, but never rose to his feet. By all appearances, he was the odd man out. Almost invisible, no one noticed him except Scarza.

Ever since his covert meeting with Rollie Masters, Jason's paranoia surfaced at unexpected moments, like this one. This mystery man might be an Admiral Masters' spy, and if that was the case, one might wonder why the Admiral would've dispatched an agent all the way to Cleveland to watch a silly show? Only one answer made sense. Quentin Masters had found out about the secret meeting, the one held in Rollie's basement.

Jason finished the show the best he could, but if his instincts about the thug were correct, the Admiral had changed the rules of the game, and the playing field. Fighting on foreign soil was one thing, but having the enemy show up in one's backyard was quite another. Now Jason would have to be concerned for the safety of his loved ones.

It was after one o'clock when they finally got home. Gramma went straight to bed while Livy and Jason wound down with a glass of wine.

Livy observed, "I thought Calvin sounded really good tonight. Much better than when I heard you guys at rehearsal."

"Well, he is a pro. A top flight musician."

"Do you think that his," she stopped to choose just the right word, "his *turn around* had anything to do with going to that AA meeting?"

Jason smiled. "Livy, it was only one meeting."

"I know, I know, but we can hope, right?" Livy patted Jason's hand. "Still, that doesn't lessen the fact that you're a really good friend. I seriously doubt that he would've gone to that meeting without you."

"Maybe, maybe not." Jason sipped his vino. "Look, we've known each other since seventh grade." He smiled. "Calvin was never a Boy Scout, but he always could make me laugh. Believe me, we've weathered a few storms along the way."

"Is there a woman in his life?" she asked out of the blue. "Any girlfriends?"

Jason chuckled. "Those phone numbers in the tip jar, that's the extent of Calvin's dating pool."

"Well, it's just that Philomena thinks he's cute. He's funny, she's funny. I just thought, maybe the two of them might hit it off."

"So let me get this straight, you're contemplating pairing a woman who reads five books a week with a man whose favorite fictional character is Batman?"

Livy smiled. "I know you're right, but sometimes opposites do attract."

"Yeah, as long as they both belong to the same species."

She finished her wine, rose to her feet, nodded toward the stairs and smiled provocatively. "Don't know if you're still interested in *the neighborhood girl*, especially after being ogled by a thousand horny women, but I'm feeling loose and easy, and totally available."

"Well, when you put it like that," Jason said as he flipped off the kitchen light, "how can I resist?"

Now standing in the darkness, he noticed a sliver of light coming from under the basement door. Normally, seeing this light would've been no big deal. People forget to turn lights off all the time. But with flashbacks of the goon perched in the corner of the Blue Note still swirling around in his head, his antennae were up.

"I'll be right up," he yelled to her, as he walked toward the basement stairs. "Wanna make sure we're all locked up down here."

After turning on every light in the cellar he still wasn't sure what he was looking for, but that didn't stop him from searching every nook and cranny. The storage area looked undisturbed, as did the laundry room, but the fruit cellar door, the one he'd jerry-rigged to stay closed, was ajar. Even more telling, the aluminum-faced insulation in the crawl space ceiling wasn't as tightly secured. In fact, one strip was hanging completely free.

"Hey, *Rock Star*," Livy called down from the top of the stairs, "is everything okay down there?"

"Just checking the hot water tank," he lied. "The water's not as hot as it should be."

"Okay, but hurry up. I warmed up your side of the bed."

Everything wasn't okay, but Jason couldn't bring himself to share his disturbing discoveries with Livy. Evidently, Admiral Masters' long, stealthy arm had reached into their home. That damn sex tape was proving to be more toxic than a vial of anthrax.

If Jason knew nothing else, he understood the subtle art of sleuthing. He also knew that *ghosts* never leave fingerprints, lights on, doors ajar, or insulation dangling. Even the brute who'd paid the Blue Note a visit had stood out like a sore thumb. He wanted to be seen. He wanted Jason to see him.

All of it left Scarza shaken. Quentin Masters wanted him to feel his presence, his hot breath. Intimidation was now the game being played.

Gramma woke up in a celebratory mood insisting the whole gang go out for breakfast. "And I don't want any arguments from nobody."

Jason, doing his best to conceal his fears about a possible home invasion, agreed to the outing, but his thoughts never strayed far from the sex tape and the diabolical Admiral. Sociopathic, well connected, and with a great deal to lose, Quentin Masters was indeed a formidable foe.

It was at this point that Scarza made a unilateral decision. The women in his life were better off not knowing about the break-in. He'd tell them when and if the situation warranted.

Gino's restaurant, featuring tasty food, picnic table informality, and lots of friendly locals, was the perfect venue to debrief Jason and Calvin's smashing musical triumph. "Check this out," Livy said excitedly as she opened the morning newspaper to the entertainment section. "It was a magical evening, raucous and pulsating! The Dueling Pianos absolutely blew the roof off the Blue Note Club. I haven't been that entertained since I saw Elton John live at the Garden."

"I don't believe it," Jason marvelled. "The paper actually sent someone to cover the show." After a chuckle he added, "I'm sure Calvin's already clipped and pasted that baby in his scrapbook."

"Well the man's right. Best show I ever saw," a very partial Gramma joined in.

"You see a lot of shows do ya?" Jason asked after kissing Gramma.

"On TV…Those count too."

"And listen to this," Livy read on excitedly, "Jason Scarza's rip-roarin' rendition of *New York, New York* did Sinatra proud, but it was his grandmother who stole the show."

"You hear that Gramma?" Livy asked. "The man thinks you stole the show."

"Stop talking nonsense. What he shoulda wrote was *there's no fool like an old fool.*"

Philomena, arriving a bit late, weaseled her way onto the bench before high-fiving Jason. "It's all over the neighborhood Jace. I heard you guys killed it. Congrats."

"And where were you?" demanded Gramma. "We saved you a seat."

She gave Gramma a quick hug before pulling a check out of her purse. "Well, I just happened to be at the Erie Art Auction last night where I collected this." She proudly held the $1300 check up for inspection. "And let me tell you that Livy's *Mansion on the Hill* piece stirred up quite the bidding war."

"I'm not surprised," Jason responded as he put his arm around Livy's shoulders and squeezed, "that painting is awesome."

Before Gramma could weigh in again, a gaunt man wearing a dapper three-piece suit walked up to their table. Livy thought she recognized him from a photo she'd seen in Balfour's office. If she was correct, Lawrence Bryson had somehow managed to track her down to Gino's, quite a feat since he'd just flown in hours earlier on the red eye from Phoenix.

"Please excuse me," the man broke in softly. With every patron in the crowded eatery focused on the stranger in their midst, he continued, "I'm sorry to interrupt your breakfast Miss Jardine…I'm Lawrence Bryson, private investigator."

"Yes, I know who you are," Livy responded pleasantly. "Whaddya doing here? How'd you find me?"

Bryson, feeling every inch the interloper, squirmed a bit. "Look, I'm so sorry to just barge in like this, but it's urgent that we talk… ASAP."

Livy, surprised by his foppish appearance and blade-thin stature, would never have put his big baritone telephone voice with the slight physique wrapped in a form fitting Brooks Brothers silk suit. "It's quite alright Mr. Bryson. I'd like you to meet Jason, Philomena, and

Gramma Scarza."

"Delighted. And again, please accept my apologies. My tight schedule has forced me to insinuate myself upon your, your apparent celebration."

Livy smiled. *Who talks like that? Who uttered phrases like,* **insinuate myself***?*

Her brief hesitation caused him to quickly add, "I can just leave the report if you like."

"No, it's okay if you don't mind squeezing in…Everybody skooch over a bit."

Bryson looked uncomfortable with the tight accommodations and picnic bench seating arrangement, but he sat down nonetheless while managing to find a place for his attaché case under the table.

Livy caught herself staring at him. He seemed so out of place at Ginos. Baryshnikov dancing the polka at a Polish wedding would have been a more likely scenario. But the bigger question still remained, *how in the hell had he found her at the restaurant?*

It was as if he'd read her mind. While smiling he explained, "It's what I do for a living."

Livy furrowed brow demanded more. "I asked your neighbor. In fact I asked several neighbors. They all directed me here."

"Well, it's nice to finally meet you." Livy said, hesitating ever so slightly. Whatever his mission, his demeanor seemed to suggest that he might be the bearer of bad news.

"Again I apologize folks," he said to Gramma specifically, "if my report wasn't so important, I would've just put it in the mail."

Jason took that statement as a cue to exit. "You know what, we were just about to head back to the house anyway… Doggie bags all around?"

"Yeah, we have to run," Philomena said kissing Livy on the cheek after handing her the check. "You and Mr. Bryson should have a little privacy to discuss whatever. We'll talk later?"

While warily eyeing the PI, Gramma mumbled something under her breath as she rose to her feet. "We'll be home Livy, just in case you need us."

Bryson was looking a little worse for wear. His Windsor knot had drooped a bit and his eyes looked bloodshot as he reached into his brief case and pulled out what appeared to be a lengthy report. "It's all in here. All the interviews with Johnny Eagle, Freddy Graywolf, and Graywolf's wife."

After thumbing through the thick packet, she threw her hands up. Deciphering a corporate contract seemed a less daunting task.

He smiled. "I have been accused of being a little too thorough. But as they say, the devil is in the detail."

Livy handed the report back. "Maybe you could condense it for me."

"Okay, perhaps I should begin with what's not in there. For starters, the Joseph Gray file."

"Who?"

"Joseph Gray. Balfour's illegitimate son."

Livy blinked, then shook her head. "Illegitimate son? No, that can't be. Robert told me that he had no children. No heirs."

"Well, he didn't know about this one. How could he? Joseph Gray's mother is Emanuelle Graywolf."

"Emanuelle Graywolf? *The* Emanuelle!" Livy's jaw dropped. "No way."

"Yes. Though I'm not aware of any confirmation of paternity yet," Bryson continued, "when I interviewed her, I found her to be quite credible. Every word seemed to ring true."

"But Robert had no idea."

"How could he?" The PI came back. "She fled immediately after their tryst, per Johnny Eagle's instructions, I might add."

Livy, still stunned, asked, "So what does this mean? And why all the urgency?"

"Isn't it obvious?" Bryson asked rhetorically. "You must strike first. How good is your attorney?"

"My attorney?"

"Miss Jardine, Robert's will lists you as the sole beneficiary of his estate, but all that was set in motion before a son popped into the picture. You know what they say about blood and water."

Suddenly, a lonely, melancholic Robert Balfour flashed before her eyes. No doubt being fixated on a long ago affair and enduring the futility of never finding his beautiful phantom had drained him. Perhaps it even shifted his focus to finding unearthly reasons for his one literary triumph. What if he'd known that he had a son? Would the boy have rescued Robert from himself?

"Have you heard a word that I've said?" Bryson pressed.

"I have. Robert Balfour has a son."

"Well then, if I were you, I'd get ready for the legal battle of your life."

Gramma Scarza went straight to the kitchen to refrigerate the contents of the doggie bags while her grandson put on a pot of coffee and turned on the kitchen television set.

"I don't trust that man," Gramma moaned. "Did you see his eyes? They were bloodshot and beady. I never trust people with squinty eyes."

Jason smiled. "Gramma the man was on an airplane all night. He was jet-lagged."

She stayed on the attack. "And he was just a little too slick if you ask me."

Jason chose to ignore his grandmother's slings and arrows as he began switching channels. "So, you want the usual?... There's still fifteen minutes left of *The Price Is Right.*"

"No, I don't need all that shouting and screaming. I need to calm my nerves. Turn on that artist guy with the beard...He soothes me."

"You want Bob Ross?"

Before Gramma could respond the local TV station interrupted its regularly scheduled programming for a breaking news report:

Early this morning, Roland Masters, ex-Navy SEAL, and the only son of Four-Star Admiral Quentin Masters died in a massive explosion at his Germantown residence. His caregiver, Wiley Kendrick, also died in the blast. Preliminary reports point to a gas leak as the probable cause. More information will be made available as the details unfold.

Scarza's stomach turned. His worst nightmare had become a reality. Both Kendrick and Rollie Masters had been eliminated, snuffed out despite their high level of expertise and experience dealing with nefarious plots and evil people. Consummate professionals—both appearing to be cautious to a fault—had been blown to smithereens with no regard to the possibility of collateral damage to nearby homes in the upscale, gated community. Being struck by lightning seemed a more probable occurrence than a natural gas explosion occurring in the middle of Philadelphia's millionaire's row.

Evidently, Rollie had gotten it right when he said that his father was a monster, a man capable of doing the unthinkable. He probably should have tacked on sociopathic, amoral, and psychotic as well. Suddenly Cleveland seemed but a stone's throw from Germantown, and maybe more significantly, Arlington Virginia.

34

DEATH COMES IN THREES

Three men of note had died within hours of one another—a Nobel winning author, the son of Four-Star Admiral, and a nurse who'd been awarded the Congressional Medal of Honor and Purple Heart for his bravery during the Viet Nam War. Their achievements and the way they had lived their lives certainly set them apart from most, as did the way they died. Mysterious explosions and baffling illnesses certainly merited a closer inspection.

Robert Balfour's death certificate initially listed the cause of his death as "unknown." The medical examiner could've taken a more imaginative route and blamed "psychosomatically induced madness," or maybe even "supernatural forces at play," but men and women of empirical science would've scoffed at such *creative* diagnoses. Fact and fiction, like oil and water, were never to be mixed.

To Jason Scarza's way of thinking, the weekend's morbidity box score should have read—two murders, and one suicide brought on by unbridled gullibility. If George Bernard Shaw could blame Don Quixote's madness on believing everything he read, then what would the playwright have said about a man who believed that he was the reincarnation of Dr. Faustus?

Livy's Monday was mostly spent dealing with the fall-out from Robert Balfour's death. There was, however, more good news from Philomena's Art Gallery. An anonymous buyer had purchased her most recent oil painting—*President Garfield's Memorial, The Citadel of Lake View.*" It would've been nice to know who the buyer was, but at this point, names didn't matter. Her budding art career had taken off.

The rest of her day was filled with the anti-climactic and mundane. Balfour's body, though still at the county morgue, would eventually find its way to a funeral home of Livy's choice. Along similar lines, the cemetery had to be put on notice to ready the burial site for Balfour's remains, the headstone etchings had to be accurate, and his epitaph double-checked. She also had to corroborate the plot number, the one Balfour had scribbled in his tattered notebook—Section 48, Plot 12.

Once all of that was accomplished, she'd pay a visit to her lawyer's office, per Lawrence Bryson's suggestion. Perhaps Joseph Gray had checked in. She had to admit that she was very curious about Balfour's boy. Anglo-American or Navajo? Prim and proper like Robert, or just an average kid sporting a shaggy mane and dungarees? She'd have to wait and see.

Her last task of the day involved disobeying Balfour's final wishes. He'd specified that he wanted no grand funerals or religious service, but to Livy's way of thinking, that seemed wrong on so many levels. Who didn't deserve some final kudos, a heads-up to the God up above that a good person was coming his way?

If Livy had any say in the matter, and the last time she checked no one else was volunteering for the final-arrangement-detail, Robert wasn't exiting like some street person buried in potter's field. Or even sadder, an unloved rich guy whose funeral lacked even a single mourner, just another footprint on the ever-sifting seashore. A cautionary tale to be sure—hermits often die alone, buried with little fanfare.

Livy wasn't having any of that. Robert Balfour would get a proper send-off, that's what friends did for friends.

35

SERIAL NUMBER 194200776531

With Livy off visiting her attorney's office and Gramma at the market, Jason had the house to himself, which gave him plenty of time to think, to plot a course of action. The subtly botched search of the Scarza home, uncharacteristically sloppy for covert operatives, had put Jason on red alert. The Admiral was definitely playing mind games with him.

Finding the tape had obviously been the *ghosts'* primary goal, but when that failed, intimidation became the new order of business. And if intimidation didn't work, God help them all.

Gramma and Livy would not become collateral damage like Wiley Kendrick, this Jason vowed. If protecting them meant distancing himself, then so be it. But how would he manage that? Was that even possible?

Uncertain what the best course of action was, he reverted back to his days in the field. Sometimes a good offense was the best defense. Various strategies began tumbling around in head, like taking the fight to Masters, challenging him on his own turf, keeping him off balance. Maybe even dial up Quentin Masters before he unleashed another lethal attack. No doubt the plan involved an element of risk, but he had nothing else. Perhaps the Admiral might even be amenable to some kind of compromise.

With the telephone in hand and his heart in his throat, he was ready to launch his offensive when it starting ringing. Livy, who always phoned mid-morning to check in, was probably finished at the attorney's office. Maybe she'd finally met Balfour's son. So for reasons unknown to him, Jason picked up the phone and playfully answered, "Just for the record maam, please state your name, rank, and serial number."

Obviously caught off guard, the caller hesitated before rattling off a robotic response, "Quentin Masters, Four-Star Admiral US Navy, serial number 194200776531…And most certainly I am not a *maam*."

Scarza was floored. Unable to confirm the other particulars, he did recognize the raspy voice. It was the *devil* himself. The brazen bastard had beaten him to the punch. Scary thoughts had to be quickly quashed. He couldn't let the fear of that moment leach into his voice. "Admiral Masters, it's been a long time."

"That it has." A pause followed. "Jason, I'm calling with some shocking news. I don't know if you've heard about Rollie?"

"Yes sir. I saw it on the news. A gas explosion, was it?"

"Yes, that's what they're telling me. He was living in Germantown. Did you know that?"

Jason hesitated. The gloves were off, let the lying game begin. "No sir, I didn't."

Another long pause followed. Masters, weighing every word, wasn't buying any of it. "Look son, I should've called you a long time ago. I know things didn't work out well for you after that Central American snafu."

Livid, Jason did his best to rein himself in. Talk about your understated, audacious insult. **Things didn't work well after the Central American snafu!!!** That was like saying things didn't work out well for the people of Hiroshima after we nuked them.

"…And being court martialed after all you did for your country, well, it was a travesty."

"Sir," Jason broke in, "I don't mean to be rude, but is there something I can help you with?"

The Admiral laughed. "No son, this call is more about me helping you."

"Okay, but I'm out the door in a few minutes, so…"

"I get it. We're all busy these days. Ya know, like hamsters on a wheel."

With no response coming from Scarza he continued, "Actually, the first order of business is me apologizing to you."

Stunned, Jason managed a cautious, "For what sir?"

"Well, for starters, we both know that you got railroaded."

Scarza almost dropped the phone. *Had his ears deceived him? Too bad this conversation wasn't being recorded!*

"...This may sound like a crock, but on my mother's grave, I always held you in the highest esteem. I liked you, and still do."

Bull dung in, bull dung out. Let the slinging of the bullshit officially begin in earnest. "I appreciate that sir."

"My son made mistakes, you know that better than anyone. Even so, it's hard for me to accept that he's gone now."

Jason, with his stomach in knots, remained silent.

"By the way, did you know that Rollie had Lou Gehrig's disease?"

Scarza never flinched. "No, I didn't."

"Yeah, it was awful seeing him suffer like that. He went downhill fast. I'm just glad his mother wasn't alive to see how much he'd deteriorated."

"ALS is a bad way to go alright sir," Jason responded with little enthusiasm.

"Listen son, we can talk for hours on the phone playing catch-up and all, but I'd like to meet, ya know, face-to-face. How does that grab you?"

They'd talked for almost ten minutes, and Jason had no idea what Masters was up to. He reasoned that the Admiral could've had him killed already, if that's what he intended. Still, meeting with Lucifer face-to-face sounded foolhardy and extremely hazardous to one's health.

The long pause on the other end of the line caused the Admiral to add, "Look, with all that's happened, I don't blame you for being gun shy, but let me assure you that I've got your best interests at heart."

More lies. Jason smelled a trap. "Oh, I'm sure you do, but leaving my grandmother alone is problematic. She's well up in years."

"Can't your girlfriend handle that? She moved in with you folks, right?"

Stunned by his familiarity with their living arrangements, Jason managed a feeble lie or partial truth, depending on how one viewed it. "Oh, that was only temporary. She's got her own place."

"Oh, that's right. The Balfour Mansion, right?"

If Masters was trying to shake Jason, it was working. "Wow, you heard about that huh?"

"Yes. Sometimes good things do happen to good people."

Jason had no response for that one except to fight back the bile that crept up into his throat.

"And she's a pretty thing, from what I understand. I've always been partial to redheads, especially talented ones. She's an artist right?"

Jason, trying to control his rage, managed a weak affirmative.

"I love that one piece … *The Garfield Memorial* oil…Do you know it?"

"Yes I do. It's one of my favorites."

"Then you know what I'm talking about. The detail is amazing… The colors are so vivid and rich. It makes me wanna come visit Lake View Cemetery, especially in the Fall."

Jason was reeling. Every seemingly innocuous statement was a veiled threat, a frighteningly folksy declaration that could only be interpreted one way—"I know where you live!"

"You might be surprised to know that I'm looking at it as we speak."

"So you're the anonymous buyer."

"Yes I am. My man says that Philomena drives a hard bargain."

The Admiral wasn't just one step ahead of Scarza, he was miles ahead. Growing tired of all the subterfuge, Jason finally let go. "Look Admiral, I don't know what game you're playing, but I'm…"

"For Chrissakes Jason, I thought you were smarter than this. Can't you recognize an olive branch when it's being waved under your nose? Meet with me, and if time is an issue for you, I'll come to you. Believe me, we'll make it all be good."

As Jason saw it, he had little choice. "Okay, where and when?"

"Good! I always knew you were a reasonable man. Are you familiar with the Cleveland lake front?"

"Been there a few times."

"The East Ninth Street pier. My boy Howard tells me there's an excellent lobster place called Captain Jack's."

Jason responded, "I know the place."

"Good. How does noon tomorrow sound?"

"Sounds good," he responded.

"Perfect. Oh, before we hang up," he said doing his best to make it sound like his next question wasn't premeditated, "I heard that you own a 1950, V-8 Ford sedan. In pristine condition."

Scarza squirmed. If Masters knew about the car, he also knew about Victor's garage. "Yes I do sir. It belonged to my dad."

"You probably don't know this Jason, but I'm a certified, car-collecting nut, and I've got a ten-car garage to prove it."

"I'm sorry sir, like I said, the car belonged to my dad. I don't see myself ever selling it."

Masters chuckled. "You know what they say, never say never. In this case never say ever." He chuckled at his own material before signing off, "I guess I'll see you tomorrow."

With the phone back on the hook, Scarza felt like he'd just gone fifteen rounds with Ali. No doubt he was rusty. It had been many years since he'd faced combat conditions. The enemies that he'd faced across the globe were formidable, but none were more cunning and dangerous than the man who'd just taken him to task over the telephone. Out flanked, out thought, out prepared and out maneuvered into what appeared to be trap.

It was now painfully obvious, Quentin Masters wanted him to know that he was smack dab in the middle of a shit storm, and squarely in the Admiral's crosshairs. He made a point of letting Jason know how closely he'd been surveilled from the time he'd stepped into Rollie's home. He knew all about the vintage Ford, Vic's garage. and his debut at the Blue Note. And most disconcerting was his familiarity with Livy Jardine. Knowing about the Balfour mansion, and buying one of her pieces went way beyond creepy.

The meeting at Captain Jack's had suddenly taken on life-and-death implications.

Livy and Philomena were in the back room of the art gallery celebrating the flurry of recent sales. Jardine was now the darling of art aficionados across the area and well beyond. Glasses of white zinfandel were being hoisted and toasts offered when the doorbell jingled.

"Shoot, I must've forgotten to put the 'closed' sign on the door," Philomena apologized as she set her glass down and hustled out into the shop. Finding a young man wearing a Chicago Bears sweatshirt admiring yet another of Livy's pieces prompted her to announce, "I'm sorry, we close at five o'clock."

Livy watched from behind the parted curtains, and though she was certain that she'd never seen the young man before, he did look vaguely familiar. The voice was also eerily similar to that of a recently departed friend.

"I'm sorry. The sign did say open... I'll just come back tomorrow."

Philomena, impressed with his soft-spoken demeanor, stopped him at the door. "Look, I've got a few minutes. Is there something I can help you with right now? One of these pieces perhaps?"

He turned back to one of Livy's painting. "I notice that the artist signed her name Livy. Can I assume that her last name's Jardine?"

That question raised Philomena's brow, and sent Livy scurrying out posthaste. "I'm Livy Jardine," she announced on the move. "And you are?"

He smiled, and extended his hand. She'd seen that smile before. "My name's Joseph Gray. Your attorney said that I might find you here. He thought we should meet."

Livy smiled, cocked her head while studying his fuzzless face. "My God, you're the spitting image of your father."

He looked uncomfortable with the comparison, so she quickly backtracked. "I mean. I know that Freddy Graywolf raised you. I just meant..."

"It's okay," he reassured her, "the idea of being Robert Balfour's son is pretty new to me, but believe me, I'm not offended in the least."

The young man turned back to the painting and said, "this one is especially good. The detail is amazing."

"Well thank you. No better subject than a stoic lighthouse guiding the seafarer safely home."

"Very poetic," Gray responded as he took a closer look. "To someone like me who's been raised in the desert, snowfall and lighthouses are kinda magical in and of themselves. Kinda like leprechauns and unicorns."

He looked around the rest of the shop without focusing on anything in particular. He seemed to be at a loss for words. "I'm sorry to just barge in here like this," he began again, but I was wondering, can we talk somewhere...privately?"

After Philomena gave her a nod, she said, "Sure, okay."

"Do you have time right now?" he asked hopefully.

"Absolutely. Do you like pizza?"

"Who doesn't."

"Good, Yacabucci's is right around the corner. We can talk over a slice."

They split a pizza and washed it down with a soda. The conversation flowed easily. "So Joseph, tell me about your childhood. You grew up in Phoenix, right?"

"Yeah, in a trailer park. We never had much. My dad was a big dreamer. Ya know, one of those guys who was always trying to beat the system, or invent something that the world couldn't do without."

Livy smiled. "Dreaming, we've all been there at one time or another."

"Maybe, but my dad took it to another level. He once got one of his brainstorms patented—a toothbrush that you load once a week. The thing dispensed toothpaste at the push of a button."

"Move over Rube Goldberg," Livy added trying to inject a little humor.

"Yup, needless to say, it was a total bust. Colgate dropped the idea before it even hit the market… Thomas Alva Edison he wasn't."

Livy chuckled. "Your mom must be a very patient woman?"

"Like Job." He paused. "My mother's a good soldier. A very strong woman. She had to be."

Livy wanted to add mysterious and maybe even promiscuous, but those weren't qualities that should be lauded.

"…For as long as I can remember, she's always worked two jobs."

Livy, whose mind kept drifting back to the night Emanuelle spent entertaining Robert in Johnny Eagle's bed, hoped hooking wasn't one of those extra jobs.

"Yup, she stuck by my dad through thick and thin." At that moment the young man's smile could've been mistaken for a grimace. "Unfortunately, there was always a lot more thin than thick."

Livy listened, as Joseph raced on. "…Then there was my dad's gambling problem."

With their little confab beginning to sound more like grist for a support group, Livy was beginning to squirm.

"…But we always managed to get by, thanks to my mother. She's a survivor. Her childhood wasn't for the faint of heart. Life on an Indian reservation can make a devout Baptist turn to drink."

Livy smiled. If she closed her eyes, it was Robert talking—same resonant voice, and the tics and mannerisms were similar, especially the way the boy constantly tugged at the tip of his nose. All of it was vintage Balfour II. Even how Joseph had turned the phrase, *a lot more thin than thick*. Robert lived on.

"So, if you don't mind me asking," she broke in, "when did you find out that Robert Balfour was your father?"

"A few days ago. I guess right after he passed."

"Your mom told you?"

"Yes. My dad was off visiting a friend in a Mesa. All pretty convenient if you ask me. Pretty awkward stuff to be sure."

"I guess so. Is it something you'd care to talk about?"

"What?"

Livy shrugged. "You know, this conversation between you and your mom. How did she explain Balfour?"

The boy looked away and then back. "You mean their affair?"

Livy was definitely interested in that conversation, but she downplayed it. "Or whatever you care to share."

"Well, it's no biggie. She didn't say a lot." He paused. "From what I understand, at the time he was a sports writer for a Cleveland newspaper. They met when he came into the bar where she waitressed. They dated for a bit." He paused. "A 'brief fling' is what she called it."

After another swig of soda he added, "I filled in the rest of the sordid details myself. With basic biology prevailing and all, nine months later, and voila," he stopped and pointed to his chest, "this bastard child was born."

Livy knew when to back off the accelerator. A house of lies often collapses with the asking of one too many questions.

"I did the math Miss Jardine," Gray volunteered without prodding. "My parents were married when my mom got pregnant." He shrugged his shoulders. "Maybe it should bother me more, but it doesn't."

Livy tilted her head, the question was on the tip of her tongue, but he saved her the trouble of asking it. "Not carrying a drop of Freddy Graywolf's blood in my veins," he stopped, a wry smile appearing, "well, it strikes me as kind of a positive thing. Not to be mean or anything, but I never could figure out why my mom was with Freddy in the first place."

"Well," Livy began reluctantly, "if it's any consolation, my dad walked out on us when I was pretty young. So, I kinda get it."

"Oh, Freddy would've never done anything like that, he absolutely worships my mother."

"And what about you? How does he feel about you?"

"I guess he loves me, like stepfathers do."

She heard it in his voice, she felt it, she'd lived it. The void, that dead spot in the middle of your chest where love was supposed to reside, was but a hollow filled with an ache. Until Jason and Gramma entered her life, that ache was all she'd ever known and felt.

He smiled. "I guess I could think of worse things than having Robert Balfour as my sire. That makes me almost royalty, at least in the publishing world."

Livy nodded, then girded herself. She sensed that he was about to lay claim to the Balfour millions.

"It's really neat. I'm an extension of a long line of great writers. Me!" He shook his head, and pointed to his wrist. "I've got Balfour blood in these veins. Their DNA is my DNA."

Livy smiled. The son was a reincarnation of the father, that much was obvious. The idea that Robert would never get to meet this bright, articulate young man suddenly saddened her. Who knew, perhaps that meeting would have saved him from his inner-demons and his self-orchestrated demise.

"Well, I'm glad that your mom finally told you. Better late than never, I guess."

The boy nodded. It soon became apparent that he was done talking about his mother. Instead he chose to ask pointedly, "You and Robert, were you close?"

"Well, I only knew him for about six weeks before he got sick."

"You didn't answer my question," he pushed without a trace of hostility.

"I guess you could say we were close, relatively speaking. Your father didn't make a habit of letting people get too close."

"He was a recluse?"

"Sort of, but he also could be quite charming, and very kind."

"Hmm…I wish I'd gotten to meet him."

"You would've liked him. And I'm sure, he would've liked you."

The boy sighed. "We'll never know."

A moment's silence prompted Joseph to open a new vein of conversation. "So, what did you two talk about?"

"Lots of things. Politics, his dog, art…"

"He ever talk about his childhood, his family?"

"Sure, especially his father…Robert worshipped the man. Wanted to follow in his footsteps."

Joseph broke into a big smile. "Of course he did. The man wrote a gazillion best sellers."

"His father's success drove him like nothing else. Robert wrote more manuscripts than you could count, but most of them weren't very good... Simply put, he didn't have his father's gift, or his stamina."

"Do you know where any of these manuscripts might be now?"

"As a matter of fact I do. They're all yours. Do with them what you like."

"I'll read everyone of them," he effused while rubbing his hands together. "Who knows, I might learn more about my father through his failures than his masterpiece."

"Then you're gonna learn a lot," Livy said as she took a peek at her wrist watch.

"I'm sorry I've taken so much of your time," he apologized. "You're a busy woman and here I am asking you all these questions."

"Don't be silly. I still have a little time. Besides, we haven't even talked about his library yet. It's nothing short of amazing."

"Really. I can hardly wait to see it."

"Robert loved books. He had one of the best book collections in the country. You just say the word, and I'll give you a tour of the place."

Livy was so impressed with the young man that she'd almost forgotten, that in all likelihood, he would be the one walking away from the inheritance war triumphantly, waving the flag emboldened with the Balfour coat-of-arms.

"So, what do you Joseph?" she asked while checking out his soft, well manicured hands. "Are you in college?"

"I graduated from Arizona State two years ago. Got a degree in English Literature. I tried to get a teaching job, but that never happened. So, by day I'm teaching on the Navajo reservation."

"Well good for you," Livy said enthusiastically.

"Yeah, I'm tutoring struggling readers. It's a real challenge."

Livy smiled. "So, saint by *day, and...* and I'm guessing there might be more?"

He smiled. "And by night, I'm trying to write a novel."

Livy laughed. "Of course you are."

"I've already submitted a novella to a small publishing house in Tucson, but I haven't heard back from them yet."

"That sounds so exciting. Robert would've been so proud."

He hesitated. His next question would be a loaded one. "Miss Jardine…"

"Please call me Livy."

"Okay Livy, I've been wondering about something, but it's a little awkward asking?"

"Ask away. I'll try to give you an answer if I can."

The boy cleared his throat. "How did Robert Balfour die? What actually killed him?"

Livy hesitated. Talking about Robert's bizarre end was a slippery slope to be sure. Afraid the answer might lead her to places she didn't want to go, she decided to dodge the subject entirely. "I really don't know exactly. The coroner's report hasn't been made public yet."

"Was he okay mentally?" shot from his mouth a little too quickly, catching her off guard. *Perhaps he was questioning Robert's mental state in order to discredit the will?*

"Why do you ask?"

He leaned closer. "He didn't commit suicide, did he?"

She hesitated to use the words *natural causes* to describe a death that was more unnatural than natural, but it certainly wasn't suicide, at least not in the traditional sense. "No, he didn't."

The boy looked relieved. It was becoming more apparent that something more than a disputed will was gnawing at his innards.

"Why would you bring up suicide?" she asked while searching his eyes.

He shrugged his shoulders. "I don't know, maybe because I think about it now and again."

"Suicide?"

He nodded.

"Whoa, Joseph, have you talked to anybody about this? Your parents need to know for starters?"

"No I haven't. It's not like I'm eating my lunch on a ledge or anything. So you can relax." He paused. "Everybody thinks about it occasionally. It's just part of the human condition."

"That's not necessarily true. You should still talk to someone. Maybe a professional."

He shifted in his seat and faced her more squarely. "As a reader and a writer," he began, "what interests me most centers around the macabre. Edgar Allan Poe, Bram Stoker, Christopher Marlowe, I love their stuff."

Livy smiled. "Like father, like son."

"Yeah, dark is my favorite color. In fact, my novella is about a love-struck vampire."

"Well then, you're gonna love Robert's library."

"I can hardly wait."

"You know what his favorite book was? *Dr. Faustus.*"

Joseph lit up. "That's absolutely crazy. I've read that book three times. Selling your soul for power and knowledge may sound crazy to the naïve, but politicians do it all the time."

Talk about deja vu. She'd had this very same discussion with Robert, which made her wonder if the madness that destroyed the father also infected the son?

"Are you familiar with Nietzsche?" He asked purposefully.

She was, but for some unexplained reason she answered "no."

"Nietzsche said that if you stare into the abyss long enough, it will stare back at you."

Livy didn't like the sound of that but asked anyway, "And that's relevant how?"

He hesitated. "Well, I believe that people eventually become what they love or fear most because they focus on it so much."

"Wow, that's very insightful. I think you've just given me your father's epitaph."

"Really?"

"PEOPLE BECOME WHAT THEY LOVE OR FEAR—if there's a better epitaph for Robert Balfour's tombstone, I can't think of it."

Joseph grew pensive, almost sullen.

"Are you okay?"

He took a deep sigh. "Not really."

She patted the top of his hand. "Joseph, you can talk to me. Your father did."

His eyes were soulful, his voice so soft she could hardly hear him. "Livy, I've never told another living soul this, but sometimes I catch myself staring into the abyss."

A VERY UNCOMFORTABLE TRU CE

The Lincoln Town Car slowly made its way down the long asphalt drive that led to the East Ninth St. pier and Captain Jack's Lobster House. With the tinted windows, and license plates that read US GOV'T, it didn't take X-ray vision or a turbaned seer to figure out that someone important sat inside the car.

Jason watched as the black vehicle pulled into the parking space next to him. His vintage Ford sedan looked puny when compared to the oversized luxury car.

The nearly empty lot, polished shiny black by a passing shower, indicated that Captain Jack's lunch crowd was meager, not really all that surprising for a Monday. It was the perfect setting for a clandestine meeting.

The rear door of the Lincoln swung open, but no one exited, or even peered out. After a brief assessment, Jason deduced that the open door would be the only invitation extended. So he exited his car and edged closer to the Town Car. The Admiral, after removing a cigar from his mouth, yelled out, "C'mon, hop in Jason." After patting the seat next to him he ordered, "and make it snappy, you're starting to draw attention to us."

Scarza, after taking note of the heavily tinted plexiglass that separated the driver from the rear seat, addressed him as "Admiral Masters." Then, for some inexplicable reason, saluted him. Everything else aside, apparently old habits do die hard.

Quentin Masters was dressed rather formally for a long road trip. He'd worn a full Naval uniform that included stars and bars on sleeves, collar, and shoulders, almost as if he needed to remind Jason that he was one of a very select few, a Four-Star admiral. Chest out, stomach in—his posture was impeccably military. His dark eyes were shiny, alert, and predatory. He looked much younger than his seventy-one years.

"You look good," the Admiral began cordially, "fit as ever."

Jason nodded, making small talk with Quentin Masters was akin to having an annual colonoscopy. It was a necessary evil.

"I see you drove your father's car."

"Yeah, I try to run it at least once a week."

Masters gave the old Ford another covetous look. "Body's perfect. No rust. Mint condition."

"Admiral, I already told you, it's not for sale."

"I get it. I'm big on family too. Most people don't know this, but actually, I'm sentimental to a fault."

Sentimental!!! What the hell was he talking about!!! You blew up your son's house, with him inside!

He pulled up his sleeve to show Jason a gold wristwatch. "It's a Bulova. My grandfather gave it to my father who passed it on to me. I wouldn't sell it for any amount of money."

As the Admiral prattled on about sentimentality, Jason noticed something that he'd never observed before. Masters' twelve o'clock shadow was black, as were his bushy eyebrows and neatly trimmed mustache, and yet the hair on his head was snow white. His crew cut stood tall and proud thanks to a healthy application of gel.

Masters rolled down his window to get a better look at the restaurant. A light fog had rolled in off the water adding a little New England ambiance to a building swathed in weathered shake shingles, several pieces of wicker furniture that occupied the porch area, a rusty old bell, and one too many windsocks.

"A Little Bit of Maine on the Shores of Lake Erie," Masters chuckled as he read the sign above the entrance. "The last time I checked, rivers don't catch fire in Maine."

"Heard nothing but good things about this place," Jason countered as if he was taking a friend to lunch, instead of squaring off with a mortal enemy.

Masters' forced smile revealed teeth that had been stained by incessant cigar smoking. "Well, if all goes well, perhaps we'll celebrate with lobster and a tankard or two."

The Admiral took a long puff on his cigar, blew several clearly defined smoke circles roofward, and turned squarely in Jason's direction. His gaze was intense. "Well Jason, here we are, mano-a-mano, dealing with a dilemma that neither of us wants. Am I correct in assuming that?"

Jason nodded. "Yes sir."

"Two sides willing and ready to negotiate their differences, that's what I call a good beginning. You agree?"

Masters didn't bother to wait for a reply. "So, let's chat. A heart-to-heart, as they say." His smile quickly vanished, it was about to get real. "You know that I have to ask, are you wearing a wire?"

Jason, anticipating the question, had already started unbuttoning his shirt. Once convinced that he wasn't wearing a wire, the Admiral apologized, "Sorry 'bout that, but trust is the foundation of any successful negotiation. And truth be told, I'm not very trusting person."

"Is that what this is," Jason asked, "a negotiation?"

"Well, you do have something that I want back, and please don't insult my intelligence by denying that you have it." He waited a moment for a denial that never came. "So, it's my job to convince you that it's in your best interest to return said item to me... That sounds like a negotiation of sorts to me."

Jason, getting impatient, shook his head. Instead of sparring, they seemed to be dancing, dancing around "little" indiscretions like multiple murders, break-ins, sexual battery, and extortion. So why not get straight to it. "Well then, maybe we should begin with some honest dialogue, about your son's death."

Masters response was a withering glare. No one dared challenge the Admiral, and Jason's tone was definitely combative. Nevertheless, the Admiral kept his composure. "Gas explosions, though horrific as catastrophes go, are more common than one might think."

"Bullshit," Jason exclaimed heatedly. "You blew up your own kid. Who does that?"

The Admiral didn't flinch. The gloves were off. "My kid went to NCIS...NCIS!" Jason half-expected flames to shoot from his nostrils as he continued venting. "He betrayed his own family. What son does that?"

"Betrayed the family? Oh c'mon. Rollie was just trying to do the right thing, finally."

He took another long puff, then explained, "He invited you to his home, and gave you the tape, which he stole from my home by the way. It became crystal clear to me that he wasn't going to stop until Masters' name was dragged through the mud. He wanted to humiliate us... Me in particular."

"You murdered your son and an innocent man," Jason repeated, this time with as much venom as he could muster, "and you're talking about your precious family reputation."

Masters, arrogant and unflappable as always, showed no remorse as he intellectualized the murders. "Let's be real here. My son had ALS. I spared him a long, agonizing end, and Wiley Kendrick? The ape was nothing but a gun-running traitor."

"What?"

"I should know. I vetted him personally. Believe me, he was scum, but his background in the Medical Corps made him perfect for my son's detail. Still, once a traitor, always a traitor."

"So he was expendable?"

Masters nodded. "You're damn right he was."

"Wow, you're one cold son-of-a-bitch."

The Admiral laughed out loud. "You got that right son."

The car intercom buzzed. "Admiral, I gotta take a leak. You good back there?"

"Yeah, go ahead. And while you're in there, give the place a once-over."

Jason watched as the muscle-bound driver exited the car, and double-timed it through a driving rain. He couldn't be sure, but the driver looked like the same man who'd sat in the back of the Blue Note on opening night.

"His name is Howard," Masters said off-handedly, "and he possesses quite an impressive skill set, one that a former SEAL can really appreciate."

Another puff on the cigar seemed to calm him. The next question rolled off his tongue almost as if it was an afterthought. "So, did you watch the tape?"

Jason turned back slowly from the pounding rain and thoughts of facing Howard in hand-to-hand combat. His hesitation was all telling.

"Of course you watched the tape," Masters said, answering his own question. "You had to find out how much clout the tape gives you. It makes perfect sense. I would've done the same thing."

"Okay, I watched it. You obviously get off on beating up women, and amazingly, you were stupid enough to tape it."

"*Get off* is the operative phrase." Masters' laugh was evil. "You're not one of those choir boys are you Jason? Go to mass on Sundays, say your prayers every night...Do it missionary style with your eyes closed."

"I saw the tape Admiral."

"They were all carefully selected. Call girls...Pros...Each and every one of them highly paid prostitutes who specialized in the rough stuff."

"C'mon, I saw them. Those women were in pain. You beat them to within an inch of their lives."

"Inch of their lives? A fat lip, black eye, and some playful bondage. Christ, half the couples in America do this kinda shit every Saturday night."

"I wonder if the Navy tribunal's going to see it that way."

The Admiral chuckled. "They'd court martial my ass in a heartbeat, and revel in it. Everyone likes to go big game hunting."

The bodyguard returned to the car and the intercom. "It's all good inside. Four patrons, total."

"Good." The Admiral snuffed his cigar out, and took a long moment to formulate what he was going to say next. He'd viewed the dialogue thus far as mere foreplay. "Let's face it Jason, my son was a major fuck-up. Physically gifted yes, but not so much mentally. When he started using drugs, I knew things were gonna end badly."

He stopped mid-sentence as a cop car took a slow pass through the parking lot. Once the black and white had gone he re-lit his cigar and picked up where he'd left off. "Just for the record, we didn't want to frame Riley Jones, but what choice did we have?"

"*We?* Rollie told me that was all you."

"Yeah, I guess it was all me. You want the job done right...blah, blah, blah."

"You ruined a good man's life," Jason shouted. "Riley Jones has four kids."

"Good man? I vetted that son of a bitch. He was a Commie."

"What? That's bullshit. He was a registered Republican. Christ, he campaigned for Reagan."

"It was all a front. Jones' grandfather ran for President on the Socialist ticket... There's no place for Commies in the United States Navy."

Convinced that he was in the presence of a truly soulless man, Jason turned away in disgust.

"...And then you, you had to go play Boy Scout...What a fucking stupid thing to do!"

"I told the truth, and I'd do it again. Jones was innocent."

"Okay, the man was a saint," the Admiral scoffed. "A man of scruples, just like you. But then you go beat my son to a pulp... If you ask me, another fucking stupid thing to do."

Jason couldn't dispute the facts. The brawl with Rollie was a huge mistake.

"Although I must admit, I was impressed. My son was a savage. Going bare knuckles with him, you had some gargantuan balls."

Jason, thoroughly repulsed by Quentin Masters, couldn't believe that one of the highest ranking men in the US military was also the worst kind of criminal. Deluded and deranged, he saw every one of his evil machinations as something done for the common good.

"You know, I wasn't lying to you on the phone when I said you were like a second son to me. And my wife too." He paused. "Too bad it had to be you who stuck his nose in where it didn't belong." The

Admiral seemed sincere as he continued. "Believe me, I hated that you took the fall, but I live by the rules of the jungle. Either you eat, or you get eaten."

"And here for all those years I thought it was Rollie who set me up," Jason said with a shake of the head.

"Nah, Rollie was too weak to take care of business."

Jason stared out the window. The rain, now coming down in gray slanting sheets, was made even more ominous by the crackling lightning and claps of thunder.

"What you've got to realize is that none of this is personal." He stopped to take another puff. "Bottom line, you have something I want. That puts you in a very unenviable position."

"Yeah but if something happens to me—"

"Cut the crap, we've had a tail on you every second since you left Rollie's house. You haven't had a chance to secure the tape, or put it into play. My guess, you probably buried it."

"You don't know that for sure, or I'd be dead already."

An evil smile fanned out his cheeks, the reptilian look was menacing.

"Okay, here's the best deal you're gonna get. If you hand over the tape, well, I'm still gonna kill you, but I'll let your cutie pie and Gramma live to see another day. If you don't give me the tape, everybody's fair game."

Scarza was shaken to his very core, but he couldn't let on. His little world was under an all-out attack, and his first line of defense was maintaining a facade of free-wheeling indifference. His mask couldn't crack, nor his voice. "Nice try Admiral. Do you honestly think I would've agreed to this meeting if the tape wasn't secured and ready for distribution? So, spare me the idle threats."

The Admiral appeared unfazed. "So, I guess that's a 'no' to our little swap?"

"You got that right. And I should warn you, when you threatened my family, the thought crossed my mind that maybe right here, right now in this fucking hearse, I should rip your heart right out of your fucking chest with my bare hands."

"And you accuse me of idle threats," he chuckled. "You should know that things are already in motion, whether I'm alive or dead."

"So," Jason shot back, "why this charade? What was the purpose of all this Tom Clancy bullshit?"

"I just wanted to get a better read. Check to see if my assumptions about you, and the tape were accurate."

"And were they?"

"Spot on."

Jason took a deep breath. For starters, he was angry with himself for meeting with Rollie Masters in the first place, and even more so for accepting the tape. But he couldn't retreat now. "So Admiral, it appears that we have a good old-fashioned Mexican stand-off on our hands."

"A very uncomfortable truce, is what I'd call it," the Admiral agreed.

Jason got ready to exit when the Admiral grabbed his arm. "Give me the tape son, and we'll see. Maybe we tweak the narrative. I'm not an unreasonable man."

Jason pulled away from the Admiral's grasp. "*Tweak the narrative!* You like playing God, don't you Admiral?"

"I'd be lying if I said otherwise... I love all the perks that come with the job," he answered as he smoothed out Jason's sleeve.

Jason didn't want to grovel or play straight man for Quentin Masters, but he was desperate. "So, when you say tweak the narrative..."

"In the new version? After I get what I want, everyone walks away, intact and deliriously happy... What can I say? I've always been a sucker for happy endings."

Scarza didn't respond. Instead he got out the car, but before he could shut the door the Admiral fired one more surprise across his bow. "Rollie's funeral, it's on Thursday. It would mean a lot if you attended."

Jason shook his head. "You're out of your fucking mind."

Masters wasn't offended in the least. "I'm just saying, he did die trying to clear your name."

Jason slammed the door shut, prompting Quentin Masters to jump out of the other side of the car. Over the roof and through the rain he shouted, "You know, he refused to be buried in Arlington. Chose to be buried alongside his mother in Erie."

Scarza got into his car drenched and shaken. There was little doubt that the Admiral was planning to kill him, and leaving nothing to chance, probably Livy and Gramma too. He had to act, and act quickly.

They ordered lobster and washed it down with a couple of shots of Jack Daniels. The mood was hardly celebratory, but it was a long drive back to Virginia, and Quentin Masters was adverse to fast food of any kind. Besides, a debriefing seemed in order. Plans had to be made, plans had to be modified. Jason Scarza was proving to be more stubborn and formidable than originally anticipated.

"So," Howard began, "do we need to make any adjustments?"

Masters waved the waiter away. He'd had enough to eat and drink. "Perhaps a tweak here or there, but first and foremost, we tighten the tail on him. Scarza shits, we hand him a roll of Charmin."

"He's gotta go after the tape soon," the bodyguard chipped in.

"I still think it's in that damn garage somewhere, or maybe hidden in the car," the Admiral stated gruffly.

Howard shook his head. "We checked out both… Nada, zilch."

"Then we do it again, this time we take things apart if necessary. He already knows we're onto to him, so a little mess won't make a difference."

"There's also the backyard to consider," the driver added solemnly.

Masters shook his head. "Not quite a needle in a haystack, but."

"So let's say he does retrieve it," Howard asked eagerly, "then what?"

The smile was thin-lipped and evil. "What do you think?"

"Okay, we have our team in place. That should be no problem."

Masters called the waiter back. "Can we have some coffee please?"

The henchman, eager to close out the Jason Scarza saga, pressed, "And if he doesn't go back for the tape, how long do we wait before we pounce?"

The Admiral looked out the window at a storm-tossed Lake Erie, its waves violently crashing up against the stone jetties. He'd always been fascinated by the complexity and majesty of large bodies of water.

On the one hand, omnipotent and destructive, capable of destroying anyone or anything standing in its path, and yet when tranquil, capable of soothing even the most troubled of souls.

The Admiral viewed the sea as a kind of god, nurturing creatures great and small, but with the turn of the wind, a raging force capable of culling the weak, or those who dared to question the natural order of things. To Quentin Masters' way of thinking, the wind turned when Scarza questioned the natural order of things. He was ripe for culling the moment he'd accepted the sex tape.

"So," Howard asked again, "how long do we wait?"

"We'll wait until after my son's funeral," the Admiral answered.

They'd met in secret and spoken in hushed tones. They'd taken every precaution. No one was supposed to make the connection between Scarza and Masters, and yet, someone had—a neighborhood guy who was celebrating his 70th birthday with a plate of lobster and a glass of wine. From his table in the corner, the celebrant watched and dissected Quentin Masters' every move, his every thought. That someone was far scarier than Jason Scarza.

39

THE NINTH LIFE

Bruno Lentoni had struggled mightily after the Gadsky boy shot himself in his home. Already ailing, and with his wounded foot slow to heal, he was close to giving up when his neighbors, the Scarzas, came to his rescue. Gramma brought him food, Livy tended to his foot, and Jason played handyman around Bruno's run-down house.

Already moved by their kindnesses, he openly wept when Livy brought him a portrait of his wife that she'd painted from an old photo. His days may have been short, but Bruno Lentoni had finally found himself a family.

November Fifth, the same day that Jason Scarza had rendezvoused with the Admiral in Captain Jack's parking lot, Bruno was celebrating his seventieth birthday, coincidentally at Captain Jacks. His brother-in-law, Nicky, had dragged him to the restaurant over Bruno's objections. "My sister wouldn't want you sitting alone in front of that damn TV eating leftovers on your birthday…Now, get your ass in the car."

Bruno and Nicky pretty much had the place to themselves, except for a trysting couple enjoying a few stolen moments off in a dark corner, and a United States Admiral and his thug appendage who were throwing down shots a million miles away from the Pentagon.

Decades of living with the sword of Damocles suspended over his head had made Bruno ever vigilant, perhaps even a little paranoid. Anything that looked remotely suspicious, like an errant member of the Joint Chiefs of Staff, he'd notice. Keep both eyes open, and trust one's instincts was a mantra he'd lived, and nearly died by on occasions too numerous to count.

As Bruno watched things unfold, everything about the Captain Jacks' scenario set off alarm bells. For starters, when he and his brother-in-law pulled up to the restaurant, they'd passed a Town Car with US Gov't plates nestled up to a Fifty Ford sedan, chartreuse green no less.

How many people in Cleveland could possibly own a thirty-five-year-old car that practically glowed in the dark? Only one man came to mind, and he never made an appearance inside the restaurant.

A half-hour was a long time to chit-chat in the back of a government car. Bruno was convinced that nothing good had happened inside that car.

Fast forward some thirty minutes, and in walks Admiral Masters with a guy built to create mayhem. It was the same guy who'd walked in earlier, and cased out Captain Jack's like he was going to rob the place.

Bruno, though unlettered and a bit rough around the edges, always had great instincts about people and what made them tick. He was a big-picture kind of guy, just one of the reasons he was still alive while many of his peers had wound up fish food.

He'd also recognized the Admiral from the news. It was his son who'd died in the mysterious gas explosion. Rollie Masters had been a Navy SEAL, just like Jason Scarza. Once again, one too many coincidences to ignore.

And if huddling in the back seat of a car in an out-of-the-way place wasn't reason enough to suspect some kind of murky goings-on, their demeanor tacked it down. They appeared to be wolves, predators on some kind of hunting expedition. Their prey? If Bruno's instincts were correct, Jason Scarza was in trouble...

Bruno Lentoni scratched his bald head. What were the odds that time and chance would converge to drop him on the doorstep of such a sinister summit. Even more uncanny, Bruno, his brother-in-law, Howard, or the Admiral, none of them had ever set foot in Captain Jacks' before. And yet, there they were, actors performing on the same stage.

He'd never been a big believer in fate, but strange happenings were afoot. Perhaps some greater power had assigned him the role of Scarza's guardian angel, especially in light of the events since Walter Gadsky became a grisly household name on Bruno's block.

Gadsky should've killed him in his own home that day. He

certainly had reason enough to snuff out the man who'd executed his sister in a most violent, detached manner. But for some inexplicable reason, he turned the gun on himself. Why? Maybe Bruno had been kept alive for no other purpose than to celebrate his seventieth at Captain Jacks, and in doing so, cross paths with Admiral Masters and his henchman.

No doubt, Bruno Lentoni had used up the eighth of his nine lives the day Walter Gadsky decided that he, not Lentoni, should die. The one life he had left, the ninth, wouldn't be wasted. Lunch at Captain Jack's had been an eye-opener. His purpose, divinely orchestrated or not, was now clearer than ever.

40

DOTTING ALL THE I'S, CROSSING ALL THE T'S

Livy Jardine, one of the rising stars of Cleveland's art community, found herself spending more time at the gallery with Philomena. To her credit, the possibility of inheriting the Balfour fortune hadn't dampened her desire to continue painting.

"A couple from Sandusky came in earlier," Philomena disclosed. "They loved your lighthouse piece."

"Really," responded Livy. "How did you leave it?"

"They said they'd come back tomorrow. They wanted to know if there was any wiggle room on the price."

"You think that $850 is too high?"

"No, I think it's priced right."

"Good, 'cause I'm still giddy about selling the James Garfield piece. I gotta tell ya, I thought you were out of your mind asking $1900."

"What can I say? I'm good. The check cleared by the way, and I finally found out who the anonymous buyer is."

Livy dropped what she was doing. "Anonymous buyer, it all sounds so mysterious, so melodramatic. So who was this mystery person?"

"Some Navy big shot. I don't recall his name right now."

"Navy guy?" Livy cringed. "It wasn't Quentin Masters was it?"

"As a matter of fact it was. Is there a problem? Do you know him?"

"Unfortunately yes, it was his son who destroyed Jason's military career. The same one who just got blown up."

"Wow, that's some back story." Philomena shrugged her shoulders before quickly moving on. "Oh well, his money's green, and that's all that matters Hon."

Telling Jason that it was Quentin Masters who bought her painting sounded like a really bad idea. Just hearing the name Masters seemed to rile him these days, and ever since Rollie died, he'd been very preoccupied, sullen even. Something was eating away at him, but he wasn't sharing any of it, and that worried her.

Fortunately, she had her own distractions, like finalizing Robert Balfour's funeral arrangements, and putting the finishing touches on the Donna Lentoni portrait.

Thank God for her art. Painting had always been a refuge for her in the most troubling of times. Unlike Picasso, her blue period stretched from adolescence through her mother's illness and death. But Jason Scarza had changed all that. Now every brush stroke was pure joy. The Lentoni portrait was especially gratifying, and Bruno's reaction priceless.

"I guess you're right. I can't control who buys my art." Livy rationalized as she removed her smock. "Even Adolph Hitler was an art aficionado."

Philomena watched as Livy packed her things up. "So where you off to in such a hurry?"

"I've gotta go downtown later this morning. You wanna come?"

Philomena looked surprised. "So where's Mr. Gorgeous?"

"He and Calvin are working on a new routine. I didn't want to bother him."

"So what, you decided to slum it?"

"Do you want to go with me or not?"

"I might be interested. What are we talking; Higbees, May Company, a little lunch and drinkie-poo?"

"Maybe later. First I've got to meet with Mr. Jimison."

"The lawyer?"

"Yeah, I guess he's got some news. Plus Joseph Gray's supposed to be there too."

"Even though I love that kid, I think I'll pass. Besides, I've got plenty to do here."

Carl Jimison's law offices, located on the ninth floor of the Terminal Tower, overlooked Lake Erie and the Gold Coast. Handling generations of Balfour legal business made the pricey locale affordable—a place to impress prospective clients without being a budget-busting extravagance.

Livy was fifteen minutes late due to a fender-bender on her way downtown. A lot can happen in fifteen minutes, as she soon found out.

Carl Jimison, who'd opted to go presidential sporting a blue suit and red tie, appeared more animated than usual as he bounced out to the waiting area to meet Livy. "Joseph Gray's already inside," he gushed.

Livy smiled. She'd never seen Jimison so animated. "Well, you did say he'd be here, remember?"

He dropped his voice a decibel or two. "His mother's in there too."

Livy, caught off guard, pulled up short. "Emanuelle Graywolf's in your office?"

With his hand on the doorknob, he whispered, "She's very nice." After a wink he added, "And quite agreeable too."

Livy had questions, lots of them. For instance, *where had the real Carl Jimison gone?* Cold, calculating litigators weren't supposed to be euphoric, jabbering ninnies.

And what did he mean when he described Mrs. Graywolf as quite "agreeable?"

The answers to both questions were put on hold as the attorney opened the door and caught mother and son standing at the floor-to-ceiling windows gawking at the far-off waterfront. Water as far as the eye could see certainly can capture the imagination, especially when one lives in a desert basin.

Jimison made the introductions, and handshakes followed. It was all very civilized and cordial as they took their seats.

"So Livy," Jimison began, "I should tell you that Joseph and his mother requested this meeting today, and just to get it all out there, I've already cautioned them that their lawyer should be present."

Joseph jumped in, "But we want Mr. Jimison to represent us."

Livy, suddenly feeling possessive, insecure, and ambushed, got ready to insist that Jimison was her attorney, when Emanuelle modified her son's statement. "We're just hoping for some honest dialogue."

"About what?" Livy asked, more confused than irritated.

"We have a few suggestions," Joseph responded, "that might help move things along."

Livy's mind was spinning. *Weren't they putting the cart before the horse? Had paternity even been verified yet?*

Jimison, reading Livy's distress, took control back by returning to square one. "Just for the record, paternity tests have confirmed that Joseph is Robert's son. Of course Robert, unaware that he even had a son, willed his entire estate to you. All of which presents an interesting legal conundrum."

Livy, not wanting to sound greedy, asked softly, "Without sounding cross, Robert's estate is worth what?"

"Six million plus in liquid assets, and of course his home on Mayfield Road. Then, there's the matter of book royalties."

Up to this point Livy had struggled to play catch-up, but as soon as things slowed down enough for her to begin processing more effectively, things and people came into clearer focus, the enigmatic Emanuelle in particular. The legendary seductress who Robert had chased across the decades came into sharper focus. Her dress was long, her heels short, her jewelry tasteful, her cheekbones exquisite. She was understated elegance.

"So Mrs. Graywolf," Livy began evenly, "you said before that you came here today seeking honest dialogue. You care to be more specific?"

"Miss Jardine, before I attempt to answer that, I first would like to thank you for the kindnesses you've extended to my son, a perfect stranger pretty much lost in a strange place. He's done nothing but sing your praises."

"Thank you," Livy responded, though questioning her motives for the unsolicited compliment. "Joseph's a good kid. Believe me, being nice to him was no big deal."

"Still, thank you anyway." She stopped and began again. "So, Mr. Jimison tells us that cases like this one can be contested for years. That the lawyers' fees are often staggering."

"Cases like this one?" Livy repeated with a slight edge to her voice. "I wasn't aware that we were at that bend in the road yet."

Emanuelle smiled. "Well, technically we're not. But it's kind of obvious where we're headed."

"And yet, you have no one here to represent you?" Livy shot back.

"That's true," she answered while smiling, "and that's by design."

Jimison, sensing tensions beginning to escalate, stepped in, his message mostly targeting Livy. "We're just talking ladies, right? Sometimes, a little banter over tea and crumpets is far more effective than calling out the troops."

Livy apologized, "Sorry, I guess I'm still a bit confused."

"Livy, the Graywolves are hoping that things can be sorted out without teams of lawyers complicating things. It's as simple as that."

Livy smiled. She found herself in legal Neverland. The proceedings thus far seemed unusually friendly, loose and informal. This kind of idea sharing could've been done at corner bar while sipping a cold one. Where was the avarice, where were the threats, the boasts that might lawyer is bigger and more powerful than your lawyer?"

"So are you suggesting." Livy paraphrased, "that we just divvy up Robert's entire estate right here, right now?"

Emanuelle smiled again. Livy now understood Robert's obsession. The woman was the perfect combination of grace and beauty, a la Jackie Onassis. "I guess I am, with Mr. Jimison dotting all the i's and crossing all the t's of course."

It wasn't that Livy objected to her folksy, homespun plan, but her curiosity got the best of her. "Please excuse me for prying, but why isn't your husband here today? You are still married?"

"Yes I am. Freddy opted to stay in Arizona."

"Actually, we fired him," Joseph joked. "He's a big fan of litigation, and Clarence Darrow in particular."

All the cards had been laid on the table. No games, no hidden agendas, just honest dialogue. So with little more to suggest, all eyes turned on Jimison as if asking, *is any of this even possible?*

The lawyer cleared his throat. It wasn't supposed to be this easy. He hadn't earned his money, but he found himself going along with Emanuelle's proposal anyway. "Well, we certainly could frame a preliminary settlement favorable to all, but I should warn you the courts are probably going to slow this process to a crawl."

Everyone in the room looked okay with that. Joseph was the first to propose something specific. "I hope I'm not out of line here, but I'd love to get the house. Livy's already given me the grand tour."

Livy understood why the young man wanted the house so badly. What better way to be a Balfour, to carry on the family literary traditions than to live in the Balfour mansion? To dream the same dreams, to write at the same desk where a Nobel masterpiece had been penned, and pore over the same classics that his father had read before him.

"I have no problem with that," Livy agreed without hesitation.

The rest of it was left up to Mr. Jimison's judgment and expertise.

Things had gone so smoothly, Livy saw no reason not to invite them to Robert's funeral. And to her surprise, both said yes.

41

THE HUNTED BE COMES THE HUNTER

Scarza, now on a mission to save his family, stormed into the Blue Note, popped a Rolling Stones tape into the boom box, and turned up the volume to a deafening level. With the lyrics of *Satisfaction* reverberating off of every surface in the room, he pulled Calvin off his piano bench and dragged him back to the cloak area.

"What the hell are you doing?" Calvin protested while practically airborne. "Is everything alright?"

"This place could be bugged," Scarza mimed, enunciating every word as though his friend was deaf.

"What are you saying?" Calvin shouted. "Can we turn down the music for chrissakes?"

Jason shook his head. "They're probably listening."

Calvin looked confused. "Who's listening? What's going on Jason?... Ya know you're scaring the hell out of me."

Jason moved his face to Calvin's ear. "Let's take a walk."

"But it's raining," he protested as he followed Jason outside.

They walked for a bit before Scarza erupted, "I'm in trouble Cal, big trouble." He paused. "And I'm pretty sure the Blue Note is bugged."

"Bugged? You're joking, right? Who'd wanna bug the club?"

Jason pushed his growing impatience aside before answering, "Some really, really bad people."

"Bad people?" Calvin mocked. "Care to be more specific?"

"I can't. It's too dangerous."

"Does it have something to do with all that nasty SEAL business," Calvin guessed. "Or maybe that guy getting blown up last week?"

He hesitated to answer. The less said the better. "You're getting warmer."

"Jesus Jason, you're involved in all of that? How?"

"Indirectly...Look Calvin, you've gotta trust me. I know I can work this thing out, but I'm going need you to do a coupla things for me."

Calvin Short was trying to trust him, trying to focus on what he was saying, but he'd known Jason for most of his life, and never seen him like this before. "Anything Bro, but I'm gonna need more. How do you expect me to help you when I'm totally in the dark here?"

Jason turned to face him. "Believe me, the less you know the better. Things could get really dicey."

"Dicey? That sounds like some kind of a euphemism. How bad is this thing?"

Calvin was throwing a monkey wrench into Jason's plan, but his request for more information was a reasonable one. "Okay, think the worst, the bloody worst."

"Jesus Jace. Who are these people? And what about Gramma and Livy? Are they safe? Do they know what's going on?"

"They know nothing." Jason studied Cal's tortured countenance. Fear had furrowed his brow and narrowed his eyes. "Believe me, I don't want to involve you, but you're the only person I can trust."

"Stop already. Of course I'll help. What do you need?"

"I'm going to Erie Pa. very early Thursday morning, and I'm…"

"Erie? What the fuck's in Erie?"

"A funeral…Just shut up for a minute and let me finish."

"Okay, I'm sorry…But you've got me scared shitless. I draw the line when people start getting whacked."

"Stop and listen to me. What I need is your car, and an alibi for this Thursday."

Calvin's eyes were pinballing, searching for villains in hiding. The man climbing the nearby utility pole merited a closer look, as did the two men fishing off of the nearby pier. Then there was the guy in the Mustang who'd driven slowly past before circling back, a shady character if ever there was one.

"Calvin," Scarza shouted, "I need you to pay attention."

"Okay, okay. What did I miss?"

"I said, I'm gonna need an alibi. I thought we could say that we were rehearsing all day long… for this weekend's show. And to make it more believable, I'll leave my car outside the club."

"Whoa, back up," Calvin demanded. "Why in the hell would you need an alibi?"

"It's complicated."

"Needing an alibi can't be a good thing," Calvin said, apparently unconcerned about stating the obvious, "especially with your record and all."

"Let me worry about all that."

Calvin got teary eyed. They'd just reconnected, best friends once again. And now Scarza was talking like a man possessed. Whatever it was that he was suggesting smacked of danger, and the kind of illegality that could bring lethal injection into the conversation.

"I'm sorry that I can't give you any more details right now, but believe me, I have no choice. I've gotta protect the people I love, and I don't want you implicated either."

"Forget that shit," the emotion just erupted as he threw his arms around Jason, "your problems are my problems. You're as close to a brother as I'm ever gonna have."

"I appreciate that," Jason responded as he pulled away, "but this time, I'm on my own."

"Christ Jason, there's gotta be another way. Can't we go to the police, or the FBI, or..."

Jason shook his head. "Listen to me carefully. I need you to park your car behind Gramma's house."

"On the other side of the cemetery wall?" Calvin asked without thinking.

Jason gave him a duh look. "Of course on the other side of the wall...It has to be there by 4:00 A.M. You got that?"

"Why not park in front of your house?"

"Because they're watching the house too."

Calvin began mumbling incoherently. Jason grabbed his shoulders before repeating, "The wall directly behind the house...Four A.M. sharp...And make sure the gas tank's full. Leave the keys under the floor mat... You got all that?"

Calvin nodded as he wiped away tears with his sleeve. He knew there was no dissuading Jason now.

While hugging him, Jason whispered, "It's going to be okay. I'll take care of everything."

A firm handshake and a desperate hug sealed the deal. The man standing before Calvin was someone he didn't recognize. The gaze was steely, the jaw set and resolute. All that was needed to complete the warrior persona was lampblack, camouflage, and an assault weapon.

The hunted had suddenly become the hunter.

42

HOME IS THE SAILOR, HOME FROM THE SEA

Gramma had a busy day. She'd shopped, cleaned her house, visited Bruno Lentoni, prepared a meat loaf, with mashed potatoes and gravy, and baked a pumpkin pie from scratch. Not a bad day's work for an octogenarian battling arthritis.

Livy, buoyed by her visit to Jimison's law offices, was especially chatty as they sat down for supper. She had Gramma's ear, but Jason, mightily distracted by Quentin Masters' baneful omnipresence, was hard pressed to stay focused. Feigning interest he asked. "So how did it go today at Jimison's office?"

"Actually quite well. I finally got to meet 'the' Emanuelle."

"Emanuelle," the old lady jumped in, "where have I heard that name before?"

Livy smiled at Jason. The G-Rated or X-Rated version? Take your pick. "Remember Gramma when I told you that Robert Balfour had a son, one that he never knew about? Well, Emanuelle is the boy's mother?"

"So, she's real then? I thought you told me that Mr. Balfour had imagined her. That he was potso in the head, or high on cactus juice."

"No, she's real, and actually quite charming."

Gramma's tsks and head shake should have sufficed, but she tacked on, "So what, after all these years, the woman just shows up out of the blue? I'm telling you, it's all about the inheritance money."

Livy disagreed. "Actually, she was a delight. Instead of a greedy shrew, she was quite gracious. To me, coming to Jimison's office without an attorney spoke volumes."

Genuinely surprised, Jason commented, "No lawyer? That wasn't very smart."

"Maybe not, but she seemed to know the law. And Jimison warned both of us that, if the estate was contested, we were in for a very long, drawn out legal battle with heavy lawyer fees on both sides."

"Those damn lawyers," Gramma spouted, "they're all a bunch of bloodsuckers."

"Mr. Jimison's different. He's one of the good ones," Livy countered.

Jason, whose mind kept drifting back to Rollie's funeral, did his best to stay engaged. "So, how did you leave it?"

Livy was beaming. "You won't believe this. It's practically a done deal."

"What's a done deal?" Jason asked while he cut into his meatloaf.

Livy threw her arms up jubilantly. "All of it…The estate, royalties… everything…All divided up fairly!"

"How's that even possible?" Jason asked. "The negotiations just got started, and they didn't even have an attorney present."

"It's unusual, but Jimison's representing both parties. We told him how we wanted the pie sliced, and he's taking care of the particulars."

Gramma, not happy with her grandson's less than robust appetite, marched around the table and ladled extra gravy on his mashed potatoes. "Now you eat," she ordered, "you're getting way too skinny."

Jason threw an arm around her and pulled her close. Even seated, he was as tall as she was. After placing a lingering kiss on her cheek he said, "I love you Gramma."

Livy was touched. His *I love you* sounded heavy-hearted, sorrowful even.

"You okay Jason?" Livy asked. "You seem distracted."

"I'm just a little tired. It's been a crazy week…Let's get back to those *particulars*."

"Yeah let's get back to the particulars!" Livy could hardly contain herself. "Now mind you, none of this is official until a judge officiates, but I do believe you're looking at the neighborhood's first, rich, starving artist."

Gramma jumped up, and pulled Livy out of her chair. Their dance, a kind of improvised jig, was followed by more hugs and kisses and an all too familiar Gramma refrain. "Now you two can get married, and start having babies."

Livy sat on Jason's lap, threw arms around him while kicking her feet and batting her eyelashes, "But Gramma, how can I be sure that your grandson wouldn't be marrying me just for my money?"

Gramma laughed. "Tell the girl that you love her Jason, and that it's okay if she's rich."

Jason kissed Livy. He wanted this moment to never end. He adored these women. He wanted kids with Livy. He wanted it all, but the Admiral's face suddenly appeared before him as a hologram, a sinister hologram. At that moment, putting a bullet between his eyes seemed more than justified.

"She already knows that I love her," he said to Gramma. Then he kissed her again. "You know I love you right?"

Gramma jumped up and scooted around them. "No one go anywhere. I got pumpkin pie, and real whipped cream."

Livy returned to her chair and did her best to clean up her plate before dessert arrived. "God, this getting rich does wonders for one's appetite."

Jason marveled at her voracious appetite. Where did she put it all?

"I still can't believe it," she effused. "I pinch myself every hour on the hour to make sure I'm not dreaming. One minute I'm walking Robert's dog, and in the next, I own the joint."

Jason nudged her on. "So when you say rich."

With her mouth full, she held up four fingers.

"Four million? Pretty impressive, what about the mansion?"

She swallowed hard. "Joseph gets the house."

"Really?"

"It seemed only right," she explained. "A Balfour belongs in that house, kinda like Dracula belongs in Transylvania."

"That's an interesting way to put it."

She nudged him. "Hey, that was supposed to be funny. Are you sure you're okay? You don't seem to be yourself these days."

"Of course I'm okay. Why wouldn't I be okay?"

"I don't know. Maybe you're losing interest in me. Ya know with all these pretty young things throwing their thongs up onto the stage and all."

Jason laughed. "Now you're being ridiculous. I'd choose you every day of the week, and twice on Sundays."

Gramma, with pie in hand, announced, "Now, we've got something to celebrate."

Livy, while watching her cut up the pie, said, "Ya know, I almost invited them to dinner."

"Who honey?" Gramma asked while serving the pie.

"Joseph and Emanuelle."

"You should have invited them," Gramma said without hesitation, "we have plenty."

"Well, I thought about it, but things got a little weird at the cemetery."

"How so?" Jason asked while refilling Gramma's coffee cup.

"It was all so anti-climactic. I don't know what I expected, but it all seemed so inadequate. Like Robert passed and nobody even noticed."

Jason didn't comment, but Livy had pretty much described Balfour's last days on earth. Dying in the arms of a cleaning woman being the final exclamation mark.

"We found the grave site okay," Livy started at the beginning, "but I gotta tell ya seeing the grave number gave me the willies. Section 48, Plot 12., the last entry in that damn notebook…It all went downhill from there. "

"Did Emanuelle join you at the gravesite?"

"No, she waited in the car. It was just Joseph and me." She paused. "I don't know why, but I was a little disappointed that she didn't join us."

"It was probably awkward for her," he offered.

Gramma interjected, "Maybe she thought you needed a private moment to say your goodbyes."

"I don't know," Livy said with a shrug of the shoulders. "But Joseph seemed unfazed by it all. The boy's very sweet, but a little strange."

"Like father, like son," Jason added.

"Maybe," Livy continued, "I wonder if Emanuelle sees it. Could be that she's worried that her son has inherited Robert's crazy gene?"

"Crazy gene?" asked Gramma, thinking a little too literally. "There's no such thing is there?"

"Let's hope not," Jason said.

"He's hellbent on being a writer that's for sure," Livy continued. "He told me that he loves the macabre. That his favorite color is dark."

"Dark isn't a color," Gramma protested. "Everybody knows that."

Livy broke into a smile as she directed the next question to Jason. "You wanna guess who his favorite author is?"

"Jason shrugged. "I have no idea."

"Christopher Marlowe. The boy's read *Dr. Faustus* three times."

Jason smiled. "Wow, that's a little scary"

As Gramma squirted whipped cream on the pie, she asked, "So Livy, what did you write on Balfour's tombstone?"

"Homo Fuge...It's Latin. It means man takes flight."

"I don't get what that means," Gramma responded.

"It's hard to explain," Livy responded. "It was Robert's idea."

Gramma sensed that Livy didn't like the epitaph. "Would you have chosen something else Livy."

"Yes." Livy suddenly got emotional as her eyes misted up. "I don't know. Like I said before, it was all just so weird. No priest to offer a prayer, no family. It was just Joseph and me standing over the grave. I didn't know what to do. So, I said a prayer, even though Robert had forbidden it."

"Prayer is never a bad thing honey," Gramma offered gently.

"Believe me, it wasn't much of a prayer. I'm way outta practice."

"God doesn't need fancy words," Gramma reassured, "it's what's in your heart that counts."

Livy nodded. She was right. The old woman, who'd launched more novenas than the London air raids, knew all about the art of praying.

"How did Joseph handle all of this?" Jason asked.

"Actually quite well. He even asked if he could recite a poem. I was thrilled. He had to fare better than I just had. What could it hurt, right?"

"Which poem did he read?" asked Gramma as though she was suddenly Little Italy's answer to Ezra Pound.

"*Requiem*, by Robert Louis Stevenson."

Gramma drew a blank as Jason smiled knowingly. "An interesting choice." He paused. "And you say that you had nothing to do with picking the poem?"

"No. I really didn't know the poem. I take it that you do?"

"Yes. It's a great choice. Very appropriate."

Livy asked, "How do you mean?"

Jason hesitated. "Go back to Balfour's obsession with death…the way he almost willed his death… Then check out the poem. They're almost in perfect sync."

"*Under the starry sky*," Livy began, "*dig the grave and let me lie… and I laid me down with a will.*"

"Robert did plan the whole thing right to the day and hour, did he not?" Jason asked though already knowing the answer.

"Yes he did. It all fits, but how did Joseph know? I didn't tell him about Robert's Faustian obsession, or the notebook."

Jason shrugged. "Beats me, but the rest of the poem is also spot on."

"*Here he lies where he longed to be*. Home is the sailor, home from the sea. And the hunter home from the hill.*"

"It's uncanny," Livy exclaimed. "The poem could've been Robert's suicide note. How did I not make any of these connections when Joseph was reading the poem?"

"It's understandable," Gramma consoled. "You were very upset."

"Actually, I was more sad then upset. After Joseph read the poem we just stood there looking at each other. Two mourners. One a person who barely knew him, and the other a total stranger. How sad is that?"

"But if it hadn't been for you," Gramma broke in, "not a soul would have been there to mourn him. You just remember that honey."

They washed the dishes, watched a little television, and turned in.

Livy and Gramma were both exhausted, and that was a good thing. Otherwise, sneaking out in the middle of the night would've been impossible. Jason had a funeral to attend in Erie.

The note he left for Livy was riddled with falsehoods, all intended to insulate her from a word too horrific to say out loud— ASSASSINATION!

Cutie,
I couldn't sleep. I'm really worried about Calvin. I think he's started drinking again. Didn't want to disturb you, so I decided to go down to the club early and start setting up for tomorrow's new set. I'll call you later this afternoon.
P.S.
Usually, rich women don't turn me on, but in your case, I'll make an exception. Crazy about you!

Love, Jason

43

RAYMOND MALCOM RYDER

—Born and raised...Brooklyn, New York

—Enlisted in US Army straight out of high school

—Special Forces. Army Ranger. Wounded in action in Viet Nam in '68

—Returned to civilian life; graduated from N.Y.U. Law School in '74

—Joined the FBI in '75

—Promoted to Special-Agent-in-Charge of Cleve. Field Office in '79

—Greatest achievement was dismantling the Cleveland mob in '83

—Low career point. Being passed over for FBI Director post in '84

—Lowest career point. Being demoted to Des Moines field office in '85

....

"So how they treating you in Des Moines Raymond?"

"Who is this," Special Agent-In-Charge Ryder asked cautiously. "And how did you get this phone number?"

Bruno chuckled. "I can't believe it. You forgot me that fast. Who else ever gave you a gallon of homemade Cribari on your birthday?"

"Well, I'll be damned! Bruno Lentoni, back from the dead."

"Just wishful thinking my old friend."

"I heard that you'd been shot, in your own house...Not true?"

"Oh it's true alright. But you know me Raymond. If they ever wrote a song about me it would've been titled— *Bullet Proof Vests and Nine Lives.*"

Raymond chuckled. "Yeah, you always did lead a charmed life.

The whole Dante crew went up the river, but you were always a little smarter than the rest."

Bruno, needing to maneuver the Des Moines SAC into a more receptive position, assumed a sympathetic role. "I was sorry to hear about what those bastards did to you, especially after the job you did nailing Enzo Dante."

"Yeah well, I guess indicting the Don wasn't enough. Or maybe, I didn't kiss the right asses."

"Well, you certainly got screwed over. You deserved better."

"Yeah, tell me about it. I was so pissed off that I completely lost it. I shot my mouth off, and it cost me dearly. Rabble rousers in the FBI are like scabs at a union rally, they don't last long."

Bruno had turned up the heat. Now he needed to let Ryder boil over.

"So, the powers-to-be looked around, and decided that Des Moines was it." After a deep sigh he tacked on disgustedly, "Not many people create their own personal purgatory."

"For what it's worth," Bruno said, "as Feds go, you're one of the good ones."

"Wow, an honest to God compliment from Bruno Lentoni, now I'm really getting suspicious."

"Don't be. I'm just sitting in front of the fire convalescing…Lots of memories, both good and bad. I'm not ashamed to admit it, I got a little nostalgic ."

The Fed guffawed before demanding the truth. "Okay Bruno, you can cut the crap. Why the call out of the blue? And if it's about granting favors, you're barking up the wrong tree. My magic wand was confiscated when I boarded the frigging plane to Iowa."

"You always could see right through me Raymond."

"Yeah, yeah, yeah. Now come out with it. What's up?"

"Okay, after I almost bought the farm, I started doing some serious thinking. Believe it or not, some of it involved you."

"Me? I'm small potatoes now. Certainly not worth a contract hit."

"Contract? No, you got it all wrong. I wanna help you. Get that wand back for you. Maybe get you out of Des Moines too."

"Help me?" The Fed laughed. "The same guy who rousted you twenty-four-seven is someone you wanna help now?"

"Raymond, I'm not joking around here…How does FBI Director Raymond M. Ryder sound? Kinda has a nice ring to it, don't you think?"

Amused, Ryder shot back, "Why stop there. President Ryder sounds even better."

"Look, I'm being serious."

"Of course you are…And I thought you didn't smoke dope."

"Maybe this will get your attention. The word's out, Director Crenshaw has stage four cancer. Won't last the year, at least that's what I'm hearing."

"And where'd you hear that?"

"CNN, Ed Bradley, Dan Rather. Take your pick."

Ryder laughed. "Bruno Lentoni, the most informed gangster I've ever known."

"If you wanna get your ass out of the cornfields, I'd suggest you start taking all of this a little more seriously."

"Okay, okay. So the old prick's dying, who cares."

Bruno came back, "With all that's at stake, you should."

"What the hell are you talking about?"

"When I heard that the Director was dying, I immediately began to mull over the possibilities. Ya know, like what would it take to get my old pal Ray Ryder back in the conversation. Maybe get him back at the top of the A-listers?"

"What A-list? For the Director's spot?"

"Why not, you were as qualified as Crenshaw, or any of the others."

"Look Bruno, truth is I'm glad you called. You're always good for a laugh. And believe me, chuckles are scarce out here in the boonies. But I've got some work to do, and…"

"Raymond, stop talking, start listening, and get a pad and pen ready."

"Pad and pen? What the hell for?"

"Because I've got names, places, and dates that will bring down every major crime family on both coasts, and some in between. Your career's about to get a big shot of adrenaline."

Though still skeptical, Ryder was no longer laughing. "I don't doubt that you can walk the walk. Why else would I court you for three years in Cleveland? All of which makes me wonder, why turn rat now? What do you want from me?"

"Funny you should ask. I need a huge favor." Lentoni hesitated. "I need someone taken out."

"That's all," Ryder answered. "I thought maybe you wanted me to do something really illegal."

Bruno ignored his sarcasm. "And believe me when this guy falls, you'll feel the tremors all the way to the Pentagon."

Ryder was both stunned and intrigued. He'd kill his own mother to get to the top rung of the FBI ladder, but he needed further clarification before he asked who the target was. "Look Bruno, I gotta tell ya, I'm confused. Since when does Luciano Pavarotti come to Perry Como for singing lessons?"

Bruno chuckled. "The answer's simple. You can get much closer to the target than I can."

44

UNBLOODIED HANDS

Having one's bones interred at Presque Isle's Shadyside Cemetery placed the decedent in very exclusive company. According to its original charter, to secure a plot in this tiny burial ground required evidence that one's bloodline could be traced back to one of the original families who settled Presque Isle, Pennsylvania. The Crawford clan was one of those founding families.

Without question, this was no ordinary cemetery. The Federal government said as much when it decreed the forty-acre parcel a national historic site.

To detractors, Shadyside was oft likened to a "boot hill." Woodsy, quaint, archaic even, less than nine hundred people had chosen to be buried there, included in that select group was Daniel Crawford—a blacksmith who helped secretly assemble Commodore Perry's fleet during the War of 1812. Building the "wilderness fleet" was a feat that many believed rivaled Perry's stunning naval victories over the vaunted British navy on the waters of Lake Erie.

Eight generations of Crawfords had been laid to rest on the wooded hillside that overlooked Lake Erie, the last being Veronica Crawford Masters—the wife of Admiral Quentin Masters. Seven years later, her only son Roland chose to be laid to rest next to his mother, passing on a much more prestigious interment at Arlington National Cemetery.

The choice of cemetery aside, Lieutenant Commander Roland Masters would be buried with highest military honors. The ceremony would feature a sermon given by a navy chaplain, a horse drawn caisson ride from the Presque Isle's National Presbyterian Church to the Shadyside gravesite, an honor guard team serving as pallbearers, a 21-gun-salute, and the playing of taps by a lone bugler.

The eulogy would be delivered by Roland's father, Admiral Quentin Masters.

If anyone dared question their strained relationship, or the mysterious circumstances surrounding Rollie's death, the lavish funeral, one personally orchestrated by the Admiral, certainly would go a long way toward squelching all the ugly rumors and conspiracy theories. By all appearances, Quentin loved his son and wanted the world to know that his boy was a national treasure, one who deserved to be memorialized as such.

Sunny and unseasonably mild for November 7th, it was the perfect day to rake leaves, ride your bike in the park, or play a last round of golf. It was also an ideal day for throwing a sham funeral.

Jason Scarza, lying flat on his belly, had positioned himself on a wooded bluff that overlooked Shadyside. He was approximately two football fields away from the gravesite, a very doable distance as sniper shots went.

Everything had gone as planned. Jason had sneaked out of his house without a hitch. Calvin Short's car was parked near the cemetery wall per Scarza's instructions. The drive from Cleveland to Erie had been uneventful allowing him to arrive early, get himself in position in a thicket high above the black-creped activities below, and assemble his weapon while waiting for the limos to start arriving.

With the Presbyterian Church being only a mile or so away, Jason knew the procession was only minutes away. He should have felt nervous, apprehensive, or in the very least conflicted. Snuffing out a life wasn't something to be taken lightly, especially for one who'd lived his faith and obeyed all the rules. Playing God was usually reserved for the godless, or those who rationalized that there simply was no other way. Scarza was of the latter ilk.

Feeling no qualms or compunctions, he calmly checked out the area around the freshly dug hole through his rifle scope while imagining the Admiral, decked out in his formal whites, coming into view. Somehow he was at peace with himself as he watched a hawk circling in the sky above—an omen perhaps, or just another hunter closing in on its prey. The ways of nature always prevailed. Survival of the fittest, *the kill or be killed* mantra, left little room for debate or remorse. If Jason had any say in the matter, Quentin Masters would not be alive to deliver his son's eulogy.

Fortunately, he didn't have long to wait. The antique caisson, draped in a huge American flag, slowly made its way up the winding, gravel road. Five black limos patiently tagged along, the new following the old.

Piling out of the first car came Quentin Masters, the chaplain, and several other high-ranking naval officers including a uniformed woman who seemed overly attentive to the "grieving" Admiral.

The other cars quickly emptied. The honor guard exited car number two. The remaining vehicles were loaded with Annapolis midshipmen, who unless Jason missed his guess, were serving as set extras recruited by Quentin Masters. The quandary of having too few mourners at a funeral befitting the son of a Four-Star Admiral required a high level of creativity and deception. And to Admiral Masters, perception was everything.

The six pallbearers, dazzlingly white and adorned with assorted stars, bars, and stripes, marched straight from the car and took their assigned positions around the coffin. The bugler stood off by himself with his shiny brass horn poised under his arm.

As Scarza shifted into sniper mode, he noted a potential problem. He'd made up his mind that the first clear shot that presented itself, he'd take. But whether it was by design or dumb luck, Masters seemed buffered on all sides. The caisson and a thicket of trees protected his rear. The Midshipmen, a veritable human shield, stood directly in front of him. And the obese chaplain and lady officer, who were closely bunched around Masters, were likely collateral damage. **No open shot yet!**

All of which meant that he'd have to stay patient. Be ready when the phalanx presented him with the necessary chink.

If all went well, the confusion that was certain to follow the shooting would allow him to escape undetected. Seeing someone's brains and bits of skull flying in all directions was one thing, having no idea where the shot had come from quite another. Even the most intrepid of souls would find themselves diving for cover, not scanning the area for the shooter, or the nearby getaway car.

So with his finger poised on the trigger, he'd remain vigilant, opportunistic. He'd watch the rest of the funeral through his scope ready for that split-second chance to do what he'd come to do. Collateral damage, however, was to be avoided at all costs. **Still no open shot!**

He preferred a head shot, just in case the Admiral was wearing body armor. The fact that he'd qualified as the best marksmen in his SEAL class might finally pay dividends. He was confident that at two hundred yards, his shot variance should be no more than inch or so from dead center. **Still no open shot!**

As he watched the pallbearers transport the coffin from the wagon to the grave, he couldn't help but wonder how much of Rollie was in that coffin. "Bits and pieces and plenty of remorse" Jason muttered under his breath as he watched the six men lift and place the casket on the elevated stand that sat next to the open gravesite. **Still no open shot!**

Next up was the chaplain. Gesticulating and bellowing, his voice disappearing somewhere between the casket and the assassin's far off summit. Being able to read lips would've been helpful. **Still no open shot!**

The Admiral, still obscured by a human stockade, paid a final tribute to his boy. Of course Jason, out of earshot, would have to fill in the blanks, but he could imagine the Admiral's line of unadulterated, hypocritical bullshit. He was one glib son of a bitch.

He'd open by praising his son. *"I'm proud that my boy was a decorated Navy SEAL. And the fact that he's chosen to be buried next to his mom speaks volumes about his loyalty and devotion to her. America should be proud also. Rollie Masters was a true patriot who'd lived a life immersed in the red, white, and blue. God, country, family! that was my Rollie. He's run the race, and stayed the course."* The Admiral's final act, a blasphemous petition to the Almighty to make a place for Rollie in his heavenly kingdom.

That's how Jason imagined the Admiral's eulogy. A series of tired old bromides laced with outlandish lies. Quentin Masters, with one final dramatic gesture, wiped his eyes with yet another prop, a white handkerchief. It was pure theater. Once he'd said his piece, he could get back to the ugly business of recovering the incriminating video tape and eliminating anyone made privy to the sordid truth. The evil never rest. **Still no clear shot!**

In the final analysis, if pinned down and asked what single emotion dominated the conclusion of his son's funeral, Masters probably would've answered, *relieved.* Rollie's disgraceful deeds would be buried forever in that fancy box, on that wooded hillside, right next to his doting mother. He was now her problem for the ages. **Still no shot!**

With the end of the service nearing, everyone's gaze turned from the Admiral to the honor guard—seven men with rifles aimed heavenward. It didn't matter that the ammunition wasn't live. As tributes went, it was still powerful and moving. Volley number one was heard as far away as Presque's village square, volleys two and three were equally resounding.

With the rifle smoke still curling skyward, the rifleman—in synchronized, robotic precision snapped their rifles back into a position adjacent to their pant leg. The 21-gun salute had been completed. **Still no clear shot!**

The ceremony was winding down, and time was running out for Scarza. His window of opportunity had shrunk to a mere peephole. Perhaps he should have planned the hit at the church, but his cover would've been limited, and his getaway much more problematic. No, this was the spot.

The bugler's rendition of Taps was stirring and poignant. As dirges went, nothing pierced the heart quite like Taps. The woman standing next to Quentin Masters was moved to tears, again. He watched through his scope as she dabbed her eyes. If she had been the target, his mission would've ended that very moment. But she wasn't the target. **Still no shot!**

How was it possible that the Admiral had remained shielded throughout the lengthy procession? Had he been tipped off, or were his instincts that good? All that remained was the folding of the flag by the six honor guards. Meticulous, deliberate, precise, twelve separate folds turned the flag into a compact bicorne gift handed to the grieving father. **Still no shot!**

The actual presentation of the flag was made by one of the other officers standing along side the coffin. Jason had been to enough service funerals to know the exact words that accompanied the flag exchange: *"On behalf of the United States Navy and a grateful nation, please accept this flag as symbol of our appreciation, for your loved one's honorable and faithful service."*

And that's when it finally happened. The Admiral stepped forward to accept the flag leaving himself vulnerable for a split second. Jason, who started to squeeze the trigger, was shocked when a single gunshot rang out from second bluff to the east of him. The bullet found its mark, dead center of Quentin Masters' forehead spraying blood on his glitteringly white uniform. Collapsing like a sack of potatoes dropped off the back of a truck, he was dead before he hit the ground.

And just as Jason had imagined it, everyone around the victim scattered and dove for cover leaving the fallen puppetmaster to face the same God he'd hypocritically petitioned only moments earlier.

Unnoticed, Jason hopped in Calvin's car and sped away. Stunned and relieved, he was going home with unbloodied hands.

A million thoughts ran through his mind as he sped down Route 90, but two questions persisted— Who pulled the trigger, and why? He realized that these were questions that might never be answered, and perhaps that was a good thing. The wicked "king" was dead!

45

THE UNLIKELIEST OF BEDFELLOWS

Special Agent Ryder entered Bruno Lentoni's home by cover of night. He'd told no one about his upcoming visit to Cleveland's Little Italy, or his pending deal with the mafia hit man. "Personal family matter back East" was cited as the reason for Ryder's two-day hiatus.

Not surprisingly, no one in the Des Moines field office seemed to care or even notice that the Chief was gone. Federal matters were handled in a fairly relaxed manner in the Hawkeye state.

As far as Lentoni's explosive revelations were concerned Ryder's agenda was straightforward, textbook even. Gather the evidence, corroborate the facts, and keep the star witness out of harm's way. Above all else, Bruno was not to be exposed as an FBI informant, at least not until he could be adequately protected from retaliation.

They were the unlikeliest of bedfellows. Lawman and career criminal sitting at the kitchen table sipping wine, noshing on aged provolone cheese and Italian bread. Oddly they were sharing war stories like they were old Army buddies.

Ryder's notebook and pen just sat there, a somber reminder that eventually there was business to be conducted and promises kept. A deal was a deal, even one that used the murder of an Admiral as currency to buy information intended to rekindle a sputtering bureaucratic career.

The old man raised his glass and managed one more tribute before the dictation began in earnest. "Arranging a high profile hit on such short notice couldn't have been easy Raymond. Here's to your resourcefulness!"

"It took some doing my friend." The G-man smiled as he raised his glass. "Very good wine by the way."

"It's the same wine I always serve. Maybe it's the circumstances that make it taste a little sweeter."

"If you're referring to me being sprung from that hayseed hell, then I heartily say, Salud!"

Bruno nibbled on the cheese and washed it down with more vino before observing, "Ya know you and me ain't so different after all. We see what needs to be done and do it."

"I think the word you're looking for is *pragmatist.*" Ryder chuckled. "Bruno my old friend, you and I are pragmatists who aren't afraid to get our hands dirty."

Bruno smiled. "Hey, you're the college guy. You know all the big words."

"That I do, but I gotta admit when you told me it was Quentin Masters that you wanted taken out, I almost swallowed my dentures."

"To be honest," Lentoni countered, "I was surprised you agreed to do it. The four-star guys cast very long shadows."

"What can I tell you, I'm a little crazy and a lot ambitious."

Bruno smiled. He couldn't disagree with either of Ryder's self-assessments. And that's when it struck him. Once the masks were removed, gangsters and Feds looked pretty much the same. Cheap beers, expensive beers, once their labels were removed tasted pretty much the same.

"So," the G-man purred through a sly smile, "you care to let me in on it? I'm dying of curiosity."

"Let you in on what?"

"Hey don't jerk me around. Why'd you want Masters hit?"

Bruno shrugged his shoulders. "He was a prick. Scum of the earth, isn't that enough reason?"

"Maybe." It was Ryder's turn to shrug. "But if you ask me, I got the easy end of the bargain. I make one phone call, and *pow!* it's done. But you've gotta do something that goes against your very core."

"And what's that?"

"Omerta my brother! Break your vow of silence."

"Yeah that's gonna be tough. For fifty years, I kept my mouth shut. Even did a stint in the slammer rather than talk." He took a deep breath. "But as the times change, so must we."

Ryder tried to wheedle more out of Bruno. "So obviously wanting old Quentin dead wasn't business as usual. It had to be very personal."

"It was."

Bruno's tone, like the slamming of a door, let the Fed know he was done talking about the Admiral. So he opened his notebook, grabbed a pen, and asked, "Well, shall we do this thing?"

And so for the next several hours Bruno supplied names, dates, places involving upper-echelon Cosa Nostra who'd been involved in activities ranging from extortion, bribery, money laundering, loan sharking, murder and mayhem of every description, even the sabotaging of a small plane carrying a couple of pesky members of the *House Committee on Organized Crime.* Bruno proved to be a fountain of information spewing forth damning evidence against mobsters who heretofore seemed untouchable.

Crime families across the country, who were fused by common interests, elicit activities, and sealed lips, proved to be surprisingly vulnerable. The bond that gave them strength was also the chink in their armor. Like a team of mountain climbers, all tethered together, if one fell, they'd all fall, and fall they would.

By the time Bruno was done naming names, thirty top mobsters were targeted and implicated in criminal activities that fell under the auspices of the RICO umbrella. Lentoni hadn't lied when he'd promised Ryder a big game hunt, one that would make the Des Moines S.A.C. relevant in Washington DC once again. *FBI Director Raymond Malcom Ryder* was a title that was sounding more and more plausible.

At three in the morning Ryder put his pen down, sat back, shook his cramped writing hand, and exclaimed, "My God Bruno, this is even bigger than I realized." He rubbed his hands together enthusiastically. "Heads are gonna roll!"

Bruno looked weary. No doubt he'd snatched Jason Scarza, and his family from the jaws of death, but in doing so, he'd sold out people that he'd known most of his life, people who had invited him to family baptisms and weddings, people who'd trusted him with their lives.

Justified or not, he was now officially a snitch, and the most despicable of all rodents—*a rat!*

"We're probably going to need you to testify," Ryder added matter-of-factly. "Are you up for that?"

Lentoni shifted his bandaged foot from under the table to a place where it could be inspected by the Fed. "You should know Raymond, I've got some serious health issues. Doctors tell me I could lose the foot."

Ryder cringed as he stared down at the bandage. Blood and pus had merged to form a sickening yellowish rainbow.

Ryder was genuinely shocked. "I had no idea. That foot looks awful."

"It's not healing. Diabetes, it's an unrelenting bitch."

"Okay, we can work around that. Maybe we can videotape some of your testimony."

Bruno nodded an okay, but his insides were now in full rebellion.

Ryder hesitated. "We've got some things to do on our end to tighten things up before we move forward anyway. So if the foot needs tending, I know a really good doctor."

Knowing there was no way out of the vise that he'd helped to create, Bruno had already begun to retreat into himself. He thanked God that Donna wasn't alive to see the disgraceful end game that loomed ahead.

"I hate to keep dropping bombs," the Fed continued, "but you're going to have to move outta here Bruno. You do know that right?"

Forty-five years living under one roof and it had come down to a puny two-word concession, "I know."

"...And of course, change your identity. Sooner rather than later."

"How long do I have before the shit hits the fan?"

Ryder thought for a few seconds, "A week, maybe ten days."

Bruno shook his head. "I can't believe I'd ever be considering WITSEC as an option. The idea turns my stomach"

"It's better than the alternative," the Fed shot back glibly.

The wheels were turning. Bruno was no novice when it came to corruption within law enforcement agencies. There was a good chance he'd never get the opportunity to testify.

Ryder studied Bruno's furrowed brow. The old gangster looked to be wavering. "Stop worrying. We'll give you a fresh start. New name, new locale, new everything...No one will ever find you."

Battered by failing health and dying a slow death expedited by abject loneliness, he was an old seventy. For these reasons starting over had no appeal to him, and his dour expression said as much.

"What did you expect Bruno. A pat on the back, mints on your pillow, a big hug. You've poked the wasp's nest. You can either get stung, or run and hide, and live to testify another day."

"Don't worry about me, I knew what I was getting into when I came to you with the deal. You lived up to your end, and I'll live up to mine."

"Good choice Bruno, your only choice really." The Fed got to his feet. "I'll let myself out. In the meantime, see a doctor about that foot, and start getting your stuff together, but think light. I'll be in touch."

46

NOT POPES OR PRESIDENTS

He knew his time in the old neighborhood was at an end. Even more significantly, his very identity was facing extinction. He had no children. He was the end of the Lentoni line. Suddenly he felt like the last man on earth. Becoming someone else was a concept that Bruno Lentoni couldn't wrap his brain around, no matter how hard he tried.

Of course he'd miss his house too, and all its cherished memories, but leaving the Scarzas and Livy Jardine would be the worst part of it.

Still, what choice did he have? The tales that he'd shared with the Feds would topple powerful men who headed billion-dollar corporations. And anyone even remotely connected to Bruno would be in mortal danger. Vanishing seemed the only way to protect friends and loved ones.

So planning his own going away party suddenly seemed to make the most sense, even though none of the invitees had any idea that this would be the last time they would ever see him again.

Even before all the hellos and hugs had been dispensed with, Bruno's wounded foot took center stage. Bloodied bandages were hard to miss, so much so that Livy immediately took him aside and began redressing the wound. "Bruno, when are you supposed to see the doctor again?" Livy asked, making no attempt to mask her concern. "This foot looks really bad."

"Next week," Bruno lied. "I've got an appointment with some hotshot specialist that Donna's nephew lined up for me at Youngstown Memorial Hospital."

"Thank God," Livy said while grimacing, "I think this thing's getting infected."

Gramma, busy preparing lunch, had been spared the gory triage intervention and Livy's preaching. Right on cue, she marched in and saved the day. "Dinner's on, is anyone hungry?"

Bruno, not very adept using crutches, struggled as he navigated the short distance from the den to the dining room table. "I didn't want you to go to all this trouble Anna Maria. I got pastry and cold cuts from DiCorpo's."

Jason and Livy exchanged smiles. It was both endearing and a bit strange hearing someone call Gramma, *Anna Maria*.

"It was no trouble Bruno. The Lasagna was already made, and we'll have the pastry for dessert. Now, everyone mangia!"

Conversation flowed easily around the table. A lot had happened recently. Some of it was good, some bad, and some too scary to talk about. On this occasion, they stuck with the good. Livy's emergence as a top commercial artist topped the list of topics.

"Philomena deserves a lot of the credit," Livy said modestly. "I don't know what I'd do without her. She sold one painting in Erie, and the very next day sold another to a Columbus woman. She's absolutely dogged."

"I love the portrait you did of my Donna," Bruno joined in. "It could be hanging in an art museum, it's that good."

"Thank you, Bruno. Your wife was so pretty, her features so delicate. Vermeer would've loved her profile."

"And she was a really good person," Gramma added a bit off topic. "Bruno you remember when the little Trippi boy came down with polio back in…I think it was '52."

"It was '54," Bruno corrected. "I remember because it was the same year the Indians won the pennant."

"You're right," Gramma said smacking her forehead. "I remember Donna didn't care if the boy was contagious or not. Even the quarantine sign didn't stop her. Every day for two weeks she was there for Mary and her little boy."

"Everybody else avoided the family like they had the plague," Bruno added, now teary eyed. "She was like Mother Teresa."

"The boy wound up on crutches," Gramma added grimly, "but he did survive, thanks to Donna's loving care."

The telling of the Trippi story, though extolling the virtues of Mrs. Lentoni, was tantamount to decorating the chandelier with black crepe ribbons and bringing in the pipers to play *Danny Boy*. The somber mood needed changing.

"Hey Bruno, you're a big Louie Prima guy, aren't you?" Jason asked a little too cheerily.

"Yeah, Keely Smith too."

"Well, Calvin and I are doing this one segment Thursday night. A tribute to Louie Prima."

"*I'm Just a Gigolo*, that's my favorite," Bruno managed with his mouth full of lasagna.

"*Old Black Magic, Nobody Til Somebody Loves You*. We're doing 'em all. How about I pick you up on Thursday about five? The Blue Note's wheelchair accessible."

Bruno scrambled to come up with another credible lie. "I can't. I'll be visiting my nephew in Youngstown. Ya know, after I see the specialist."

That exchange brought quizzical looks around the table. "So how long are you staying at your nephew's place," asked Livy, trying to disguise an interrogation that had now begun in earnest.

Unfortunately, Bruno wasn't cooperating. "I have no idea."

"I saw the stuff you packed in the back room," Jason inserted delicately. After a chuckle he added, "It looks like you're really traveling light, kinda like an army on the move."

Bruno didn't smile, instead he stretched the lie even further, "I probably won't be down there long, so I won't need much."

When the phone began ringing Bruno breathed a sigh of relief. One too many questions, way too many lies. About ready to plead the 5th Amendment, Livy came to his rescue, "It's some guy named Raymond. He says he's a friend of yours Bruno?"

Bruno, obviously caught off guard by the call, grabbed the phone and moved to the farthest corner of the den. Though the whispered conversation was brief, it was enough to shake Bruno. "Anna Maria, do you mind if I pass on dessert? With my sugar levels being what they are, the cannolis might be a bad idea."

"Of course not, Livy and I will clean up in here. You men go relax."

They headed out to the front porch and sat down. It was sweater weather, but the chill in the air was welcomed by Bruno, who still appeared somewhat flushed and frazzled. The phone call had apparently upset him a great deal.

"Are you okay Bruno?"

Bruno nodded as he lit up a cigar. After a few puffs he tried rationalizing the filthy habit. "I gave these up years ago on doctors' orders." He laughed. "Like a hundred other things aren't gonna kill me before these things do me in."

The silence between them was surprisingly comfortable. Bruno puffed away while scrutinizing his tiny front yard, for what Jason didn't have a clue. Perhaps it was the bushy-tailed-squirrel busily burying acorns for the leaner times ahead. Finally, the old man turned to face Jason. He was smiling when he asked, "Jason, do you remember Jupiter?"

"Of course I remember him. Goofy black Lab, howled like a coyote. He was your wife's dog."

"He was a good dog. My wife rescued him from the pound."

"I didn't know that."

"I'm ashamed to admit it, but I mistreated him. Well, you saw for yourself." He dropped his head. "No excuses mind you, but Donna had just passed, and I wasn't myself."

"Yeah well, that was a really tough time for you."

Again Bruno smiled, apparently another memory had surfaced. "That lilac bush over there, Donna planted it just before she got sick... I've fertilized that bush twice a year ever since."

"It shows," Jason said. "Without a doubt, it's the biggest lilac bush in the whole neighborhood."

"Between you and me, I don't think it's just the fertilizer...She's still here. That bush is Donna's living memorial."

"Well, it certainly is doing a lot better than your grass. I think you've got grubs."

Bruno appeared unfazed by the grub threat as he continued

reminiscing, "You remember that day you called me out? It happened right over there."

Jason followed Bruno's crooked finger to the weedy remnants of a once flourishing flower garden. Both men were smiling as Jason answered, "I sure do."

"Yeah, you just showed up outta the blue, and backed me down like no man had ever done before. And you were just a kid." Bruno chuckled again. "You had cantaloupes for balls, I'll tell ya that."

Jason laughed. "Well, I'd just graduated from high school. Talk about being completely full of yourself."

Bruno's mood turned melancholy. "You know, I used to check on that dog from time to time. Walked past Livy's house like I was just taking a stroll."

"I know, she told me."

"Livy was a good choice," he said patting Jason on the back. "She took real good care of Jupiter."

Jason smiled. "You know, it was my idea to change his name to Milo."

Bruno's furrowed brow caused Scarza to add, "Ya know, like they say on *Dragnet,* to protect the innocent."

Both men laughed.

"I liked the name Jupiter better," Bruno confided. "It's strong. What kind of a name is Milo anyway?"

"I don't know, but he did live to be sixteen."

"That was all Livy's doing," Bruno said lovingly. "She's a strong girl. Never had it easy. Believe me, she dealt with a lot growing up. The cops were always at her house."

"Well, her mother was troubled."

Bruno took another puff on his cigar and then asked out of the blue, "Are you happy with her?"

The conversation was taking on a father-son feel. It was a little strange, but Jason liked it. "Very happy. She's terrific."

"Smart, talented, pretty. She reminds me of my wife, before she got sick."

Jason nodded sensing that more Donna Lentoni anecdotes were on the way, more reminiscing too. "Like Livy, she used to paint. Did you know that?"

Scarza shook his head.

"Mostly landscapes… Never sold a one of them." He chuckled. "They're hanging all over the house. Signed them *DBL*…Donna Beth Lentoni."

Jason handed Bruno a handkerchief, patted him on the back, and waited for the old man to collect himself before switching topics. The segue was as calculated as it was clumsy. "Speaking of your house, you want me to look after it while you're in Youngstown?"

Bruno, apparently still mired in poignant memories, apologized, "I'm sorry, what did you just say?"

"Your house, yard…You want me to look after it while you're gone?"

"That would be great. I'll pay you for your time."

After waving off the idea of being paid to help a friend, he asked, "Are you sure you really wanna do the *Youngstown* thing? I mean, you really love this house. There are so many memories here."

Bruno struggled to get the words out, "No choice kid."

Jason didn't quite grasp how prophetic that statement would prove to be over the next twenty-four hours, but he did sense something was terribly wrong, so he stayed the course. "Does this Raymond guy have anything to do with this *move* to Youngstown?"

Fearing that Jason was beginning to put it all together, Bruno answered obliquely, "Well my man Raymond, he is kinda in the moving business, so yeah, I guess you could say he's helping me move."

"Look Bruno," Jason began more assertively, "tell me to shut up if I'm outta line here, but it feels like you're running from someone, or something. Am I wrong?"

"We're all running from someone or something kid. Most of the time it's ourselves."

More double talk, Jason thought. Bruno was doing an excellent job of stonewalling. Pinning him down was like trying to corral a greased pig in an open pen.

"From the second we're born," he philosophized, "we're all trying to outrun death, but no one's ever done it. Not popes or presidents, and certainly not mob grunts like me." He paused to smile. "I guess the same could be said for admirals too."

Admirals!!! That one caught Scarza between the eyes. "Interesting that you'd mention admirals, especially after what happened to Admiral Quentin Masters."

"Well, it was all over the news," Bruno responded casually. "Some sniper got him, right?"

Jason wasn't sure how Bruno was involved, or even if he was involved, but all signs seemed to point in his direction. He couldn't come right out and ask if he had any part in the assassination, so he took another path, one much closer to home. "I've always wanted to ask you about something Bruno."

After another long puff, he responded, "Sure, ask away."

"It's about the Mangini brothers."

"You mean *Dumb and Dumber*. What about 'em?"

Jason hesitated. How often does one ask another human being to confess to committing a double homicide? "That was you right?"

Bruno did poker face well. No tells, no tics, no giveaways. "I paid for their funeral, if that's what you mean. Their mother couldn't afford a proper funeral, and I was feeling charitable."

Jason ignored Bruno's song-and-dance and plowed on, "The hit on Heidi Gadsky gave it away. Anyone involved in the billiard hall beating was taken care of, including her. That's why her brother showed up on your doorstep. Am I right?"

"A very entertaining theory Jason," Bruno answered while smiling. "Not quite big screen material, but maybe a good made-for-TV movie plot."

"How about taking out an admiral? Would Hollywood buy that storyline?"

Bruno turned and faced him. "Look Jason, big shots get to be big shots by stepping on a lot of people on their way to the top. Make one too many enemies, and sometimes, people get whacked."

Bruno smiled as if to say, *nice try kid*, then continued to muddy the waters. "Take Julius Caesar for example. Stabbed right there on the floor of the Senate. They were probably lined up around the forum to do his ass in… No doubt he was a big prick too."

Jason fell silent. He knew now that Bruno would never admit to any of it, not directly anyway.

"Sometimes in this life," Bruno continued on, his tone softening, "a man gets lucky, real lucky. He finds himself surrounded by good people, kind people. People he probably doesn't deserve to have as friends."

Bruno's eyes welled up as went on. "We're talking about friends who do good things, like rescuing family pets, or bringing meals when you're sick. They welcome the shunned, like my Donna did with the Trippi boy. They're people who look past all the rumors and whispers, peel away the tough outer shell and look into the heart of a man."

He stopped and put his meaty paw on Scarza's shoulder. "I've known very few people like that in my life. Four to be exact." He held up an open hand wiggling four fingers before closing them into a fist. "Donna Mangini, your grandmother, Livy and you. A pretty short list by anyone's measure."

It was Jason's turn to get misty-eyed. "Look Bruno, whatever, or whoever is behind this exile to Youngstown, or whatever place you're really being shipped off to, let me help you with it. It's the least I can do after all you've done for my family."

"I appreciate that more than you'll ever know, but I've got it covered Jason. You help me with the house, and we're square."

They sat in silence for a long moment before Bruno tacked on, "Who knows, maybe someday the place will be yours."

Jason didn't like the sound of Bruno's last words, a weighty postscript to be sure, but he also recognized it was Bruno's not-so-subtle way of saying *let's change subjects, let's move on, let's enjoy what's left of this day*. The burrowing squirrel had their full attention until the wind shifted ominously, and the skies darkened. A storm was on the way.

47

"PUT ON YOUR COSTUME AND POWDER YOUR FACE"

Seeing Jason, in a Cleveland Browns' hoodie, grilling burgers on the front porch caused Livy to quicken her pace and sharpen her wit. "Hey Chef Boyardee," she shouted out from the bottom of the steps, "does your grandmother know what you're up to?"

She was up on the porch and kissing him before he could respond, "Hey, the cook-out thing was Gramma's idea. I'm guessing it's her way of keeping her hallowed kitchen safe from my rather questionable culinary skills."

"Hmm. So, she's off on a mission somewhere?"

"Yeah. I guess Carmella's got a situation."

"When doesn't Carmella have a situation?" Livy sniped while glancing down at the charred meat patties. "Well, it's certainly not Anna Maria's chicken piccata, but it does smell pretty good. Almost edible even."

"Talk about your ringing endorsement," he shot back as he flipped the burgers. "Remind me not to cook for you ever again."

She laughed. "I like your scrambled eggs, doesn't that count for something?"

"No, breakfast is fail proof fare, but the better question is, why haven't you cooked for me yet?"

"You know why. I scorched a pan. In Gramma's eyes, no greater sin and all that."

"Well, it is her kitchen." The curl of pungent smoke stung his eyes momentarily backing him away from the grill. "Sorry about earlier," he said while rubbing his eyes. "I couldn't shake free."

"It's okay. I took the Rapid… Twenty minutes, and I was right there on Carl Jimison's doorstep."

"So, what was all the urgency? Is there a problem with the settlement?"

"No, everything's right on schedule. He had a few more papers for me to sign." Livy rearranged her shopping bags as she took a step toward the front door. "Look, why don't I go in and start setting the table. I don't think I can screw that up."

He gently grabbed her arm. His tone was mischievous. "If I were you, I'd ditch the purple bag, you know the one you've been trying to hide from me."

"You mean this one?" she teased while dangling it under his nose. "After an evil giggle she initiated the seduction. "I guess we're going to find out later if *Ambiance* is truly for lovers."

He smiled. "Lest you forget, Gramma thinks it's her god given right to sneak a peak at any and all contraband that enters her home, especially the purple ones. "

Livy scoffed, "Actually, the sexy nightie was her idea. She said black lace was the way to go."

Jason laughed. "And how in the hell would she know?"

"Beats me. Maybe she's been reading *Cosmo.*"

"Before hell freezes over," he said as he reached for the purple bag. "Let me have a look."

She slapped his hand playfully. "Patience is a virtue."

"There's another old expression that comes to mind," he said. "We must strike while the iron's hot." He gave her a quick kiss before adding, "Who knows how long Gramma's gonna be gone."

"You're kidding right," Livy asked incredulously. "This whole evening's a Gramma Scarza production…It's a set-up."

Jason's stupefied expression caused her to add, "The black lace underwear, having the house all to ourselves…you don't see a master planner at work here?"

"I do now," he said while wrapping his arms around Livy.

"The woman's a pitbull with a one-tracked mind." Livy paused. "Grandkids by hook, crook or sexy lingerie!"

He grabbed her hand and placed it on his burgeoning crotch. "Believe me, if you were dressed in a burlap sack, babushka, and galoshes, you'd still be the sexiest woman on the planet. Who needs black lace anyway?"

She patted his cheek as though he was someone to be pitied. "You really are horny, aren't you?"

"Horny and ravenous."

"Hold that thought," she responded enthusiastically. "I've got a quick errand to run first. Then maybe we postpone the barbecue. How does pizza in bed sound?"

"Hold on a sec," he said. "Backup. Did you just say something about an errand?"

"I did, but we're talking about a really, really quick little detour. Maybe fifteen minutes max. Then I'm all yours."

The kiss he planted on her lips left her weak kneed and wavering. Thinking that he had her on the ropes, he begged, "Maybe the errand can wait until tomorrow?"

"Sorry love, it's not something that I can just blow off. It involves Bruno."

"Bruno?"

"Yeah, remember when I promised him a frame for his wife's portrait?" She opened the second bag exposing an ornate, gold picture frame. "I thought I'd give it to him before he left for Youngstown."

"That's really thoughtful," he said while trying to disguise his disappointment.

"Maybe the frame can wait. I'll give it to him tomorrow."

"No," Jason responded firmly, "the old man doesn't ask for much, and we owe him big time…Problem is, I'm pretty sure he said that he was leaving really early in the morning."

"I figured as much," Livy responded. "That's why I thought I'd run it down now. When I get back, I promise I'll model that little black ditty for you."

Jason took the bag from her. "I've got a better idea. You order the pizza and douse the fire while I run the frame down to Bruno. Hopefully, he hasn't turned in yet."

With visions of Livy cavorting around in sexy underwear, Jason was a man on a mission. Get to Bruno's place and back as quickly as possible.

. . . .

His pace was brisk, as was the dropping temperature. From his vantage point on Bruno's front lawn, the house appeared to be completely dark, the one exception being a single light in a second-floor window. He checked his watch—7:35. *Could Bruno have turned in already?*

As he got ready to knock, Scarza could hear classical music filtering through the closed front door. He recognized the aria, Habanera from *Carmen*. Bruno may have liked Louie Prima's scat style, but opera had always been his passion. And evidently, this night he'd decided to share it with his neighbors.

Being loud and demonstrative had never suited Lentoni's style. The man, nicknamed "The Shadow" by mob associates, had always prided himself on staying beneath the radar. Shunning the bright lights was more than a way of life, it was a survival tactic that was dictated by the bulls-eye that never left his back. All of which made the blaring music somewhat puzzling.

Jason rang the doorbell several times before tapping on the glass with his Annapolis class ring. When that didn't work, he peeked through the living room windows and spotted a pair of metal crutches that were illuminated by a single beam of moonlight. Propped up against the side of the bannister, the idle crutches begged the question—where was the wounded old timer? A very perplexing separation indeed, a hobbled man without transport.

So, around to the side door he went. More knocking proved fruitless, as did repeatedly calling out Bruno's name. A look through the kitchen window was sketchy at best. With the help of a low wattage oven light, he could barely make out appliance silhouettes and a very tidy kitchen. No surprise there, Lentoni was compulsively neat.

Everything looked ship-shape. Windows and doors were all secured. All signs pointed to an early bedtime, which made sense if Lentoni was leaving at the crack of dawn. Or, after conjuring up images of his infected foot, perhaps his prescribed pain meds had mercifully induced sleep.

So back on the front porch he went. There'd been a change of music—*Carmen's* aria had given way to Nessun Dorma. Luciano Pavarotti even sounded great through walls and glass. After listening for a bit, Jason deduced that the music was most likely coming from the lighted room on the second floor.

Fearing the worst, he reluctantly reached for the house key that Bruno had given him only the day before. Though circumstances seemed to warrant a closer look inside the house, he was still apprehensive about unlocking the front door and barging in uninvited. What if this frantic search was little more than a case of runaway imagination?

Filled with uncertainty, he'd retreated to the front walk, but when he took a last look back, the second floor light was still beckoning. His gut told him that something was terribly wrong inside that house, and there was only one way to find out for sure.

Fortunately, the key opened both the door lock and the deadbolt. Once inside he gave a shout out before inching his way across the living room floor, never forgetting that Bruno had a formidable gun collection that included big ones, little ones, and every caliber in between. It wouldn't have been the first time that an unannounced visitor had been mistaken for an intruder, and most certainly not the first time Lentoni had put a bullet in someone.

"Bruno, it's Jason Scarza," he called out tentatively from the bottom of the stairwell. After moving up one step he repeated, "It's Jason, Bruno. Are you up there? You still awake?"

The ensuing silence left him little choice. It was time to face whatever ugly truths were lurking at the top of the stairs. So up the creaky, uncarpeted steps he trod, every step bringing him ever closer to the music and the truth. A stirring aria from Pagliacci added power and melodrama to a tense situation that needed neither.

After reaching the upper landing he stood and peered down the dimly lit hallway. He could see that the bathroom door was ajar, open just a crack really. Obviously he'd found the source of the light and the music, but for some reason he hesitated even though every fiber of his being told him that something horrible awaited him at the end of the hall.

Finally standing outside the bathroom, he called out to Bruno, this time loud enough to be heard over the music. Bruno still wasn't answering. So a peek through the narrow opening revealed an open linen closet, a scale, and pair of men's trousers crumpled up on the floor. There was no sign of Bruno.

Suddenly Pavarotti's powerful voice reached out to him. *"Vesti la giubba e la faccia infarina. La genti paga, e rider vuole qua."*

Jason, who spoke fluent Italian, understood the meaning of the words. *"Put on your costume, powder your face. The people pay, and they want to laugh."*

While feeling Pagliacci's pain, various scenarios sped through his mind. They were all bleak. Perhaps Bruno had a heart attack, or stroked. The tile floor looked wet. He could've fallen and hit his head. Worst case scenario, the body of a dead friend was waiting to be discovered.

Finally, he pushed past his fears and entered the bathroom. Finding Bruno wide-eyed, ghostly white, and sitting up in the tub was completely unexpected. The fact that his bath water was crimson turned his stomach. After steadying himself, Jason took note of Bruno's bloodied right arm, the one dangling from the tub's rim. It was almost as if he was pointing to the straight razor that lay next to the tub, the one stained with blood.

Though the next few minutes were a blur, Scarza managed to check for a pulse that wasn't there, no signs of respiration either. Bruno, already cold to the touch, was gone! His spirit had already left his body, hopefully on a quest to re-unite with his beloved Donna.

Badly shaken, Scarza grabbed the sink and held on for dear life. He couldn't take his eyes off of Bruno who looked like a man taking a soak after a long day. His countenance was serene enough, his eyes locked in on a photograph of his wife. Curiously he'd gone to great pains to prop up the photo of his wife on the nearby clothes hamper. *An odd thing to do*, thought Jason.

The man who'd taken many lives in his extended tour with the mafia had evidently taken one more—his own. The instruments of death were a welcoming warm bath and a glittering, pearl handled razor.

48

I WAS NEVER HERE

With Pagliacci's resounding score quickly becoming an assault on the senses, Jason turned off the radio and collapsed onto the closed toilet seat. The profound silence that followed was pierced by a persistent faucet drip, one that gently rippled the bloody bath water.

His initial shock soon gave way to disbelief. He'd just spent quality time with Bruno. They talked about life, love, Jupiter, and happier times. Granted his infected foot had slowed him, maybe even depressed him, but Jason was convinced that Lentoni wasn't the suicidal type. He'd always vowed that death would have to come get him, not the other way around.

And yet, there he sat immersed in his own blood stripped of any semblance of dignity. Jason, who desperately wanted to yank him from the water, cover his nakedness with a blanket, and mercifully shut his eyelids, knew better. Nothing was to be touched or altered in any way. Bruno's bathroom was now a potential crime scene until proven otherwise.

So there was nothing he could do for his fallen friend except make a phone call that would, once again, turn Bruno's house into a three-ring circus. Unfortunately, waiting for the police to arrive was a duty that he'd inherited by stumbling onto the body first. For the moment, Jason was a person of interest simply because he'd brought a gift to a friend.

The fact that Jason was a convicted felon might also complicate things, especially since dead bodies seemed to be piling up around him like battlefield carnage. The Mangini brothers, Heidi Gadsky, and now Bruno—they were all dead. Mere coincidence, a wrong place-wrong time scenario, bad luck, or *something else?* Hopefully, the police wouldn't dwell on the *something else.*

Despite his reservations he knew what had to be done. It was time to call the police, but as he made his way toward the telephone, he heard the front door slam shut. Either someone had just entered the house, or he'd left the door ajar and the wind had intervened.

After a moment of reflection, he reasoned that whoever entered the house couldn't be police. Even if someone had called complaining about the loud music, or the neighbors had mistaken Jason for a prowler, the cops wouldn't have entered the premises without sufficient warning. So, who was in the house?

The answer came quickly from somewhere near the bottom of the stairs. "Hey Bruno, are you ready?"

Jason, completely flummoxed, tiptoed out of the bathroom debating his strategy. He was uncomfortable with just blurting out, "He's dead, Go away!" Instead he asked forcefully, "Who's down there? Identify yourself, now!"

From his years in the field, and with peril having been his constant companion, Scarza's senses had been honed to hear a pin drop, the squeak of a leather shoe, or even the rustling of one pant leg against the other. It wasn't surprising that, even though separated by a flight of stairs, he'd heard and recognized the sound of a gun being unholstered, and its safety released. The creaking steps sent him scrambling for cover.

"I'm with the FBI," shouted the intruder from somewhere below. "Please show yourself!"

It was a standoff. Knowing about Bruno's colorful history, ancient or even more recently, it was very possible that the invader could be another hit man, or government assassin posing as a Federal agent.

Jason, feeling naked without a weapon, tried bluffing his way onto more equal footing. "I've got a gun, and I'm licensed to use it."

The nerve-racking silence allowed him to hear the man panting heavily. Probably overweight and out of shape, Jason deduced. Though a definite advantage for Jason, the gun was more than an equalizer.

"…And I should tell you that the cops are on their way," Jason continued, feigning strength of position. "So, either get the hell outta here, or toss up some identification."

A long moment passed before an FBI badge landed on the top

landing. Scarza's bluff had worked. A voice from below explained, "My name's Special Agent Raymond Ryder. I was supposed to pick Bruno up at 7:30. Who am I talking to? And where's Bruno?"

Jason relaxed a bit. Raymond Ryder, that was a familiar name. The same man, who'd interrupted last Sunday's dinner with a phone call, was now lurking in the darkness below. His badge corroborated his story. Special-Agent-In-Charge Raymond Ryder was out of the Des Moines field office begging the question— what the hell was he doing in Lentoni's home?

"My name's Jason Scarza," he shouted back. "I'm a neighbor." Jason stopped short. He'd become a lot more than a neighbor. "Actually, I'm a friend of Bruno's."

Another long pause followed. "Is it okay if I come up Jason?"

"Come up, but be prepared. It's not good."

Ryder, after securing his weapon, hustled up the stairs where Jason pointed him toward the bathroom.

After one step into the bathroom, the Fed stopped dead in his tracks and cursed, "What the fuck have you done Bruno? You've gone and ruined everything."

The man's broad shoulders slumped a bit as he took in the scene from the doorway. He made no attempt to get a closer look, to check for vital signs, to survey what could have been a crime scene. The only thing that apparently interested him was a walking, talking FBI informant who was relevant for only one reason—to revive Raymond Ryder's flat-lined career. The dead informant was capable of neither walking or talking.

The Fed finally wheeled back in Jason's direction. His flushed face reflected devastating loss, but not the kind that might accompany the death of a loved one. No, his grief was more about the loss of a highly prized asset. Seeing one's diamond ring disappear through a sewer grate would be difficult to deal with, but for Ryder, Bruno Lentoni's death was tantamount to losing the Hope Diamond. His one shot at becoming the Director the FBI was about to swirl down the drain along with the last drop of Bruno's blood.

It took Ryder a few minutes to speak. Finally he managed, "How long since you found him?"

"Ten, fifteen minutes?"

He sounded thoroughly defeated as he asked, "Did you really call the cops?"

"I was just about to when you showed up."

The agent nodded, then zipped up his jacket "Well, go ahead, call them."

"Are you going to talk to them," Jason asked hopefully.

"No, you found the body, you talk to them."

Jason shook his head in disgust. "So let me guess, you're not sticking around, are you?"

"Even more than that Mr. Scarza, *I was never here*. You got that? Never here."

As they walked down the stairs together, Scarza could see a car parked outside. A shadowy figure was behind the wheel. "Can I ask you a question Agent Ryder?"

"Yeah sure, but make it quick."

"Bruno said something about staying with his nephew's family in Youngstown. Was any of that true?"

Ryder laughed. "Bruno never was very creative. WITSEC has a reputation to maintain. We start relocating people to ghost towns and nobody's ever going to turn?"

Jason shook his head. WITSEC! He couldn't believe that Bruno had agreed to the flip. He'd always detested informants.

Ryder winked and pointed a finger at Jason. "I can see that you're surprised by all this. Believe me, the old man had his reasons."

Jason, wondering if this whole tragedy had something to do with the Quentin Masters' affair, asked timidly, "Care to be a little more specific?"

"I can't. Remember, I was never here," he laughed, "so how can I get more specific."

The Fed headed out the door, then turned slowly back. "Ya know, for a ruthless gangster, Bruno wasn't such a bad guy. Who knows, in another life, we might've even been friends."

Jason thought otherwise. Bruno had more integrity in his trigger finger than Ryder had in his entire duplicitous body.

The wind kicked up as sleet began to pelt the front porch. Special Agent Ryder pulled up his collar as he marched out onto the porch. Scarza was right on his heels. The G-Man took a long look at the wintry scene before slowly turning back toward Scarza. "You wanna know what really killed Bruno Lentoni?"

Anticipating an answer that might border on the profound, Scarza drew closer.

Though his smile was wistful, the Fed's tone was biting. "Fucking friendship!"

49

Bruno Lentoni's suicide was more than loss of life. An old friend had passed away in a most tragic, puzzling way. Questions remained long after he was buried, questions about his last night on earth, his clandestine involvement with the Bureau, and his unlikely relationship with the morally bankrupt Raymond Malcom Ryder.

Jason's lone encounter with Ryder left him searching for answers. There was something about the way the Fed looked at Scarza as the two parted on Bruno's front porch. He knew he wasn't paranoid; Ryder's gaze had been accusatory. It was as though Jason had somehow been responsible for Bruno's suicide.

"Bruno had his reasons," those were Ryder's exact words. When pressed he deflected as a coward might, immediately washing his hands of Bruno's messy demise, and even Bruno himself. It was all as easy as declaring himself a non-persona. *"How can I tell you more when I've never even been here?"* As disclaimers went, it was foolproof. Quantico had taught the slippery Agent well.

If the thorny G-man could've magically disposed of Bruno's hard-to-explain corpse by simply pulling the bathtub stopper, Jason lamented, then he would've yanked the plug without a second thought, or flicker of remorse.

Ryder, not satisfied with leaving Scarza to face the police inquiries, chose to shoot one last guilt-dipped arrow. "Ya know what actually killed Bruno? *Friendship.*"

Raymond Ryder might as well have plunged the knife into Scarza's back and finished him off with the tired old taunt—*With friends like you who needs enemies!.*

Exactly five weeks to the day that Bruno passed, Jason's questions were answered via a newspaper headline—**FOURTEEN MOBSTERS**

INDICTED! The story went on to name Special Agent Ryder as the lead investigator, making him a hero once again. The Bureau's prodigal son had triumphantly returned, the laurel wreath placed on his head by Bruno's dead, cold hands. And Ryder had said as much when he credited Lentoni's testimony as the key to breaking these cases wide open.

Quite the footnote! The last piece of the puzzle had fallen into place. Every major question was suddenly answered including, who ordered the hit on Quentin Masters? Why did Bruno take his own life? What was the connection between the old gangster and Raymond Ryder? All answered with one credit listed at the end of the lurid "movie"—**"None of this would have been possible without the help of Bruno Lentoni."**

The old mob foot soldier had obviously struck a deal—his considerable treasure trove of mob secrets in exchange for the head of Quentin Masters. Quid pro quo, this for that.

Of course, the fact that Bruno took his own life instead of testifying in open court put a dent in Ryder's coup. Certainly many more underworld kingpins escaped the FBI's sweeping net when the old man opted for a warm bath and some serious blood- letting. Ryder would have to be satisfied with a career booster, rather than a career maker.

The embittered G-man wasn't wrong when he said that it was *friendship* that killed Bruno, his unlikely friendship with Jason Scarza to be more precise. To Jason's way of thinking, the fact that an FBI Agent, a man sworn to uphold the United States Constitution, had ordered a hit on a Four-Star Admiral wasn't as shocking as Lentoni turning informant.

Bruno Lentoni was old school gangster. Omertà, like his precious reputation, meant something to him. He was a vault. Secrets in, secrets sealed. The Feds, especially Raymond Ryder, found that out in the purge of '83 when Bruno, interrogated for months and threatened with hard prison time, never gave the Feds a thing.

Fast forward a few years, and what changed? A friendship.

Ultimately, the safety of Jason Scarza's family meant more to Bruno than omertà, old mob friendships, and life itself. Sure he'd give Ryder enough to initiate the hit on Masters, but when it came down to testifying in open court, that was never going to happen. A dead man couldn't be subpoenaed.

Epilogue

Four years had passed since Bruno's suicide sent shock waves through the close-knit neighborhood, but Little Italy, like it had done countless times before, moved in its own inimitable way.

For Livy and Jason Scarza, so much had changed, yet so little. Their tiny hamlet, the one that time had evidently forgotten, was quite capable of creating such contradictions.

The Scarzas recognized and appreciated the uniqueness of this place, especially as they pushed the double stroller past Bruno Lentoni's old house. They half expected to see Bruno sitting on his front porch smoking a stogie, instead, a woman came running down the path clutching a pie in both hands. "Jason, Livy. I was hoping you'd pass by."

"Hello Miranda," Jason responded. "How are you?"

"Good, thank you." Before handing over the pastry, she dropped down into a squat position to get a closer look at the twin babies. The pinch of the cheeks was almost reflexive.

"Oh my God are they cute," she cooed as she stood up revealing a black eye that was beginning to fade into a yellow and purple memory. "How old are they?"

"Six months," Livy answered, apparently having grown weary of the question.

Miranda Ulman's eyes darted back and forth between the babies. "They really are identical aren't they? It's gotta be so hard telling them apart."

Livy tried to stay patient while an amused Jason looked on. He was obviously entertained by his no-nonsense-wife being forced to deal with the inane questions that came with having adorable twins. "The blue ribbon is James," she responded, "the pink one is Anna Maria."

"Anna Maria," Miranda repeated with a kind of hushed reverence, "that's such a beautiful name. Kinda has a saintly quality to it."

Jason finally pitched in, "We named her after my grandmother."

"Yes of course," Miranda responded. "Gramma Scarza. I've heard such wonderful things about her…She's a legend in the neighborhood."

Jason teared up and looked away. Nearby was Bruno's lilac bush covered in fragrant blossoms, no big surprise since Jason fertilized it twice a year, carrying on the tradition that Bruno had started decades ago.

"I'm really sorry for your loss," Miranda consoled. "Not all that long ago, from what I understand."

"Thank you," Livy responded.

"I hope she at least got to see the little ones before she passed."

"She did," they both answered in unison.

Livy and Jason stared at the pie hoping to expedite things, but Miranda wasn't quite done with the small talk. "Was James your father's name?" she asked Livy.

Livy was stung by the question. The inquiry wasn't rude or that far afield, but it did bring her father back into her stream of consciousness. Keeping his memory dead and buried was something she'd really worked hard at. Her snappy response said as much. "Oh no, no, no. The baby's named after Jason's dad."

"So you gonna call the little tyke Jim?" Miranda asked, while chuckling at the prospect. "Jim, kind of a manly name for such a little guy."

Jason responded patiently, "We call him J.B."

"Jaybee?" Miranda repeated, as if questioning the choice. "Kinda like Albee."

Jason smiled. "No, J.B. as in James Bruno Scarza."

"Ah, I see," she exclaimed as she looked back over her shoulder at the house that she was temporarily inhabiting. "Bruno, as in *the* Bruno Lentoni."

"Yes," he answered haltingly, unsure of her inflexion and its meaning. Hypersensitive to any Bruno bashing, he quickly added, "he was a dear friend of our family."

Like everyone else in the neighborhood, the battered woman had heard all the conflicting stories about Bruno. Black-hatted villain, or legendary folk hero? It just depended on your source. As far as the battered young woman was concerned, it really didn't matter. She had a roof over her head, a roof that had once belonged to Bruno.

"Which reminds me," Miranda said to Livy's relief, "I baked this apple pie just for you two, ya know, to show my appreciation."

"Thank you," Livy responded sincerely, "you didn't have to do that."

"It's the least I can do since you're letting me stay in the house, rent free. I really appreciate it. And, I just wanna let you know that I'm working with the people at the woman's shelter. They said they'd help me find a place, and a job."

Jason took her hand in his. "Listen to me Miranda. You stay as long as you like. There's no pressure, okay?"

She threw her arms around him, then stepped back. "God bless both of you, and when you see Philomena, tell her I said thanks for everything."

Jason carried the pie, while Livy pushed the stroller back up the hill to the Scarza house. "So, Miss Miranda," Livy began gently, "what's the end game there?"

"I have no idea," he responded. "I know she gets a small Social Security check and food stamps. But her life's a train wreck."

"Poor thing. Did you see the shiner? Philomena told me that her husband's a real piece of work. Slapped her around, cleaned her out, and then just took off."

"She's been through a lot," he agreed.

Livy nodded. "Philomena said that she had some kind of breakdown?"

"She's bi-polar," Jason clarified. "But she seems okay now."

Suddenly, the vacant eyes of Livy's mother were staring back at her as she offered a suggestion. "Look, Bruno left you the house, so it's your decision to make. But I have no problem with letting her stay on indefinitely. She looks like someone who could use a break."

Jason gave her a kiss. "You read my mind."

They walked into the house half expecting to hear Gramma shout out that supper was on, but those days were gone. In some ways it was difficult to live in a place filled with so many warm memories, but Gramma, on her deathbed, made Jason promise to never let the house go to strangers.

That meant that the mantle of family historian would now be his to wear. Years down the road he'd be sharing stories with his children, identifying the people in those many sepia-toned photographs. Of course, pictures of Jason's parents would be prominently displayed, but Gramma's photo would always be positioned at the top of the Scarza pantheon.

And so, by tweaking the narrative, very little had changed for the Scarzas. They resided in the family home, were still blissfully in love, and Bruno, at least in name only, lived on in their baby boy. Of course Anna Maria Scarza still ruled the roost with a pair of disarming dimples and big green eyes, instead of a wooden spoon.

The family car, the vintage '50 Ford that had belonged to his father, was parked in Victor Trammel's garage like it had for almost forty years. And Quentin Masters' damning sex tape, wrapped in a waterproof plastic bag, remained buried under the gravel floor of the garage. Exposing it to the light of day seemed both wreckless and counter-productive. Nothing could reverse Jason's court martial and the felony that besmirched his reputation, so why exhume the Admiral's evil deeds.

And lastly, young Joseph Gray had his name legally changed to Robert Balfour III. As one might guess, sightings of Joseph were about as common as spotting a bald eagle perched on your backyard swing. From the reports Livy was hearing, the young man was busily cranking out manuscripts, none of which had been published yet. It all sounded so familiar, so right. Once again, an eccentric Balfour clansman looked down upon them from the top of the hill.

So, full circle they'd all come on a harrowing journey filled with unpredictable twists and a surprisingly complicated cast of characters. No one behaved as advertised, neither hero or villain, lawman or hitman. The packaging had often been mismarked.

And so, in the telling of this tale, the lines that separated fact and fiction, truth and lies, delusion and reality were often blurred, or erased entirely, proving that things rarely are as they seem.